W9-AZW-336

Adam Smith and the Tower of Justice

Book One of the Tower of Justice Series

Copyright 2016

By William Stafford

Cover Art by Todd Elofson
Editor Heather John

For my friends and my wife, let Justice be done.
For my father and mom, let Justice be done.
For my daughters and son, let Justice be done.
For our future as one, let Justice be done.
For the Fatherless souls, let Justice be done.
For the weak and the bold, let Justice be done.
For the lost and the cold, let Justice be done.
For the ones who must fall, let Justice be done.
For the poor, most of all, let Justice be done.

Table of Contents

iv

1
Cold Beginnings

Adam Smith—or at least the boy who called himself that—woke up... and groaned.

His fifteen-year-old body ached everywhere. It felt like someone was jabbing sticks in the naked skin of his right shoulder and right hip and right calf. He stretched and rolled around, trying to get the discomfort out of his everything. When rolling around didn't work, he sat up and pushed off his four mismatched blankets.

He loved the blankets. The one on the bottom was the best. The Campground-Lady had given it to him on the day she'd discovered him sleeping on her property. He still wasn't sure why she'd gifted it. Perhaps she'd had an extra.

The Campground-Lady was an older woman, very thin, with severe lines. Her hair was black and gray and ended level with the angle of her jaw. She had dark, piercing eyes that seemed to see through everything. She'd been carrying an oxygen tank, but removed the tubing from her nose to smoke and negotiate. The blanket she'd provided looked old but it was heavy and bore a strange picture of a man supporting the whole world on his shoulders. Adam found the weight comforting.

The next blanket up the pile was a quilt. Or, at least, it had been once. It had holes and loose threads and its pattern was faded beyond recognition. He'd discovered it half-buried in leaves and mud in a ditch on the side of the road months back. Rainfall—his unloved traveling companion—had washed it clean long ago. The third blanket was white cotton. He'd found it in a dumpster two weeks ago. It was covered in blue stains like a map of indigo continents on a white fabric ocean. Washing it in the lake hadn't improved its appearance much. He kept it sandwiched between other layers to contain the pond scum smell. The top blanket was a thick, army green, wool affair which was remarkably warm but made him itch. He'd discovered that beauty on a particularly lucky day in the City, piled next to a trash can waiting for pickup.

Adam had traveled to the City every day for the last several months, mostly to look for work. Unfortunately, he'd found nothing reliable. Everyone seemed afraid to employ him.

He lifted thick, straight, black hair out of his eyes and sighed. His appearance wasn't helping.

Adam unzipped the tent flap and slipped out into the chill morning. He looked back at the faded, tattered, patched tent that was his home. The Campground-Lady had rented him that when she'd found him sleeping under the sky. She'd said that some other campers had abandoned the tent long ago but she'd kept it around in case someone needed a spare. He'd thanked her for the loan of it—thinking at the time that it was a huge upgrade compared to sleeping in the open. Looking back, though, it was more than just an upgrade—he might not have survived without it.

Adam did jumping jacks outside the tent. His body was lean. His skin lay directly over muscle without any fat separating the two. He could make out the individual strands in his whipcord muscles as he exercised—which was cool. Perhaps that leanness explained his impressive agility. Like an alley cat, he could change directions at the speed of thought or go from standing motionless to a full sprint in a single heartbeat.

"I'm not ugly," he reassured himself as he pulled all four blankets out of the tent.

"I'm just hungry."

That was an understatement, and something of a mantra.

He wrapped the heavy pile of cloth around his shoulders, took a deep breath and—before the breath was even half-expelled—was instantly moving at top speed. He raced barefoot along a narrow dirt path around the lake adjacent to the camp site. While running, he wondered idly if the blankets made him look like Superman. Probably not. For one thing, he wasn't flying. For another, Superman was tall and heavily muscled. Adam shook his head to clear the depressing comparison and pushed his feet to move faster.

After a while he started to sweat. He pulled the blankets around tighter and kept running. When he was positively overheated, he ran past the tent and bowled the blankets through the open entrance. Without slowing, he altered direction toward a large rock that jutted out in the lake. In three rapid strides, he traversed the rocky outcrop and leaped—completely naked—over the frigid water.

"SO COLD!" he gasped as the water embraced him.

His words came out as bubbles that floated up toward the surface. He did not follow them, however, because his muscles had all locked up. He sank to the bottom.

An instant later, he could move and started scrubbing his body vigorously with his hands. After thirty seconds of intense scrubbing, he stood up and took a great, gasping lungful of air. Thick, spongy mud pushed up between his toes. He lurched toward the bank with all the stuttering speed his body could muster.

Shivering and dripping, he scurried away from the lake to the nearby tree line. He broke through the brush to the hidden spot where his clothes had been drying all night—strewn across branches.

"Crap... maldito..." Adam groaned when he noticed his clothes were still damp. He took a deep breath for courage, then quickly pulled the moist shirt over his head and the clammy pants over his legs, followed by the soggy socks and damp shoes. A heartbeat later, he was running back toward the campsite. His feet were numb so it felt as if he was running on the stubs of his ankles. Without slowing, he dove through the tent opening and under the unruly pile of blankets. With trembling fingers, he tried to pry the tent zipper closed, but failed. Resigned, he curled up—a human burrito—and shivered.

After about twenty minutes his teeth stopped chattering and he reluctantly climbed out from under the blankets and left the tent. He zipped the tent closed, then walked over to the cottage where the Campground-Lady lived. He grabbed some firewood along the way from the nearby, half-collapsed barn that served as a roof over her piles of cut wood.

Adam passed through the back door of the cottage—which was never locked—and entered the small mud room. He stacked the cords of wood neatly inside the mud room. This ritual of wood stacking was the little chore the Campground-Lady had given him in exchange for use of the campsite and the tent. Just to the left of the entrance door was a second door that led to a tiny bathroom with a sink and toilet. A third door—opposite the entrance door—led to the rest of the house, but it was always locked. The Campground-Lady told him he could use this little out-bathroom any time, so long as he kept it clean.

He leaned over the sink so the faucet poured water directly in his mouth and gulped down as much as he could without throwing up. He swished water around his mouth for sixty seconds before spitting it out and scrubbing his teeth with a finger. He hoped to find a toothbrush someday—even a used one would be awesome. While he fantasized about a toothbrush, he wiped down the faucet and the sink and the toilet—in that order—with a square of folded toilet paper, in exactly the manner the Campground-Lady had shown him. After cleaning, he tossed the makeshift rag in the toilet and flushed it. The room didn't exactly sparkle, but it was clean—cleaner than him, truth be told.

He kind of envied the tidy sink for a moment, then looked up at the mirror. Dark brown eyes with a hint of purple iris stared back. His face, somewhat lean at the moment, was scored with thin, pale scars across perpetually deep brown, tan skin. The longest scar began underneath his left eye and followed a horizontal path across his cheek before ending several centimeters in front of his left ear. A smaller, diagonal scar interrupted his right eyebrow near the center. A vertical scar adorned the left side of his chin. Taken together, the scars made him look several years older, he thought.

Feeling good about looking older, he turned and went back the way he'd come.

Outside the cottage, Adam smelled wood smoke and something salty—perhaps bacon—in the air. It smelled amazing. His stomach cramped painfully.

He tried to remember when he'd last eaten—two days ago, maybe? He couldn't remember and he couldn't do anything about it, so instead he checked that his shoes were tied tight and started walking the 0.8-kilometer dirt road that led away from the campground.

He crossed to the right side of the street and slowed his walking pace, as per their ritual.

An aging, yellow 2006 Volkswagen Beetle pulled up beside him and stopped. He turned to face the passenger window. It was already rolled down.

One of the prettiest girls—*señoras*, he corrected himself—he had ever seen smiled at him.

"Need a ride today?"

Her name was Anne. She'd told him that during their first conversation earlier in the week, but he thought of her as the Volkswagen-Saint.

He looked up and down the road a couple times, as if considering her offer, then said, "I thank you, ma'am, but I think I'll pass today. I'm feeling good, so..."

She broke eye contact with him and looked down at her phone. Before he could finish his standard refusal, she cut him off saying, "The weather forecast calls for rain today."

She didn't look up, just turned her phone so he could see it.

'70% Chance of Rain' the phone read.

He gulped. He really didn't want more blisters. He wasn't sure he was eating enough food to heal the ones he had already.

Adam warred with himself for five more seconds, then reached for her door and got in the passenger seat.

"Thank you," he said and gave her a brief, seated bow.

The Volkswagen looked—from the outside—like a large soap bubble with four small soap bubbles for wheels. The inside was surprisingly roomy though. As he closed the door and buckled his seatbelt, Adam noticed that the inside smelled like apricots, and spring rain, and something else he couldn't name. It was nice. He looked over at Anne who had started driving. She was wearing the tiniest of smiles. He felt comfortable with her.

Anne started talking almost immediately. Words flowed out of her in the same way wind blew by the car at high speed. Once they started, they just kept rolling.

Anne had owned her car since college. She'd bought it new and loved the sheer uniqueness of it. She liked *unique*. *Unique* made life fabulous. She had a fabulous life. She said so several times. She'd eaten an egg burrito that morning and had already done forty minutes of exercise.

He caught all that in the first sixty seconds. She didn't let up for the rest of the ride.

Following the torrent of information that flowed out of Anne would have been hard work, but she didn't seem to require any response from him. Which was perfect, because he didn't want to say anything. It might cause trouble for him later. She had a nice voice.

He wished his bed was as soft as her passenger seat.

The next thing he knew he was being shaken gently. He awoke with a start and sat bolt upright, looking around feverishly. The car had stopped and Anne was leaning toward him with her hand up— simultaneously defensive and pacifying.

"You fell asleep," she said quickly in what must be her calming voice. "We've arrived at the City. I wasn't sure where you wanted to go so I stopped at the bus station. You can get anywhere you want from here. The buses are free in the City."

Adam already knew that. Free bus rides were a charming feature of the City. Still, he usually walked. Even so, this was a good place to start his day—if for no other reason than he knew where he was.

He turned in his seat so he was facing Anne better and gave a small bow.

"Thank you so much for the ride. I am in your debt."

"Nah," she waved her hand like a princess shooing a fly away. "You were good company. We're even. What's your name, by the way?"

Adam blinked once and pasted on a smile.

"Adam," he lied. "Adam Smith."

He hated the necessity of lying, especially to someone who'd just helped him out. But he had no choice. Every time he thought of his true name or his true past a cascade of horrible memories crushed him. Sometimes the tsunami of uncontrollable emotion left him unmoving and uncaring for days. He couldn't afford crippling depression like that. He had to eat, and that meant he had to work, which also meant he had to keep moving, which is why he used a borrowed name.

He got out of the car and tossed the leftover fast food bag in a nearby trash can. When he turned around, the Yellow-Bugmobile—his new name for her car—was driving away. He waved at its taillights.

She'd said he was good company, but hadn't he been asleep almost the entire time he was with her? He shook his head. Nothing he could do about it now. He looked up at the clock on the bus terminal sign. It read 08:20. He'd never made it to town this early before. He thought for a moment, then headed toward the center of the City.

3
Humble Work

The center of the City was a district with a large number of food establishments. Adam ducked in the alley behind a long row of restaurants and started knocking on back doors one by one.

Whenever someone opened one of the doors he bowed and recited his offer.

"I am Adam Smith, a humble worker in need of work. I am the best dish man in the City and would gladly work for an hour in return for one of your fine meals."

He didn't actually know what kind of meals they served or if they were fine. He didn't really care, honestly. He couldn't afford to care.

Most of the time, no one opened the door. Sometimes whoever opened it would cut him off mid-sentence and turn him down. Sometimes the door didn't belong to a restaurant. It was hard for him to tell from the back of the building and he couldn't be seen at the front of these businesses so he just had to swallow the embarrassment each time he made a mistake.

The problem, his dad had been fond of saying, *was the government*.

Some well-meaning politician had come up with the brilliant idea that children shouldn't be allowed to work. Obviously that politician hadn't been thinking about kids who needed to work to stay alive. Not only that, even if he lied about his age, Adam usually couldn't get work because of the minimum wage law. The law says no one can work for less than $7.50 an hour. The trouble was he was pretty green when it came to working and usually couldn't produce enough value for a business to justify paying him $7.50.

It was like, "Hey, Mr. Business Owner, I'll give you $5-an-hour worth of work and, in exchange, you give me $7.50 an hour. Great deal, right?"

But it wasn't a great deal and Adam knew it. And no businessman who took deals like that on a regular basis would be in business for long.

It was also possible the color of his skin was working against his job prospects. He wasn't certain and he couldn't have done anything about it even if he had been certain. On the other hand, he had a slightly easier time finding work at Spanish-speaking establishments.

So those were the facts. Anyone who hired Adam was literally breaking at least two laws. That's why he was at the back door—not the front. If you were asking people to break the law, the least you could do was come to the back door.

He got lucky that morning and a Chinese take-out spot needed help. Apparently, they got most of their business at night and had almost zero customers in the morning, so they let their dishes pile up at night and did them the next morning when there wasn't much else to do.

Immigrant businesses were usually his best source of work. He wasn't sure why. Perhaps they cared less about the law or just didn't understand it. Probably, though, they just worked really long hours every day with no days off and got really tired. When you're tired, getting a little help—even from a kid just starting out—can be huge. At least... he thought that might be the case.

Adam worked for an hour, was given permission to grab a meal, then ate some leftover Chinese take-out from the fridge. Fried shrimp first thing in the morning was a little odd, but he ate it and asked for more. They offered him a second hour of work for $3 an hour if he wanted it. That was less than half of the minimum wage. Adam didn't even have to think about it. He took the job. But when all the dishes were clean, they cut him loose.

That was the real problem with labor laws. It's not that they kept him from finding work. They didn't. It was that they kept him from finding *steady* work. No one would hire him full time for fear that the police or some health department raid would expose them, fine them, and close them down. No one wanted to risk their job just to give *him* one. So Adam was cut loose after two hours. The rest of the businesses didn't need a dishwasher that day. One needed a floor scrubbed so he earned another $6 over the next hour and a half. Then he got another "free" meal.

Adam was a hard worker. Everyone told him that, but no one had any more work for him. An Italian joint told him to come back around dinner time—that there would be dishes for him then.

4
Girls and Gangs

Adam took some of his newfound wealth and hid it between loose masonry in a concealed part of the alley behind dumpsters. He kept $2 and went out on the main street to find more food. He only kept what was needed on his person. That way, if he was robbed, he wouldn't lose everything.

At a grocery store he bought health bars off the clearance rack. They were huge, dense bars of bread and nuts. He almost cracked a tooth on the first one. No wonder they were on the clearance rack. Also, they tasted like cardboard. But he was pretty sure they'd taste like that right out of the oven. He got a free glass of water in a plastic cup from one of the restaurants and sat at a black iron table outside a restaurant that was closed.

"¡Salud!" he said, lifting his glass toward the empty chair across the table.

He dipped the rock-hard health bar in the glass of water, let it soften, then chewed thoughtfully. What was he going to do if he couldn't get regular work? He didn't want to live in a campground his whole life.

The noise of a buzzer blaring from far away drifted down the street. Adam followed the sound with his eyes to a massive, three-story, square building surrounded by a long, high fence. The building looked old but well-maintained. He thought it might be a factory until hundreds of young people around his age—all wearing school uniforms—poured out the front doors.

Even from a distance, the students were impressive. They were—almost to a person—athletic-looking. They moved with grace and precision. Their uniforms were navy blue with gold accents. They moved in small groups, chatting amiably, laughing. Some of the groups were all-male, some all-female, but most were coed. He felt a pang in his chest each time he saw a guy talking to a girl.

What is that feeling anyway?

Some of the students passed in front of Adam's table. None seemed to notice him. Perhaps he was invisible. This close up, he could make out the features of girls as they passed by. His mouth went dry. They were gorgeous! And they smelled so clean. That clenched it. He needed to go back to school.

How to get in though?

Perhaps he could ask some of these students. He was about to stand and introduce himself when he glimpsed his reflection in a car window and froze.

Adam's normally straight hair was a bushy mess. His clothes looked faded and ragged. His front was splattered with small stains from the dishwashing he'd done that morning. He sniffed at the shirt. It smelled like lake water and Chinese food.

Could be worse, he figured, but might not make a good first impression.

He shrank back in his chair and tried to hide behind his water cup.

Over the rim of Adam's plastic cup, movement to the left pulled his eye. A thin boy in an oversized, hooded sweatshirt—walking against the flow of student traffic on the same side of the street as Adam—stubbed his toe on... the sidewalk maybe? And stumbled and fell through a group of female students. While falling, he got tangled up with a particularly stunning blond. His arms flailed against her for support before he regained balance. He apologized without making eye contact and walked on quickly.

All good, Adam thought.

But he felt uneasy. Something about that exchange felt unnatural. He tried to replay the scene in his mind.

The hooded boy had stubbed his toe on the ground but there was no irregularity in the sidewalk. What's more, he looked to have perfect balance while falling. If anything, the fall looked acrobatic rather than clumsy.

"Why fall then...?" Adam mumbled to himself. Then he saw it. The boy's arms weren't flailing for balance—they were patting the girl down and, just before regaining his composure, he'd removed something from her pocket.

Adam's attention snapped back to the world at large. As luck would have it, the hooded boy was passing directly in front of where Adam was sitting. On impulse, he stuck out a leg.

The hooded boy tripped—again—but this time the fall looked decidedly more genuine. He landed with a *thud*. Adam winced and had second thoughts about his hasty plan until he saw what looked like a feminine wallet slide over the sidewalk.

Adam stood to retrieve the wallet, but the young man was already scrambling toward it. Adam kicked the boy's feet from behind, sending the lad sprawling to the ground a third time. Adam took two quick steps past the fallen thief and kicked the wallet soccer-style. It went skidding under one of the iron restaurant chairs.

The hooded boy followed the path of the wallet with his eyes, then glanced back at his harasser.

Adam did his best to look menacing and took a step forward.

The thief abandoned his prize and sprinted away—bumping students aside who were unfortunate enough to get in his path. Adam was reminded of a white-tailed deer he'd frightened by his campsite—a flash of white, then gone.

Adam shook his head and reached under the sidewalk chair to retrieve the wallet, then jogged after the gaggle of girls.

"Excuse me?" Adam said loudly enough to be heard over the ladies' chatter once he'd caught up.

As one, the girls stopped talking and turned to look.

"Yes?" the striking blonde at the center of the group asked, curiosity and caution coloring a smoky voice.

Adam licked his lips—mouth suddenly very dry. The school girl was nearly as tall as he was. She wore a tight-fitting school uniform which did nothing to hide her broad shoulders and sculpted musculature. She had green eyes and wore no makeup.

Adam stood unmoving, mesmerized.

The girl lifted one eyebrow and narrowed her eyes.

Adam, unthinking, held out the wallet.

The girl's eyelids blinked dumbly at the object, then crinkled in confusion, and at last grew wide with alarm.

Before he realized she'd moved, the wallet was gone—his hand empty.

"That was impressive," Adam said, staring at his empty hand.

Her reflexes must be amazing.

He'd barely seen her move.

"Where did you find it?" she asked, clutching the wallet to her chest.

"Back there," Adam said, looking over his shoulder—half to indicate the direction and half to make sure the hooded boy hadn't returned with friends.

"It fell into that boy's pocket after he stumbled against you. I... asked him to return it."

She stared at him for a long, searching moment. Then her shoulders relaxed perceptibly and she smiled.

"Oh yeah! That clumsy boy. I didn't realize I'd dropped my wallet. He took it, you say? What luck you saw it happen! Not everyone would be so brave and honest. Thank you so much!"

Then she stepped forward and gave him a grateful hug.

Adam stood frozen—uncertain how to react. Should he hug her back? Was this okay in public? Would the stains on his shirt rub off on her uniform? Would it bother her if they did?

If I move will she stop hugging me?

He decided it best to remain still.

She smelled like strawberries.

"I wouldn't survive without *this*," she said, stepping back and pulling a large plastic rectangle from her wallet.

Adam tried not to look disappointed.

"I keep my calendar in it. And my money," she continued. "Actually, the calendar and the money are both *on* the ID card. I live and die by this thing. Plus it works as my access to everything at school. I couldn't get anything done at school if I lost it. Well, okay, I could have bummed help from my friends, but... you know how it is. I don't want to bother any of them."

The other girls surged forward giving assurances they would be more than happy to help her anytime.

Adam suddenly found himself near the center of the whole group of girls.

"You're my hero! You know that?" the girl told Adam after thanking her friends for their kindness. "What's your name?"

Adam—bad with names at the best of times—couldn't, for some reason, remember his own right then.

A small, concerned frown appeared on the beautiful blonde's face.

Adam, agonized that he might have disappointed her, focused all his considerable powers of concentration.

"Adam," he managed to say though his voice cracked.

She smiled.

"I'm Asuna. So where are you from, Adam?"

Before he could think to answer such a complicated question, one of the other girls tapped Asuna on the shoulder, then pointed at her phone clock.

"Oh! Right," Asuna said. "I have to run or I'll miss my bus!"

She batted long eyelashes at Adam in apology and grabbed his right hand with both of hers.

"I owe you one, Adam. I'll repay you for helping me one day. You'll see."

She squeezed his hand affectionately. Her grip strength was extraordinary. When she released Adam and turned away, the crowd of girls followed behind her like ripples in water behind a boat.

Time passed. Adam wasn't sure how much. He felt like his head was in the clouds among rainbows and his feet floated above the ground. Next thing he knew, he was standing directly across the street from the imposing, three-story school building. He couldn't recall how he'd gotten there. He didn't really care. He wanted to go there. He looked around for a sign that might reveal the school's name. No name was obvious, but an inscription—carved in marble over the entrance—read, 'Where Justice Leads, Prosperity Follows.'

Serio, Adam thought.

Movement below the inscription pulled his focus down. Four students wearing reflector vests and carrying portable stop signs exited the building, blew whistles, walked in the street, and stopped traffic in both directions. Each wore a bright orange armband with a gold stylized compass at its center. The back of their brightly colored vests read 'Charter 7'. A wave of uniformed students crossed the street. After all students crossed, the guards left the street and traffic resumed.

Charter 7? What kind of a name is that?

Perhaps that's what they called their crossing guard—a charter. That didn't sound likely. Perhaps he should ask someone. However, the thought of talking to a uniformed stranger filled Adam with anxiety.

I'm tired after tussling with that bandito, he rationalized.

Plus, on reflection, he was still overwhelmed after being so close to so many new, beautiful people. Also, he was not dressed for proper introductions. They'd likely run him out for trespassing or maybe just for being Latino.

I should go home, he decided.

But before he'd moved a centimeter, loud, abrasive, confident speech floated past his ear. Adam bristled. Something told him all that bravado was for his benefit. Reluctantly, he looked over his shoulder. A group of four young people approached. He sized them up at a glance. Three looked manageable, but one big fellow looked formidable. None were wearing uniforms. None looked like they were in good shape, judging by their strides.

Adam moved to get out of their way, but the group stepped to the side so they were on a collision course. Adam moved again, but all four shifted again so their paths would certainly meet.

Adam sighed.

Here comes the accounting, he thought. Yin and Yang. Good and Bad. Help and Harm.

He faced the oncoming group and waited.

The one at the front of the group looked—to Adam—like an enormous string bean wearing a leather jacket. Adam guessed the string bean was probably the leader of the group given his position forward of the others. That probably meant he was the one talking at an obscene volume a moment ago. Adam decided to call the string bean *Loud-Talker*.

Standing to Loud-Talker's right and about ten centimeters behind, was a taller, fatter, stronger boy—also in a leather jacket—whom Adam decided to call *Ogre*. Positioned to Loud-Talker's left and twenty centimeters back was an unhealthy, thin boy with red, angry scabs all over his face and neck and forearms. Adam also noted scabs on the backs of his hands. The scabby fellow twitched. Adam dubbed him *Scabby*. The fourth person—the would-be thief from earlier—stood just under a meter behind everyone else. He was the only one without a leather jacket. Adam named him *Bandito-Aspirante*.

Adam figured he could take out Loud-Talker, Scabby, and Bandito-Aspirante if it came to fighting, but Ogre would be a problem. Adam knew how to fight. He knew how to fight well. But he also knew he didn't *want* to fight.

The newcomers stopped just under two meters away.

"Hey, kid!" Loud-Talker said, loudly. "Do you go to school there?"

The lead boy indicated the school across the street with a flick of his chin.

"No," Adam said neutrally. "Do you?"

Loud-Talker laughed as if Adam had said something funny. The other three started laughing with him—like an echo.

"Hear that?" Loud-Talker said to Ogre. "He thinks we're students."

Ogre laughed again.

"No, kid," Loud-Talker said, "we don't go there. We don't go to school. We escaped from those prisons and are out on our own. Free."

"Really?" Adam said, mildly curious while still considering escape options. "I thought everyone went to school."

"Oh no, not everyone," Loud-Talker said, conversationally. "Some kids can't go to school because they hurt people."

At this, he indicated Ogre.

"Or they use drugs."

He indicated Scabby.

"Or because they try and poison their teacher."

Here, Loud-Talker flicked his eyes over his shoulder toward Bandito-Aspirante.

"Or maybe because they *sell* drugs."

Loud-Talker put his right hand over his own chest.

"There are lots of reasons kids don't go to school. Incidentally, you're not wearing a uniform. What did *you* do?"

"I just moved here," Adam half-lied, "and I haven't gotten registered yet."

"Oh, is that so?" Loud-Talker said. "So you're new here but thought it was okay to interfere with my boy's business?"

Adam, not knowing what to say, said nothing.

Loud-Talker considered Adam, frowned, then spoke again.

"You know what? I think you're lying."

Adam blinked, amazed.

How had he known?

"I think you're a spy for the Blood-Devils."

"Oh," Adam said, relieved. "No. I've never heard of them."

"Really?" Loud-Talker asked. "And I suppose you've never heard of the Street-Angels or the Night-Gang?"

"I've never heard of any of them," Adam repeated. "I'm new here."

"Well," Loud-Talker said, shrugging, "allow me to school you. We're the Street-Angels and this is our turf and you have interfered with our business."

Adam tensed, but no one made aggressive moves.

Loud-Talker continued.

"But I heard how you handled my boy back there—smooth. Easy. Clean. Even managed to get some attention from the girls. I respect that."

The hooded boy in the back scowled at the ground.

"Listen, kid," Loud-Talker said to Adam in what must be his charming voice. "This is your lucky day. We're recruiting, as it happens, and we could use people like you. Smooth and clean and all that. If you pledged yourself to us right now, I'd even forgive your trespass and your interference. This way you'd avoid the thrashing you've got coming and we'd protect you from those other, vicious gangs. What do you say?"

"Ah," Adam sputtered, strangely amused. "I'm not gang material. I'm a scholar."

"Scholar, huh?" Loud-Talker puffed. "You sure don't dress like a bookworm."

"Well, the thing is..." Adam started to say.

Loud-Talker interrupted.

"The thing is we don't care what you call yourself, kid. There are really only two groups of people on this street—Angels and enemies. And you really do *not* want to be our enemy."

Just then a whistle sounded.

Loud-Talker paled. The other boys tensed and looked around. Adam saw his chance and took it. He stepped backward off the sidewalk, then spun on his heel and walked forward, passing the four crossing guards on their way out to block traffic. Once on the other side of the street, he paused to look back.

Loud-Talker's mouth curled in a sneer. Ogre frowned and stared with beady eyes. Bandito-Aspirante looked furious. Scabby just looked distracted and twitched.

Adam turned his back on them—his decision made—and headed through the gates of the school.

5
Greene's Turf

Past the gates, Adam climbed a long set of stately steps, trying not to look like a harried animal. At the top of the stairs, he walked through a large swinging door—one of several arranged side by side across the center of the front of the building—and found himself in a large air-conditioned hall with a high ceiling. The well-worn floor was gray marble with specks of white. Ahead was a rope strung across the hall which broke in the center to make way for an empty door frame. A bored security guard sat next to the odd door frame.

Adam slowed his pace, trying to figure out what to do next, which drew the attention of the security guard.

"New here, are you?" The guard asked with an Irish accent.

"Yes," said Adam. "I'm looking to enroll here."

Adam looked over his shoulder to make sure there was a clear path back to the entrance doors in case he needed to run. He hoped he wouldn't have to. The Street-Angels probably hadn't left yet.

"Great!" beamed the security guard. "Let me be the first to welcome you to Charter 7, or what most of us affectionately call the 'Tower of Justice'. I'm Officer Ben. No weapons or alcohol or cigarettes allowed on campus. Do you have any of those things on you? No? Okay, step through this metal detector, please."

Adam did as instructed.

Once he'd cleared the frame of the metal detector, the guard pointed to a glass door just to the left.

"That's the administration office. Go there first and they'll help you."

The administration office had a long counter across the front with several ladies sitting behind it, working on computers. Adam walked up to the counter and waited. No one seemed to notice him. After a while, the waiting grew uncomfortable and one of the ladies behind the desk looked up.

"Well?" she said shortly. "Log in."

Adam just stared at her dumbly.

She lowered her reading glasses to focus better on his eyes.

"With your ID card," she said slowly and deliberately.

Adam bit his lip.

"What's your name, student?" she said with an angry edge to her tone.

"I'm not a student yet," Adam said shyly. "I'm here to enroll."

"Oh. Oh! Why didn't you say so?" she said, practically jumping up out of her chair. Her body jiggled like Jello when she moved.

"Wait right there."

She went through an opening in the back of the room and disappeared down a well-lit hallway. After about thirty seconds, she bobbed back in the room, leading an enormous black man in a navy blue suit. He was half again as tall as Adam and probably three times as wide at the shoulders. He had the body of a professional football player except for a huge belly hinted at by the girth of the suit jacket. He had short, salt and pepper hair and a salt and pepper goatee. The instant he saw Adam a great grin spread across his face. He came around the counter in three strides and stuck out a meaty hand to shake. The man's hand, like the rest of him, was huge. It swallowed Adam's as they shook. His grip was strong but not painful—reassuring and steady.

"A new student! How wonderful!"

The man in the suit beamed.

"I am Mr. Greene, the principal of Charter 7. Where are your parents?"

Adam resisted the urge to shuffle his feet.

"They work during the day, so they sent me over to get the paperwork and whatever else I need to enroll here."

He regretted the necessity of lying. He hated lying. But he had a good life right now and didn't want it taken away.

"Oh," Principal Greene said, "Not a problem."

He turned and said to Jello-Lady, "Gladys, a new student binder, please."

She was handing Mr. Greene a thick binder before he even finished the sentence. He startled a little, then took the binder.

She looked pleased with herself.

"Thank you, Gladys."

The principal turned to Adam and handed over the binder.

"That's everything we need to get you started. We're already halfway through the first semester. But if you hurry, we might be able to get you through all the red tape and the government's hurdles in time to get you started mid-term."

Adam felt surprise. Did Mr. Greene really say two months to get through administrative hurdles was 'hurrying'?

Mr. Greene seemed to pick up his mental vibes.

"We can process paperwork—start to finish—in about two hours."

He stood a little taller when he said that.

"But then we have to get okayed by several government boards, the teachers' union, and the city, state, and national Boards of Education, respectively. They are bureaucracies, so they move slowly even at the best of times. But for us, I think they take great pains to be… well, great pains. They are all relatives within the public school system, after all, and we are a charter school. Do you follow?"

Adam didn't, but he nodded anyway.

Mr. Greene seemed to guess his confusion.

"Charter schools," he explained, "are independent. They run themselves. The public schools are all run by committees and government bureaucracies, most of which are not even located in a school and have little or no interaction with teachers and students."

He leaned forward and lowered his voice conspiratorially.

"Charter schools are the competition of the public schools. But they can't compete with us. They're too big, old, slow, fat, and expensive. Since they can't compete any other way, they try to compete by slowing us down. Thus, anything we have to do that requires their 'okay,' they drag out as long as legally possible."

An annoyed look crossed over the face of everyone in the office. It passed quickly and Mr. Greene's big grin returned.

"Do you follow now?

Adam smiled back and nodded twice. Politics he didn't understand, but competition—that was something he grasped down to his bones.

"I understand," Adam said cheerfully. "You're a strong competitor. Like a fast wide receiver on a football team. Since the defense can't keep up with your speed, the only option left is to trip up your feet or hold your uniform to slow you down just off the line of scrimmage. So you don't get too far ahead."

Mr. Greene roared out a great belly laugh that filled the room.

"Hear that, Gladys? He's talking football. This kid might be a genius. I want him here!"

He clapped a huge hand on Adam's shoulder. The impact ran down Adam's spine, then his legs, and finally out through his heels.

Mr. Greene continued, "You just get those papers filled out soon as you can. We'll take care of the rest. Paperwork is one of the things that—out of necessity—we are good at."

Adam nodded again.

"In that case, I'll get started... I mean, I'll have my parents get started right away."

He then made a half-turn as if to go, paused as if in afterthought, turned back and said, "One more question. How much does it cost to go here?"

Mr. Greene pursed his lips. His eyes rolled toward the ceiling as if running figures in his head.

"Well, I'm guessing you'll be a freshman?

"Yes."

"Freshman tuition averages $6,500 this year."

Adam felt his jaw drop open.

Mr. Greene added, a touch defensively, "You won't find a better deal anywhere, especially for the quality of education we provide. Our students do really well in life after school. Our college entrance rate is nearly 60%. Our job placement rate is close to 100%. Now, to be fair, not all charter schools are this good—some even go out of business—but Charter 7 is among the best of the best in the whole nation."

Adam hadn't heard anything past '$6,500'.

"Does that include meals?" Adam asked, a little hoarse.

"No," Mr. Greene said. "Meals are extra."

Adam made a choking noise.

"But we accept the state school vouchers as partial payment toward meals and tuition. You are a resident of the state, right?"

"Absolutely," Adam lied. "Thanks for everything. I can't wait to become a student here."

And, with that, he turned on his heel and hurried out of the office.

"Wait!" Mr. Greene called after him. "There's more!"

But Adam was already gone.

6
Rules of the Game

Adam paused at the Charter 7's front doors and peered through one of the little windows in the door. He couldn't see any Street-Angels. He chewed his lip.

Have I given them enough time to leave?

He felt a presence enter his personal space to the right and turned his head in that direction. He caught a glimpse of red hair, then heard the now-familiar Irish accent of the security guard.

"See something out there?"

"No," Adam said, "Just... ah... seeing if my friends were waiting for me."

"Friends. Right," said Officer Ben. "Well, since your friends aren't out there to walk you home and you're new to this school, you probably don't have anyone to walk with. I only mention that because there has been increasing gang activity in these neighborhoods recently."

"Yeah," Adam sighed. "I've heard that too."

There was a pregnant pause before Officer Ben said, "Listen, I'm about finished with my shift. If you don't mind waiting a few minutes, I can walk you as far as the bus stop. I live near here and the bus stop is on my way home."

Adam turned to eye him more closely. Officer Ben pretended to ignore the inspection and kept looking out the window. He was probably in his thirties. His uniform looked pressed and well-maintained—nothing out of place.

Can he be trusted?

He was an employee at the school, so they must trust him. He was something of a question mark, but the Street-Angels were a sure thing. Adam decided to take the chance.

He made a coughing sound in his throat. Officer Ben looked over at him.

"I would be grateful for your company," Adam told him. "I get lost easily and I am pretty new to this part of town. I'll just text my mom and let her know I will be a few minutes late."

Officer-Red smiled and said, "Okay. Just take my picture and send it to your mom. Make sure my badge is in the picture. It has my name and ID on it. That should give her comfort."

Adam turned quickly away from Office Ben to hide his embarrassment.

"That's a great idea, but my phone doesn't have a camera. I memorized your ID so I'll just text that to her."

"Okay," Officer-Red said, shrugging. "Just wait here a few minutes. I'll be right back."

When Officer Ben had gone, Adam let out a breath he didn't realize he'd been holding. Already he was being caught in the web of his lies. He didn't have a cell phone, much less a camera phone, or even anyone to text to. He'd lost all contact with his family half a year ago—best to keep that to himself though.

While waiting, Adam looked around till he found a water fountain, then drank as much as he could manage. He even pulled the crumpled plastic cup he'd been using earlier out of his pocket and filled it with water. It was a long way home and he wasn't sure he could find water again this easily before leaving the City.

A few minutes later Officer-Red returned with a briefcase in one hand and a lunch pail in the other. They headed out to the street. The walk to the bus stop was only two blocks and it went by in amiable silence. Adam filled the time by keeping a vigilant eye out for gang members. He saw none. Officer-Red waited till the bus arrived, then waved and walked off as Adam climbed on the public transit.

Adam regretted having to take the bus this early. He'd hoped to return to the back door of the Italian restaurant to work more, but he felt the risk of getting caught again by the Street-Angels today was too high.

7
Dumpster Diner

Adam woke the next morning when water splashed his face. His eyes snapped open in alarm. His groggy brain tried to figure out who on earth would crawl in the tent to splash him with water. He rubbed his eyes and looked around. There was no one in the tent but him.

Just then another drop of chilly water hit him on the forehead. He looked up and noticed condensation forming along the insides of the tent. Occasionally, the little drops of condensation would merge to form a big drop of water that abandoned the tent wall to leap at his face.

Adam sighed. Condensation probably meant it was colder outside than inside the tent. He summoned courage and left the shelter. It was colder for sure. He had goose bumps instantly. Interestingly, the lake water felt warmer than ever. That, at least, was nice, even if only an illusion. Getting out of the water was harder, though.

Once dressed, Adam hiked away from the campground. He was still shivering but too motivated to take the time to warm up under the blankets.

Instead of heading for the City—which was his usual routine—he headed for the small town between the City and the campground. Adam called it *Cow-town* in honor of all the cattle farms and pickup trucks hauling livestock. He asked around in the only diner in Cow-town. A waitress told him where to find the library. It was just one room of an old storefront on the street everyone called 'downtown'. The size of the library was not terribly important to him. What *was* important was internet access.

He found the library open and entered. The inside was... humble. It had three shelves—half full of books—two desks, and a check-out counter. No librarian was around. Along the back wall of the library were two ancient computers. Adam sat down and tried one. It worked right away and didn't have any security requirements. The Internet was slow, but he had time. He wasn't in school after all.

His stomach tried to get his attention but he ignored it.

Adam used search engines and the folder Principal Greene had given him to research how to get a voucher. It mostly came down to having an address, school-age dependents, and a government-issued ID. Additional queries revealed that families moving in and out of school districts were a common phenomenon all year round due to job changes or address changes or parents going to jail or other financial difficulties forcing families to move in together or move apart. So starting in the middle of the year was not unusual.

He felt a hint of a plan form but couldn't concentrate enough to give it shape. His stomach wouldn't tolerate any more distractions. He needed to eat. Immediately.

He walked back to the Cow-town diner and snuck around back. He found a hiding spot in some tall weeds and waited. When all was quiet in the neighborhood, he sprinted toward the diner's trash dumpster, jumped over its lip, and landed atop a pile of sealed plastic bags. It smelled horrible and there were flies everywhere. He grabbed the top-most bags and ripped them open. He shifted aside the normal restaurant trash until he found what he was looking for—fresh, half-eaten diner food.

Eggs and buttered bread flew in his mouth. Adam continued to fill his hungry maw to bursting, then looked for more. He found more bread, grits, part of an omelet, and fried potatoes. He noticed steak but ignored it. Meat made him sick more often than other kinds of food, so he avoided it like the plague.

Once both his hands were stacked with food, he crawled back out of the dumpster using his elbows and tried—vainly—to avoid getting anything smelly on his clothes. Adam hit the ground on his feet and ran back to his hiding spot in the weeds. When it looked like no one had seen, he emptied about three quarters of the contents from his mouth—unchewed—on top of the pile already in his hands. He chewed two times, swallowed, waited only half a second, then attacked the food in his hands. Some of it got caught in his throat. His eyes watered. He gagged and coughed it back up in his hands, then drank it down again a second later.

For a blessed moment, the cramping, aching stomach pain disappeared, but it was quickly replaced with a new kind of pain—a stretching, tearing discomfort. Adam fell over and curled up in a ball on the ground. He stayed there for a half hour. When it finally eased and he could move again, he snuck to the back of the diner and stole water from a hose attached to the back wall. As an afterthought, he washed his face and hands.

After the bird bath, he hiked back to the library. Inside, there was a bathroom where he washed again, this time with soap. He also found a few ugly smudges on his clothes and washed them too. Finally, he put his face to the sink and filled up on water. Once clean—well, cleaner—he set about cultivating a plan.

First, he was off to the local license branch to see what it would take to get an ID card.

"$10, a birth certificate, and a letter from your parents," the clerk at the license branch told him.

Second, Adam went to the small motel on the edge of Cow-town called The Rockytop Inn and talked with the proprietor. She agreed to let him use the hotel as his home address for $2 a month. He could just come by and pick up his mail any time they were open. He didn't have the $2 on him, so he said he would be back with it in a couple of days.

Third, he went back to the library and looked up websites that would help him forge a birth certificate. There were several to choose from. He chose one that was free and loaded his information in the computer. He used his actual social security number, place of birth, date of birth, etc., but used 'Adam Smith' as his name and John and Jamie Smith as his parents. He printed it. There was an honesty-box next to the printer with a paper taped to the side that read, '10¢ per page'.

Adam frowned at the box, then ignored it.

Finally, he wrote a letter from his parents saying it was okay for him to get a government-issued ID. He printed it.

The honesty-box beside the printer drew his attention once more.

Character, Adam's father had once told him, is what you do when no one is looking.

Adam's chest ached.

He pulled a scrap of clean paper out of a trash can and scribbled two IOU notes. He put one IOU in his pocket and the other on top of the unyielding honesty-box.

The little library had ancient computers but its printer was brand new. The forgeries looked great. All he needed now was money.

9
Winning Absent Virtue

While walking back to the campground that evening, Adam looked at his new ID card. He noticed that the young man in the picture looked older than he remembered—also tanner and with longer hair. Most worrying, he looked much, much skinnier. He wasn't hungry, but he stopped and immediately ate the leftovers from the diner. He hoped he wouldn't always look so thin.

That evening he read more of the documents in the Charter 7 entrance binder until the light grew too dim, then performed his nightly cleaning and laundry ritual. Afterward, he lay on his back with his head sticking out the front door of the tent. He could feel pine needles on the back of his head. They smelled green, tangy, and sweet. He stared up at the stars. They were remarkably bright this far away from the City.

He listened to his emotions in the darkness. He thought he should feel elated. He'd overcome a lot of hurdles that day. He was making steady progress toward his goals. He was playing the game and, by all measurable standards, he was winning. But all he felt was—for the most part—uneasy. Why? Did it not count as winning because he had to lie to pull it off? He didn't know. He figured a world where he had to lie to succeed wasn't ideal, but it was all he had. He couldn't change it. Not yet, anyway.

Adam pulled his head back in the tent and zipped up the entrance flap. He wadded up one blanket into the shape of a pillow and buried his head in it, feeling miserable. His dad would have been disappointed.

He hated lying.

10
Watch and Learn

Adam spent the next two weeks walking to the City each day looking for work. He changed his sales pitch to include cleaning bathrooms and scrubbing floors in addition to washing dishes. He asked for $5 per hour. Ironically, he found it easier to get work even though his price had gone up.

Go figure.

On the few nights he was in the City late, he found work at the Italian restaurant. Their automatic dishwasher frequently broke down so they needed extra hands doing dishes all the time. One evening while working there, he heard the owner call in a repair man. He heard the owner say he would pay $45 an hour in addition to whatever the parts cost. When the repair man arrived, Adam had already shifted a large stack of plates and cups to a part of the sink with a good view of the automatic dishwasher. Adam closely watched everything the repair man did—taking careful note of the tools he grabbed and how he used them.

His eavesdropping was complicated by long hair dropping down in his eyes. He had to repeatedly brush it out of the way with soapy hands. He watched the different places on the machine the repair man touched to open panels and expose inner parts. At one point, the repair guy seemed to have difficulty and asked the Italians if they could spare someone to help. The owner pointed at Adam, then at the machine. Adam nodded and rushed over to assist.

The repair guy—Adam decided to call him *Handy-Dan*—had Adam hold a wrench in place while he turned a screw on the other side of the machine at some impossible angle. After that, any time Handy-Dan needed assistance he would call Adam over. Adam paid special attention to the names Handy-Dan gave each of his tools and what those tools were used for. Eventually Handy-Dan finished and the machine worked properly. The restaurant owner forked over a $100 bill. The two men shook hands and parted.

Increíble! That was a lot of money!

Adam wondered if he could break into that field. He'd need tools... and a phone... and a car to get around town... probably a website... some experience.

He sighed.

Not today.

11
Bruises, Bad Deals, and Bad Luck

In a mere hour, the automatic dishwasher flexed its muscles and the dirty dishes dried up. Adam was paid and sent back to the street.

It was dark behind the restaurant. He stepped carefully to avoid tripping. When his eyes adjusted to the dim light, he looked up and down the alley, noticed no one around, then ducked behind the trash cans. He found the loose masonry and pushed his fingers as far in as they would go. They brushed some of his previously stashed money. He smiled, then stuffed most of the money earned today there as well, keeping $5 on him for needs. He needed to find new clothes—especially socks. Oh, and soap. He still hadn't purchased any soap.

Once the coast was clear, he snuck out from behind the dumpster and headed back to the main street.

He hadn't been there thirty seconds when he heard an overly loud, abrasive voice behind him say, "Hey, kid. What do you think you're doing here?"

Adam turned slowly to see Loud-Talker, Ogre, Scabby, and Bandito-Aspirante approaching. Loud-Talker was spinning a chain with something metallic and shiny on the end. Scabby's twitch seemed more pronounced. Bandito-Aspirante still didn't warrant a leather jacket. Ogre looked, well, the same—big and ugly and intimidating. There was a predatory hunch to the shoulders of everyone in the group.

Adam sighed. This was not going to end well.

"Oh, look what we have here," said Loud-Talker to his little group. "It's the scholar. Hey, Mr. Scholar. I thought we told you this was Street-Angels turf. Have you decided to join us or do you have a death wish?"

Adam knew it wouldn't matter, but he tried anyway.

"I'm just here for work. I'm a dish boy."

"Oh, you're a dish boy, eh? Not a scholar then? Well, your story keeps changing. That's pretty suspicious if you ask me."

That must have been Scabby or Bandito-Aspirante. He couldn't see which one.

"Okay, let him up."

The hands holding him down suddenly released. He stood up slowly so as not to startle anyone. Keeping them calm was his best way out of this unhurt.

"Well, kid," Loud-talker said while shaking his head sadly. "You don't get paid very well. You really should join us. You could do a LOT better working in some of our side businesses. They are VERY profitable."

"Thanks," Adam said while dusting off his shirt and pants, "but I'll earn more than that someday. I'm still learning."

Loud-Talker shrugged.

"Whatever. Here," he tossed a dollar toward Adam.

It landed on the ground.

"It's not right to take a man's last dollar. You made a good purchase though," he said while waving the $5 bill in front of him.

"This little exchange buys you our protection this week. Not the whole month, mind you. It's not enough for that. But this week you can feel safe. If anyone bothers you, tell them Gil has got your back. If they don't back off, they'll answer to me."

Gil—Loud-Talker—slapped him on the right shoulder in an exaggerated friendly gesture.

"Nice doing business with you. See you next week, maybe."

With that, the meeting was over, and Adam was left alone, rubbing his bruised pride and bruised right hip. His new, folded $1 bill rocked back and forth on the sidewalk, mocking him.

With only that dollar left on him, Adam decided new socks were no longer on the menu. Soap, though… that might be possible. And perhaps some food. Come to think of it, he should have asked the Italians for food to take home after work.

"Stupid. Estúpido," he berated himself. "You need to think ahead."

He thought about raiding one of his stashes for more money but he was having bad luck this evening and didn't want it to spread. He took a bus to a part of the City with a supermarket and found some Ivory soap for a quarter and a small bag of peanuts for the other 75¢. The tax put him over a dollar though.

Taxes, he decided, were going to kill him.

He was about to throw in the towel when the sales clerk told him there was a take-a-penny/leave-a-penny pot. Perhaps his luck wasn't all bad. But the penny-pot was empty.

Yep, all bad.

Adam left the peanuts and bought the soap and left a penny in the pot. He took the bus to the edge of town and started to run home. His right hip hurt from where he'd fallen earlier so he had to slow down and walk. He was striding unhappily along the roadside when someone driving by scored a hit with a half-filled drink cup. Cola and frigid ice soaked the left side of his head and the back of his shirt. He picked up the cup in a fury and threw it at the sky yelling, "What else could go wrong?!"

Then it started to rain.

Adam just stood there for several minutes with his eyes closed— feeling the rain fall over his face. Then the rain picked up. The drops were huge and fell so fast they hurt. He could not see three meters in front of him. His clothes grew cold and heavy instantly as they took on water. He started to cry. Tears he could not feel were washed away by the rain. He sat down in the ditch beside the road and rolled to his side, sobbing.

"What do you want from me?" Adam yelled at the driving rain. "What am I supposed to learn from this?"

A list of possible lessons started scrolling through his mind. Annoyed, he pushed the thoughts away and lay there feeling sorry for himself. Eventually the rain stopped and he decided he needed to get up and get moving. He got to his feet.

Just then a car passing in the dark hit a puddle and splashed up a great wave of water. The torrent came down right on top of Adam like a dirty waterfall.

He stood there stunned for a moment, feeling only numbness inside. Then he felt a new emotion bubbling up. He started to laugh.

"Okay, God," Adam said dryly. "That last bit was funny."

12
Luck be a Lady

It had been two months since Adam sent in his application for a school voucher. Since then, it had become part of his morning ritual to run over to the Cow-town motel and see if any mail had arrived. This morning was looking up. The sky was clear. The sun was warm. The lake water even seemed warm! So he was in good spirits when he asked the motel clerk if any mail had arrived for him. The motel clerk—this morning it was Yellow-Beard—looked at him dumbly through bloodshot eyes. His eyes were always bloodshot and he always smelled of alcohol. Today he smelled a little less strongly than usual. After a few seconds, Adam's question seemed to register and Yellow-Beard picked up a letter from behind the counter and handed it over.

Adam would have hugged Yellow-Beard if the counter wasn't between them. Instead, he grabbed the man's yellow, sun-spotted hand and shook it vigorously.

"Thanks!" he gushed.

Then he ran out of the motel and ripped open the letter. Sure enough, it was an official-looking letter with the words 'School Voucher' across the top and his name and birthday written in the middle. There was a third page that seemed like a long list of things it couldn't be used for under penalty of prosecution. He spun around in the gravel parking lot with the letter held over his head until he got dizzy and fell down.

He'd done it. He was going back to school.

Adam ran back to the campground and grabbed his Charter 7 application binder, then started walking toward the City. Along the way, he found a plastic bag in which he placed the school voucher and his school application binder. After that, he started jogging. He'd made about half the distance to the City when he heard a familiar high-pitched horn beep at him from a distance.

Adam grinned, switched to the right side of the road, and slowed to a walk. A yellow Volkswagen Bug pulled up next to him with the passenger window rolled down.

"Need a lift, Adam?" said the VW-Saint behind the wheel.

His smile grew even wider. He liked hearing VW-Saint's voice. He hoped the Saint would talk a lot today.

"Thank you," he said. "I could really use a ride today. And I even have some money to trade for your trouble."

He fished in his pocket.

Anne motioned energetically for him to get in.

"You don't have to pay me anything, silly. I just want someone to talk to. This road is so boring."

"Not always," Adam said with a mischievous hint to his voice. "This road is never dull for me. Speaking of 'not-dull', it's great to see you again."

Adam had to give himself points for turning her complaint around to a compliment in a mere three sentences.

She blinked at him twice and looked a little uncertain. He could tell her mind was doing some work behind those eyes. He felt like she was reassessing him, perhaps re-categorizing him. Then a sly grin crossed her lips.

"Well said, Adam."

Anne started driving.

Adam noticed in his peripheral vision that her hair was in a tight bun on the back of her head today. Also, she was wearing a long dark skirt and a black t-shirt. The t-shirt was form-fitting. He couldn't tell for sure, but he thought she was wearing a lot of dark makeup.

The Saint seemed about ready to start talking but Adam blurted out, "Guess what came in the mail today?"

Something in the back of his mind told him to stay silent, but he totally ignored it. He was surfing on a tidal wave of excitement.

"What?" she asked curiously.

"My school voucher!"

He withdrew the voucher from the plastic bag with reverence. He held it up to her right side so she could see it and the road at the same time.

"Oh," she said. "That's cool. Where are you going to school?"

His eyes glittered as he gazed at his voucher.

"I'm not certain yet. The instructions that came with it say that I can use it at any school in the state. Originally, I thought I would use it to go to Charter 7."

The VW-Saint made a small sound in the back of her throat like a whimper, a hiccup, and 'eep' all at the same time.

"What?" he asked.

"Nothing," she said. "Go on."

"Well, I was originally going to go to Charter 7, but now I think I need to find a school where I can earn some money. You know, like in a Work/Study or something. I'm not sure what schools—if any—have programs like that, but I think I should research it before I make any firm decisions."

"Well, you know," the VW-Saint sounded a little strangled, "I've heard that Charter 7 has lots of work opportunities for students. They're pretty famous for that, really. Students can work for other students, or for teachers, or even for the community. And they get paid for their work. Not only that, some teachers pay their students real world money when they get good grades."

Adam was not sure he could take any more awesome in one day.

"Really?! Money for grades?! You've got to be kidding."

"Definitely not kidding," Anne said confidently.

He sat back hard in the seat and stared straight ahead. Instead of seeing the road, though, he saw the future. A future where he not only went to school, but actually got paid for going. He sat dumbstruck, shaking his head at the wonder of it all.

The VW-Saint chatted amiably in his silence the rest of the trip. She didn't seem to mind that he didn't reply much. He judged they were both pretty happy.

The Saint dropped him off at the bus stop on the edge of town, turned down his offer to pay, then waved and drove off.

He felt somewhat sad as he watched the Yellow-Bugmobile turn a corner out of sight. It was only his second time riding with the Saint, but he really enjoyed her company. He only wished there was something he could do for her in return for her help. She wouldn't take his money. Perhaps he could buy her a gift instead. He got on the bus and headed toward Charter 7.

As the bus made its way to the City center, Adam pondered girls. What do girls like anyway?

Not money, apparently. Jewelry? Didn't matter, he couldn't afford it. Candy? Perhaps. Flowers? Might be on to something there. He'd have to ask VW-Saint if he saw her again.

13
First Day of School

Adam Smith stepped through the entrance of the Charter 7 school building. The entrance hall felt smaller and less imposing today than it had on his first visit, perhaps because it was bursting at the seams with students and parents and teachers and staff. They swirled around like eddies in a stream. Sound echoed off the tall ceilings.

He caught a hint of red hair through the crowd and followed it down to the face of Officer-Red who was standing, as before, near the metal detector arch. Adam waved to him. Officer-Red noticed the wave, smiled back in recognition, and pointed for him to queue at the end of the shortest line in the room under one of the signs that read 'New Students'.

The line moved quickly and, in short order, Adam was at the head of the line.

A young man in a school uniform with a purple armband displaying a gold embroidered symbol of a shield, sword, and scale half-yelled at him, "Name, please!"

"Adam Smith."

The student worker behind the desk looked up at him and then back down at the paper then up at him again. He turned his head ninety degrees to the left and yelled, "Mr. Greene!"

The huge form of Mr. Greene—wearing a navy blue, double-breasted suit and gold tie—turned and started walking toward them. In spite of his size and height, he moved slowly, as if wading up to his chest in a stream flowing the other direction.

Adam tried to wait patiently but felt like a large firecracker of excitement was lit inside his chest. He hoped it wouldn't explode, but didn't want it to go out either.

After what seemed like hours, Mr. Greene arrived and said to the student worker, "What is it, Johnny?"

"This student is not in our database, Mr. Greene."

Mr. Greene's eyes looked up at Adam. Adam thought he saw regret reflected in them.

The wick on Adam's internal firecracker started to burn faster. He needed to act. He spoke up quickly.

"I have the voucher right here. It came in the mail today."

The student worker—Johnny, Mr. Greene had called him—took the voucher from Adam and handed it to the principal. Principal Greene looked at it a moment, then pursed his lips and let his eyes roll up toward the ceiling.

It was the same thing he'd done when performing math in his head the first time Adam met him.

After a few seconds he shook his head. His eyes grew focused again and he handed the voucher back to the student worker.

Mr. Greene took in a breath and let it out slowly before he said, "The timing is not good. It takes months to get a new student squared away with the government. And this is the first day of the semester."

He reached up and massaged the bridge of his nose.

"Perhaps we could get him in at the start of next year."

Adam found he was on his feet with hands planted firmly on the small desk in front of him. He didn't remember standing. He felt like the firecracker in his chest had morphed—now his whole body was one large keg of gunpowder.

"Wait," Adam said, reaching in his plastic bag. He pulled out the new student binder Mr. Greene had given him on his first trip here.

"I have this all completed."

Johnny opened and leafed through it. His eyebrows rose a little.

"Nice handwriting."

Adam looked up to see the principal staring thoughtfully at the binder. Mr. Greene's eyes shifted over and looked at Adam's clothes, his long hair, and his dark eyes. Then he seemed to make a decision.

"Add him to the roster, please" Mr. Greene said in an authoritative, deep voice. "We'll make this work somehow."

Then he smiled at Adam and put out his enormous hand.

"Welcome to Charter 7, Adam. We are so glad to have you."

The principal winked as they shook hands.

"You did well," he said, then turned and waded back in the river of people.

Johnny spoke over the noise, "What is your address, new student Smith?"

Adam recited the address of the motel in Cow-town before providing the email address he'd set up at the small rural library. Once all his vitals were gathered, Johnny took Adam's picture with a digital camera, copied some numbers off the voucher in the computer, waited a few minutes, then produced a large, dense plastic card which he slid across the desk.

Adam picked up the card and noticed his name and photograph were on the front. On the back was a flat display screen. On the border of the display screen was the school motto in tiny script: 'Where Justice Leads, Prosperity Follows.'

Johnny turned and waved a girl over from a queue of older students lounging against the wall.

Adam's eyes went wide. The girl striding toward him had wavy, mellow brown hair a little past her shoulder that bounced with her step—giving the illusion that her hair was blowing in a gentle breeze. Her eyes were large and her irises were a smooth, dark brown. Her body was all curves, as if her sculptor had refused to allow any angles. The lines of her shoulder, the sweep of her legs, the angle of her chin and jaw, the place where her neck met her clavicle—all were graceful arcs.

"Jenny," Johnny said. "This is Adam. He is a new student in the freshman class. Adam, this is Jenny. She is a junior this year and was the valedictorian of her class last year. She will show you around."

With that, Johnny started waving for the next student in line.

Adam moved around the desk to meet up with Jenny. He noticed her focus linger on Johnny a moment before she turned.

Incredibly, she was even more amazing close up. She had faint blond highlights in her brown hair. She was the same height as Adam and had a wide mouth with thick lips and a graceful nose. Her skin looked flawless. Her cheeks were pink. She looked like something out of a makeup commercial—except he was pretty sure she wasn't wearing any makeup.

Her school uniform involved a knit, navy blue sweater and a flowing navy blue skirt that ended just above the floor. Like Johnny, she wore a purple armband with the gold embroidered symbol of a shield, sword, and scale on her left arm. Unlike Johnny—or anyone else in the room at that moment—she had a navy blue armband on her right arm that showed a golden laurel crown.

When Adam finished his inspection of her uniform, he looked up and found Jenny looking him over as well. She looked at his hair, his shirt, his pants, and shoes. Her left eyebrow rose higher and higher with each new article of clothing she observed.

Adam suddenly felt very aware of the worn state of his clothes— the holes in his shoes, the ragged length of his hair, the tight fit of his jeans, even the white powder dusting him from the dirt road he'd walked beside. He groaned inwardly.

Jenny looked him in the eyes. She wore a lopsided grin that only turned up at one corner of her mouth.

"Okay," she said like a professional about to take on a large project. "Come with me. Let's get you cleaned up."

14
Worth the Price of Admission

Adam followed closely in Jenny's wake as she led him down a crowded hall to a large stairwell. He wondered if there was a hole along the way he could jump in and die. At the bottom of the stairs they took a hard right, then walked a short distance before stopping in front of a doorless entryway next to a sign that read 'Men's Locker Room'.

"I can't go in there," Jenny said frankly. "Let me see if I can find someone to show you this area."

She glanced up and down the hallway, then waved over her head and yelled, "Patrick!"

Adam wondered if she won beauty pageants with that wave.

A boy who'd been further down the hall turned at her voice and jogged toward them. When he was close, Adam noticed he had on an armband the color of orange construction cones. On it was stenciled a symbol of a compass.

"Pat," Jenny said to the newcomer. "This is Adam. He's a freshman transfer student starting midway in the year. Today is his first day. Would you please show him the locker room while I wait out here?"

Patrick looked at Jenny and grinned, then glanced over at Adam. His grin slipped a bit. He looked back at Jenny and his grin widened again.

"Sure thing, Jenny. Anything for you."

Patrick was a little taller than Jenny and had muscled arms lined with veins. He walked with a purposeful stride. His uniform fit snugly. Adam noticed the point of what might be a tattoo emerging from under the collar of his shirt on the left side. He had a hole in his left ear where he might have had an earring recently. His hair was cut and combed in a close approximation of James Dean's look. He waved for Adam to follow.

The men's locker room was enormous. It must have been half the size of a football field. There were lockers lining the walls and in stacks through the center of the room. Each had a long bench beside it. The room smelled of soap and bleach and sweat. Patrick led him to the farthest corner in the back of the room.

"The lockers back here are for freshman. Don't use any others or you'll make trouble."

Patrick then led Adam to an adjacent wall made up entirely of shelves filled with folded uniforms.

"These are the school uniforms. You have to wear them, although there are quite a variety of styles to choose from. You can change out your uniform as often as needed. Most people average two or three changes per day. The dirty laundry goes here."

He pointed to a large basket on wheels at the end of the wall of uniforms.

"You'll probably need to shower several times a day, so follow me and I'll show where."

The "where" was a circular room with tile floors that sloped toward a central drain. The walls were interrupted at regular intervals by short, perpendicular wall segments extending in the room off the outer wall. An opaque glass door stretched between each divider. Adam, curious, opened one of the doors. It was heavier than it looked. There were not one, but seven shower heads in the cramped space—two on each wall and one overhead. Patrick came over and pointed at a red glowing circle on the floor of the shower stall.

"That is a pedal," he explained with unnecessary bravado. "That turns on water mixed with soap. When you let up, the sprayers turn off. After you scrub, you step on this other pedal."

He pointed at a blue glowing circle on the floor.

"This activates the clean water. No soap with the blue pedal. Blue will rinse you off. The whole affair takes about one minute, most of which is spent scrubbing. The soap and rinse only take about three seconds each. Towels are on the way back to the wall of uniforms. If you are the first person in the morning to use the showers, then..." he trailed off. "Well, I'll just let you find that out for yourself. Freshman are usually the ones fed to the Cold-Monster."

Adam laughed, impressed by the whole setup and not intimidated by cold water. The lake he bathed in each morning was frigid. The water here couldn't possibly be that cold. He was about to say so, but Patrick spoke first.

"Okay, new guy," Patrick said with finality. "Pay up."

Patrick held out his hand, palm up.

"Pay?" Adam asked.

The only money he had on him was three quarters. He'd been planning to buy something for lunch with it.

"But why?" he stammered.

"Look," Patrick said. "You're new here so I'm going to spell it out for you. This is a trade. I just taught you something. Now you are in my debt. I don't *want* you to be in my debt. So pay up or I'll do something unpleasant to you."

Adam thought about tying Patrick up as a pretzel, but admitted to himself that he really had learned a lot. He fished out a quarter from his pocket and handed it over to Patrick. Patrick frowned at the quarter, then sighed and put it in his pocket.

"Fine," Patrick said. "We're square. Now hurry up and shower and change into a uniform. If you keep Jenny waiting long, I will consider it a personal offense. And that would be bad for you. I am a hall monitor."

He pointed at the compass on his armband.

"You really don't want to make us mad. We can make life pretty unpleasant for you. Got it?"

Adam looked at Patrick calmly. If the older boy would just stop talking, this would go much faster.

"Got it. I'll be fast," Adam said and got moving.

He grabbed some of the uniform clothes off the wall, along with underwear and socks. Too bad shoes weren't provided as well. He ran to the shower room and noticed there was a half-height shower stool stationed just outside each stall. Beneath each stool were three small shelves. Adam considered the little shelves for a moment, then put his shoes and dirty clothes on one shelf and his new uniform on another. He couldn't figure out what the third shelf might be for.

Adam stepped in the shower and closed the door. He found the red glowing circle on the floor and stepped on it. An enormous amount of water hit him from all sides at once. He let off the pedal and sputtered. Soap ran in rivulets down his skin. The intensity of the water was such that he didn't feel he needed any scrubbing, but Patrick told him that was the way to do it, so he followed directions. He then pressed the blue pedal, and in three seconds he was completely rinsed. A huge, toothy smile spread across his face. This shower alone was worth the price of admission.

It was only when Adam stepped out of the shower he realized he'd forgotten a towel.

"Maldito," he muttered. "That's what that third shelf is for."

Since he was under pressure for time, he dried off with his street clothes, then jumped in the school uniform.

The new fabric felt at once slippery and cool, but also thin and light. It clung to his body like a second skin. It wasn't exactly the spandex superheroes wore in comic books but it was eerily similar. Adam could swear he felt it breathing. It was fantastic.

He thought he must look good so he searched out a mirror. His reflection looked anorexic. Oh well, at least he was clean.

He looked around the room, found an empty locker in the "freshman section" and stuffed his old clothes in it. While stuffing, he felt something hard in his laundry pile and pulled out his new ID card. He noticed a dark patch of cloth on his uniform shirt that looked the same size as the ID card. The dark patch felt different than the rest of his shirt and was situated in front of his right shoulder. He touched the ID card to the dark patch and it stuck like a magnet.

"Que chido," he said out loud, impressed.

He took a mental picture of the surroundings so he could—hopefully—find his way back later, then jogged out to the main hallway. The new uniform felt weightless while he ran. It was made for action... like him.

15
Urban Jungle

Adam found Jenny still waiting in the hallway. She was chatting with Patrick. Jenny looked up at Adam and smiled.

"Much better," she said with mock relief.

Adam smiled back. He felt great.

Patrick, on the other hand, looked annoyed.

"I gotta go. See ya later," he said to Jenny.

Jenny waved at Patrick pleasantly, then stepped toward Adam and looked him up and down. Still smiling she said, "Big improvement!"

"Yeah, yeah," he rolled his eyes. "I can take a hint. Thanks."

Jenny led him to a large indoor pool farther down the hall. It was big and... wet. No one was using it at the moment. Then she led him back up the stairs and to the left. She stopped in front of a wall of doors which opened on an enormous room filled with tall tables and chairs.

"That's the cafeteria," she said and walked in.

The cafeteria was three times the size of the entry hall—nearly as big as a football field. Glass-enclosed buffet carts were lined end to end parallel to one wall. Along an adjacent wall, there was a long line of sinks and sprayers separated from the rest of the room by a thin stainless-steel counter. Throughout the middle of the room were separate, tall round tables with barstool-height chairs.

The upper half of all four walls was taken up by large banks of computer screens and electronic signs. The monitors displayed lists of names. Some of the lists had prices. Other lists were joined up with titles and accomplishments and dates. There was a scrolling bar of information circling the entire room. The whole setup reminded him of the New York Stock Exchange. He incidentally noticed Jenny's name at the top of one of the lists, next to the title 'Sophomore Valedictorian'.

Adam nodded toward her name on the monitors.

"Is that you at the top of the list?"

She nodded, seeming not to care.

"Students' achievements are posted and updated in real time. We take competition here very seriously. Everything that matters gets published in rank order lists. I happened to get the top spot in my class last year and the year before that," Jenny said offhandedly.

Adam still got the impression that she didn't care much about her achievement. He found himself wondering what she *did* get excited about.

"All this information is compiled and tracked by the Master-Mind—or part of him, anyway. The Master-Mind is the computer program that matches students with their classes and jobs, keeps track of workout times, maintains bank account ledgers and money transfers, and updates prices in real time for each of the services sold here at the school. It does other stuff too, but you'll learn all of that in time. For now, let's keep going."

They exited the cafeteria and turned left, walking a long while before the hall opened up to an enormous gymnasium. The gym looked to have multiple tiers and tracks. At just a glance, Adam saw parallel bars, basketball goals, volleyball nets, a running track, treadmills, exercise bikes, racks of weights, and weight machines. Further up, he saw nets around indoor batting cages. In addition to all the exercise equipment, there were wires running all over the room. It looked like there were designated paths through the forest of exercise equipment and bundles of wires. The whole scene struck Adam as a three-dimensional cubist rendition of a jungle.

"Look at this," Jenny said as she led him down one of the paths and stopped at a treadmill. "You make everything in this school work by logging in. Put your badge right here."

Adam pulled off his ID badge and held it before him, confused.

Jenny grabbed his wrist and guided his hand close to a gold plate that was affixed to the side of the machine. His wrist tingled where she'd touched it. He heard a soft hum as the machine came to life. Dials and readouts spread across a panel at the front of the treadmill. A television/computer monitor blinked on at eye level in front of the machine. Jenny motioned for him to step on the moving belt.

"The Master-Mind will automatically keep track of all your vitals and statistics and will let you know when the next class period is coming. You can access this keyboard if you want to work on a computer."

She pulled a keyboard out from under the treadmill's dashboard.

"Or you can use this other shelf here as a writing desk."

She pushed the keyboard back and pulled out a sliding desktop from somewhere under the keyboard slot.

"You can turn on these fans manually."

She pointed to several small fans at different parts of the treadmill.

"Or you can ask the Master-Mind to operate them for you in response to your body temperature and heart rate. When you're finished with the equipment, just flash your ID over the plate again or simply walk away from the machine. Everything you do is instantly updated to your student profile. Statistics are processed on your performance, and all sorts of comparative data comparing you and your classmates is published in the cafeteria. Competition is fierce, so no slacking."

She gave him a mock stern look, then laughed before heading out of the gym.

On the way back toward the school entrance, they passed a lengthy series of doors. She turned and pushed one open to reveal a short tunnel which ended in a second string of doors. They proceeded through the second set only to discover yet another short tunnel ending with an identical array of doors.

"Creepy," Adam said.

His voice echoed around the enclosed space. He felt claustrophobic.

"Yeah," Jenny agreed.

After passing through the third door, they emerged outside the school.

"This is the Play Yard," Jenny said.

She made a broad gesture that encompassed an enormous outdoor complex of what looked like every possible sort of sports setup.

"Why all these doors?" Adam asked, indicating the tunnel through which they'd just come.

She shrugged.

"Maybe to save electricity as people come and go out of the air-conditioned building all day long? Every student has two PE periods each day. That's a lot of coming and going."

Jenny turned around and led the way back through the tunnels and into the Tower. She turned left again. They had almost reached the front entrance to the building when they passed a large, sliding glass door. It opened soundlessly as they approached.

"This," she said grandly, "is the library."

The first thing Adam noticed when he entered the library was a dry, musty smell and a separate, crisp lemon oil smell. The second thing he noticed was a long desk near the front of the room where several librarians and a handful of students stood sorting and filing books. The long desk was raised more than a meter off the ground so it looked very tall and imposing, as did the people who were standing behind it. He wondered if the desk was designed to make an impression. He could think of no other practical reason to build a counter that high.

The room itself did not seem particularly wide but it was very long. He could barely make out the back of the elongated chamber. There were great shelves filled with books that ran parallel to the length of the room. There was a small desk on which a computer sat positioned between the ends of each set of shelves.

Adam felt eyes on him and glanced up to see a young woman staring at him through long, dark eyelashes. Her hair was black and she was wearing a black ribbon around her neck. From this angle, it was tough to see her hair, but it looked straight and black and shiny, and he thought he could make out a hint of some black ribbons nestled among twin ponytails. She had a slender nose on a slender face with Asian features—perhaps Korean. Her dark eyes had a slight tilt, and she had a tan complexion. He put on what he hoped was a charming grin and waved at her. The corner of her mouth twitched and she gave a little four-finger wave in return.

Adam startled when he realized Jenny was talking to him. He looked toward her and caught the end of her sentence.

"...so most of the books are in a basement underground. If you can't find what you want just ask a student librarian and they'll get whatever you need. The computers are self-explanatory. Be careful what websites you visit. The Master-Mind keeps track of that too."

Jenny looked at him. He nodded his understanding. Then she turned and led him out. Adam looked over his shoulder and found the pretty student librarian was watching him leave. He decided to name her *Ribbons*.

"Now comes the really important part," Jenny was saying, "and the thing that really sets this school apart from other schools. Let's sign you up for classes."

16
Bargain Hunting in a Healthy Market

Jenny led Adam up another flight of stairs to the second floor of the school. Like the rest of the school, the halls were packed full of students, parents, teachers, and staff.

As he followed Jenny, she filled him in on some of the particulars of the school.

"The teachers at this school are independent contractors. None of them are employed by the school. The teachers here rent space from the administration. Functionally, that means each teacher is an independent school—so Charter 7 is really a conglomeration of, like, 200 schools—all under the same roof."

"Why do they set it up that way?" Adam asked. "It doesn't sound typical."

"I'm told it is to encourage competition between the teachers. Competition drives prices down for us but pushes quality up. It's a big win for students."

"The other great thing," Jenny continued, "is there are no regulations telling the teachers how they have to do their job. Since no one tells them what to do, they can get creative. You'll find classes in this school run like nowhere else in the world. Sometimes that's great—sometimes not so much—but it's never boring."

"Wait," Adam interjected. He needed some clarification.

"If there's no regulation of course content, what prevents a teacher from, say, feeding candy to kids and showing movies all day long instead of teaching?"

Jenny turned, smiling, and walked backward.

"Two things. The consumers and the competition."

"The... students and the other teachers?" Adam asked in a tentative translation.

"And parents," Jenny added. Which made Adam wince. Jenny didn't notice.

"The students and their parents could buy a relaxing period of brainless entertainment if they wanted. It's their money. But why would they spend money on frivolity when they can get the same thing at home for nearly nothing?"

"Good point," Adam admitted.

"Also," Jenny continued, on a roll. She swung herself around a quarter turn and performed a graceful grapevine shuffle while explaining.

"In a free market like this school, if a teacher is below par, the other teachers competing for students will relentlessly advertise the weak teacher's deficiencies. Bad press like that can force an ineffective teacher to lower their price and maybe even drive them out of business."

She lifted her chin and held up an index finger as if lecturing.

"The businessman's *competition* protects the consumer from the businessman."

Adam grinned.

"And that works as well as regulation?"

"Better," she winked and turned to face forward again. "See for yourself."

Adam looked around and noticed teachers standing in front of each classroom. He tried not to openly gape. Some of these teachers were stunning. The men were tall and gallant. The women were statuesque and glamorous. All of them were dressed for success. Most were interacting with students and parents. Some were shaking hands vigorously and smiling like their lives depended on it. One teacher who wasn't talking with anyone at that moment was shouting out his course offerings.

On one side of each classroom door was a display that served as an advertisement for the course offered by each teacher. Most of the advertisements in view were large, flat computer screens displaying movies and pictures promoting the class and its teacher. All of the ads looked professionally produced. They had soundtracks and music scores. One teacher had a small laser light show drawing attention to his advertisement. The best, Adam thought, was a three-dimensional hologram extending out from the wall. It showed a teacher soaring through space like Peter Pan, with students flying behind like ducks in a 'V'. Under each advertisement was an electronic display of the class price. Under each price was a label that read 'per semester'.

Not surprisingly, the better-looking teachers had prominent shots of themselves in the photographs moving across their class display. One of the male teachers even had an ad that was just a big, smiling glamor shot of his face. Adam was only partly successful at choking down his laugh.

Jenny turned around to see what was ailing Adam, noticed the picture on the wall, and started to giggle too.

The scene reminded Adam of an outdoor market—albeit one staffed by big budget politicians and salesmen, with a bit of a carnival thrown in as well. There was a vibrant energy in the air. Adam found himself smiling.

After they walked further down the hall, Jenny leaned to Adam's ear and half-yelled, "Did your parents put any extra money toward your classes or is the voucher all you have?"

"Ah, well... that is... no," Adam stammered.

She nodded her understanding.

"Okay then. These popular classes will probably be too expensive for you. I'll take you toward some more affordable teachers."

She looked at his shoes and reconsidered.

"Perhaps the bargain wing would be best for you."

Adam wasn't sure what the 'bargain wing' was, but it sounded just right.

Jenny turned back the way they'd come and led him up another flight to the third floor of the building. From there, she guided him toward the very, very back of the hall of classrooms.

The stark contrast between the second floor and the top floor was startling. First of all, there were far fewer students, so it was much quieter. Secondly, the teachers in this hall were homely. Their clothes were practical and clean, but the styles were traditional and conservative, or else relics of a long-lost clothing fad. Third, the ads beside the doors contained fewer pictures of the teacher and more images of students at work or students holding up their finished projects and smiling. Many of the advertisements were clearly self-produced and a bit amateur. Finally, many of the prices per semester were half of what was listed for classes on the floor below.

Jenny spoke in his ear again—she didn't have to yell this time.

"How much do you have in your account?"

He shrugged.

"I'm not sure. How do I find out?"

"It's on your card."

She showed her own to demonstrate. She flipped it over so the back was facing up and slid her thumb over the portion that read, 'Where Justice Leads, Prosperity Follows.'

The text vanished and a number display lit up. Hers read '$7,500'.

Adam pulled his ID card off the front of his shirt, flipped it over, and ran a thumb over the inscription.

His display read '$3500'.

He looked up and saw Jenny's mouth had assumed a tight, flat line.

"What's wrong?" he asked.

"It just makes me mad, is all," she told him with a small growl.

"The state pays state-run schools $6,300 per student per year, but only gives $3500 to charter students per year. The unfairness of it is staggering."

She let her anger out in one long breath, then seemed more relaxed.

"Okay then. Desperate times call for desperate measures. Come with me."

Jenny led him deep down the long hall.

As they walked, Adam noticed subtle changes. The lights, for example, got progressively dimmer. Some were flickering. The temperature started to rise too, along with the humidity. Perhaps the air conditioners didn't work up here? The teachers, too, were aging. Some were not engaging students as they walked by. The prices on the wall were a quarter of the prices he'd seen on the second floor. The advertisements beside each door were paper posters or corkboard presentations.

Adam was delighted... at least with the prices.

They passed by an old man with pure white hair, hearing aids, thick glasses, and a cane. He was sitting in a chair outside of a classroom notable for having the lowest posted price Adam had yet seen—$100. The old man was slumped forward over a cane. His skin was the color of a wax model. Adam stopped in front of the professor and looked closely to see if he was still breathing. The nametag hanging from the wax model's shirt collar read 'Mr. G'.

The old man's eyes flashed open and Adam jumped.

"What do you want?" asked the professor in a voice like dried leaves crackling over a burning fire.

"What do you teach?" Adam asked.

"What did you say?" asked the old man, cupping his ear.

"WHAT DO YOU TEACH?" Adam yelled.

"Oh, I teach Economics. The dismal science," he cackled.

"What is useful about economics?" Adam asked.

"What did you say?"

"WHY DO I CARE ABOUT ECONOMICS?"

"Oh, economics is the best! It is full of tools to help you understand yourself and the people around you—the decisions we make and the outcomes those decisions produce. It also has tools for making predictions about what policies will make us better off as a society. And which ones make society *worse*. But most of all, girls dig it."

The professor cackled again, then stopped abruptly.

"I may have fibbed that last bit."

"YOU HAD ME AT $100," Adam told him.

A huge grin stretched across the professor's face.

"Young man, you have the makings of an economics genius. What's your name?"

Adam flashed his ID card over the gold plate in front of the room, guessing that this was how he told the Master-Mind he wanted to join the class. His ID card lit up briefly, displaying the name of the class and the price quoted on the wall. Then the price on the wall increased to $105.

"ADAM SMITH. My name is ADAM SMITH."

The professor stared at Adam, apparently dumbstruck. Then his eyes started watering and he was guffawing so hard that Adam worried he might hurt himself.

"And I'm the Pope. Pleased to meet you," the old man wheezed between bouts of devilish laughter.

Jenny tugged on Adam's arm.

"We need to keep going. You have more classes to choose."

"Yeah," Adam said, then waved to *Mr. Geezer*—Adam decided that was his name—who was still cackling and wheezing as they walked away.

17
Biology

Further down the hall they came across two remarkable teachers, one on the left side of the hall and the other on the right.

The one on the left was a woman dressed in flannel workout pants and a matching flannel workout jacket, both in school colors. She wore a whistle around her neck and had bad hat hair as though she'd recently taken off a baseball cap. Her hair was thick and curly and black with slashes of grey. She reminded Adam of a football linebacker. Her hips and shoulders and neck all looked like they were fashioned from square blocks. She had a square jaw with a big, round, pink nose at the center of her face. She had thin lips and a hint of hair on her upper lip. She had a single long eyebrow spanning her whole forehead. A traditional paper collage poster on the wall next to her showed pictures of students tending to plants and animals of all sorts.

Adam glanced through the door and got a sense that there was a lot of green stuff in the room. He thought he saw a kitten peek out, but it was gone in a flash. Perhaps he'd imagined it.

The price outside her door read '$160'. Adam slid his card over the wall plate. The price on her door jumped up to $180.

Ms. Squarepants—Adam decided that was her name—smiled and clapped him on the shoulder. He thought he felt something break.

"Glad to have you," she said in a low baritone.

"What do you teach?" Adam asked her.

Her eyebrow lifted.

"Why, Biology, of course."

Then, after a moment, she said, "Did you really just sign up without knowing what you were signing up for?"

"Excuse me," Adam said, blushing. He really didn't know how to answer. "I have to go pick more classes."

He turned quickly and walked away before she could say more.

18
Statistics

Adam nearly ran into the tall, spindly man on the other side of the hall. The teacher was so thin and so tall a light breeze would likely knock him off his feet. The thin man wore a white, button-up shirt and had near a dozen pencils and drafting tools sticking out of his left-hand pocket. Adam decided to call him *Pencil-Pocket*. Pencil-Pocket had thick glasses and a sharp nose. He had on well-worn khaki pants. His belt and shoes were well-worn brown leather. Adam fancied he saw calluses on the fingers of his right hand. He had small, dark, beady eyes which were staring at Adam's ID badge. The advertisement next to the door showed a large graphic that looked like a Taco Bell logo except with sunglasses and a smiley face.

"Care to learn statistics, Adam?" said Mr. Pencil-Pocket.

"What is statistics, sir?"

"Statistics," Pencil-Pocket beamed, "is practical mathematics. It is a collection of tools for dealing with uncertainty and chaos and randomness. It is useful for making real-world decisions since the world is full of uncertainty and chaos and randomness."

"I like tools," Adam said. Then after a moment's thought, "Do many girls take this class?"

"The smart ones do! I wish more did!"

Adam peered around Pencil-Pocket—it didn't take much—and saw the price on the wall read, '$110'. Apparently nobody took this class, boy *or* girl.

Well. The price was right. Adam signed up. His card flashed the class details, and the price on the wall went up to $120.

"You are a wise man," Pencil-Pocket said, smiling ludicrously and shaking Adam's hand. "You made a good choice. You won't regret it."

19
Economics of Cooking

Six doors down from the Statistics class was an advertisement that read 'Home Economics'.

Adam swiped his card over the plate.

Jenny looked surprised.

"You're interested in cooking?"

Adam went pale.

"This isn't another Economics course?"

Jenny's eyes sparkled. A muscle in her jaw twitched. She remained silent. Clearly her mood had improved.

His shoulders slumped.

"It's not, is it?"

Jenny shook her head from side to side.

"Oh crap," he said as he noticed for the first time the price by the door—$250. He turned green and felt a lump in his throat. He stuck his head through the door to see what he'd done.

The room was large and oddly furnished. There were ovens up and down the left wall and large square desks with range tops at their center. The middle of the room was dominated by chairs and the front wall of the room was taken up by shelves covered with boxes of diapers, racks of food, and what looked like infant dolls.

Adam was about to ask Jenny how to undo his selection when he noticed the pictures advertising the class. They included images of food and pastries and quilts and crafts all being proudly displayed by beaming students. Adam leaned closer to study the food and realized there were, like, two guys at most in all of the photographs. A class full of girls baking every day sounded like some kind of heaven on earth. He fantasized about a line of girls in aprons and oven mitts walking by his desk, asking him to taste their latest food creations.

He turned to Jenny and answered her question from earlier.

"Yes," he said solemnly. "I'm very interested in cooking."

Jenny's eyes narrowed suspiciously.

Adam turned away to hide his grin and continued walking.

20
Language of Love

Adam figured they were getting near the end of the hall because it was almost too dark to see. He was about to turn around and head back when a familiar smell made him pause. It was apricots and spring rain, and something else he couldn't name. He looked around and was startled when he noticed there was a small goblin of a teacher standing right next to him.

He turned his gaze upon a hunchback—albeit a petite one—with stooped shoulders and long, dark curly hair that hung nearly to the ground. She had enormous glasses with round lenses that covered half her face. She wore a floor-length skirt and a dark shawl that draped over her arms before it followed her hair to the ground like a waterfall cascading off her shoulders. Her shawl and skirt were both midnight blue—which might explain why he hadn't seen her in the dim light. The whole ensemble reminded him of the witch in *Snow White*—the one with the poisoned apple.

The hunchback looked up at him. Her nose came up to his chin. The smell of her hair filled his nostrils. It smelled like cedar and dust with undertones of apricots. Her eyes looked big as coffee cups viewed through her glasses. She had a large wart on her nose. She sniffed at him. Her hands, which were surprisingly strong, reached up and gripped his forearms. She squeezed his arms like the witch in *Hansel and Gretel*—the one who tried to fatten the kids up for stew.

While he imagined himself as Hansel, the witch made a *'tsk'* sound.

He looked down and noticed she was looking at his shoes. The shoes, he knew, were ragged. He was ready to explain why he wore such tattered things on the first day of school, but the lie died instantly when he saw that she was smiling.

Playfully Adam said, "You can't have my shoes."

She lifted a magnified eyebrow and rotated her head like a curious bird.

"They're in high demand," he said disingenuously with a hint of sarcasm.

"I've already sold them once today. I can't bring myself to part from them a second time, even for pretend. So please control your envy."

"My... 'envy'?" she said, nearly coughing.

Adam held up a stalling hand. "Don't even offer. I can't bring myself to part from them for any price."

He heard her say in a British accent, "You're my people."

Now it was Adam's turn to look confused.

"Your... 'people'?" he queried.

"I found you. Yes, I did," she said triumphantly.

Just then Jenny grabbed Adam's arm from behind and hauled him back.

"Get away from him, Miss Anne. He's not interested in your class."

Miss Anne—apparently that was her name—looked down her nose at Jenny through the enormous lenses of her glasses.

"What? I think you are mistaken, Ms. Valedictorian."

As she spoke, she reached out and grabbed Adam by his wrist again. Adam briefly felt like the rope in a tug-of-war match.

"He's perfect for my class."

"Adam," Jenny said, still not letting go of his arm, "do not join this woman's class. She is a... a... faker."

"Now, Jenny," Miss Anne said tersely. "I am simply trying to scare away students so I can keep my price low enough for the truly destitute. Mine is a labor of love not to be questioned by one so pretty, young, smart, and fortunate as yourself."

With that, the old crone tugged a little harder on Adam's wrist. Neither lady was giving any ground.

"Um," Adam spoke to no one in particular, "what class is this?"

"It's Language and Communication! The tools of love," Miss Anne practically sang out in that adorable British accent.

Adam had a polite refusal on his tongue, then forgot it as Miss Anne suddenly released him. He fell back into Jenny momentarily— not an unpleasant experience. He was about to apologize to Jenny when he noticed Miss Anne had taken up an odd posture against the wall. Her hands and eyes and neck and waist were all pointing to her left. Adam followed the lines of her body like he might a painting until they landed on the focal point which—in this case— was the price on the wall.

$90.

"Okay," Adam said while a chuckle bubbled up from deep in his belly. "You win. I'm your people."

He strode forward and waved his badge over the wall. His card flashed its acknowledgement.

Miss Anne made a deft, hunchbacked curtsy to Adam.

Jenny tugged on Adam's arm again and he followed her back up the hall a bit. She frowned over his shoulder, then looked Adam in the eyes and said, "Why didn't you listen to me?"

Adam shrugged and looked down bashfully.

"The price was right."

Jenny sniffed.

"Do you even know what a price is?"

Adam, taken aback, thought a moment.

Then he replied, "It's the numerical obstacle that keeps me from getting everything I want."

"It's the ratio at which an exchange takes place," she said, not quite burning him with the intense look from her smooth, dark brown eyes.

Adam raised an eyebrow.

"Say again?"

"It's the ratio at which an exchange takes place," she repeated, though with less heat the second time. "It's not just a number. It's a number that you agree to in order to make an exchange for something else. An exchange with a particular person at a particular time in a particular place."

Adam nodded, partly understanding.

"I get the 'particular person at a particular time in a particular place' part, but where does the ratio come in?"

Jenny sighed in exaggerated exasperation.

"A ratio is one value over another with a line between them. It's just a relationship. When you signed up for that woman's Language class..." her eyes flicked toward the old crone still standing by the door, "you agreed to pay $90 and she agreed to teach you language skills."

"$90," she made a slash in the air, "over her language class is a ratio. The whole ratio is closer to: $90 paid by you for one semester of Language class provided by Miss Anne this semester, agreed upon today at this specific time, in this specific place. But that's a whole lot of words. By convention, everyone just shortens it to $90. The rest of it is just sort of understood by you and Miss Anne because you were both there when it happened."

"What happened?" Adam asked.

"The exchange," Jenny retorted.

Adam gave a long, appreciative whistle. "I get it now." He grinned.

"You're saying that if it had been a different time or a different place, or some other teacher by that door, or some other student besides myself, then that exchange we made might not have occurred."

"It *could not* have occurred," Jenny said, stressing the 'could not'.

"Oh," Adam said, eyes widening at the implications.

"Wow."

"Yeah," she said, looking chagrined. "There's an enormous amount of information in each and every price, hidden in plain sight. Nobody sees it."

Adam squinted, seeing it.

"But that would mean," he said, thinking the ideas through carefully, "that prices are not generic, easily-transferable numbers."

"Yes," she said.

"When does *your class* start?" Adam asked, star-struck. "I'd love to sign up for it."

She gave him a guarded look, then relaxed. When she spoke again, she no longer sounded angry.

"You know how to sign up for classes now. This concludes my obligations as a student council representative. Master-Mind will take your selections and design a schedule. It will be ready by the end of the day when everyone else has finished signing up as well. If you have any questions in the future that your teachers," she cast another brief glare in Miss Anne's direction, "cannot answer, you can call or text me."

With that, she picked up her phone and pointed it meaningfully at Adam.

Adam looked at her phone, then at her, then back at the phone, confused. She was clearly waiting for something.

"Your phone, silly," she said.

He didn't budge.

"Show me your phone so we can swap contact info."

Adam blinked in confusion, then blushed fiercely. He muttered, "I don't have a phone."

"WHAT?!" Jenny blurted out. "Everyone has a phone. How do you not have a phone?"

"Um, well…" Adam started to explain.

"Oh, never mind that."

She pulled a piece of paper out of a hidden purse under her sweater and scrawled out her number.

"Use a school phone if you need to. Also, you can text from any computer in the library. Now let's review: what is a price?"

"The ratio at which an exchange takes place," Adam answered by reflex before he'd even registered the question.

She nodded—a self-satisfied look on her face.

"It was nice to meet you."

Jenny turned on her heel and walked rapidly out of sight back down the hall.

Adam watched her recede, pondering the turbulent, brilliant girl. After she was out of view, he turned to speak to Miss Anne and found himself nose to crooked nose with her. He startled and fell backward.

Miss Anne's eyes—magnified several times over by her ridiculous glasses—sparkled with mischief.

"I'll see you tomorrow in class, Adam. Don't be late."

She whirled around and went back to her spot by the classroom door.

Adam turned and headed down the hall—back toward the library—wondering how ladies, young and old, had such a knack for knocking him off balance.

21
Amy

Adam got lost twice looking for the library again. Cursing his lack of direction sense, he broke down and asked for directions both times. He got there eventually and found students everywhere—between the stacks, at the computers, congregating around the elevated desk at the front. Adam briefly saw a flash of narrow eyes, then black ribbons disappeared behind the front desk. A moment later the tall, slender girl who had waved to him earlier in the day appeared next to him. She wore a dark ribbon tightly around her neck which drew his eye. Her neck was attractive. The lines of muscle drew triangles under her jaw, in front of her throat, and along each side of her shoulders, just over her clavicles. Her hands were clasped behind her back and she was leaning toward him, smiling in a very girlish gesture.

"I'm Amy," she practically sang. Adam just stared. "I'm a library assistant here."

She pointed to a brown armband around her left arm that displayed an image of a half-open book.

"Can I help you find anything?"

"Oh, yes please," Adam responded. "I would be most grateful if you could help me find my schedule for tomorrow. And also help me check out a book to read tonight on the way home."

"I'd be happy to," she said as she rocked back and forth on her heels like a cheerful rocking horse.

"Just follow me."

Amy turned and led him down a corridor with bookshelves on each side. She had long, straight, shining black hair that drifted to below her waist. Her hair was tied in twin ponytails—each adorned with a wide, black ribbon that ran parallel to, and the entire length of, her hair. Adam found the sway of her hair mesmerizing.

She stopped and motioned for him to sit in front of a computer. She indicated a gold panel beside the computer desk. Adam swiped his card. The computer lit up instantly, revealing a profile page. It had all kinds of information on him like his age, height, vitals that morning, grade level, classes, a picture, and a box that read 'Biography' that was presently empty.

Down the right side of the display was a list of the classes he had selected, all color-coded. Next to each class was a grade percentage—all of which read 0%. He touched one of the classes with his finger and it expanded to give details on the teacher, the class description, a link to the syllabus, the cost of the class, homework assignments, supplemental readings, etc. The whole setup was very intuitive.

Ribbons leaned forward and pointed. "Touch right here to display tomorrow's schedule."

He did so and was rewarded with a calendar. At the same moment, his ID card lit up and showed the same schedule. Adam felt pleased at this small accomplishment.

He turned to Ribbons to thank her but only got out, "Thank…" before he cut off speaking abruptly.

She was very close—closer, perhaps, than he had ever been to any girl. She smelled like spearmint. Her eyes looked very large, very dark, and very intelligent this close. She didn't move away, but fiddled with one of her ponytails and waited for him to recover. He blushed furiously and turned his head back toward the computer.

She went on as if nothing had happened.

"Now, the library access portal is down here," she pointed to the lower left corner of the screen where there were many tiny icons. Some of those icons resembled the symbols he'd seen on different students' armbands, including one that looked like a half-open book. He touched the symbol of the book and it expanded to fill the whole screen with a webpage strikingly similar to an online book distributor, but without any ads.

Ribbons explained, "You enter the book title or the author or any other search criteria in this line and select the media format you want over here. When you find what you want, just click 'Add to cart', then 'Checkout'."

She waited to see if he understood.

He nodded.

"If you have any problems, just find me. Remember, my name is Amy."

Oh crap, Adam thought to himself. She couldn't possibly know how bad he was with names. He repeated her name over and over in his head—hoping it would stick but knowing it wouldn't.

She seemed to read his mind.

"A. M. Y."

With each letter she spoke, he felt her write the same letter on the back of his hand with an ink pen. Then, she stood up abruptly.

He hurriedly stood as well and gave her a formal half-bow.

"Thank you very much. You were a great help to me. And thank you for this." Adam turned her name on the back of his hand toward her.

The corner of one side of her mouth went up before she said quietly, "So formal."

She bowed toward him as well—more of a tilt of her head, really. Then she put her left hand behind her back, leaned forward at her waist like a rocking horse again, and said warmly, "You are very welcome, Mr. Adam Smith."

She tapped her name on the back of his hand, then twirled and walked quickly away—ribbons fluttering behind her like a cape.

Adam took a long, hard swallow. Amy was... impressive.

22
Justice

Adam sat back down at the computer desk and contemplated what he would like to read. He looked around at the nearby bookshelves, trying to think of something that interested him or some problem he needed to solve. He saw his ID card sitting on the desk with the school motto facing toward him.

Where Justice Leads, Prosperity Follows.

What was justice anyway?

He keyed the word 'justice' in the search line, selected 'book' for his preferred type of media, and hit enter. A list of books appeared. He scrolled through them—looking for one that sounded interesting—then stopped at *The Theory of Moral Sentiments* by Adam Smith.

Adam Smith? Seriously?! ¡No manches!

He selected *The Theory of Moral Sentiments* and it shot over to his virtual cart. Then he checked out the way Amy had instructed. Nothing happened. He looked around for a slot or some directions as to how to collect the book he'd ordered but could find none. As soon as he stepped away from the desk, the computer went dark.

Bah, he thought irritably. It looked like he'd need to ask Amy for help already. That kind of perked him up.

He wandered back up to the front desk. Ribbons was nowhere to be seen. He asked another librarian how to collect a book he'd ordered and she pointed to one of the many gold plates on the face of the elevated front desk. He flashed his card across it and heard a book thump behind the wood of the desk. A slot he'd not noticed till then opened directly under the gold plate. He reached in the slot and grabbed his book.

"Thanks," he said to the librarian who had already gone back to her work.

She may or may not have heard him.

Adam followed his stomach back to the cafeteria. Jenny had mentioned that they left food out even after mealtimes. He found the place sparsely populated. There were some trays filled with food in the glass-covered carts along one wall. He grabbed a tray and went through the line.

There were three different vegetarian selections and two fruit selections. There was yogurt and milk available as well. There was no one serving, so Adam just spooned huge portions of everything on his plate. He took his weighty tray to a cash register and flashed his ID card over the ubiquitous gold plate. A middle-aged, mildly overweight balding man in a white uniform totaled his food. It all rang up to $6. '($6.00)' appeared briefly on the back of Adam's ID card, then faded.

Adam reckoned this was a good price. He'd purchased a lot more food than he saw served at the restaurants he'd worked and it was about half the price of a meal at those establishments, too. Even so, he clapped his hands together before eating and sent up a silent thanks to God—once again—for his voucher.

Adam was famished. He'd not eaten at all today—perhaps not yesterday, either. He couldn't remember. The vegetable dishes tasted exotic, but also healthy. He tried to eat slowly but failed miserably. After only a few minutes he felt kind of stuffed and slowed down. He drank some milk from a carton and opened his library book, *The Theory of Moral Sentiments*.

The book was well-written but the language was old and some of the spelling different, which, he guessed, was to be expected in something written over 200 years ago. Adam—the student—was looking for an explanation of 'justice'.

He went to shift the book and felt something solid on its back cover. He turned the book over and noticed a miniature version of the gold plates that were all over the school. Curious, he ran his ID card over it. The display on the back of the ID card came to life to reveal the cover of the book he held in his hand. He put the book down and examined the display on his ID. He slid his finger over the display and the page turned just like in a real book.

"Qué chévere!" Adam said to himself.

Next he noticed a small magnifying glass in the bottom corner of the display. He touched it and a text line expanded on the screen with the word 'Search' at the start of the line and a virtual keyboard under it.

Curious, Adam typed the word 'justice' in the text box and hit 'Enter' on the virtual keyboard. The screen flashed and displayed, '93 paragraphs found.' He slid his finger over the screen and paragraphs rolled by, one after another, with the word 'justice' highlighted in each.

"Ooooh," Adam cooed. "This is sweet!"

Adam read in Section II.II.5, "The violation of justice is injury: it does real and positive hurt to some particular persons."

Adam pondered that. He concluded that when Justice is violated, someone gets hurt.

In Section II.II.9 of the book he read, "Justice is, upon most occasions, but a negative virtue, and only hinders us from hurting our neighbour."

So justice, Adam decided, was not an active virtue in the way giving to the poor is an active virtue. Justice was more like the absence of action—specifically the absence of actions that hurt others. That explanation reminded him of the phrase, 'Do no harm,' that doctors say as part of their creed.

Perhaps 'Do no Harm' was a good definition of justice.

He rolled his school ID card around in his hand and reread the school motto, 'Where Justice Leads, Prosperity Follows.'

Given his newfound understanding of justice, the school motto might mean, "When we don't hurt each other, we all get rich."

Adam raised his eyebrows. That sounded pretty good. He'd have to run it by a few other people, but he thought he might be on to something.

He tucked the book under his elbow and fixed his ID back on his shirt. He took his tray over and dropped it where he saw other students leaving their trays. At the last second, he grabbed a half-eaten apple off someone else's discarded tray, ate the whole thing in two bites—core and all—and left for home.

23
Asuna

The next day, Tuesday, was Adam's first day of class. He was so excited that he got up, bathed in the lake, carried firewood, brushed his teeth, drank his fill of water, folded his blankets, zipped up his tent, and headed for school—all before the sun rose. The walk to school was uneventful aside from the fact that the sun came up a magnificent purple, then red, then yellow. It made the sky look like a canvas and the clouds colorful blobs of paint.

He had no trouble in the City either. Once at the school, he waved to Officer-Red and pulled up the day's schedule on his ID. His first class period was Physical Education. He tapped the name of his class on the ID card and it pulled up a map showing him where to go. The map had him going to the locker rooms first.

In the locker room Adam realized he had a half hour before first PE, so he went over to the showers still wearing his street clothes. He went through the whole shower routine, but instead of washing his body, he scrubbed his clothes. Afterwards, he took off the soaking apparel, wrung it out as best he could, and hung it to dry in one of the freshman lockers. Then he took another shower—this one for his body. The school uniform he picked today was a tank top, running shorts, ankle-high socks, and some grey boxer-brief underwear. Next he went by the library and dropped off the book he'd borrowed the day before. Then he followed the map on his ID card out to the Play Yard.

Still early, he sat down in the grass and pulled *The Theory of Moral Sentiments* up on his ID. Apparently he didn't need to possess the physical library book to read its contents. He picked up reading where he'd left off the previous day.

"Whatchya reading?" a happy girl's voice interrupted him.

Adam looked up and saw a familiar broad-shouldered, athletic female with blond hair and green eyes looking in his direction. She was stretching.

Adam's eyes widened in recognition.

The girl—he couldn't remember her name—glanced up, blinked twice, then gave him an enormous, bright smile.

"Adam!"

Adam nodded, unable to prevent his own face from grinning back at the happy girl. She looked much as she did the day he'd rescued her wallet from Bandito-Aspirante, the pickpocket. Her hair was straight and long enough to reach the middle of her back. She had a button nose and an average-sized mouth on an oval face. When smiling, her upper, central-most teeth looked larger than the adjacent teeth, giving her a faintly bunny-like appearance.

"Asuna," she said. "My name is Asuna. Do you remember me?"

He nodded enthusiastically.

She stopped stretching and sat up straight.

"I remember you too. You rescued me from certain disaster when I dropped my wallet. I'm still grateful. My friends say I'd lose my feet if they weren't attached to me. I had no idea you were a student at this school. Have you always been a student here?"

Adam shook his head and took a breath to answer, but Asuna kept talking.

"I came here early because I like this class. Phys Ed, I mean. I like PE. And I'm good at it. You look fit, Adam. I'll bet you're good at PE too. I'll bet you're fast. You look strong."

Adam blushed and said, "Thanks. You do too."

"Me? Strong?" Asuna asked conversationally. "I guess that's true. I'm stronger than all the girls at this school and most of the boys."

She flexed her left arm absentmindedly. Adam could see the striations of her prominent muscles.

"But I've always been this way. It's just how I'm built. Some girls don't like it though. They think muscles only look good on men." She looked thoughtful and started stretching again. "I think they're mistaken. It's fun being strong, and besides, I think muscles look pretty on women too. I like the way I am."

"I like the way you are too," Adam blurted out without meaning to.

She responded with a smile, this one warmer.

"That was nice."

She stood up and walked over to stand directly in front of Adam.

"Let's do formal introductions. I'm Asuna Flyer. Pleased to meet you... again."

Adam stood up and took her offered hand.

"Adam Smith. Pleased to meet you also."

They shook. Her hand was warm and strong and sweating.

"Where are you from, Adam?" she asked.

"Cow-town," he said, then corrected, "I mean, I'm from out of town, about sixteen kilometers outside the City."

"'Cow-town', huh?"

She looked amused.

"That's a funny name. I like it. I live pretty close to the school. I walk to school with my friends in the morning, but in the afternoon I take the bus to my Gran's house. My dad is a fireman."

She waved over Adam's shoulder at others who were walking toward them.

Soon the whole class was present and talking. Then a whistle blew and everyone looked over to see Adam's new Biology teacher, Ms. Squarepants, walk over.

So she was his coach too?

Adam mentally amended her name from Ms. Squarepants to *Coach-Squarepants*.

Coach-Squarepants spent the next twenty minutes telling them all the rules expected of students on the Play Yard. All the rules, she assured them, existed to help them avoid injuries.

"Ignore the rules all you want," she said, "just so long as you're the only one getting hurt. Ignore the rules and get someone *else* hurt," she said with a menacing air, "and you will fail this class instantly."

She also gave them practical instruction on what to do when someone broke the rules anyway and got hurt. She handed out handkerchiefs and newspapers and demonstrated how to make splints in the event someone broke a bone. She then asked everyone to pair up.

Most of the pairs were boy-boy or girl-girl, but there was an odd number of both boys and girls. When Coach-Squarepants asked for a girl to pair up with a boy, Asuna volunteered. When no boy volunteered, Asuna walked over to Adam, smiled at him, grabbed his wrist and hauled it above his head.

"He'll do it," Asuna told the coach.

Adam was amused. He'd never met anyone so extroverted in his life. He nodded to Coach and he and Asuna practiced splinting each other's arms and legs. Asuna had an incredible physique. She could have been a model for an anatomy textbook. She kept up a steady stream of conversation.

"It's a good thing I was here to save you, Adam. Who knows who you'd be stuck with otherwise?"

She pursed her lips, lifted her eyebrows, and looked around at their classmates conspicuously. Then she giggled.

"Just kidding. You look pretty fit, Adam, but—if you don't mind me saying so—kind of thin. Are you a cross country runner or something?"

Adam pondered the question, then said, "No, but I walk or run over thirty kilometers each day. Plus the food at my house is not very good. I'm hoping the food here is better."

Asuna brightened and was about to say something when Coach-Squarepants whistled and started to explain how to manage big cuts and bleeding. She taught them how to bandage a wound and how to stop the bleeding. Then they broke off again and practiced.

Asuna whispered excitedly, "I work in the cafeteria. I mostly help clean, but I sometimes get to cook! Maybe I'll see you there sometime. I can tell you which food is good."

Adam was trying to continue to talk but found he was more than a little distracted by the exercise. He was supposed to find areas on her body where there were big arteries and press on them really hard. One of these areas was over her upper arm and the other over her upper leg. He tried to look away while pushing on her leg, but only succeeded in making her giggle.

"It's over here, silly," she said. She guided his hands over her hip until he could feel her pulse—strong and slow and regular—beneath his palms.

He blushed furiously.

"Thanks."

Coach-Squarepants whistled again and told them all to run for the last five minutes of class.

Adam was mildly alarmed when he saw all the cheerful humor run out of Asuna's features while she pulled her hair in a tight ponytail just before the start of the run.

"It's time to get serious. I won't be holding back, Adam, so give it your best. I'll see you at the finish."

Asuna was much faster than Adam at the start of the run, but he had great endurance from his daily walks and he was really light, so it didn't take much effort for him to maintain a fast run. After a few minutes he caught up to Asuna on the track. She scowled at him and picked up her speed. He grinned and tried to keep up. In the end, Asuna won the race handily. When he crossed the finish, Adam found her lying on her back on the ground, breathing hard and fast. She pulled an inhaler out of her pocket and took some deep puffs on it. Adam walked over and sat next to her on the grass. He wasn't breathing too hard, but then, he didn't have asthma either.

Coach-Squarepants whistled the end of the class. The whole class walked toward the showers together. Asuna let her hair hang loose again as they walked. Her smile returned and she started talking amiably with everyone.

After a quick shower, Adam changed to another set of the school uniform, then headed to his next class, Language and Communication.

24
Lee

Adam followed the map on his ID card to the last room at the farthest end of the hall of the highest floor in the building. The map was especially helpful given the lighting was so poor on this end of the building. He poked his head in the room to see if he had the right place.

Sitting near the center of the room, surrounded by half a dozen other girls, was Asuna—whom he'd just spoken to the previous period. Outside the first ring of girls was a second, looser ring of girls and boys. Some of the students in the outer ring had their own smaller rings as well. The whole affair reminded Adam of the rotation of the planets around the sun and the moons around the planets.

Something caught Asuna's attention and she looked up straight in Adam's eyes. Instantly the smile on her face grew broad.

It seemed to Adam that the light in the room was brighter. He even went so far as to glance up at the ceiling to see if someone had turned on additional lights. When he looked down again, Asuna had broken free of her planets and was moving toward him—dodging tables and chairs athletically and quickly.

Adam suddenly felt nervous. He couldn't take his eyes off Asuna coming toward him and he could see in his peripheral vision that everyone else in the room was following her progress too. In mere moments he would be the intense interest of everyone in the room. Adam briefly entertained the idea of running. He'd miss the class though, and she could probably catch him. Running was no good.

In the middle of his moment of indecision, she arrived. He felt the air pushed ahead of her brush by his skin. She smelled of strawberries. Her smile was nearly too bright to look at. Her eyes were sparkling green gems.

"Adam!" she exclaimed and punched him playfully in the shoulder. "We're in this class together too!"

Adam, for his part, was struck speechless.

Asuna continued, "We really need to do something about this hair of yours."

She fluffed the long ends of his dark, thick hair with one of her hands.

"It hides your eyes. You have pretty eyes. I hope you'll let me cut it. I've been wanting someone to practice on."

She winked at him, spun, and headed back to her seat just as the teacher, speaking with a German accent, started to chastise.

"Take a seat, Adam. Hair is important, true, but we need to begin class."

Adam followed the sound of the voice to the front of the room. The voice sounded familiar—in spite of the accent. Then his jaw dropped.

He'd expected the old crone—bent back and huge round glasses. Instead, he found the Volkswagen-Saint standing at the front of the room dressed like Albert Einstein. She wore a long white coat over a white shirt and blue tie. She wore navy blue pants and a blue belt. Her shoes were sensible leather flats. Her hair today was stark grey and frayed up in all directions as though she'd spent all morning absorbing the static electricity from every piece of clothing in the City. She even had a tiny mustache on her upper lip. At that moment, her eyebrow was raised and she looked slightly perturbed.

"Pick a seat, Adam."

Adam closed his mouth with a click and took the first open seat he could find. All of the seats near Asuna were taken, so he ended up on the third—rather sparsely-populated—outer ring.

"Now, class," the VW-Saint said, waiting for the students to settle down.

"Welcome to the study of language. I am Miss Anne. You may call me 'Miss Anne' or just 'Anne' if you don't mind losing a finger. Language is native to each of you. Built in our genes, you could say. So we often take for granted how truly complicated it is. For example, the word 'language' can refer to written text, which is simply a string of symbols we all agree to associate with particular ideas or sounds or events or a whole manner of other features of reality. Language can also refer to the words we speak to each other, which is a different kind of symbol—a sound-symbol. Speech sounds and written symbols are stored in different parts of the brain. They are treated differently by our brains. They are—very obviously—quite different from one another, but we still apply the word language to them as if they are the same.

"Add to that that some people cannot hear, others cannot speak, and for them, language may be gestures or bumps on a flat surface. Language, as you can clearly see, is a very broad subject. One commonality between all of these uses of the word 'language' is symbols connecting experiences between people. So that is the definition we will use throughout the rest of the year. 'Language' is 'symbols people use to reflect common experiences'."

She repeated the definition slowly, emphasizing each part distinctly.

"Symbols... people use... to reflect... common experiences."

She waited a beat.

"So today I would like you to ponder that definition and begin honing your language skills by getting to know the people in this class, especially their names. Names being the symbols used to reflect the common experience that is your classmate. Ready, set, go!"

There was brief silence in the room, then Adam heard Asuna start talking to someone next to her.

"Hi, I'm Asuna. Nice to meet you..."

Adam was up and out of his chair in an instant. He made a direct line for the teacher.

Saint-Anne was just taking the chair behind her desk when Adam arrived.

He pitched his voice low and said, "Anne, when did you pick up a German accent?"

She frowned, displeased, and meaningfully looked down at his fingers.

"Which one would you like to lose?"

Adam paused briefly, confused, then remembered what she'd said earlier about how she wanted to be addressed.

"Oh, sorry," Adam said, deferentially, "Saint-Anne..."

He squinted his eyes shut as he realized he'd made another mistake with her name.

"I mean *Miss Anne*," he said, with eyes still closed.

"'Saint-Anne'," she mused in her German accent. "I like that one. You can keep that one if you like. Now tell me, how have you been?"

"Really good," Adam said honestly. "I'm really grateful to be here. I have a lot to learn, but everyone I've met seems really nice."

Patrick was not so nice, he remembered, but had been very helpful nonetheless.

Saint-Anne gave him a gracious smile.

"I'm so glad to have you in my class, Adam. How did you like my costume yesterday?"

Then she giggled like a young girl.

Adam looked down bashfully.

"You had me fooled. I think it was great."

Saint-Anne clapped her hands together in delight.

"Adam, I am simply giddy over all the fun we are going to have this year. But I cannot monopolize your time for my own enjoyment. Do make your rounds and try to get to know as many of your classmates as you can."

With that dismissal, she sat back and waved him away.

Now—for the record—a free-for-all meet and greet is not an introvert's idea of a good time, and Adam found the task daunting. Fortunately for him, though, most of the students in this class knew each other—at least in passing—so they were most eager to meet the few students—like him—who were new to the school. Most of the students in the class came to him and introduced themselves. For whatever reason, having strangers initiate contact with him was far less anxiety-producing than if he approached them. After chatting with a few of them, Adam noticed a very tall, thin, blond male student near the edge of the classroom. He was sitting in stony isolation. Seeing someone even more introverted than himself gave Adam a sense of power and courage with which he was generally unfamiliar. He decided to act on it. He walked over and sat across from the quiet gentleman and introduced himself.

"Hi, I'm Adam Smith."

The other boy looked up from the drawing he was making, which put him looking down at Adam.

Adam smiled at the irony.

"Hi as well," the towering boy said with apparent calm—although his body language looked anything but calm.

"My name is Lee. Lee Jorgan. What made you smile just now?"

The way Lee asked the question did not perturb Adam. In fact, he felt pretty at ease chatting with the taller boy.

"I was thinking it was ironic that when you looked up from your picture, you were looking down on me. Literally. What were you drawing?"

Lee turned his picture over toward Adam. It was a picture of Saint-Anne standing in front of the class behind the lectern. Much of the picture was just loose lines, but the illustration grew more detailed around her face. There were outlines of students in the foreground and sunlight streaming through windows in the background.

"Wow," Adam said, "that's really something. You've got talent."

"Thank you," Lee said, "but it is, 'You've talent,' not, 'You've got talent.'"

Adam just blinked at him.

Lee explained, "The abbreviation is throwing you off. Get rid of it."

Adam said slowly, "So it's, 'You have talent,' instead of, 'You have got talent'?"

"Right," Lee said triumphantly. "And great work catching the irony before. A lot of people don't know the meaning of irony and don't use it correctly."

"So I did good?" Adam asked.

"You did *well*," Lee corrected.

"Wow," Adam said. "If you are as talented with language as you are with art, I feel really lucky to have met you."

That got a grin out of Lee.

"Oh, and thank you for teaching me," Adam said. "I am pretty weak when it comes to language."

Which was true.

"It is one of the reasons I chose this class."

Which was not true.

"Well," Lee said, "since you are a man of uncommonly good taste in art and companions, I insist you sit next to me. If language is indeed a weakness of yours, you will find I am an uncommonly good resource... and also uncommonly modest... which is—I am sure you will agree—also ironic."

Adam laughed. Lee was a hoot—kind of over-the-top smart, but funny about it.

"I thank you and I will," Adam said as he plopped himself into the seat next to Lee.

"I can trade you for your company with my own. And although I am weak in the areas of your strength, I also have areas in which I excel."

"And what might those be?" Lee asked nonchalantly.

"Uncommonly good looks, for one," Adam said deadpan. "Obviously."

"Obviously," Lee agreed around a crooked grin.

After a few moments of amiable silence, Adam asked, "Lee? If you are done with it, could I trade you something for that picture you just drew? I like it."

Lee sighed.

"Alas, no one could fault your taste, good sir. But I am required to turn in any drawing I make to that teacher over yonder."

He waved a hand roughly in the direction of Saint-Anne.

"She tells me there is something a little wrong with drawing in a Language class, but she accepts my drawings in place of actual writing assignments."

"Really?" Adam was taken aback.

"Why on earth would she let you do something other than write in her writing class?"

"Language and Communication class," Lee corrected.

Then he went on, "I wasn't kidding when I said I was good with language. In fact, Miss Anne says I'm *too* good. She thinks I have— let me try to remember what she called it—'real talent'."

"I'm sorry," Adam interjected. "I am confused. Why are you in this class again?"

"Because I love to write," Lee said grinning—though he sounded depressed. "Obviously."

25
Trading is Work. Work is Trading.

Adam stood in the hall outside Saint-Anne's classroom looking down at his schedule. His ID told him his next period was 'Work/Study'. He didn't know what that meant exactly. He touched the class period on his card and was rewarded with an on-screen message that read, 'See advisor.'

What is an 'advisor'?

He racked his brain for a few minutes, then had an idea.

He jogged down the hall to the stairs, bounded down to the main floor, then walked to the main office. Jello-Lady was behind the counter. Her real name was Gertrude or Gladys or Godzilla—he couldn't remember.

Adam reached in his pocket and pulled out the piece of paper Jenny had given him the day before.

"May I use the phone, please?" Adam requested, using his best manners.

"What for?" Jello-Lady asked.

"I need to call Je... my advisor," Adam told her.

She gestured to the phone on the counter and looked back down at her paperwork.

Adam dialed the number. It rang twice, then Jenny answered.

"Jenny here. How may I help you?"

Adam cupped his hand over the receiver and spoke quickly.

"Jenny, this is Adam. Adam Smith."

The phone line was silent.

"The freshman you showed around yesterday."

More silence.

"You gave me your number and said I should call if I had any trouble?"

"Sure, I remember you, Adam. I would be happy to help any way I can. What do you need?"

Adam told her, "I have three 'Work/Study' periods open on my schedule and I don't know how to sign up for them."

"Oh, that's right. You won't have heard of those," Jenny said. She paused a moment.

"Odd, though. Work/Study classes are usually worked out between parents and administrators several weeks before the start of the new semester."

"Ah," Adam said. "That would explain it. I applied for school on the same day you showed me around, and my parents couldn't be there."

Jenny clucked her tongue over the phone.

"Well, let me think. I can help you sign up for them but I'll have to miss part of my class to do it. What will you trade me for the information?" Jenny asked.

Adam pondered that question. He was starting to get used to how students at this institution traded with one another for everything.

"Well, I was wondering…" Adam stammered, "Do you like flowers?"

"Of course I like flowers," Jenny said, nonplussed. "But I can't pay for college with flowers."

Adam drummed his fingers on the phone for a second.

"Do you like candy?"

"Are you trying to make me fat?" she joked.

"Jewelry?" he asked in desperation.

"Can you *afford* jewelry?" she asked dubiously.

"Girls like to talk, don't they?" Adam asked hopefully. "I mean, everybody likes to talk from time to time. How about I agree to listen to fifteen minutes of anything you want to talk about?"

The phone line was silent again. Adam thought he must have upset her somehow—perhaps because listening wouldn't pay her bills either.

Stupid. Muy estúpido.

He took a deep breath—intending to apologize—but she cut him off.

"Make it thirty minutes and you've got a deal."

Adam let out a cheer and hopped in the air.

"Yes!"

Jello-Lady gave him a cold stare over her reading glasses.

"Sorry," he mouthed silently, trying to swallow his celebration.

"I'm friending you," Jenny said over the phone.

"Really!?" Adam asked, uncertain he'd heard correctly.

"Look down at your ID."

Adam pulled the ID card off his shirt. On the back a message displayed, 'Jenny Longwillow would like to be your friend. Do you accept?'

Not what he'd been hoping for, but not bad either.

Adam hit the 'OK' box.

"Done," he told her.

"Now touch the little grey picture of a face in the bottom right corner."

He did so and the face expanded to reveal a list that read 'Friends' at the top and had Jenny's name underneath it. Next to her name was a classroom number.

"Now touch the classroom number next to my name."

Adam touched the classroom number and it expanded to a map.

"Now just follow the map to me. There is a computer here you can use to sign up for classes."

Adam hung up the phone and thanked Jello-Lady who waved without looking up. He followed the map toward Jenny but somehow still managed to make two wrong turns. Eventually he arrived at a chemistry lab.

There were glass instruments on shelves all around the room and a Bunsen burner on each desk. Each 'desk' was more like a table—about the size of four normal desks shoved together with a sink in the middle.

Jenny sat at one of the large desks in the center of the room. She was wearing plastic goggles and a long white lab coat. She had several glass tubes filled with different colored liquids in small stands arrayed out in front of her. She looked up at him, smiled, and removed the safety goggles, which left big red circles on her face. It made her look kind of like a red-faced raccoon. A cute one. With great hair.

"First," she said, "let me show you how to trade. Look at your ID and touch the dollar sign symbol in the top right corner."

He touched it. The symbol expanded to a text line.

"Now touch the 'Friends' icon still displayed in the bottom right corner of your screen, then my name."

Adam followed instructions and her name popped in the text box. He touched 'Enter' on the virtual keyboard. Two pull-down boxes on either side of a '<==>' symbol appeared. The first pull-down read 'Promise' and the second read 'Consideration'.

He touched 'Promise' and was given two options: 'Currency' and 'Other'.

He selected 'Other' and typed 'Listening, 30 minutes, any subject' in the text box that emerged. Then he touched 'Consideration' on the other side of the screen and was given the same options. He selected 'Other' again and typed 'Show Adam how to sign up for Work/Study'. Then he hit 'Accept'.

"Done," he told Jenny triumphantly.

She looked at her ID and touched it a few times.

"Well done. I accepted your offer. Now you will see a little picture of hands shaking just under the dollar symbol on the right side of your screen. If you touch the shaking hands, all your outstanding agreements will display."

Adam touched the shaking hands icon and it expanded to a list containing his new agreement with Jenny.

"Now, come over here," she said and led him to the side of the lab where a computer station sat idle. He lit it up with his ID card. Jenny directed him to his schedule and had him touch his first Work/Study period. It expanded to a long list of job openings. The list ran off the page.

"Wow," Adam said overwhelmed, "there are so many choices."

Jenny sat in a chair behind him resting her chin in her hand. She was tapping her cheek thoughtfully with her index finger.

"Well, these are jobs. You get paid for them. So the better or faster you are, the more likely you will get paid well. Do you have any skills that you are especially good at?"

"I can do dishes," Adam said without hesitation. "And I've been taught how to clean bathrooms and floors."

"Janitor or dishwasher," she said and continued to tap her cheek. "Choose one of those as your first choice. Now, for your second and third choice, answer this question: Is there anything you WANT to get good at?"

"I want to know how to fix broken equipment," Adam said.

He wanted to know how to repair things like the broken dishwasher at the Italian restaurant.

"And also solve problems," he added.

"Maintenance... Counseling... Perhaps medical services," Jenny said, translating his preferences into options. "Do any of those sound good to you?"

She was staring at the computer screen.

Adam could see the lights in the room reflected in her eyes. He thought Jenny looked kind of like the statue of *The Thinker* in that pose—except female and attractive. He felt his cheeks grow hot.

"Those all sound good."

Jenny nodded, satisfied.

"I know the nurses in Health Services. They are nice to work with, and once a week a doctor comes and gives personal instruction to the health staff after his open lecture to the school. You'll learn a lot."

Adam turned away from Jenny and selected 'Janitorial' for his first Work/Study period, 'Health Services' for his second, and 'Maintenance' for the third.

"Don't be surprised," Jenny told him, "if Master-Mind changes the order around. He tries to spread out the work evenly so there aren't a hundred people working one period and none the next."

"What do these jobs pay?" Adam asked with anticipation.

"That depends," Jenny said.

"On what?"

"It depends on you. Or rather, it depends on if anyone wants to hire you. Students and teachers and staff can make you offers for your services, just like the contract you and I just made—except usually for money. You can accept or decline them as you please. Usually at the start of each shift you can check your department's website for work requests and the prices offered for completion of the requests. You choose the work you think you can do at prices you are willing to accept. Once the person who posted the work signs off that it's done—and fills out a satisfaction survey—the money is transferred from their account to yours. If you get a good reputation, people might post work requests specifically for you— rather than the department. Or they might give you tips or allow you to make counter offers. Don't worry about the details too much right now. You will pick it up quickly. I can tell."

She gave him a reassuring smile.

"I think I have it," Adam said. "When do you want me to fulfill my side of the bargain?"

"I'm pretty busy during school hours," Jenny told him candidly. "Can you come to school a half hour early on Thursday?"

"No problem," Adam said, taking her cue and talking frankly. "Where shall we meet?"

"Let's meet out on the Play Yard. There's a picnic table under the tree by the south lawn. The friend tracker on your ID will show you where."

Adam nodded and turned to leave but Jenny put a hand on his wrist. The unexpected contact pleased but confused him. He looked back at her askance.

Jenny was looking down at her ID card and manipulating it with her free hand.

"I just informed Master-Mind that I completed my end of the bargain. Now he sends you a survey. Look at your ID. You should see the shaking hands symbol flashing."

Adam touched the flashing symbol. It expanded to a list where the first and only entry read 'Adam Smith – Listening, 30 minutes, any subject' <==> 'Show Adam how to sign up for Work/Study – Jenny Longwillow'.

His side of the agreement was solid red. Her side of the agreement was flashing yellow. He touched her side of the agreement and it expanded to a short survey.

'1) Services rendered as agreed? 2) Services rendered in expected time frame? 3) Comments?'

At the end of the first question and the second question, there were five empty stars all in a row. Adam touched the fifth star in each line and the preceding stars all turned yellow. In the comments section after the third question Adam wrote, 'Beautiful'.

The screen shrank back down to the description of their agreement except now Jenny's side was solid green. His side was still solid red.

"This trading tool is amazing," Adam said.

"It sure is," Jenny said—wrinkling her nose but looking pleased as she read his posted comment.

"It's one of the many things that sets this school apart from all others," she said, smiling.

Adam faced her squarely and gave her a respectful bow.

"Thank you so much for taking the time to show me the ropes. I look forward to repaying my debt to you."

Jenny ruffled his shaggy hair.

"So formal. Always bowing. Your parents must have raised you right."

Adam—still bowing—closed his eyes.

His parents were dead. For once he was grateful for long hair. It hid his pain.

26
Epiphany

Adam missed his entire first Work/Study period and part of the next period because of his meeting with Jenny. His ID directed him to go to his next class anyway. Economics. That was Mr. Geezer's class—the old guy with the cane—if he remembered correctly. He climbed the stairs to the top floor, walked through the classroom door, and entered a zoo.

The room was full of people talking to each other. There were spitballs and paper wads flying through the air. Mr. Geezer was standing at the front of the class writing on the chalkboard and talking—apparently to himself.

Adam entered the maelstrom. No one seemed to notice his arrival. The only open seat was front row, dead center. Adam sat down and looked around. He didn't know anyone. He wondered why this class was run so differently than his other classes. Then he remembered that Mr. Geezer had hearing aids. He felt a little bad for the old man. This class was disrespectful.

From his position in the center of the room, Adam could not see around Mr. Geezer to get a look at the board. He was curious, though. And no one seemed to be following any rules anyway, so he got up and stood next to Mr. Geezer to see what he was writing on the chalkboard.

Mr. Geezer's handwriting was small and precise—almost like typewriter font. The text on the board read, 'What is Justice?'

There was also a bunch of writing under it, but it was too small to read, even up close.

Adam turned toward Mr. Geezer and said, "I did some reading on that question just yesterday."

Mr. Geezer stopped what he was writing and turned to face Adam.

"Oh, it's you. What's-Your-Face, the father of economics."
He barked a staccato laugh.

"You made it here. Good for you. Now what did you say?"

Adam leaned in close to his ear and yelled, "You asked," he pointed to the board, 'What is Justice?' I JUST READ ABOUT THAT YESTERDAY."

The classroom had quieted down some. Apparently everyone was entertained watching Adam yell at his teacher.

"And what did you learn?" Mr. Geezer asked, sounding skeptical.

"DO NO HARM," Adam yelled. "JUSTICE MEANS 'DO NO HARM.'"

Mr. Geezer blinked several times before speaking—quietly and to himself. "'Do no harm.' That's not bad. I can use that."

Mr. Geezer turned to face the classroom.

"Do no harm. Repeat after me, class. Justice is... Do no harm."

The class echoed him reluctantly.

Then Mr. Geezer thumped his cane on the ground. It echoed around until the room was completely silent. The silence felt immense in the absence of so much noise just a moment ago.

"Justice is the concept of 'Do no harm,' but it also carries the expectation of *remedy* when harm is done."

The class stared at him stupidly.

Like a viper, Mr. Geezer's hand flashed out and his cane wacked a stunned student in the front row gently on her forearm. She cried out in a voice more startled than hurt.

"Ouch!"

Mr. Geezer shuffled his feet toward her desk then lowered himself so his chin was resting on the top of his cane and his eyes were level with hers.

"Did that hurt, young lady?"

Tears of embarrassment filled her eyes. She rubbed her forearm.

"Yes," she whimpered.

"So was justice violated by my action?" he asked.

"Yes," she said with more confidence than a moment ago.

Mr. Geezer cackled with glee.

"Very good. You are smart. But what now? What happens next?"

"She calls the cops!" a boy from further back in the classroom said, sounding righteous.

"Bah," Mr. Geezer said dismissively, though he looked pleased. "Watch and learn."

He stood up straighter and handed the cane to the girl in front of him.

"Use it, smart girl. You know what to do."

She looked at the offered cane like it was a snake. Then her mouth firmed in a straight, thin line. She took the cane from Mr. Geezer. She looked right and left for support from those around her, then squared her shoulders and used the cane like a pool stick—poking him in the ribs.

Her strike didn't look fierce to Adam, but then, neither had Mr. Geezer's.

Mr. G jumped a little and shouted in exaggerated alarm.

"OUCH! You hit me."

He rubbed his chest theatrically then held out his hand. The girl frowned but handed the cane back. Then Mr. G spoke to the class as a whole.

"She hit me. She hurt me. Has she, then, also violated justice?"

A murmur ran through the class, then the righteous boy spoke again, muttering, "No."

"Smart boy. Why not? How come she hurt me but justice was not violated?"

"Because she was righting a wrong," another girl in the class said.

"Precisely," Mr. Geezer said, thumping his cane once on the ground. "Justice is 'Do no harm' but also 'Remedy harm done.'"

He had the class repeat the definition several times.

"Smart girls and smart boys, this lesson is the most important lesson economics has to teach. Remember it well. Justice is the key to prosperity. Its absence—*in*justice—ultimately leads to poverty, hunger, injury, misery, and death."

Adam felt something flimsy inside him snap under the weight of the words Mr. Geezer had just spoken. He sucked in a sharp breath. He felt like he couldn't see with his eyes. Was he blind? He felt like he wasn't standing in a classroom any more. Instead, he was floating in space, surrounded by swirling images on all sides. He knew the images were memories of events in his life—poverty, hunger, injury, misery, fear—along with pride, joy, exaltation, laughter, happiness, pleasure, accomplishment—but the events flew by so quickly that they blurred.

Adam felt terrible vertigo—like he was falling and spinning without any reference points or sense of direction. He felt nausea. Then he heard a tiny, clear bell ring through the space followed by a strong force that jerked all-that-was-Adam roughly. His mind grappled desperately with the new force—trying to tame it. The fighting sent him spinning even faster—even more out of control. He wanted to vomit.

Then he shifted.

He stopped fighting the force and, instead, used it to orient himself—to map direction in that void. The force became his gravity. Adam's mind began sorting his life relative to the new gravity. He experienced a sensation like bridges falling in place across chasms in his mind. It was as if his whole mind was reorganizing itself at light speed—adjusting to a powerful new reality. He suddenly suspected the messy, unknowable, complex, frightening events of his life made a tiny bit of sense.

Chemical emotions—a relaxed, calm satisfaction followed by a nearly overwhelming sensation of limitless possibility—swirled through his blood vessels.

"Ay, Dios mío," Adam said out loud in the void. He heard his voice echo around inside himself. It sounded full of wonder.

"Are you all right?" a concerned female voice said from outside him.

Adam abruptly found himself back in class standing beside the teacher. Everyone was staring at him.

The lingering sense of serenity still swirled through his body, so he felt no shame at finding himself the center of attention.

Mr. Geezer whispered hoarsely, "You see it, boy?"

"Yes," Adam told him, grinning tiredly. "I see it."

"Class dismissed," Mr. Geezer said abruptly and loudly.

The class, confused about ending early, began to gather up their notes and books.

"Ruminate on justice tonight. Repeat what you have learned. And try your hardest to catch up to What's-His-Face, here. He is light-years ahead of the rest of you."

27
Apprentice

Adam was only vaguely aware of the other students filing out of the room or that he was sitting on the floor.

When had he sat down?

He heard a chair scrape next to him and felt Mr. Geezer settle in it.

Mr. Geezer leaned forward and rested his chin on his cane. He looked out the window and said, "I know what you are going through."

Adam turned his head slowly and wiped tears off his cheeks with his sleeve.

When had he started crying?

Why was he crying?

Then he noticed Mr. Geezer was crying too. The old man's eyes were turned up toward the ceiling but seemed far off. The corners of his mouth turned up in a fond grin.

"I remember it was like waves crashing inside my mind, leveling what I thought were mountains. I remember the sensation of tumblers in locks falling in place—as if I had discovered a key that opened all doors. Until today, though, I've never seen anyone or even met anyone who had a similar experience. It is why I devoted my life to the study of economics. It is why I spend every ounce of what remains of my life trying to teach its mysteries to these," he waved his hand at the empty classroom, "young people."

Adam said, "It just keeps going."

Mr. Geezer nodded.

Adam continued slowly, "I can only see some of it, but I can feel the potential unfolding outward ahead of me."

Mr. Geezer nodded again, then said, "You will be the crowning achievement of my life. Don't be late to class again. I don't want to waste even a moment."

Adam nodded, then stood to leave.

Mr. G spoke a question before Adam had gone two steps.

"How did you know what justice is?"

"I read it," Adam said.

"Where?"

"In *The Theory of Moral Sentiments* by..." he coughed as he said, "Adam Smith."

Mr. G looked impressed.

"Adam Smith, the father of economics? You read one of his books?"

"A little of both of his books, actually," Adam admitted. "But not all."

"I see," Mr. G said as he tapped fingers on the handle of his cane. It looked like he was struggling with a decision until—all at once—the drumming stopped.

"Would you be willing to do extra reading for this class? Would you be agreeable to take on assignments that the other students don't have?"

"Yes," Adam said, genuinely excited. "I want to know more. Please teach me all you can."

Mr. G grinned.

"Very well. Just remember, though... you asked for it. Start with *The Making of Modern Economics* by Mark Skousen."

Adam grinned devilishly. "Why do I feel like I'm getting a leg up against my competition?"

Mr. G shook his head almost imperceptibly.

"These kids—your peers and classmates—are no longer your competition. Keep your focus and do this work, and you'll find yourself in an altogether different league entirely."

28
Pretend Parents

Adam made his way a short distance down the hall and entered the Home Economics room. He was one of the first students in the room. He saw a diminutive girl with the build of a soccer player standing next to one of the cooking tables in the back of the room. She was already wearing an apron.

Adam waved to her and she waved back.

"Take a seat anywhere you like," the young lady said.

Adam picked a seat in the back row. Because of the arrangement of the ovens and sinks and tables behind the desks, his seat was very close to the center of the room.

Other students started to file in.

"ADAM!" he heard an excited voice say from the doorway. He looked up and saw Asuna coming toward him.

"You're in my cooking class too! How awesome is that?"

To his amazement, she sat down at the desk next to him and started talking.

"I had a Work/Study just before this one. Would you believe I got to *cook* in the cafeteria? I spent the last half hour working on meal prep and now I've come here. Isn't that crazy? Two food classes in a row. What was Master-Mind thinking? It's okay though. I like cooking. Perhaps I'm destined to be a chef someday. Your eyes look kind of red. Do you have allergies?"

"No," Adam told her, "I just had an... epiphany, I think."

"Adam," Asuna said. "You're so deep. I don't even know what that means, honestly. Was it painful? Are you okay?"

Adam caught sight of something large out of the corner of his eye and looked up to see Lee taking the seat farthest from the front of the room, closest to the door. Lee was looking at Asuna cautiously.

Adam waved him over.

Lee stayed where he was, but said to Asuna, "He means he experienced a sudden and striking realization. Like a scientific breakthrough or a religious revelation."

"Hiiiiii theerrrrre," Asuna said to Lee, stretching the words out as if they needed to cross a great distance to get to him. "You look familiar. I'm Asuna. I think we're in the same Language class together."

"We are," Lee said while smiling.

Adam thought Lee's smile looked sad. How ironic was it to have a sad smile? People usually smiled when they were happy. Was it even possible to smile when sad? Lee seemed to really live for irony.

"Asuna," Adam said joining the conversation. "This is Lee. Lee, this is..."

"Asuna. I know," Lee said.

Adam wondered if Lee was trying to be rude by interrupting. He didn't think so since he was trying to smile and make eye contact. Maybe he just didn't have good timing when talking.

"Hey, Lee," Adam said. "I was just thinking you had a sad smile."

Lee blushed and looked angrily over at Adam. Adam was momentarily puzzled by the reaction, but then realized he must have embarrassed the big man in front of a lady.

Adam spoke quickly, "I didn't mean any insult by that comment. I only shared it with you because I thought you would like the irony in the phrase."

Lee's brows furrowed for a moment, then lifted in surprise. Then his smile grew larger and close to genuinely happy.

"You used 'sad' as an adjective for 'smile'. That's pretty remarkable. Thanks for sharing that with me."

Adam shrugged and glanced sideways.

Asuna looked back and forth between them, appearing a little confused.

"Lee is a genius with language... Well, written language, anyway," Adam explained to Asuna. "And he likes irony. A lot."

"You might say it is the underlying theme of my life," Lee said.

Asuna blinked and continued to look confused.

Adam found this whole interaction delightful. Lee—the most introverted person he'd ever met—trying to have a conversation with Asuna—the most extroverted person he'd ever met. The whole thing was playing out like a well-written farce.

Just then a strong voice rang out from the front of the room.

"Good morning, class. I am Miss Erica. I want to welcome you to Home Economics."

There were a few seconds of general confusion as everyone looked around to see who was speaking. Eventually every eye settled on the petite woman with the apron standing in front of all the desks.

Adam's eyes grew wide. It was the student he'd seen when he first entered the room. Well, not a student then, but she must be the smallest person in the room and she looked like the youngest too. This was going to take some getting used to.

"Your first assignment is to care for a baby," Miss Erica said with a smirk.

'Baby' did not sound like 'food' to Adam. He thought this was a cooking class. What had he gotten himself into?

Miss Erica held up a baby doll with a plastic face and cloth body.

"You have to prove you can handle *these* before I can trust you with a real baby."

Miss Erica started to hand out baby dolls.

Adam pondered his teacher as she worked. She was memorable, but her name wasn't. He'd need something more unique to label her in his memory bank.

Perhaps Miss-Tiny-Person?

No. Utterly boring.

Miss-Dynamic?

Better, but too many syllables.

Miss-Super-Adorable-Put-Her-In-Your-Pocket-And-Take-Her-Home?

Ugh. He hated his brain. Why couldn't he just remember a name?

Adam watched his miniature teacher carefully. When she turned her head, he got a view of her profile. She had a dainty neck packed tight with muscle—like an athlete—yet retained graceful, feminine lines.

Miss-Foxy?

Too explicit. He'd get in big trouble if he accidently said that one out loud. She did look kind of like a fox, though, with red highlights in her hair and a narrow face and sharp nose. Also, foxes were carnivores and he sensed a dangerous edge to her.

Little-Fox?

"These baby dolls," Little-Fox said, "are super special and you're going to love them."

Adam smelled a lie. He and this elfin teacher were kin.

She continued, "For this assignment, you must keep this baby within two meters of you at all times for the next week. It senses proximity to your ID card. And—before any of you get any bright ideas about leaving it on top of your ID card while you go out partying—it can also tell if the ID card is on you or not. Don't ask me how."

There was a general groan from the class.

"Wait!" she said. "It gets better. These babies have needs. They need to be fed. They need to be burped. They need their diaper changed. They are programed to cry periodically when they need one of these things, but it is up to you to figure out which one. Sounds easy, right? Except—just like a real baby—they will have these problems at all hours of the day and night but—unlike a real baby—all you have to do is touch one of these magic bottles," she started handing out baby bottles, "to the baby's lips and the baby is instantly satisfied."

She went on talking, ignoring the moans and grunts of the less ambitious students.

"In case any of you are flirting with the idea of disliking me during this project, realize that there is a setting that requires you to feed the baby for twenty minutes each time it gets hungry. Currently that setting is turned off. Let's keep it that way. Be on your best behavior."

A hand went up. An—as yet—unnoticed third boy in the class with crew cut hair was connected to the raised arm. He was situated deep in the popular section of the class—about as far as possible from where Lee sat.

"A question from the minority gender," Miss Erica said, looking over at the student. "Patrick, isn't it?"

Patrick! Adam thought. The same hall monitor who had shown Adam around the locker room on enrollment day.

Miss Erica preempted Patrick's question. "It's refreshing to see more men stepping up to shoulder the challenges of childrearing."

When she stopped speaking, Patrick cleared his throat and stood to speak. Half his mouth was turned up in a cocksure grin.

"Instead of pretending a doll is a real baby by pretending to feed them, change them, and burp them, can't we just leave them here on the shelf and *pretend* we did all those things?"

Subdued laugher floated anonymously from some students around Patrick. He returned to sitting.

Little-Fox smiled. Except it didn't look like a smile. It was more a showing of teeth.

Adam looked toward the door and wondered if it was too late to withdraw from the class. His motion caught Miss Erica's attention. She seemed to read his intent and moved quickly to the exit and stood in the door.

"None of you can leave the class, especially you boys. I've never had three men in my class at the same time. So I will refuse any request to drop out."

Adam narrowed his eyes. He thought he'd already detected one lie from this teacher. She was probably bluffing this time too.

"Childrearing is hard and not—generally—gender-specific," she went on nervously. "It takes a village to raise healthy children. There aren't nearly enough positive male role models in this world. So you all, especially you three boys, must stay. The future of mankind might depend on your preparation and participation."

Lee sat up straighter in his chair.

Adam frowned. Developing child-raising skills was not anywhere on his radar or to-do list.

Miss Erica looked him directly in the eyes.

"Women appreciate men who are good with children," she said, seemingly out of desperation.

Adam blinked, taken aback.

Girls like men who are skilled with children? Could that be true? Or was she lying to keep him in class? And how did she know he cared deeply about such things? Was he that transparent?

He looked around. There were a lot of girls in this class. Many of them were nodding agreement and demonstrating support for Miss Erica's statement.

Perhaps these really were skills ladies valued in men.

Adam settled back in his chair.

She'd won. He couldn't pass on the chance at even a possibility of becoming more attractive to women.

When no one made any further protest, Miss Erica relaxed and walked slowly back to the front of class where she finished handing out babies and their bottles.

In short order, Patrick had his baby hanging by the neck from a small cord tied to the back of his chair.

"Not appropriate," Lee growled in a low volume that carried toward Patrick.

Many of the other girls took notice and threw vocalizations and body language in support of Lee's intervention.

Patrick scowled at Lee and removed the baby from the noose and laid the doll on his desk.

"It was just a joke," Patrick mumbled to no one in particular.

Several of the girls gave Lee admiring looks.

Adam frowned down at the mock baby in his lap and tried to imagine—without success—how a stuffed doll could possibly make him more attractive to girls. He remained in that logic puzzle until the period bell rang, signaling the end of class.

29
Anger Issues

Adam's next period was PE class Number Two.

He picked up a couple of plastic bags out of his locker, triple-bagged the baby doll and baby bottle, then absentmindedly stuffed the bags back in the locker.

Adam's ID drew a map toward the baseball diamond. He noticed twin ponytails with black ribbons already at the diamond. He rubbed the faded letters on the back of his hand and threw a silent thanks up to heaven. He really loved school.

When he arrived at the baseball diamond, he found Amy turned just enough in his direction that he suspected she could see him in her peripheral vision. He thought he caught a ghost of a smile on her lips before she quickly turned away.

He took that as a good sign and changed course so he could walk up beside her. At the same moment, however, someone stepped in his path and then proceeded to bump him—hard.

"Hey!" he heard a girl's voice complain in his direction. "Watch where you're going, oaf!"

The voice came from a brunette with short buzzed hair on one side of her head and long hair on the other. She had a scowl on her face. She looked like a rock star with toned legs and lean shoulders and arms. She had piercings in her tongue, lips, ears, and several in each eyebrow.

"Sorry!" Adam said apologetically. "Are you all right?"

"Of course I'm all right!" she said defensively, some of the anger dissipating already. "Do I look fragile to you?"

"No, no," Adam assured her while holding his hands up in a consoling gesture. "Not fragile at all. I'm Adam, by the way. I think I saw you in my Home Economics class."

"Oh yeah? Is that right?" She looked him up and down as if appraising a side of beef. "Then where's your baby?"

"Oh crap!" Adam exclaimed. "Where did it go?!"

He spun around in panic, then remembered leaving it in a locker.

His shoulders slumped and he bowed his head while running one hand through his shaggy hair. The very next class hadn't even started and he was already failing his baby-watching assignment.

Kat smiled evilly and said loudly enough that others could hear, "So you can't keep track of your baby and you can't keep track of where you're walking. What's the pattern? Are you absentminded or just dumb?"

Adam bestowed on her—in that moment—a new name. Henceforth she would be called *Anger-Management*.

The instructor for the course was a thin, ripped, middle-aged man with a buzz cut who spoke like a Marine and introduced himself as Mr. Slaven. Adam decided to call him *Sergeant-Slaven*.

Sgt-Slaven had everyone in class line up in rows for attendance. Adam raised a hand.

"Yes, Adam Smith. What is your question?"

"Coach Slaven," Adam ventured, "why does everyone at this school have *two* physical education periods? Most schools I've ever heard of don't have any."

The coach put down his tablet and answered in a crisp, clear, clipped manner that carried his words effectively over the whole class.

"Excellent question! You must be new to Charter 7."

Adam nodded patiently.

"The aim of this school—of every school, really—is to prepare each student to survive and thrive once they graduate and enter the competitive adult world. To that end, daily exercise is highly beneficial. Exercise improves sleep. Sleep improves concentration. Concentration is required for learning. Furthermore, exercise increases the number of connections in your brain. More connections mean more learning. So exercise makes you smarter. Exercise also makes you more attractive to other people, which you may find useful and desirable someday. Additionally, humans treat each other differently based on perceived health. If you are healthy in appearance and bearing, you will have better luck getting hired following job interviews. You will require fewer sick days away from work. You will have an easier time establishing and maintain working and social relationships. And if that weren't enough, daily exercise reduces anxiety and increases adaptability under stress. All useful attributes predicting greater likelihood of success in life during and after school."

"The only downside to regular exercise," he added in a well-rehearsed afterthought, "is heat, sweat, faster and deeper breathing, and time lost for other endeavors."

"Yes. But why *two* periods?" Adam pressed.

"Again, great question. Observational data on the few remaining hunter-gatherer societies remaining on this planet—tribes of the rainforests, aborigines in Australia, plainsmen in Africa—suggests the members of those societies average two to three hours of moderate to intense exercise every day. Since humans have been hunting and gathering for most of our existence on this planet, it is probable that we are still designed for roughly that much exercise each day. The fact that two to three hours of exercise is not required for survival in modern society does not change the fact that we were designed to move. When people do not get enough exercise, strange things happen. Like diabetes and infertility and early arthritis and heart attacks. Avoiding as many unnecessary ailments as possible increases the likelihood of your success here and after school. Much of being healthy is avoiding the unhealthy."

"So," Adam asked, doing the math in his head, "we should have four, thirty-minute PE periods a day?"

Coach Slaven held up a hand and continued.

"The educators at this school—myself included—think one hour of exercise a day is a bare minimum for healthy living. We give you close to that while in school as well as instruction on how to set your own goals and monitor your progress against those goals if you desire additional exercise after school hours. We also sponsor numerous after-school sports and intramural leagues for anyone interested. And though it is true that additional hours of exercise while in school would likely make each of you healthier, it might also cause our students to appear to fall behind in the short-term competitive academic race against other students at outside schools. Schools where students do no exercise whatsoever. Thus, by only requiring one hour a day, we are attempting to strike a balance between your potential short- and long-term outcomes."

Coach Slaven waited.

"Thank you," Adam said loudly to the pause.

Sgt-Slaven smiled.

"Exercise is my passion. Let's see if I can make it yours as well. Today's workout is kickball."

Sgt-Slaven spent the next few minutes explaining the rules of kickball in a loud, clear voice while standing in perfect military posture. Adam got the distinct impression that breaking any of the rules would instantly and unceremoniously lead to the end of the world.

Kickball involved a lot of standing around and watching. Since watching was unavoidable, Adam didn't feel particularly guilty for doing it. Amy, for example, was perfection in motion.

First of all, she was really fast. When she ran, the ribbons in her hair flew out behind her, giving the impression of speed lines in her wake. She was also strong. When she kicked the ball it went far. Furthermore, she played smart. No one ever caught the ball when she was up to kick. Finally, she was healthy. The thin sheen of sweat on her skin after running the bases caused the sunlight to highlight her neck and collarbone and the muscles in her arm.

Adam was vaguely aware that he was not the only one who found her distracting. In fact, every guy—with the possible exception of Sgt-Slaven—seemed to follow Amy's progress through the game. It caused problems. One boy on second base took a ball full in the face when he was watching her run the bases. Even some of the girls seemed to stumble or miss a step when she passed by.

Anger-Management, though, was a different story. She was barely-contained fury. Muscles tight everywhere in her body all at once. Teeth showing. Ball exploding off her foot in completely random directions. Growls and spittle flying from her mouth. When fielding, she showed no strategy outside of hitting the runner with the ball as hard as possible. Watching her was like watching cannons fire—loud, chaotic, and primal.

Adam thought of himself as somewhat in between the two ladies. He was a strategic player in the field and tried to place his strikes when up to kick, but had only average strength and above-average speed.

When the game was over, Sgt-Slaven dismissed the class. Literally he said, "Dismissed!" like a drill sergeant—dragging out the -issed sound at the end.

Adam gravitated toward Amy. He was trying to fight down his grin. She glanced at him sideways, then sat down to adjust her sock. Adam was pretty sure her sock needed no adjustment but he wasn't going to criticize anything that was so clearly working in his favor.

"Impressive," he said to her.

At his word, her head spun up quickly as if noticing him for the first time. Her ribbons followed the arc of her head beautifully. He wondered if she practiced that move.

"Thanks," she said. "You're not bad yourself."

Adam looked up at the sky and scratched his head.

"Thanks."

He didn't feel like he deserved much praise but was happy she had words for him.

Just then he heard Anger-Management speak from behind.

"Don't compliment him too much. He might get to thinking he's too hot to handle."

Adam noticed Amy's smile falter. Her eyes slowly, reluctantly moved over to look at Anger-Management. Ribbons finished fussing with her socks and got to her feet.

"Kat," she said. "You played a good game. You might be losing your touch though. You didn't manage to cripple anyone. Are you sure you're feeling well?"

Anger-Management sputtered something incoherent before a new voice entered the conversation.

30
Schoolyard Rumble

"Oh dear, look who they let out of jail."

Adam saw a dark cloud drift across Anger-Management's face. They all turned to see two boys walking toward them. The one in the lead, who was speaking, was new to Adam, but the trailing boy was Adam's classmate from Home Economics, Patrick. Both boys had the same construction-orange colored armbands with a stylized compass on the outside.

"What did you say?" Anger-Management asked quietly.

Adam thought she sounded more menacing when quiet than when yelling.

Before the newcomers could answer, Adam saw the flutter of ribbons out of the corner of his vision and heard Amy say, "Back off, Dave. You are out of line."

When the motion halted, Amy stood between Anger-Management and the two boys. She'd assumed a staggered stance with one shoulder more forward than the other and her arms crossed. It was a defensive posture. She was taking this seriously.

Adam stepped beside Amy, hoping they presented a unified front.

The lead boy looked at Adam with contempt. Patrick—trailing—looked away as though embarrassed.

"You must be new, brown boy," the lead boy said, "but you've chosen to side with Crazy-Kat."

He spit on the ground.

"Bad decision."

Then he turned to Amy, reached out, grabbed her wrist, and tugged her toward him.

"Let's go, Amy. These people will stain your reputation if you stand too close to them."

Amy let out a sound that was simultaneously alarmed, affronted, and pained. Adam found the first two objectionable. The last qualified as injustice and required a response.

As Adam started to move, though, Anger-Management surged forward and shoved the lead boy, Dave, in the chest, yelling, "Get your hands off her, creep!"

Time slowed.

Adam read brief shock on Lead-Boy's face, followed by annoyance. Then the bully shoved Anger-Management hard in the chest and shoulder. She flew backward, collided with Amy, and they both tumbled to the ground, a heap of arms and legs.

Adam stepped in the space left vacant between them, grabbed the right wrist of the lead boy with both hands, and twisted hard to his left. At that same moment, he sent a roundhouse kick at the boy's right ankle. The boy's feet were already partly unseated from the ground by the violent torque on his wrist. The simultaneous sweep of the ankles sent the boy spinning in the air. As soon as his feet were directly over his head, Adam tugged down hard on the captured wrist, sending the inverted boy to the ground head first.

Lead-Boy's body crumpled unevenly. As he settled, Adam moved to crouch over him, one knee planted firmly on his neck, his left hand curled in the other boy's hair, and his right hand ready to deliver a strike to the face. He never delivered the strike, though. Dave was clearly already out of the fight.

Adam relaxed his grip on the hair. Before he could stand up, however, he felt someone tackle him from behind. Thinking it must be Patrick, Adam grabbed the wrist of the arm wrapped across his chest and prepared to throw him over his shoulder.

Except something was wrong. His body wouldn't move. Adam waited the milliseconds required for his brain to sort out the sensory information and tell him the problem. Answer: The wrist was too small, the voice yelling in his ear was female, he could smell spearmint, and there was a small black ribbon wrapped around the wrist.

Adam released her wrist and started to raise his hands—open and facing outward in the traditional gesture of surrender—when Patrick appeared in front of him. Patrick landed a punch in Adam's exposed abdomen, followed quickly by a hook to his right jaw. The air vanished out of Adam's lungs, his vision grew dark around the edges, he saw stars, felt pain in his face on the right side, and then he was falling left. Amy's arm was still around him, so she was pulled down too.

Then time returned to normal.

Adam tried desperately to expand his lungs and get to his feet. He knew he was horribly vulnerable. But his body wouldn't work. He couldn't get untangled from Amy. He needed time to recover and he knew he didn't have it. He waited for the axe to fall.

Then Anger-Management threw herself on Patrick's back, growling and scratching. Patrick was much stronger and easily tossed her off to the side. She landed heavily on her back, rolled a bit, and groaned. Her attack—though ineffectual—seemed to take the fight out of Patrick. Instead of finishing Adam off, he knelt beside Dave to see if he was all right.

After about fifteen more seconds, Adam was able to take a deep, gasping breath and sit up. He heard Amy crying behind him and Anger-Management muttering off to the left.

He saw Patrick helping up Dave, who looked pale and unsteady.

Amy stepped around in front of Adam. She put her hands on his shoulders and kept repeating, "I'm so sorry. I'm so *so* sorry."

She had tears in her eyes. Adam hoped she wasn't hurt by the fall. Her hand traced over his face. He winced.

"I thought the fight was over. I was trying to prevent you from killing Dave, but all I ended up doing was restraining you while Patrick hit you."

Adam tried to smile.

"Honestly, Amy, I'm not sure it would have mattered. Patrick is really amazing."

He heard a snort from the direction of Patrick, who was helping the other boy to his feet. Patrick looked over at Adam and said, "Right back at you. That move was spectacular."

Adam looked Patrick in the eyes for a moment, then nodded respectfully. Patrick nodded back deferentially.

Adam put his right hand on Amy's left shoulder to comfort her.

"I'm okay," he said. "Can you check on Anger-Management over there?"

Katrina scowled at Adam from her seat on the ground but kept quiet.

Amy stood up and went over to Anger-Management. Adam heard Kat saying from the ground, "I'm fine. Nothing injured here but my pride."

Patrick said, "I'm going to take Dave to get checked out at the nurse's office. You all can see to yourselves?"

"We can," Adam said cautiously. He didn't quite trust this new, unexpectedly reasonable side of Patrick.

"Good," Patrick said. "If you want to file a complaint, do so at the front office before the end of school today. If you have not, I will be filing a report regarding a 'sporting accident' during PE. Unless you think differently, please let anyone who asks know that this was an unfortunate Ultimate Frisbee accident."

Adam saw Dave nod agreement. Adam, too, nodded agreement. The girls followed Adam's lead.

"Agreed," said Amy.

"Whatever," said Anger-Management.

Then the two hall monitors walked slowly off the Play Yard.

31
Between the Lines

Adam and the two girls got to their feet, brushed themselves off, and started walking toward the school. Adam rubbed his jaw. Amy glided along with her hands clasped in front of her and stared at the ground. Anger-Management fumed to herself.

"Thank you both for sticking up for me," Anger-Management eventually said to the air in front of her. "No one has ever done that for me before."

Ribbons continued to stare at the ground a few more steps before she picked up her chin and lengthened her stride till she pulled ahead of the group. She abruptly turned back and bowed at the waist. Her hair drooped like the branches in a willow tree.

"Thank you both for sticking up for me also."

Adam stopped and looked first at Anger-Management, then at Amy.

"Same here. Thank you."

Amy returned to upright.

Adam reflected, "We earned a pretty favorable outcome, all things considered."

Amy's chin dropped slightly. She put on a pretty smile that didn't quite reach her eyes and said, "I'm late to class. I need to rush. I'll see you later."

She turned in a spiral of ribbons and jogged away.

Adam watched her go. Once she was out of sight, he heard Anger-Management kick some grass. He turned.

"Listen," Kat said, "that thing you did back there was… effective. Could you teach me to do something like that? You know, for when I'm in trouble? So I could defend myself… or someone else."

"You fought pretty well," Adam said.

Anger-Management waved a dismissive hand.

"He threw me off like a three-year-old. If he'd wanted to, he could have totally destroyed me. I was nothing back there. I was less than nothing."

"Don't be so hard—," Adam started to say.

She cut him off angrily, "Can you teach me or not?"

Adam looked her in the eyes for several seconds, then slowly, carefully, probed, "You've had similar situations in the past? Before today, I mean?"

Anger-Management's eyes turned flat and grey. She repeated in a whisper, "Can you teach me or not?"

Adam sighed.

"It took me years of daily practice to earn a black belt."

She wilted.

"But there are a few useful tricks I can teach you."

Some color returned to her eyes.

He pulled off his ID.

"We have to trade, right? That's how things work in this school? What can you trade me to teach you self-defense?"

She lunged forward and grabbed his shirt in the front.

"Anything," she said. "Whatever it costs, I'll pay it."

Adam looked down at his t-shirt wadded up in her fists and grinned ruefully. Just then his stomach growled. He rubbed it thoughtfully and said, "Can you cook?"

"No," she said, "but I can spread peanut butter. I'll make sandwiches for you the rest of the year if you'll teach me this one thing."

"Well," Adam said, "I could really use something to eat on the way home from school each day. Could you pack me a lunch each day? I don't really care what's in it. I'm not a picky eater."

"Deal!" she shouted in his face and kissed him on the lips, then released him and pulled the ID from her shirt. She touched it several times.

Adam, flustered, stepped back to make a little space. He gathered his wits and accepted her friend request on his card. Then she entered the contract details and he accepted that too.

"When?" she asked, with restrained excitement in her voice.

"How about after school on Friday?" he returned—tasting cherry on his lips.

"You find me Friday," she said, tapping the edge of his ID with her index finger. "Don't let me down."

Then she turned and disappeared in the building.

Adam, emotions all entangled, touched his lips. His first kiss with a girl hadn't gone at all the way he'd imagined.

32
Asuna to the Rescue

As it happened, Adam had missed his entire next period, which was Work/Study Number Two. So his ID card directed him straight to lunch. After two PE classes and a brawl, he was starving. He hadn't eaten since the previous day.

The cafeteria line had four vegetable options made up of two vegetarian entrees—today's being hummus and tofu in curry—and two plain vegetables—broccoli and carrots. There were two fruit options—apple slices and peaches—and two dairy options—yogurt and 2% white milk. There were also two starches—spaghetti and brown rice, both conveniently placed next to marinara sauce and soy sauce. There was a meal plan where Adam could choose four items, but he got a serving of everything.

"ADAM!"

He heard an excited squeal from across the serving line and saw Asuna spooning out tofu for him.

"Asuna!" he said, delighted. "You work this period?"

"Yeah," she said and stepped back from the line to show off her apron uniform.

"I like to cook so I chose this as one of my Work/Studies. Well, it turns out I accidently chose *two* cafeteria Work/Studies. *And* I'm in Home Ec. I'm not sure how I made that mistake, but maybe I'm just meant to be a chef!"

She leaned forward a little and said in a conspiratorial tone, "I might know who made this tofu curry that you see here in front of you. If you like it, let me know and I might just tell you who the cook is."

Just then he heard someone in the line growl, "Move along! You're holding up the line."

Adam and Asuna both blushed. She rolled her eyes and said, "See you around."

Adam sat down at a nearby table, too hungry to care who else was sitting there. He inhaled his food in a manner that would make a vacuum cleaner jealous. He ate so fast that he forgot he was supposed to form an opinion about the curry.

Ah well, he thought, it must have been delicioso. There's not a drop of it left anywhere.

He leaned back in his chair, happily breathing short and shallow around his too-full tummy. He let his eyes roam the room till they found Lee sitting off in a corner. Even sitting, Lee towered over everyone and stuck out like a flashlight on a dark night.

Adam picked up his tray and walked over to where Lee was sitting. From a distance, Adam thought Lee was alone, but up close he saw another student sitting next to him. Where Lee was tall and thin, the other student was short and wide—not fat-wide, more like barn-is-wide. The student had really broad shoulders and long, thick arms. The skin on the back of his neck and ears was red. His face and the back of his hands looked tanned. It appeared to Adam that the school uniform did not fit the boy well. It was tightly stretched around his neck and shoulders and chest, but overly loose—even baggy—around his trunk and waist. Neither Lee nor the other boy appeared to be talking... or even seemed aware of each other, but Adam thought he could feel an air of familiarity between them, as though neither was unhappy to be sitting and not talking.

Adam reintroduced himself, "Lee! Hi, it's me, Adam. From Language class. And Home Ec."

Lee turned shrewd eyes on him.

"Ah yes, the scholar with an appreciation for irony. How are you, my old man? And what brings you to this forgotten corner of the universe?"

Adam tried to sort through what Lee had said, gave up, and said, "Mind if I sit here with you?"

Lee remarked, "Well, you see, there is a long line of applicants desiring that seat which you have just now occupied. But since you have the good fortune of being a classmate of mine, I think I can pull some favors and get you to the front of the line."

Adam couldn't quite bring himself to laugh at what he thought must be Lee's joke, so instead he leaned across the table and extended a hand to the other boy there.

"My name is Adam. Adam Smith."

The other boy didn't move for a moment, only looked up at Adam, then slowly, arduously, his body started to shift and his arm came out to shake.

"I'm Hal," he said, then squeezed.

The strength in Hal's hand was phenomenal. With just a brief squeeze Adam was quite sure he'd broken bones. He retracted his wilted hand and examined it for the damage.

"Impressive grip," Adam said, trying to decide if Hal had been showing off.

"He was holding back," Lee explained, reading his mind. "I suspect he didn't want to hurt you."

Adam watched Hal pull his arm back to his side—ponderous and inevitable. He wondered if that was the same motion tectonic plates made when viewed from space over long periods of time.

"Hal is a farmer," Lee explained. "He just graces our school with his presence because the law requires him to be in school and he thinks this one has the most farm-friendly curriculum anywhere in the country.

"Ah," Adam said, "that explains your grip and your arms. You must use them farming."

Hal nodded his head, sucked on a toothpick, and said, "Yep," between his teeth.

Lee sighed and rolled his eyes theatrically.

"Please forgive my friend, Adam. His enormous vocabulary and unceasing word barrage can be overwhelming to even the greatest of linguists."

This time Adam did laugh. Hal, for his part, only cocked his head a little and looked up at Lee through the corners of his eyes. He sucked on his toothpick twice then settled back in his previous, neutral position.

Suddenly Adam heard Asuna's familiar female voice approaching from behind. He was about to turn and greet her when he noticed a look of horror come across Lee's face. He thought this might be another of Lee's jokes. But then he noticed a sheen of sweat break out across Lee's body. His pupils dilated and he turned pale. He looked terrified. Adam turned to eye the source of Lee's terror.

Asuna came to the table carrying a water pitcher in one hand and dirty dishes in the other.

"Adam. Lee. Hal," she addressed them all in turn. "I saw you all sitting over here together and then I realized that you might need some water since this is so far away from the water fountain. So I thoughtfully grabbed a pitcher and came to rescue you."

She beamed a smile at the table of boys. Adam looked up at the ceiling to check why the light in the room had suddenly gotten brighter.

Lee cleared his throat, "None of us drink water, dear Asuna."

"I'll take some," Adam said cheerfully, unable to remove the smile from his face.

"Yes, but you don't have a glass. Adam, perhaps you should go and..."

Asuna smiled at Adam and pulled out an empty glass from the front pocket on her apron.

"I thought I could see that you didn't have a glass, Adam. Which could have been an issue given how much food you ate. I didn't want you to choke."

Lee made a choking sound.

"So I brought you a glass. You know, just in case you needed saving... from choking."

Asuna looked over at Lee curiously. "Or even just thirst," she added hastily and blushed—breaking eye contact and looking down at the table. Then she took a great big breath and stood up again. "I have to get back to work."

She gathered up their trays and plopped the pitcher of water on top. Then in rapid-fire speech she said, "I told you I'd pay you back for rescuing my wallet. I hope this begins to satisfy my debt. I hope I get to see you again. It has been a pleasure serving you."

Asuna curtsied, smiled quickly, spun, and dashed away.

Hal whistled quietly.

Adam followed Asuna's progress through the room as she moved between tables. It was easy to tell where she was at any given moment because everyone at the table around her was smiling.

Lee's panic attack must have passed because he let out a long, slow breath and collapsed in a puddle on the table.

"Oh, Adam," he said, resting his head sideways on the table. "The most disreputable company follows in your wake. I fear your presence in this corner of the room may be a herald of warning that it is no longer safe for Hal and myself."

Hal chewed on his toothpick.

Adam felt confused and a little hurt. Lee seemed serious. Or was that part of another joke? It was so hard to tell with him. That really *had* been a panic attack though. Adam was sure of it. You can't fake that stuff. Adam knocked on his forehead with his knuckles, trying to make sense out of Lee's behavior. He couldn't figure it out. So he did the next best thing. He asked.

"What's the problem?" he asked a little loudly and not without some heat. "Asuna is one of the kindest, most delightful people I've ever met."

Lee squirmed a little in his seat. "Well, that's the problem, you see."

"No, I don't see," Adam said, really getting angry now.

"I'm reserved," Lee said almost pleading. He looked as though he'd just pulled his heart out of his chest and laid it on the table. "And she's not."

Now he sounded petulant.

"He means *shy*," Hal said helpfully.

Adam's jaw dropped.

"No way! Lee, you're what? Two hundred centimeters tall?"

"One hundred and ninety-six centimeters," Lee admitted.

"One hundred and ninety-*four* centimeters," Hal corrected.

Adam continued, "You couldn't possibly hide in any crowd anywhere in the world. You know that, right?"

"Yes."

"So you're saying that your emotional nature desires to be invisible, but Mother-Nature has made any such hiding technically impossible?" Adam asked, trying to use big words Lee could understand.

There was a long silence.

Then Lee said, "Yes... Rather unfriendly of her, don't you think?"

"Oh," was all Adam could think to say.

Hal nodded sagely on the other side of the table.

The three boys sat in silence after that, each in their own thoughts. Adam spent the remainder of the lunch period pondering Nature's sense of humor—and irony.

33
If it Sounds too Good to be True...

Adam arrived on time to his next class, Statistics. He entered the room and found it surprisingly well-attended. The center seat in the front row was unoccupied so he sat in it.

In front of the class stood a pencil-thin, 188-centimeter tall man with a mousy, thin face, large triangular nose, and thick glasses. He had an impressive number of pens, rulers, and tools sticking out of his left shirt pocket. He looked up from his computer pad and addressed the class.

"Perfect attendance. Exceptional! My fame as a teacher must be spreading. Or is it? As it happens, perfect attendance on the first day of class of the second semester is well within two standard deviations of the expected value for classroom attendance *regardless* of who is teaching. Meaning perfect attendance is decidedly NOT exceptional, and I am confusing random coincidence as proof of my teaching prowess. Correlation—two things happening at once—is not evidence of causation—two related things happening at once where one triggers the other. It happens that your brain—and mine too—is wired to *think* correlation is causation. But they are not the same thing.

"Once you understand the flaw in the reflex assumption, you will discover this pattern repeated hundreds of times in yourself and everyone around you every day of your life. So let's explore it a tiny bit more.

"I am teaching. Attendance is perfect. These two notable events happened at the same time. Other events also happened in that same moment. I picked up chalk. You blinked. You took a breath. Your heart beat. Some of you shifted in your seats. A bird flew over the school. In reality, an infinite number of events happened inside and outside this class room all at the same moment in time. The vast majority of those events were completely unrelated to each other. Did your heartbeat cause perfect attendance today? Did a bird flying over the school cause perfect attendance in this class today? Did my teaching prowess cause perfect attendance in this class today?"

He drew a large circle on a chalkboard at the front of the classroom.

"This large circle represents the infinite number of events in the universe that happened at the same moment."

He drew a much smaller circle inside the previously drawn large circle.

"This smaller circle represents the tiny fraction of events that happened at the same moment that are somehow related to each other. My mind, poor thing, likes to assume that the large circle and the small circle are the same size. My brain automatically assumes a relationship exists between my teaching and perfect attendance today. My intellect weaves these two simultaneous events into a story where attendance today is perfect *because* I am teaching. But, on the first day of class each semester, perfect attendance is the norm *regardless* of who is teaching. Which means my teaching did not cause the perfect attendance. My teaching and the perfect attendance were only correlated but not causally-related."

He dropped his arms, faced the class, shook his head slowly, and grinned.

"Correlation is not causation. The circles are not the same size, no matter how much my lazy brain wishes they were identical. Oh, how science humbles even the greatest among us."

Pencil-Pocket then introduced himself as Mr. Hayek before pushing a button on his desk. A screen lowered in front of the room. The lights dimmed.

A projector in the back of the room threw a picture of the very same man standing in front of the very same room on the screen. The projected Mr. Hayek then proceeded to give an introductory lecture on statistics. The lecture was smooth and polished.

"Statistics," the video version of Mr. Hayek said, "is a branch of mathematics devoted to taking large bodies of information and processing that information so that it can be—ideally—more easily understood, manipulated, and transmitted to others."

As the teacher spoke, cartoons and images appeared and disappeared around him on the screen. When he said the word "data", a video clip expanded on the right showing people dropping voter cards in a ballot box. When he spoke of "Understanding, manipulating, and transmitting data", the video clip changed to people around a table counting the results of the election. That image morphed to a bar chart with 'Candidate Names' along the bottom and 'Total Votes' along the side. The bar chart then drifted up until it occupied the left-hand corner of a news broadcast where an anchorman described the outcomes of that election.

The newscast faded and the image of Mr. Hayek dominated the screen again.

"Human beings have brains that do some statistical processing naturally and effectively."

Beside the professor a small inset video appeared of a man successfully jumping across a gap several meters wide, hitting a ball with a bat, and playing table tennis.

"But there are other statistical processes that humans are either poorly designed to handle or wired to handle incorrectly."

The teacher shrank to the bottom left corner of the screen, replaced by clip after clip of cars crashing, motorbikes missing their landing, airplanes colliding in the sides of mountains, high-wire walkers falling off their tightrope, and government officials and newscasters giving statements followed immediately by actual footage of events that revealed they were completely wrong.

Mr. Hayek filled the screen once more.

"This class will show you a few techniques and tools for managing pools of data intelligently, but the lion's share of the class will be spent demonstrating the litany of common errors made by people—including professional statisticians—in the collection, processing, interpretation, and understanding of data."

"In other words, you won't be a statistician after this course, but you *will* know when statistics are reliable and when they are deceptive—regardless of whether the deception is intentional..."

A rerun of an old commercial played where a depressed man tipped back a beer and suddenly found himself surrounded by three stunning models in bikinis. The ladies were all wildly excited to touch and talk to him.

"...or *un*intentional."

The scene flashed to a gambler pounding his fist on a slot machine and shouting, "I've lost so many times I can't have any bad luck left. I'm due for a win!"

Then Mr. Hayek took the center of the screen again and began to formally teach.

At the end of the class, the real Mr. Hayek brought up the lights, stood in front of the class like a traditional teacher, and answered questions.

Adam raised his hand and asked in a somewhat awed voice, "How long did it take you to make that video?"

"Oh," Mr. Hayek said, "I started making them back when I was in college. I knew what I wanted to teach, you see, so I had a head start over other teachers. And I've continued to make new videos as I learn more about statistics. Then I edit the old ones. Did you like it?"

"Did I ever!" Adam exclaimed. "That was like watching the best lecture a man ever presented overlaid with thoughtful supportive evidence and delivered with precise timing and artful presentation."

An amused grin rose up on Mr. Hayek's face. "Really? Is that all?"

"Can statistics really tell the difference between truth and lies?" Adam asked.

"Do you mean correlation and causation?" Mr. Hayek asked.

"That too," Adam beamed.

Pencil-Pocket squirmed a little, then said, "At its best, statistics will do a better job of distinguishing truth from lies and correlation from causation than any other method known to man. But the devil is in the details. There are many steps involved in gathering, compiling, interpreting, and presenting data. Every step is a potential entry point for errors and bias."

Adam pressed, "But if everything is done perfectly, then will it tell the difference between truth and lies?"

Mr. Hayek looked at his computer pad.

"Absolute certainty, Mr. Smith, is a luxury of the gods. Mortals like us have to settle for probabilities."

Adam took a deep breath, let it out slowly, then mused, "So I take it drinking beer won't cause a large crowd of bikini-clad ladies to join my fan club..."

Pencil-Pocket choked, then let out a deep, heartfelt laugh.

"Adam, if it did, I certainly wouldn't be in this classroom teaching you statistics."

34
Hippie Cheerleader

Adam entered his next class, Algebra, feeling anxious. He hadn't signed up for this class. It had showed up on his schedule though, so he followed the map on his ID card to the second floor. Adam was under the assumption the classes on the second floor were too expensive for him, but the price on the wall outside this room was closer to the least expensive third-floor classes. $50.

Adam entered a room resembling a warehouse floor. The room was at least three times the size of a normal classroom. It was packed tightly with computers in long rows. There were large fans at the end of each row. Adam saw oversized air conditioner ducts along the ceiling. He looked around for a teacher and saw a man near the front of the room sitting back with his legs propped up on a cheap desk.

He had round, John Lennon-style, thin-rimmed glasses and long hair that went to his mid-back. He was middle-aged, with mostly grey stubble all over his face. He was wearing a loose, tie-dyed, short-sleeve shirt that buttoned up the middle. He had the buttons undone down about halfway so the middle of his chest was open. He wore an oversized medallion of a dollar symbol on a thick gold chain around his neck.

Adam walked up to the man and said, "I'm Adam Smith. Is this Algebra?"

The man looked up from his *Knitting Hemp* magazine.

"Yes, it is."

Then he went back to reading.

"Um..." Adam said.

The man sighed and looked up again.

Adam continued, "I didn't sign up for this class but it showed up on my schedule. Is it all right if I'm here?"

The man put down his magazine.

"Sometimes Master-Mind sticks students into classes it thinks would benefit them if they can't count high enough to figure out how many half-hour classes they need to sign up for to fill a six-hour day. It's just my opinion, but Master-Mind seems to favor math and science courses with low prices. It also seems to take into account the other classes a student has chosen and the star ratings of the teacher. My star rating is only mediocre but the price of my class is rock-bottom, so I get all kinds of lost children."

He waved his hand vaguely at the classroom.

"You might call me the Pied Piper—leading the children who can't read directions away to other worlds. Anyway, take a seat, turn on the computer, the rest is obvious. I'm just your cheerleader."

Adam walked over to an empty computer wishing his cheerleader were nicer, better-looking, and the opposite sex. He sat down and flashed his ID over the ubiquitous gold plate in the console. The computer sprang to life.

On the computer screen was displayed an empty room with stone walls. There were flaming torches set equal distances from one another along the walls. In the center of the room was a large gold throne. Sitting on the throne was a roughly human-shaped lump of clay.

Letters flashed across the screen.

'Put on the headset.'

Adam looked around. Seeing no headset, he opened a drawer on the desk and found a headset within. He put it on and immediately heard some gentle 1980s synthesizer music. He heard a voice come over the headset that sounded a lot like *Hippie-Cheerleader* who was still sitting at the front of the classroom.

The disembodied voice said, "Enter your weight."

Adam guessed 60 kilograms for his weight.

"Enter your height."

He entered what he wished was his height.

"Stand up with your arms out to your sides."

He did so.

"Now wait."

He waited thirty seconds, then Hippie-Cheerleader's voice said, "Now flap your arms like a chicken."

Adam did as instructed until the voice said, "Just kidding about the chicken part. You look silly. Now sit down and stare at the screen."

Adam blushed and sat.

"Turn your head right."

He complied.

"Now turn your head left."

He turned left.

"Well done," the voice said. "Now marvel at thyself."

The image sitting on the throne changed and stood up. On the screen was a small, computerized replica of Adam Smith. Adam's avatar was thin, wiry, and muscular with approximately the correct dimensions except for better-looking abs. It also had approximately correct facial features.

Oh, and it was wearing a loincloth.

"I know what you are thinking," the voice said in his headset. "You're thinking, 'I don't really look this good.' That's okay though, because it's not real. It's just an imaginary little person made up of pixels on a computer screen. Think of it as a doll. One you are free to alter in any way that makes you happy, but not right now. Right now, your better-looking pixelated pal is stuck wearing a loincloth and looking a lot like you. To change that, you will have to learn something. When you learn something, your avatar will earn experience. Experience leads to levels. Levels lead to new stages of the game. New stages of the game mean better loot drops for your pixel-pal. Got that? Getting smarter equals getting cooler. Just wait. You'll see. And you'll like it. But first you have to pick your back story."

A list of stories popped up to the right side of the screen. Adam touched the first and it expanded to a text description that read, 'You are the last child of a royal line of kings. Your parents and siblings were all killed in a coup d'état when you were an infant, but your nanny snuck you out and hid you until you were old enough to venture out on your own. You are ready to enter the world and show it who is master, intending to someday retake the throne. But, for now, you are just trying to survive. Your nanny did not have the foresight to take any of your royal inheritance when she spirited you away, so you enter the world with only a loincloth, your wits, and your royal blood to protect you.'

Adam hit the second choice.

'You are the son of a beggar. The beggar trade did not work out for your father though, and he passed away from consumption. Tuberculosis. You have no remaining family, no money, and only a loincloth to protect you from the ugly world. But you are young, strong, clever, and have a burning desire to learn and grow and exit poverty.'

Adam chose the second option. Hippie-Cheerleader's voice gave him instructions on how to get around and interact with the world. Adam walked his avatar around the virtual room, then pulled on a torch that looked different from the others. A door appeared in the wall, revealing a set of stairs. He walked down the creepy, Dark Ages-style, spiral stairwell and eventually came to another door. He pulled on another unlit wall torch and he heard a booming voice in his headset say, "What is your name?"

Adam noticed some small print on the bottom of the screen that read, 'Say your name out loud.'

"Adam," Adam said out loud.

"Adam," his avatar said back to him. Then the door opened.

He was standing at the edge of a large open meadow. He stepped out in the grass and heard a door closing behind him. He turned around and saw the seamless trunk of a tall tree where a door had just been. He looked around and noticed other people, similarly clad, all running in the same direction. He followed them a short distance to a clearing that was filled with enormous wasps. There were loincloth-clad boys and girls wearing homespun bikinis all moving in what appeared to be slow motion. They were engaged in hand-to-hand combat with the giant wasps. He noticed one of the girls looked remarkably like Ribbons.

Adam was suddenly very glad he'd chosen this class.

Just then a wandering wasp took notice of him and charged over. Time slowed in the game. The screen showed a giant angry wasp at the center. All around the edges of the screen were different postage stamp-sized pictures with small labels beneath them.

One read 'Calculator' and showed an image of a calculator. Another showed a man's smiling face and read 'Instructor 1'. Another smiling person—pictured below the first—was titled 'Instructor 2'. There were five instructors visible and it looked like there might be more scrolling off the screen.

There was a long red bar above the angry wasp, and a long green bar over his avatar's head. There was also an hourglass to the right of the angry wasp that was rapidly emptying.

Along the bottom of the screen, a math problem was displayed that read, '2 + 2 = x. Solve for x.'

Adam hit the number '4' on his keyboard. He was rewarded with a friendly chime and his avatar executed a left-hand jab at the angry wasp. The wasp shuddered, and the red bar above its head shrank a little. Also, the hourglass beside it refilled, reset, and immediately started emptying again.

A new problem was displayed on the bottom of the screen.

'2 + x = 8. Solve for x.'

Adam hit '6' on the keyboard and heard the happy chime again. His avatar did another left jab and the wasp shuddered again and lost more of its health.

This continued for a while with each new problem proving more difficult than the last. Eventually the problems got so complex that he didn't know the answer. When the hourglass ran out, the wasp stung him and his avatar lost some of its health. The pictures of faces along the side of the screen started flashing. Adam touched 'Instructor 1'.

Time stopped for the wasp and Adam's avatar, and their images turned grey. The 'Instructor 1' picture expanded to cover most of the page and a smart-looking man of Indian descent with a mellow voice started giving a detailed explanation of the type of problem Adam had just failed to answer in time. The instructor drew examples on the screen using different colored markers and walked through the solution like a traditional teacher might.

Adam thought he could get the answer right but hit 'Instructor 2' just to see what would happen. A female instructor with a Swedish accent gave a similar lesson but in a different teaching style, using different methods. She told funny stories and used descriptive body language and drew pictures, whereas the first instructor had relied more on rules and formulas. Adam could see the value of having these different teachers. This system seemed well thought-out.

He touched the screen and the instructor went away. Time started again and color returned to the slow-motion combat. A new math problem was written along the bottom in the same style and complexity as the one he'd just missed. This time he answered correctly and the wasp made its last shudder, then fell on the ground before slowly fading away. His little avatar gave a cheer that sounded roughly like Adam and a gold, vertical experience bar to the left of the avatar filled a small amount.

Adam went around and defeated five more giant wasps, at which point fireworks went up and exploded over his avatar's head. The words 'Level Up' in gold letters flashed across the screen and the sound of a stadium crowd cheering came through the headphones. Then a little store icon on the left side of the screen started to blink. He touched it and the game turned grey again as a generic market interface appeared on screen. There were headings for all sorts of different goodies for his avatar organized in categories including: 'Clothes', 'Tattoos', 'Makeup', 'Haircare', 'Skills', 'Weapons', 'Titles', etc.

He touched the 'Skills' category and a second long list of options overlapped the first. Everything on the new list was greyed out but the first selection which read 'Right-hand Jab - $1'.

Apparently he'd earned $1.25 killing those angry wasps and the first option was the only one he could afford. He bought the right-hand jab, then looked around for something he could purchase for a quarter. About the only thing available was a feather to put in his hair. Adam purchased it thinking it might draw attention away from the fact that he was only wearing a loincloth.

When he closed the shop, color returned to the game world and his avatar now sported a feather in his hair.

Adam liked this game.

He searched out and fought another wasp, but it didn't give him much experience this time. So he left the little clearing and looked around for something else to fight. He found some porcupines a little ways away and picked a fight with one. The fight mechanics were the same as the wasp, but the problems were different and harder. He had to use the instructors right away. He was about to return to combat when the class bell rang.

Adam's avatar turned, faced him, and waved goodbye. Then the screen went blank.

Hippie-Cheerleader, still at the front of the classroom, waved to the large crowd of students exiting the room without looking up from his magazine.

35
Striving

Adam's last period was Work/Study Número Tres. He'd missed his first two work shifts so he was determined to make it to the last one.

His trusty ID card led him to the bottom-floor hallway just outside the swimming pool. There he joined a small group of students gathered around a short African-American woman with an enormous afro. She was wearing a janitor's uniform, blue gloves, and curved, clear, plastic safety glasses. She reminded him of someone on TV, but the celebrity's name escaped him. He tried to think of a nickname for her.

Janitor-Teacher?

Perhaps 'Boss' rather than 'Teacher' made more sense—this *was* a Work/Study period, after all.

Janitor-Boss?

Getting warmer. She was the head janitor. Janitors were professional cleaners.

He smiled, pleased with her name.

Boss-Clean.

Her name, she told them, was Jalena Singer, but they were to call her Ms. Singer. She pointed to the ID on her uniform where it read 'Ms. Singer' over the right pocket. The ID showed her smiling face wearing the same clear glasses.

Boss-Clean told them they were all children and that she would treat them like children until they had proven themselves. Most of the students who started working for her, she told them, were lazy and spoiled and couldn't tell a clean toilet from a dirty one even if they had to eat off it. But she planned to change all that. She would make them into great men and women by showing them the greatness of work.

To begin with, though, they had to understand that she had very high expectations for them. Expectations so high, in fact, that they could not possibly meet them the first time out of the gate... Nor the second... Nor the third. Only through repeated striving for improvement, she explained, could any of them hope to ever meet her lofty expectations.

"Work," she told them, "is striving. Striving to grow. Striving to learn. Striving to improve. Striving is key to a successful life."

She immediately called on a young girl whose eyes had glazed over at the beginning of the speech.

"Child, what is work?"

"Um," the girl turned bright red and sputtered, "something you do to get paid?"

"Not even close," Boss-Clean told the girl. Then she pointed straight at Adam.

"Child, what is work?"

"Work is striving," Adam repeated.

"Excellent," she said, then pointed at the first girl again.

"What is work?"

The girl squeaked out, "Work is striving?"

"Excellent," Boss-Clean said again. Then she pointed to a third student.

"Striving for what?"

"Erm," the young man said. "Striving for money?"

Boss-Clean shook her head and frowned.

"Striving to learn," Adam said, tiring of the slow pace. "Striving to grow. Striving to meet your expectations and exceed my own."

"Young man, what is your name?" the boss asked.

Adam realized he'd been promoted from 'child' to 'young man' in that last address. That was a good sign.

"Adam."

She grunted and gave him a grin with only half her mouth. After that, she gave a tour of an enormous storage room and assigned each student one of the cleaning carts that were lined up in the center of the room.

Each cleaning cart was the size of a riding lawnmower. They looked kind of like miniature versions of the ice-paving machines that groom a hockey arena, except without an engine. Each cart had shelves and hooks and holes and slots and bins all full of supplies and tools. It also had a trash can. It rolled on four caster wheels. Boss-Clean had all the students write their name on a piece of paper and tape it to the front of their cart.

Next Boss-Clean introduced them to the different tools on their cart. Mops, brooms, dustpans, rags, trash bags, soaps, squeegees, spray bottles, etc. were all examined and explained one at a time. Ms. Singer went in great, loving detail on the uses for each tool and also how to clean and maintain each one after use. She had every student practice cleaning each tool and then storing it. They repeated the process of pulling out a tool, cleaning it, then storing it over and over again until she was satisfied they had it down. Then she moved to the next tool.

Near the end of the period she went over the different chemicals and sprays they had on their carts. She had graphic stories about the horrible things they could do if handled improperly, like burn the eyes, possibly leading to blindness. Some cleaners could blister the skin and cause pain. Or catch fire. She showed them where all the first aid supplies were and had each of them squirt themselves in the eyes at the eyewash sink for one minute. They all had red, mildly irritated eyes after that experience.

"Anything gets in your eyes," she told them, "wash your eyes out at the nearest sink for twenty minutes before you even *think* of going to the nurse."

Then she showed them where the eye protection was on their cleaning cart. She had them put on eyewear and protective gloves. A few students snickered.

"Not getting hurt," Ms. Singer said authoritatively, "is the best medicine in the world. It costs the least. It hurts the least."

She looked meaningfully in the direction of the students who had snickered.

"I know kids your age aren't in the habit of thinking past the end of your own nose, but consider how 'cool' you'd look wearing an eyepatch the rest of your life."

Boss-Clean held up both her hands off to her sides, palms up.

"In one hand, you have the certainty of wearing safety glasses and gloves for a few minutes each day."

A pair of plastic safety glasses appeared in her right hand.

"On the other hand, you have the possibility of having to wear an eyepatch every day for the rest of your life."

She made a motion with her left hand as if it contained something very heavy, then closed her eyes and walked around the room staggering into objects until she tripped and fell on the floor.

There was some nervous laughter around the room.

"If you lose your sight," she said from the floor with her eyes still closed, "it's not the end of the world. Some people are even born that way and they make do. But *you* have a choice."

Boss-Clean opened her eyes slowly and deliberately, then put on a pair of safety glasses.

"I just hate to see young, healthy, educated, smart, pretty people scarred for life on account of carelessness, laziness, or overconfidence. Wear the Personal Protective Equipment while you work."

She had them take out all their safety gear, put it on, take it off, clean it, and store it over and over until each person could do every task fairly well even with eyes closed.

Then Ms. Singer had them put their carts back in storage. As they were leaving the spacious storage room, she asked each of them a question. If they got it wrong, she made them go back to the end of the line. The question she gave Adam was, "What is Work?"

"Work is striving," he told her confidently.

"Well said, young man."

36
An Evening with Singer

Adam's first day of school had officially ended.

After everyone answered their questions correctly and left for the day, Adam walked back in the central storage room and approached Boss-Clean.

"Did you forget something, Adam?" Ms. Singer asked.

"No," Adam assured her. "I was just wondering if there was some paying work that I could do after school. Now that I know how to use and care for the tools."

"Well," she said, "that depends. Have you ever done this kind of work before? Is there anything you're already good at?"

"I cleaned some bathrooms before and had a really good teacher—high expectations, I mean. She made me do it over and over till I got it right. So I guess I'm probably best doing that, starting off anyway."

"And you don't mind cleaning bathrooms?"

"No, ma'am. I am just starting out. I still have a lot to learn— even about cleaning bathrooms. Truthfully, I've found even simple jobs have something to teach me right now. I just have some experience with bathrooms already, so I'll be strongest there to begin with."

"I like your attitude, Adam. Grab your cart and come with me. I'll pay you a dollar for every fifteen minutes you work for me, as long as you're working hard. Less if you're slacking. As you get better, faster, and more reliable at the different jobs, you can approach me to discuss a pay raise. But for now, at the beginning, you're not going to be much real help. So I'll pay you a pittance and I'll keep you close to me. Your duties in the beginning will be simple tasks. That way I can see what you do, catch your mistakes, teach you how to work, that kind of thing. Just leave your pride right here at the door. If you think you're going to be great, you're wrong. You're going to be terrible, but that's the only way to grow. Understand?"

"Yes, ma'am. But there's one thing I need you to know."

"What is it?" she asked.

"I have to keep this baby with me in case it needs anything."

He held up the baby doll from Home Economics class.

An enormous, bright grin split Ms. Singer's face. She looked as though she were trying to force down a laugh.

"No problem, Adam. I'll keep you in my sight. You keep that baby in yours."

Boss-Clean was true to her word. She kept Adam close and had him do simple things within her eyesight. She kept up a constant stream of instructions and stories. The characters in her stories were her kids, her students, and sometimes herself. Some of her stories were of triumphs. Most, however, were about trials. Trial after trial and the things she learned from them. Adam liked her stories. They were kind of like fables, only personal.

Adam had no trouble with the tools or following instructions. He had the most trouble figuring out when to stop. His intuition about when a task was done was almost never correct, and in most cases, after several tries, Ms. Singer would have him stand aside and watch how she did it, explaining everything she did as she went. Then she would have him try again.

"Repetition is learning," she told him… Repeatedly.

Adam had the baby doll sitting on the top of his cleaning cart. In the middle of the afternoon it started crying. Adam tried giving it a bottle but it didn't seem to want it. He sat down on the ground and took off the diaper but couldn't figure out how to get it back on. Boss-Clean noticed his consternation and came over and gave him directions.

He was sitting on the ground with a baby doll in front of him—its diaper on backward— and she was standing over his shoulder giving stern instructions. The scene reminded Adam of a football coach shouting plays to the quarterback. After several mistakes, Adam managed to get the diaper on well enough that the baby stopped crying. He let out a long breath and wiped sweat off his brow.

"Now do it again," she told him.

He looked up at her with something approximating horror. She walked away laughing. He changed the diaper again.

After two hours of mopping floors and cleaning the locker rooms, Adam said he needed to head home for the night.

He didn't want the sunlight to disappear while he was still trekking home. He'd seen newly killed deer on the roadside some mornings when walking to the City, but never while walking home in the evening. The deer were hit in the night, he reasoned. He didn't want suffer the same fate if he could avoid it.

Boss-Clean told him he'd done a good job and transferred $8 to his personal account.

"Thank you, Ms. Singer," he said, holding the mop to the side and bowing a moderate degree, "for teaching me this trade. I look forward to learning from you again tomorrow."

When he straightened, she tapped the long handle of her broom against the end length of his mop handle. Their implements clanked like swords crossed in salute.

Adam smiled at the exchange.

Ms. Singer grinned too.

"Good job, Adam. Clean and stow your tools the way we practiced in class. I will see you tomorrow."

37
Burping Babies for Beginners

Thanks to the work he'd done with Ms. Singer, Adam was able to buy food at a supermarket. His ID card, it turned out, also doubled as a debit card. He bought a frozen pizza, a box of granola cereal, and a box of matches. He ate most of the granola while walking home. He tried the pizza once it thawed but it was mushy and didn't taste good.

At the campground he built a small wood house out of fallen, dry, dead branches in a fire pit. The campground had fire pits everywhere. Adam filled the small log cabin with tiny twigs. Atop the twigs he piles sticks of progressively greater thickness. The roof of the cabin he made from small logs. He used a single match to light the twigs at the bottom of the pile. They caught fire easily. The fire spread up through the sticks and eventually to the logs on the top. Adam then hauled a large, flat rock up from the lake and set it close to the fire. Once the rock was hot, he placed pizza slices on it, two at a time, until they were cooked.

The flavor was divine.

After eating close to heaven, Adam set about getting ready for bed. He didn't need to wash his body or his clothes in the lake since he had unlimited shower usage at school now. He fell asleep that night marveling at how far he'd come in such a short time.

He awoke in the middle of the night to the sound of a baby crying. Confused, he looked around and noticed the sound was coming from just outside his tent. He opened the tent flap and pulled in a crying bundle of grocery sacks. Half asleep, he opened the bundle, pulled out the noisy baby doll, and looked for an off switch.

How was this supposed to work again?

Memory came to him slowly and he fished around for the bottle. He put it to the baby's mouth but it kept crying.

Okay, there were two other things that were supposed to work. What were they?

Adam tugged its little diaper off and put it back on, but it kept making noise. He rocked it in the air to no effect. He thought back to the class and remembered he was supposed to burp it.

But how do you do that?

He ran little circles over its belly area but that didn't do anything. He patted its diapered bottom, but no luck. He tickled its feet... Nothing. Desperate, he tried blowing on the baby's face. When that failed, he took one of his blankets and buried the baby doll under it.

Then he went back to sleep.

The next morning, loud bird chirping woke Adam before the sunrise. He heard the muffled sound of the baby still crying. Why on earth had he chosen that class again?

He worked out the sore spots in his muscles before rolling from under the blankets... then scurried back under the covers. It was chilly! If winter was coming this soon he might be in serious trouble. He needed to buy a winter coat. Perhaps some more blankets too. Gloves. Thick socks. Scarf. Hat.

The list went on and on.

Just then his stomach churned. He ground his teeth with frustration. Was there ever a moment of the day he wasn't hungry? He thought about his bargain with Anger-Management. If she came through on her end... he slipped away to a fantasy where, no matter where he went, he always had a lunch box and it was always overflowing.

Eventually the morning chill and the ache in his stomach motivated Adam to get moving. Perhaps he could find some leftovers in the cafeteria at school. It couldn't hurt to ask. His hand snaked out from under the blankets to unzip the tent flap. Then it padded around blindly in the dirt till it found his shoes. He pulled them in, shook them hard to flush out any bugs, shoved them over his feet, then frowned.

They hadn't felt that tight the previous day. Could they have shrunk? Could he have started growing after only two days of decent food?

"Bah," he grumbled. Now shoes that fit were another thing he needed to purchase. He needed to get to work... or rather, school, so he could earn some money.

Adam left the tent and was about to start off at a run when he heard the baby crying. He wasn't sure which made him angrier, that he had to bring it with him or that he'd almost forgotten to bring it... again. He ducked back in the tent and grabbed the baby, the bottle, and the plastic grocery bags. Then he stacked wood in the mud room for the Campground-Lady, brushed his teeth, and headed for school—still-crying baby in bag.

Adam sprinted the first leg of the sixteen kilometers to kill the chill. When he started to feel warm he slowed to a jog. When the first bit of sweat formed on skin, he started to walk. Just then he heard a familiar horn from a good distance behind. He looked over his shoulder then crossed the street and waited at the edge of the road.

VW-Saint pulled up and rolled down the window.

"Need a lift?" she asked, cheerfully.

"Do you know how to burp a baby?" he asked through the open window.

She developed a stunned look and pointed an index finger toward herself in question.

"I'll take that as a 'no'," Adam said and got in the passenger seat. He took the baby doll out from the plastic bags and showed it to her.

"May I see that?" Anne asked.

Adam handed the wailing doll over gratefully.

She bounced it on her knee, rocked it in her arms, whispered "Shhh, shhh" in its little ear, and rubbed its plastic head. The baby was still crying. She stuck out her lower lip and handed it back, holding it at arm's length.

"Thanks for trying," Adam said. He stuffed it under his seat—which muffled its noise considerably. "It's been at this all night."

"I'm guessing you didn't sleep well," she said.

She turned the radio up to cover the remaining baby doll noise. Adam laid his head against the door and closed his eyes.

"Too true."

Then his eyes popped open and he asked, "Do you like flowers?"

She spit out some of the coffee she'd just been sipping, then said, "Sure, I guess. Who doesn't?"

Anne wiped coffee off the dashboard and the front of her clothes.

"What about candy?"

"Only the kind with sugar."
She closed her eyes tightly, grinned, and held up an index finger—as though she'd just scored a point. "I'm picky that way."

Adam laughed. "Lee would love that wordplay."

Saint-Anne put the car back on the road and looked at him sideways.

"He thinks irony is really funny... I think. It's hard to tell for sure, but he employs it about every other sentence, so I think he must," Adam explained.

"You're making friends then?" Saint-Anne asked.

Adam thought about his first two days at school and nodded.

"Many," he admitted, then turned his face away feeling embarrassed.

Her question had touched something raw inside—a vulnerable spot he was not aware existed until just that moment. In truth, he was surprised at all the amazing people he'd met in the Tower, and even more surprised by their acceptance. It was as if they didn't notice his dark complexion, slight accent, worn shoes, faded clothes, irregular hair, or even his scars. His delight felt delicate and fragile. He was not ready to let it face real scrutiny.

Saint-Anne waited a bit longer, then let the topic drop.

"I heard you had—what was it?—a 'sporting accident' yesterday on the Play Yard."

Adam's mouth went dry.

"Are you okay?" Saint-Anne continued obtusely.

Adam rubbed the right side of his face automatically, then froze and deliberately lowered his hand to the arm rest.

"Just a bruise," he said. "I've had much worse."

"Have you now?" Anne asked.

Adam nodded, "Yeah." Then he turned away and fell to silence again.

After about fifteen seconds of quiet, Anne puffed air out her nose, sounding a little frustrated. Then she pulled in the driveway of the bus station.

"Do you want off here again?"

Adam thought about all the things he needed to buy but didn't have the money to purchase. He thought about asking for a ride straight to the school, then had an even better idea.

"I'll get out here," he said as he climbed out of the car. "Thank you again, Miss Anne. You saved me a bunch of time this morning. How can I repay you?"

"You already have," she said. "I told you, I enjoy your company. I'll see you in class."

38
Witnessing Her Moment

Adam took the bus a few blocks, then got off. He thought there was a flower shop somewhere along the bus route. He found it quickly and picked out three roses—one red, one yellow, and one black. They were $2.50 each. Adam sighed and put them back.

He walked the rest of the way to school and arrived forty minutes before the first period. He checked his Friends List on the school ID. Jenny was near the locker rooms and Anger-Management was not yet on campus. He headed toward the locker rooms and found Jenny walking out in his direction.

"Oh, you're here early," Jenny said in her usual, friendly tone.

"I got a ride," he said, hoping she wouldn't ask from whom.

"Listen, Jenny, I owe you a half hour and have about that much time before my first class. Is now a good time for you?"

Her face lit up with excitement as she grabbed his hands in both of hers.

"Yes!" she said enthusiastically. Then she turned and tugged him along behind her.

"It's too cold to go outside this morning, so let's go to the auditorium. No one should be in there now. Theater types aren't usually morning people."

Adam hadn't seen the auditorium before. He hadn't even realized there was one. Jenny led him quickly up to the main floor, then past the gymnasium. She pushed open some heavy, large doors on the left side of the hall next to a ticket window cut out in the wall. They entered a tall, quiet space, dimly lit by recessed lighting in a ceiling two stories up. There were velvet, red padded seats in rows on a black floor. The floor sloped sharply down toward a stage at the front of the large room. Adam could see dust floating around in the air. The whole place smelled like starched linen and sawdust. It seemed to swallow sound.

Jenny took a seat in the front row and had Adam sit next to her. Her eyes sparkled and she looked like she was having trouble containing herself. Adam wiggled around till he found a relaxing way to sit, then twisted and lifted his hand in her direction, palm up—hoping she would see it as a gesture that he was ready to listen.

She started like a sprinter exploding out of starter blocks.

"I thought a lot over what I'd like to talk to you about and I decided I want to talk to you about my faith."

Adam kept his features mildly pleasant, but otherwise neutral, and nodded encouragement.

For the next half hour, Jenny, the valedictorian of her class, told him all about the journey of her faith—the day she accepted Christ, the day she was baptized, her first mission trip. Her desire to serve others but also be an example to others. Church camp experiences and the first time she'd ever witnessed to someone. Her feelings for the divine. During this time, she required no prompting or encouragement. The words poured out of her, inexhaustible.

Adam tried not to think while she was talking. He didn't want to miss anything she said. He felt—through a kind of sympathy-of-sentiment—her joy. In a surreal touch, the recessed light from the ceiling hit her hair and caused it to glow exactly like a halo.

In no time, Jenny's phone alarmed that thirty minutes was up. Abruptly she stopped talking. Her cheeks were flushed. Her brown eyes sparkled. She was breathing fast. Her pulse pounded in the notch of her neck. Adam marveled—she was breathtaking.

She reached down and pulled out her ID card, touched it a few times, and put it back in her pocket. Adam looked at his ID. She'd given him five stars on her satisfaction survey and written 'Trustworthy' in the comments.

He grimaced briefly, feeling a fraud. No one who lied as often as he did deserved such a noble title.

When he glanced up she was standing, still looking vibrant and alive.

"Thanks," she said breathlessly. "I really needed that."

"Thank *you*," he said honestly, "for sharing this experience with me. I really enjoyed seeing you so... passionate about something."

She smiled brightly, turned, and strode out of the room at a rapid clip—waving briefly at the door before disappearing.

Adam lingered in the room for a minute—absorbed in the silence—remembering Jenny in her moment.

39
Blessed Silence

Adam ran to the library in the ten minutes still remaining before his first class. He checked out the book Mr. Geezer had recommended—*The Making of Modern Economics* by Mark Skousen—directly to his ID card. Then he ran down to the locker room where he washed his clothes in the shower, washed himself, changed to the school uniform, and hung up his old clothes to dry in his locker—all in five minutes. He was impressed with the time but couldn't shake the feeling he was forgetting something.

Given the temperature outside, Coach-Squarepants told her first-period PE class to exercise in the gym. Adam chose an exercise bike and read his new book on the back of his ID card while riding. The period passed quickly.

When Adam entered his second class, Language and Communication, no one else was there. He pulled *The Making of Modern Economics* up on his ID. Before he got anywhere in the book, a baby doll came crashing down on the desk in front of him. It was crying.

Adam looked up to see Saint-Anne, red-faced and flustered. She'd changed her clothes to something like a Southern belle, complete with hoopskirt and parasol. Her dress was bright yellow with white lace on the bottom of the skirt and the cuffs of the sleeves. Her hair was braided tightly behind her head and she had on a large, white sun hat.

In a rich Southern accent she said, "Hun, you left this in the car. I tried everything I could think of, believe you me, but I couldn't get it to stop."

They both stared at the supine baby doll. Adam looked horrified and Saint-Anne looked helpless and overdressed.

Lee arrived and sat in the chair behind Adam. He followed the line of focus around from Adam to Saint-Anne and down to the baby doll. Then he reached effortlessly across the distance and gently picked up the doll with his long-fingered hand. Adam followed the doll through the air with his eyes, then his head, then his whole body, until he'd turned completely in the chair and looked straight back at Lee. Lee had the baby over one of his shoulders and patted it on its little back with a hand at least as large as the baby.

Blessed silence filled the room. Adam and Saint-Anne let out a shared, "Oh."

Lee looked pleased and bashful as he handed the baby back to Adam, supporting its neck with the fingers of one hand in the shape of a 'C', with the rest of its body supported on his forearm—a move that Adam thought looked practical.

"Nicely done," Saint-Anne said and clapped.

Her dainty golf clap sounded muffled given she was wearing white gloves.

Adam stood up, clapped his hands together in a gesture like prayer, and bowed his head over his hands saying, "Thank you so much. You may have just saved my life."

Lee grinned shyly.

"It's nothing, really. I just like kids."

Adam peered at Lee with one eye through his shaggy hair and whispered, "Are you sure you're not forty years old?"

He regretted it as soon as he said it, even more so when he felt a folded up parasol hit his right shoulder blade.

Lee's eyes widened and he said in mock outrage, "Not even close, you illiterate Neanderthal."

Adam quickly resumed his previous half-bowed, prayer posture.

"I'm so sorry I said that out loud after you so recently saved my life."

Lee grinned evilly—rather like the Cheshire Cat from *Alice in Wonderland*—then started to say, "If I had…"

But Saint-Anne cut him off and primly wacked each of them in the head with her still-folded parasol.

"Enough, y'all!" she said in that rich Southern accent. "We need to git class rollin'."

40
Bubbly-Boss

Two periods later Adam entered the nurse's office where he was greeted by a pleasantly plump young lady who asked if she could help him.

"My name is Adam," he said, bowing slightly at the neck and shoulder.

"My ID told me to report here for Work/Study in 'Health Services'."

The nurse clapped her hands together and bounced in her chair, looking delighted.

"Bravo," she said. "I love formal types. I'm Nurse Kacey. You'll be working with me out of this office. Do you have any experience in healthcare?"

He shook his head.

Negativo.

"Perfect," Nurse Kacey said happily, "then I won't have to break you of any bad habits. Listen, Page-Boy... By the way, I'm going to call you Page-Boy from now on because I think it is funny on so many levels. Would that be okay with you?"

Adam was trying to decide what he thought of his new name when Nurse Kacey continued talking.

"Perfect. I knew you'd like it. So anyway, Page-Boy, this is my part-time job. In my grown up life, I'm the head nurse at the ER at Lady of Peace Hospital. Have you ever been there?"

Adam shook his head again in the negative.

"Well, that's probably a good thing. Means you're healthy. In any case, what I'm trying to tell you is that I've got loads more experience than your average school nurse, so we are going to do a lot more in this school health clinic than is typical for a school clinic. Can you handle the sight of blood?"

Adam shrugged.

"Well, you'll get used to it. In any case, don't worry. I work under the supervision of a doctor, so we won't do anything here that's dangerous. His name is Dr. Roberts. He's a great doctor. He comes here once a week to help out at the clinic and gives a free hour-long lecture in the auditorium. I'll try to work it out so he gives his lectures during this period so you can make it to all of them if you want. Now," she said, rubbing her hands together, "Let's get busy."

The first few patients that came through were sick kids with viruses. She had Adam give Tylenol or ibuprofen or Pepto-Bismol or antihistamines, depending on their complaints. Some she sent home, some she sent back to class.

A student came in with a scraped knee from a fall in the Play Yard. She had Adam wash it with soap and water, rinse it, pat it dry, and cover it with antibiotic ointment and a Band-Aid. The whole time he worked, she kept a running commentary on what he was to do next, how well he was doing at present, and peppered her instructions with frequent, short, usually humorous medical stories.

The period went by quickly.

Nurse... now what was her name?

Adam decided to call her *Nurse Bubbly-Boss*.

Nurse Bubbly-Boss tapped her computer pad.

Adam looked at his ID and found he'd been paid $2. His face brightened with a smile. He looked over at Nurse Bubbly-Boss and said, "Thank you for teaching me."

"You did well today, Page-Boy," she said, laughing at the sound of the name she'd given him. "I've got a good feeling about you. See you tomorrow."

41
Win-Win

Adam's next class was Economics where he found Mr. Geezer standing on a chair writing, 'Win-Win' in tiny letters on the chalkboard—underlined twice.

Adam sat down in the center desk, front row as the bell sounded.

Mr. Geezer turned toward the class but did not step down from his perch.

"Class," his voice crackled like an old-timey record player.

"Imagine for a second that What's-His-Name here," he pointed at Adam, "has a ring—a sparkly, super valuable, diamond ring. And also imagine that I want to get married."

A girl student said, "Gross," quietly. Several people snickered.

"Bah," Mr. G grumbled, "don't act so surprised. I'm still young at heart. Anyway, I want that ring and that's a problem for me because he has it. In economics, we call that problem 'scarcity'."

"Scarcity," he went on, "is a problem all living creatures must deal with. Most animals deal with this problem violently: If they want it, they take it—if they can—without regard for what happens to the original owner. Justice—the 'Do No Harm' topic we discussed yesterday—is laughably absent in nature. But we are human beings," he continued. "We are different—special." He barked a laugh.

"So my special young people, let's brainstorm. Think like advanced creatures and see how many different solutions we can think of that end with me in possession of that ring."

"You could offer to buy it from me for money," Adam suggested.

"You could take it from him while he's asleep," a girl offered.

"You could kill him and take it," a boy suggested.

"You could make your *own* ring," an affronted girl huffed.

"You could trade him for something of equal value," a different student said.

"You could wait until he dies, then dig up his grave and take it," a boy said.

"You could marry him and he'd give it to you," a girl said, giggling.

"You could do some work for him and ask for the ring as payment," another student threw in.

"You're doing great," Mr. Geezer beamed.

"Additionally, I might hire thugs to go and take it. Sue him in court and ask for the ring as reparation. Or—you're probably all too nice to think about this—I could kidnap his family members and threaten to hurt them if he did not give over the ring as ransom."

Adam frowned darkly at his desktop. His family was beyond kidnapping now, but thinking about them hurt terribly.

"Mr. G!" a girl said, sounding disturbed.

"I know, I know," said Mr. Geezer. "That's ugly talk. But the point of this exercise is that there are different ways humans solve the problem of scarcity. In economics, we call that 'rationing'. Rationing means deciding who gets what. Some of our brainstorming produced the natural, no-holds-barred, winner-take-all, violent rationing solutions. But not *all* our ideas were violent or mean. In some of them, What's-His-Face came out pretty well."

Mr. Geezer hopped deftly down from the chair.

"This interaction we've been contemplating between myself and…. What was your name again?"

"Adam."

"Right. This interaction we have been contemplating between Adam and me is called a 'two-party trade'. He is a party and I am a party to the trade of a ring. Now let's generalize and categorize. If one of us is better off after the trade, then it's a 'win' for that person. If one of us is worse off, then it's a 'lose' for that person."

Mr. Geezer picked up some chalk to write something on the board, then changed his mind and asked Adam to do it.

Adam popped out of his seat and strode to the blackboard.

"Draw a large square," Mr. Geezer told him, "then write your name above the square and my name to the side of it."

Adam did as instructed.

Mr. Geezer spoke loudly to the class.

"Each of us can either win or lose from the rationing of the ring. So draw a vertical line down the center of the square so there are two columns. Above the left column write 'Win' and above the right column write 'lose'."

Adam complied.

"Perfect," Mr. Geezer said. "Those are the outcomes from your perspective. Now draw a horizontal line through the middle of the box making two rows. Label the top row 'Win' and the bottom row 'Lose'. Those are the two possible outcomes from my perspective."

"Finally," Mr. Geezer said, "fill in each square at the intersection of a row and column with the appropriate trading outcomes: 'Win-Win', 'Win-Lose', 'Lose-Win', and 'Lose-Lose'."

When Adam finished, Mr. G waved for him to sit down again.

"This outcomes table," Mr. Geezer tapped Adam's drawing on the board, "is pretty unique in nature. Most living creatures are unable to contemplate anything but their own desires."

He covered up Adam's name.

"But we are humans and—for the sake of this class—we are economists. So we have the ability—though we do not always use it—to spare a thought for our neighbor."

He took his arm off the board so Adam's name was visible again.

"If I kill Adam and take his ring, it's a 'Win' for me but a 'Lose' for him."

He pointed to the upper right hand box on the board.

"If I save his dog and he gives me the ring as a reward, it's a 'Win' for him and a 'Win' for me."

He pointed to the top left hand box.

"If I try to kill him, but only manage to injure him and he kills me in self-defense, then it's a 'Lose' for him and a 'Lose' for me too."

He pointed to the bottom right box.

"What's-Your-Face," he pointed at Adam again. "What is justice?"

Adam yelled back so Mr. G could hear him.

"Do no harm. Remedy harm done."

"Good," Mr. Geezer said. "So in that Win-Lose scenario I gave earlier, the one where I kill you and take your ring—did that violate justice?"

"Definitely," Adam said.

"Right," Mr. G agreed. "So we now have a second, valid definition of justice—'Win-Win'. By extension, we also now have several additional definitions of *in*justice—'Win-Lose', 'Lose-Win', or—God forbid—'Lose-Lose'. Which leads us to the main question in the study of economics: Is there a simple, inexpensive, effective way to guarantee a 'Win-Win' in every trade, all the time, for everybody? Put another way, how can we guarantee justice for all?"

After a brief pause, Mr. Geezer continued, "It took humanity tens of thousands of years, perhaps even hundreds of thousands of years, to find a stable solution to the scarcity problem. But figure it out they did. And now I'm going to tell you their secret solution."

He crouched a little, cupped his hands in the shape of a megaphone, and said in an exaggerated whisper, "Citizenship."

He waited. Chairs creaked. People shifted uncomfortably.

Adam raised his hand.

"Professor, what is citizenship?"

42
Highs and Lows

The bell rang and Adam did not get his question answered, which was irksome.

Mr. G, though, looked delighted.

"The key to humanity's long-term prosperity will have to wait till tomorrow," the old professor said as students collected their belongings.

"Don't miss it! Not for anything!"

Adam didn't have far to walk before he was in Home Economics.

The teacher had a crib set up in the front of the room and was standing next to it. Adam idly thought she could probably lay flat in the crib and fit comfortably. For some reason he found picturing her in the crib amusing.

He set down his plastic bags and unloaded his baby doll. He said a quick prayer that he could turn it in today, but was denied.

Adam was gratified to see that many of the other students filing in the room had big circles under their eyes too. At least he wasn't the only one.

Little-Fox's eyes sparkled with mischief that morning as she asked how everyone had done with their babies. A general groan came from the audience and she laughed at her own joke.

"Tut-tut," Little-Fox said. "The path to adulthood is through suffering. And these babies only give a hint of the suffering that awaits you as new parents. You will overcome this. You will get stronger and smarter for the effort."

She struck a super hero pose with both fists on her hips.

"Don't give up."

Adam tried to imagine her in a spandex superhero costume complete with mask, baby doll in one hand, and a cape fluttering behind. He snorted out loud, then blushed as the whole class turned to look at him. Little-Fox gave him a suspicious, reproachful look.

Then she pulled a baby doll off a shelf and gave instructions on how to hold a baby. How to burp a baby. How to feed a baby. How women breastfeed a baby. She actually demonstrated latching techniques on a naked female torso mannequin.

Adam practically held his breath through the demonstration. Even a model of a naked female torso was an alarming and intriguing sight.

"Breast milk," Little-Fox explained, "is nearly perfect food. It's easy for babies to digest. It tastes good to the babies. It costs far less than baby formula. And, most importantly, breast milk contains antibodies. Moms pass along a lifetime of disease fighting antibodies to their infants through the breast milk. This is important because the infant's immune system has never experienced any diseases. Breast-fed babies get sick less often and, when they do get sick, have less severe symptoms than formula-fed infants."

"That's the up side," she continued. "The down side is it's hard. My sister has an infant right now and she says breastfeeding is the hardest thing she has ever done. Also, not all women are capable of breastfeeding. But for those that can, breastfeeding is a great advantage to the babies."

Next Little-Fox taught how to dress a baby. How to undress a baby. How to swaddle a baby. And on and on for the whole period. After each small bit of instruction, she had the students practice on their dolls.

Intermittently throughout the class someone's baby would cry and one of the students would frantically try to figure out what was wrong so it would quiet.

When the class ended, Adam packed up his baby in the plastic bags and headed for the exit.

"Adam," he heard Little-Fox say behind him, "a word, please."

He turned but—at first—couldn't find the teacher. Then he looked down. She was right in front of him—naturally.

"I looked at your baby recording, Adam. You are supposed to keep the doll with you at all times."

"I did," he said, shoulders slumping a little. "I just didn't know how to burp a baby. It cried forever. But no worries. I was right next to it."

She looked at him sideways with a serious look on her face.

"Well," he admitted, "I *did* forget it in my ride's car this morning on accident. That won't happen again though. I'll get better."

"Chin up," she said with a reassuring smile while she patted him on the shoulder and ushered him toward the door. "You couldn't get any worse."

Adam stepped out of the Home Economics classroom depressed. The hall was full of students traveling upstream like fish. He was about to let himself get swept away in the current when the flutter of something black in the corner of his vision caught his attention. Gloom forgotten, he altered course and chased two pigtails through the crowd. In a matter of seconds, he caught up to, and fell in beside, the elegant lady.

"Hi," he said good-naturedly.

Amy glanced at him out of the corner of her eye while walking.

"Oh, hi," she said, sounding surprised and pleased. "I didn't notice you there."

Then she slowed and scrutinized his face closely.

"You look... harsh," she said with a touch of concern in her tone.

"I had a long night," Adam admitted, grinning like an idiot.

"How come?" Ribbons asked.

"*This* woke me up," he grumbled, pulling the baby doll out of the plastic bags.

"It needed something. Burping, I think. But I didn't know how. So it kept on crying. It took me, like, ten hours and my entire friend network to figure out how to burp a baby."

Ribbons put her hand over her mouth to hide a giggle.

"I know," he said. "Someday, when I'm not so tired, I'll find it funny too."

Just then Adam's baby started crying. He held it at arm's length, frowning. Ribbons laughed and took the baby from him and patted it on the back. It kept crying, so she stopped walking, crouched down in the middle of the hall, and proceeded to change its diaper. Students flowed around her like water around a rock. The doll kept crying. She looked around as if searching for something, noticed the bags in Adam's hand, reached over, and fished around in them. She pulled out the bottle and gave it to the baby, finally silencing the little demon.

Adam let out a breath he didn't realize he'd been holding.

"Thanks," he said as she put the baby and its bottle back in the plastic bags. "You're a lifesaver."

She rolled her eyes a little, smiled, and stood up.

"Any time," she said whimsically before entering the girl's locker room.

He imagined the ribbons trailing her were waving goodbye as they vanished out of sight. Oblivious to the people all around, he held up the plastic bags and spoke to the baby doll inside.

"Perhaps you're good for something after all."

43
Shop Boss

After his second PE period that day, Adam showered and changed, then followed the map on his ID to a room on the second floor. He entered a good-sized open room set up markedly similar to the Home Economics room one floor above it. In place of baby dolls and foodstuff, though, this room had shelves full of wood and metal and tools and nails and all manner of building materials. Along the back of the room, instead of ovens, there were large industrial tools set meters apart from one another. Mounted to one of the large industrial tools was a pair of safety glasses enshrined in a clear plastic box. The glasses inside were arranged in such a way that they showed off nicely the chunk of metal sticking part way through one of the lenses. In addition, the room was plastered everywhere with warning signs and poem fragments like, 'Touch this wrong and your finger is GONE.'

Adam was imagining one of his fingers amputated when he heard footsteps enter the room. He turned to find a 190-centimeter muscular giant striding through the door with several wooden planks on one oversized shoulder.

The newcomer had brown hair that was cut short and spiked on the top. He had a prominent, triangular nose and a solid jaw with a hint of stubble. He had thick eyebrows, brown eyes, and a grin that revealed perfect white teeth.

"Hi there, young man," he said, "I've not met you before. I'm Mr. Keynes, the shop teacher."

Adam took a step back unconsciously.

"I'm Adam."

He had no idea men could get that big. Adam briefly wondered if his whole body even weighed as much as one of that man's arms.

"Well, Adam," Mr. Keynes said, "what needs fixed?"

Adam blinked in puzzlement.

"You know," said the giant man, "what's broken? Which beautiful teacher sent you to seek my aid?"

"Oh," Adam caught up to speed, "I'm here for Work/Study. I signed up for 'Maintenance'."

"Ah, great!" the giant roared. "I'm glad to have an understudy. Here now, you can start by helping me put these boards away."

The giant had Adam slide each board off his shoulder one at a time and place them on the shelves. As they worked, Mr. Keynes kept up a running stream of commentary and instruction.

"The best and easiest route to success in life is to read and follow the directions. Got that? Good. Because I never read directions. I always intend to, but I get so excited about the project that I skip over that first little step and just jump right in. And I ALWAYS regret it! So your job, Adam, while working with me, is to read the directions for me! Then tell me what I did wrong so that I can get the job done right. Got that?"

Adam tried to puzzle through the logic that had just been thrown at him.

Mr. Keynes misread his body language and said, "You *can* read, right?"

"Certainly," Adam said defensively. "Can't everybody?"

"Well," the Shop giant said, "I guess what I really meant is, are you smart? Can you process what you read and turn it into useful directions? You know. Can you read for understanding? Can you handle technical reading?"

Adam shrugged. "Probably. Some of the economics books I've read were a lot like stereo instructions—all dry and precise and exact."

"Excellent," the giant said while beaming his perfect smile at Adam. "Then come over here."

Mr. Keynes led Adam to one of the large machines in the back of the room. It looked shiny and new.

"This beauty is my brand new table saw. The old one died after I tried to fix it. So I want to set up this new one properly so it won't need fixing. That way I can't break it."

Adam nodded. He was starting to understand the problem here.

"I'd like you to read this manual," Mr. Keynes said as he plopped down a thick pile of paper on a table next to Adam, "and tell me how to set this up. Can you do that?"

Adam had a feeling very few people had ever said no to this man.

"Yes sir, I'll do it."

Adam spent the rest of the period reading the instructions and telling Mr. Keynes how to make the machine work. In the short spaces between each of Adam's relayed instruction, Mr. Keynes would try to guess what needed to be done next and start tinkering. His guesses were almost never right and they had to backtrack several times to undo some damage he'd caused. By the end of the period, though, they had it operating like the well-oiled machine it was.

"Fabulous," said Mr. Keynes. "You're a prince. I would never have gotten that done so quickly without you."

He went over to a desk at the front of the room and touched the pad lying on it.

Adam found he had another $2 in his virtual wallet.

"Together," said the Shop giant, "we'll solve all kinds of problems and the girls will love us! Trust me, Adam, there's no shortage of girls in this world and all of them," he winked, "have problems that need fixing. And they are super grateful when someone comes along with the skill," he flexed his bicep, "and the talent," he showed off his perfect teeth, "to get the job done. We're going to be a great team. You'll see."

Adam grinned and blinked, uncertain how to feel. He couldn't tell, just yet, if he was now the sidekick of a super hero or a super villain.

44
Fear of Math

Adam worked with the janitor staff for an hour and a half after school that day, earning a few more dollars. When he quit work, he set out for the City, on the hunt for a winter coat... Or some shoes. Maybe some socks. His pants were getting short too. And he still wanted to buy those flowers.

Before leaving the school, he briefly considered wearing or sneaking out some of the warmer school uniform clothing to layer against the cold. After a moment's consideration, he dismissed the idea. The school uniform was distinctive. Anyone seeing him wearing the uniform would find him memorable, easy to identify, and, therefore, easy to track. To remain invisible, he needed to blend in the background like a chameleon.

He tapped his ID card and noted he had $12.

Enough to buy... nothing.

Still, he could map out what he was going to buy! So he set out to go price shopping.

Adam walked up and down the sidewalks of the retail district. He stopped in clothing shops and shoe shops. Very quickly, he had more information than places to store it in his brain, so he snagged a discarded pen off the ground and a piece of paper out of a trash can and started writing furiously the things he'd seen, the stores he'd seen them in, and the prices at each store. It made a table, which was elegant—in a mathy kind of way.

At one of the shoe stores a sales clerk approached him and offered to tell him his shoe size. Adam said, "Sure," and discovered his shoe size was a full inch longer than the shoes he was currently wearing. That explained a lot. The sales clerk snorted and said Adam's current shoes only fit because they were so worn out. Speaking of worn out, Adam's socks had holes in them. The clerk helping him looked embarrassed when he saw the holes in Adam's socks.

Odd, Adam thought, since he isn't the one who has to wear them.

Still, Adam felt embarrassment sympathetically and mentally added yet another pair of socks to his list of things to buy. When Adam told the sales clerk what kind of prices he could afford, the clerk looked even more embarrassed and told him the least expensive shoes he had were $66 on clearance. Adam tried not to gape. It would take months before he had enough saved to buy their clearance shoes! It would be winter by then.

Almost casually, the sales clerk mentioned that Adam might want to check out the local, church-run thrift store.

No matter where Adam looked, the prices were always too high. What he really needed was someplace inexpensive… preferably free. He asked around for directions to the thrift store and was told there was one two blocks east. Adam headed off in that direction.

It was amazing how much the City could change in just three blocks. The landscape went from being pretty storefronts with clean sidewalks to dark saloons splattered with who-knows-what, then to run-down residential housing with narrow lanes tightly packed with parked cars.

Something about the residential area made Adam nervous. It was nothing like the roomy, well-maintained, friendly, manicured suburbs where he'd grown up. Here, unpleasant smells drifted out of homes and alleyways. Many doors were sagging on their hinges, many windows broken. Directionless, muffled sounds of dogs barking echoed down the street. The sound of screams and gunfire and cars crashing streamed out of open windows. Adam was relieved to see the shimmer of oversized televisions when he looked for the sources of violence.

Occasionally he saw adults walking or standing around. Most seemed idle—taking care not to make eye contact with anyone. The clothing worn here was unique. Half the time the style was baggy long sleeves and hoods that hid every detail of the person. The other half of the time it was tank-top t-shirts with gold chains, oversized rings, and medallions the size of hood ornaments. Maybe they *were* hood ornaments!

After walking down the residential street a bit, Adam came across the thrift store. He entered and found himself staring across a large, open room packed end to end with racks of clothes of all colors and styles. The room smelled like mothballs and old people. There were a few women, one with two children running around her, picking through the racks. The women wore clothes in a similar state of wear to his own. He scanned the walls and found they were covered with shelves holding crates and boxes of miscellaneous items in something slightly more organized than random. There were signs over racks and attached to boxes that read: '$1', '$2', '$3', '$5', '$10', '$12'...

Adam's eyes sparkled.

"Jackpot," he said out loud and commenced his search.

First priority was a coat. There were fewer of them than other types of clothes and there weren't any good thick ones. Adam tried on thin ones. There were lots of thin ones that looked nearly new and fit well. He tried layering them one on top of another. He started sweating instantly. That was a good sign. He took them off and walked up to price them at the register. The relaxed, plump clerk told him they were $2 each for a total of $6.

He left the coats at the front counter and continued his search through the store. He pulled out the shopping list he'd made earlier. He had to prioritize—shoes were next.

He found shoes piled haphazardly in boxes. Fortunately, the boxes were labeled with sizes. He picked a shoe at random from a box labeled one size larger than the shoes he was already wearing. It fit nicely—too nicely. He took the shoe off and tried the next half size up. A little loose, but he figured he'd need room to grow. He commenced to dig through that pile and picked out a newish looking pair of hiking shoes. He took them to the register and discovered they cost $5. That left $1.

He grabbed an adult set of mittens for 50¢, a pair of socks for 25¢, and a toboggan hat for 25¢, which put an end to his shopping spree. Extra blankets would have to wait.

He walked to the checkout and pushed all his items toward the sales clerk.

She totaled them and announced, "$12.72."

Adam looked shocked and confused. When he found his tongue he said, "No. There is some mistake. I added them all up and they came to $12 even."

"There's a 6% sales tax," the clerk said apologetically.

Adam groaned.

"Okay," he said, "how much can I afford if I have a total of $12, so that sales tax won't put me over?"

The clerk looked at him with a mixture of irritation, confusion, and terror. Adam recognized that look. Fear of Math.

He made a calming gesture and quickly said, "Sorry. Didn't mean to alarm you. The total has to be less than $12 and the previous tax at $12 was 72¢. That means my max will be a little less than $12 by 72¢, or around $11.28. I'll take the three coats and the hiking shoes and one pair of socks. The gloves and hat I can get another time."

The terror left the clerk's eyes and she looked briefly grateful before she returned to her previously pleasant demeanor.

Just then the demon-baby doll decided to start crying. Adam shut his eyes and took a deep breath and said, "Excuse me, I have to take care of this. I'll go to the back of the line once I'm finished."

Adam went over and hid behind one of the clothing racks and pulled out the demon-baby. Burps and food didn't help, so he replaced the diaper and it shut up. He wiped sweat off his brow. A couple of ladies in the room hid smiles behind their hands.

Adam went to the back of the line. When he was back up to the register, the clerk added his coats and boots and socks and said, "$11.93."

He handed over his ID card.

"What's this?" she asked.

"It works as a debit card," Adam explained. "See the strip along the edge?"

"But we don't take credit cards," she huffed. "Cash only." She pointed to a sign taped to the front of the register.

Adam smacked his forehead with his hand. Being poor was full of all sorts of inconveniences.

"I'm so sorry," he said, "for taking so much of your time today, but I would really like to get these things. Can you please keep them in a bag behind the counter for me? I will come tomorrow with cash."

She rolled her eyes and said, "Fine."

She stuffed the things in a bag then thrust them under the counter.

Adam said, "You have been really helpful and really patient and really kind with me today. Thank you for being such a beautiful person."

Adam must have done something right because she softened a bit and even smiled slightly.

"Go on," she said. "It'll be here for you tomorrow."

Adam walked down the street, not really paying attention to his surroundings. He was trying to puzzle out how to get cash off his card when he heard a familiar, grating, high-pitched voice say, "Well, look who the cat dragged in..."

Adam didn't wait. He just ran.

"Hey!" he heard Loud-Talker say behind him, then heavy footsteps in pursuit.

He wasn't carrying anything heavy and his body had grown stronger and faster with the school food. He flew down the sidewalk, hearing the wind whistling past his ears. He couldn't remember ever running this fast and he was pleased to find he was not tiring.

Faintly, he heard Loud-Talker yelling, "You think you're safe in that school, Scholar, but you're not. This is *my* city. You just wait!"

Adam kept running, and eventually the sound of footfalls behind him faded and stopped altogether.

Adam kept to the shadows after that till he found a bus stop. He hid in a doorway till the bus was close and only stepped out to flag it at the last second. Even on the bus, he kept his head down. He couldn't afford to be robbed all the time. He really needed to do something about these gangs.

What is citizenship, exactly?

45
When in Doubt, Ask.

Adam woke the next morning before the sun rose, shivering. He opened his eyes and saw white puffs of smoke come out of his mouth with each breath.

Oh crap, he thought.

"It sure would be nice to have a coat!" he yelled up at the ceiling of the tent.

A curious bird chirped a playful song in response.

He sighed. There was nothing for it but to get a move on.

He rolled around under the blankets, trying to loosen up his sore muscles. He carried wood up to Campground-Lady's house. He brushed his teeth and flattened his hair—*tried* to flatten his hair—without success. He gave up and went outside. It was starting to get light and he saw there was frost on the ground. His skin prickled with goosebumps. His short sleeve-shirt was not going to cut it today.

He reached in the tent and pulled out one of the blankets, wrapped it around his upper body, then headed for school.

He hadn't gone three meters before he stopped, turned, and went back to the tent to collect the demon-baby doll.

Blanket and baby in tow, Adam made it to school early.

He found Officer-Red at his post by the detector and waved to him.

"Oh, hi, New-Kid," said the officer as he lounged in an uncomfortable school chair.

"Adam," Adam told him, happy he wasn't alone in the world of name-forgetting.

"What?" asked the officer. "Oh, right! Adam. Sorry. I'm Ben. Or Officer Ben. Or Been-Nice-Knowing-You."

He grinned at his own joke.

Adam shuffled his feet, not quite sure how to respond to lame jokes.

"Nice blanket, by the way. Planning to sleep here?"

Adam blushed and futilely tried to hide the blanket behind his back.

"My winter coat is in storage. This worked in a pinch."

That is at least half-true, Adam told himself, feeling kind of guilty.

In fact, though, the blanket had worked remarkably well. Perhaps he didn't need to buy a winter coat after all.

"Uh huh," Officer Ben said. "Well anyway, what brings you to these lofty halls," he gestured in an arc over his head, "so early in the morning?"

"Well," Adam said, "I need to find out how to get cash out of my Work/Study account."

Officer-Ben scratched his chin theatrically.

Adam continued, "I need to buy some school supplies and one of the stores won't take credit."

"Oh," Officer-Ben exclaimed, suddenly standing from his chair. "Why didn't you say so? Look right over there."

He pointed Adam to a cash machine built in the wall of the school's entrance hall. There was a gold plate next to it. Adam scanned his ID over the plate and the machine activated. It asked him his birthday, street address, and mother's maiden name before having him set a pin code for future use. Adam entered the pin code, '1776' and a screen showed him how much was in each of his accounts. He pulled the $12 out of his debit account—thrilled to see the machine dispensed small bills and charged no fee—and shoved the cash in his pocket for later. He thanked Officer-Ben and headed into the school.

He went to the lockers first. He picked out a school uniform with long pants and long sleeves and also grabbed a workout jacket. Next, he went to the showers and washed his clothes and his blanket, then washed himself. He squeezed as much water as he could out of the blanket and the clothes, then toweled off and put on the uniform. He hung his wet laundry in a locker and took the damp blanket down the hall to the storage room where his janitor cart was housed. He laid the blanket over his cart. He hoped someone would think an overzealous student janitor had chosen to put a dust cover over his cleaning cart.

That done, he headed to the cafeteria to eat before school started.

46
Sometimes the Patient Turtle Wins the Race

First period was PE. Adam thought it might be too cold to go outdoors, but he was proven wrong. Cold temperatures, Coach-Squarepants told the class, make for great running weather. So that is what they did. They ran around the track. Speed of running wasn't stressed, so most people—Adam included—jogged.

However someone flew past Adam in a blur, cut in front, then slowed down hard.

"Ack!" Adam exclaimed as he lunged to the side to avoid colliding with the back of the other runner.

"Oh," Asuna grinned innocently over her shoulder as he regained balance. "I didn't notice you there."

Adam grinned back at her sheepishly.

"Sure you didn't."

She fell in beside him.

"It is your own fault though," she said with mock seriousness. "With your hair falling down in your eyes like that, I'll bet you run into people all the time."

"Heh," Adam made a weak chuckle, "it's funny you mention that. I was thinking about the offer you made the other day to cut my hair. I really would like this mop tamed. Would you cut it for me?"

"Well I think I *have* to," Asuna said, "as a public service to all the women of the world. Otherwise you might run into one of us... even when she's right in front of you."

He rolled his eyes.

"After school come to the Home Economics room on the third floor," she told him. She had her ID out and tossed him a friend invite. Remarkably, her pace didn't slow in the slightest while she concentrated on her ID.

He accepted her invite.

"You should feel lucky," Asuna told him. "I don't friend just anyone."

Adam snorted and said sarcastically, "Right. And I don't like to eat."

She reached over and patted his washboard stomach.

"You'd better not get a belly. You won't be able to keep up with me if you do."

And then she took off.

Curious, Adam sprinted after her. He gave it his all, wondering if he could catch her. For about 200 meters, he gained about three centimeters on her with each stride. But then his aerobic endurance gave out and Asuna pulled away. Asuna continued around the track and came back around, then slowed beside him.

"You'll have to work... much harder than... that... if you think you're going to... catch me," she told him between gasping breaths.

"Or..." Adam replied, breathing only slightly slower than Asuna, "I could just wait for... a day when you forget... your inhaler. Even Achilles had a... heel."

She shot a glare coupled with a half-grin, half-snarl in his direction. Then—while still looking directly in his eyes—took out her inhaler and took two puffs.

47
The Needle that Pricks Forever

Language and Science classes passed without incident. Fourth period was Work/Study in the nurse's office.

A student came in supporting her left wrist with her right hand. She looked pale and her left wrist looked swollen. The girl told Nurse-Boss that she'd slipped on a wet patch of floor and landed on her outstretched hand. Her pain had started immediately.

"First," Nurse Bubbly-Boss explained to Adam as they looked at the girl's arm together, "you have to assess the skin around the fracture. If the skin is intact, it's called a 'closed fracture', but if the skin is broken, then it is called an 'open fracture'. Open fractures get infected, which is bad. And closed fractures don't, which is good."

Adam looked the wrist over without touching it. The skin was intact all the way around.

"Good," Nurse-Bubbly said. "Second, give this young lady some Tylenol and ibuprofen. That's got to hurt."

"Both?"

"For sure," Nurse Bubbly-Boss replied. "Each works in a different way, so taking them together is complementary. Acetaminophen and NSAIDS combined is quite possibly the strongest over-the-counter pain medicine known to man. Also, get her a large glass of water. Look how pale she is."

She had the student lay back on a reclining chair while Adam fetched the items.

Afterward, Nurse Bubbly-Boss had Adam—she still liked to call him Page-Boy—size the girl for a Velcro wrist brace. After they got her in the brace—which was no easy task since even tiny movements of that left arm made the girl cry out—Nurse-Boss taught Adam how to check for nerve and vascular function.

"*Vascular* refers to the blood vessels and blood circulation," Nurse Bubbly-Boss told Adam. "The capillary beds under our nails are small blood vessels that are easy to see and test. If you press on the finger nails, you force the blood out of the capillaries and the nail beds blanch white. See?"

She demonstrated on Adam's nail beds.

"And when you let up, the blood returns and they turn red again. That's called 'capillary refill' or 'cap refill' for short. If the circulatory system is intact and operating properly, the nail beds should return to their normal red color in less than two seconds. Try it."

Adam pressed each of the girl's fingernails and counted the seconds out loud till they turned red again. Each finger took about one second.

"Excellent," Nurse Bubbly-Boss said, clapping her hands together. "Now gently brush the tips of each of her fingers and ask if the sensation she experiences is normal or not."

Adam did as instructed, and the student told him they all felt normal.

"You're doing great, Page-Boy. Now, I will call the doctor at the emergency room and you will tell him everything that you know about our patient. Name, birthday, what happened that caused the injury, her appearance and vital signs, the appearance of the injury, what we did for it, and her nerve and vascular status. Okay?"

Adam was terrified, but Nurse-Boss had him write everything he was going to say down on paper. She added a few pointers to what he'd written, then made the phone call and handed Adam the phone. Adam read his prepared report to the doctor over the phone. The doc praised him for an excellent job and asked that the nurse send the young lady over to the walk-in clinic beside the hospital or to her regular doctor to get an x-ray. She would not have to come to the Emergency Room.

"Nice job!" Nurse-Bubbly beamed. "We've saved the young lady a trip to the ER. That's a big deal. It costs ten times as much to go to the ER as a regular doctor."

"TEN?!" Adam said, wide eyed.

"Not joking," Nurse-Boss told him. "Ten times. Sometimes more. Now I'll call this student's parents and you can tell them the same thing you told the doctor. Also pass along the instructions the doctor gave to you. I'm sure her parents will appreciate the advice."

Adam did as directed. The student's mother came quickly and whisked her daughter away to get x-rays.

Nurse Bubbly-Boss sighed happily as she paid Adam's wage.

"That sure was exciting," she said. "Now spend the rest of the period writing notes on what you learned and saw. No names or identifying info in your notes though. As health professionals, we have to strictly protect the information patients give us. That means you can't talk about this with other students. That will be hard, I know. This was cool and you will want to share it with everyone—plus everyone will want to know. But you can't. And if you do, you're fired. Understand?"

"It's a secret?" Adam asked, feeling somewhat confused. "But half the school must have seen her swollen wrist on the way here. Can't I even tell them she's going to be all right?"

"You can't even tell them that you were the one she saw in this clinic today, or that she came in this clinic at all. The provider-patient relationship is private. Pretend this last half hour of your life never happened except when talking to me or her or that doctor or her mom. I can't stress how important this is. Do you understand?"

Adam didn't understand but he nodded.

"To the world, she was not here. I did not see her. I know nothing about her or how she was treated," he said almost robotically.

Nurse Bubbly-Boss stared in his eyes for a few seconds, then sighed.

"We get to see and do some of the coolest things on the planet, Adam. But we can only talk about the things we see and do with the people directly involved in the care of each patient. It's like the prick of a needle that you must get used to because—as long as you work in healthcare—you can never remove it."

48
Citizenship for Idiots

Adam's next class was Economics. He loved economics but he was still riding on a high of adrenaline from treating the broken wrist. He couldn't talk about it with anyone though, which sucked. It was like the information had a life of its own and wanted out—especially when he heard people in the halls talking about what they'd seen or heard about the accident. Their information was incomplete at best, outright wrong most of the time, and he knew the truth. Trying to hold it all inside—to keep all that excitement and knowledge to himself—felt selfish and unnatural. Still, Nurse-Boss said this was the way healthcare worked. So lots of people, including Nurse Bubbly-Boss, must deal with these feelings all the time. If they could do it, he could do it too.

Adam tried to focus on his immediate surroundings. The desks in his Economics class were rearranged so that some of them made a circle facing outward and the rest were tightly packed inside the circle. Adam picked the one closest to the front-center of the room. When everyone arrived, Mr. G took them through a review.

"What is justice?" he asked and pounded his cane once on the floor.

"Do no harm, remedy harm done," the class responded.

"What virtue is required for prosperity?" he asked and pounded his cane twice on the floor.

"Justice," the class replied.

"What is the Big Problem?" he asked and pointed his cane to a random student.

The random student said, "Um, taxes?"

Mr. Geezer put his face in his hand and shook his head a little. Then his head shot up and he pointed at Adam.

"What's-Your-Face, what is the Big Problem?"

Adam sat up and said, "Scarcity—there is not enough to satisfy everyone's desires all the time."

"Super," Mr. Geezer said. "And what is the Prosperity Problem?"

Adam spoke up without being asked, "Prosperity attracts thieves like blue lights attract mosquitos."

"Ha!" Mr. Geezer cackled. "Not bad. Perhaps you're not an idiot."

Adam wrinkled his nose.

Mr. G then pointed at the previous student who'd spoken about taxes and asked her, "What is the Prosperity Problem?"

This time she said, "Prosperity attracts injustice."

"Close enough," Mr. Geezer wheezed. Then he elaborated, "Scarcity requires rationing. Rationing is the mechanism that decides who gets what. Rationing is *not* optional. We *must* choose a method of rationing. The method we choose can cause people to win or lose—depending on the method chosen and the person of interest. If we insist on justice, then we will only accept 'Win-Win' rationing solutions. When we have lots of 'Win-Win' trades going on, prosperity grows. But prosperity is an irresistible lure for violence.

"Now, class," he continued, "I told you yesterday that it took tens of thousands of years—perhaps even *hundreds* of thousands of years—for humanity to solve the Prosperity Problem. Have you, little geniuses, figured out the solution?"

Adam raised his hand.

"Justice?"

"Yes, yes," Mr. Geezer said testily. "We've established that already. But how do we ensure justice for all? How do we deal with the people who are not willing to enter a common agreement not to harm each other?"

"Citizenship," Adam said with more confidence than he felt.

Mr. Geezer's jaw dropped open. He looked stunned.

"That's right! How did you know that?"

Adam felt embarrassed for Mr. Geezer and said hesitantly, "Mr. G, you told us yesterday in class."

"Oh, I did? Of course I did," Mr. Geezer sputtered.

"Now then, write this down on your paper. Tattoo this on your skin. Burn this on the surface of your heart. Secure it in your brain right next to keeping your heart beating and your lungs breathing. Repeat after me class. Citizenship..."

The class said, "Citizenship..."

"...is a verbal contract..."

"...is a verbal contract..."

"...between two or more people..."

"...between two or more people..."

"...who agree to not harm the other members of the contract..."

"...who agree to not harm the other members of the contract..."

"...AND—and this is the *big* idea—to aid the other members of the contract who are threatened."

"...and to aid the other members of the contract who are threatened," the students concluded.

Mr. G let silence echo around the room for a few seconds. Then he drew a large circle on the board.

"I'm going to tell you a fable," he said, facing the class, "that I adapted from Chapter Three of Adam Smith's—the Father of Economics, not the student—masterwork *An Inquiry into the Nature and Causes of the Wealth of Nations* published in 1776."

He traced an outline of the circumference of student desks in a broad, all-encompassing gesture with his right arm.

"There was once a large island in the sea with many port cities. Traveling by land across the island was slow, thorny, hilly, and very, very dangerous."

He grabbed a small step stool positioned against the wall and used it to step up on top of a student's desk. He then mimicked difficulty walking across students' desktops. Students all around Mr. Geezer held up their hands and shouted alarm and warning until he finally stepped back down safely to the floor.

"Water, on the other hand," he said, mildly winded, "is often flat and relatively easy to traverse. So the people of this island—especially the people living along the shore—got to know each other as they all boated around between towns."

He picked up a large, construction paper cutout of a rowboat off his desk. He walked around outside the circle of desks with the rowboat cutout in his left hand and used his right to shake hands with some of the students at random who were facing outward.

"And each town," he resumed, "had a contract with the other towns that they would not invade or attack each other's boats or steal each other's cargo. Justice was universal, and prosperity followed."

He returned to the chalkboard and drew a big dollar sign inside the circle he'd drawn earlier.

"But there is a dark side to this story. Outsiders saw the wealth of the island nation and grew envious."

He tapped the dollar sign on the board with his cane. Then he pulled a helmet decorated with fake horns coming off the sides from behind his desk.

"Vikings came across the ocean and invaded the towns along the shores—killing, stealing, and burning, then going back to wherever they came from."

He walked over to where Adam was sitting and grabbed his wrist, tugging him out of his seat. He made an exaggerated stabbing motion with his cane, took Adam's plastic bags and baby doll, and told Adam he was now dead and needed to go sit over on the side of the room.

"It was the Prosperity Problem. I.e., universal justice led to prosperity but attracted violence, which then pulled everyone back toward poverty. Normally the people of a nation like this would raise an army to drive off the invaders, but the Vikings were clever. They came only infrequently and at random intervals, and it was impossible to know which town they were going to attack. Not knowing when or where to defend against an attack prevented a standing army from positioning itself effectively."

He pulled out a plastic sword and shield from behind his desk, gave them to a student in the center of the desks, and told the student to defend the island.

"The Vikings would invade, kill, and steal."

Mr. Geezer went over to a random desk on the outer ring wearing his Viking helmet and made a stabbing motion with his cane. He pulled the mock victim out of his chair, took his backpack, and sent him to sit on the side of the room next to Adam.

"Then they would leave before an army ever had time to mobilize."

He directed attention to the student defender wedged in the middle of the circle, unable to get to the invading Mr. G in time.

"For the same reasons, maintaining a navy was an ineffective solution to the Viking problem. So, not only was the standing army or navy expensive, it was also impossible to deploy effectively. So, for perhaps the first time in history, people couldn't use a standing army as their solution to the Prosperity Problem. Without the standing army solution, people on the island had to get creative. Eventually, some genius came up with an alternative. He or she approached their neighbors and said, 'Listen, we've already got an agreement not to hurt each other. But why don't we expand that agreement a bit so that if you get attacked, I will come over and help defend you? And, in return, if I am attacked, you will come over and help defend me. In the worst case scenario, you won't die alone. In the best case scenario, we will outnumber the attackers and drive them away.'

"Enough people found this contract extension agreeable that it took hold in one of the towns. Then, in the way ideas often do, it spread to the other towns. Eventually every coastal town was part of the same agreement. So when the Vikings came again, the first person attacked yelled for help, and the entire island nation rose up against the invaders."

Mr. Geezer had everyone in the circle hold hands. Then he mimed attacking with his Viking helmet but was unable to steal anyone away from the linked circle.

"In retrospect, this idea of common defense was an elegant strategy in that it was both inexpensive and effective—particularly when the time between invasions was long, invasion parties were small, and the location of invasion was unknown. This defensive arrangement relied on overwhelming numbers, not on specialization in the arts of violence. That meant the people of the island nation could continue to specialize in productive occupations rather than committing large numbers of its young men to nonproductive service in an army. Which meant even more prosperity than ever before *and*—ironically—more security than ever before."

He let this conclusion sink in on the students for a minute.

"So," Mr. Geezer said, beaming a smile toward his class, "now that you know that fable, you know citizenship."

He turned to Adam again.

"What's-Your-Face, what is citizenship?"

Adam said tentatively, "An agreement not to hurt each other *and* to defend each other against threats and violence."

Mr. Geezer took off his Viking hat and had the other student sitting against the wall come over and stand in front of him.

Mr. Geezer held up his hand and said, "I solemnly swear to take no action which will cause you harm, to remedy any action I take that accidently causes you harm, and to aid you in any way I can— even at the risk of my own life—if you are ever threatened.

"Now you say the same thing to me."

The student in front of him held up his hand and repeated the words verbatim, though with pauses as he struggled to remember the exact words.

Then Mr. G turned to the class.

"There, you see? He and I are both citizens in a two-person nation."

Mr. G then went over and had another student stand up and repeat the same agreement.

"Now there are *three* citizens in this little nation of ours. And that's how it grows. The nation grows as the agreement spreads."

49
Haircuts in Heaven

Adam entered the Home Economics classroom next period. Little-Fox was standing beside the door holding her computer pad. As Adam walked by she said, "Much better, Adam. Your future children—should you choose to have or adopt them—might have a chance after all."

Adam just looked at her darkly, then remembered he had a question for her.

"Teacher," she looked up from her computer pad, "Asuna—who is also in this class—offered to cut my hair. Are there any clippers and scissors I could borrow?"

Little-Fox took a step forward so she was just in front of him—looking up. This proximity caused Adam to squirm because she was, after all, rather adorable. She didn't seem to notice. She was looking at his mop of hair, which she reached up and fluffed nonchalantly. Adam thought he saw evil glee glimmering in her eyes.

"Oh my, yes," she said. "Adam, I've got an idea. It's not every day I get such an unkempt specimen in my class."

Adam grimaced.

She continued, "If you are willing, I will change the lesson plan today from 'fetus growth and maturation in utero' to 'hygiene and hair maintenance.' Would you be the hair model for the class? I'll let Asuna do the cutting and I'll give instruction over her shoulder."

Adam didn't think Little-Fox would be able to see over Asuna's shoulder, but he kept his mouth shut and agreed.

Con buena hambre, no hay mal pan. Beggars can't be choosers.

That class was the most humiliating and delightful of his life. He spent the next half hour surrounded by 29 females all focused entirely on him. Well, on his hair. But anyway, he was literally the center of attention.

Asuna nervously cut Adam's hair as Miss Erica—standing on top of a small ladder—barked instructions over Asuna's shoulder. Little-Fox was impatient and funny. She gave lots of running commentary on how bad Adam looked, play-by-play. When Asuna's hand shook too much to cut safely, Anger-Management stepped up and did some clipping. But whereas Asuna's cuts were too tentative, Anger-Management's cuts were too aggressive. She even managed to nip Adam's right ear with the scissors, which made him jump and made Little-Fox fall off her ladder laughing. To her credit, she looked to make sure Adam wasn't hurt too badly. Anger-Management was then relieved and several other girls in the class took turns.

Near the end, Lee took a turn. His fingers were longer than the scissors, but he managed them deftly.

"Have you done this before?" Adam whispered.

"Quiet," Lee hissed. "I'm making art here."

Little-Fox didn't have anything bad to say about Lee's work. And, when Patrick declined to touch Adam's hair, Lee did the finishing touches around the ears and neckline.

When it was all done, the strong consensus was overall improvement.

Adam was floating on a happy cloud.

Patrick brought him down.

"Now that his hair looks so much better, is there anything we can do about his face?"

Adam was pleased to note that nearly every girl in the class gave Patrick a dirty look in unison.

Little-Fox projected her voice toward Patrick.

"How about we cut *your* hair tomorrow, pretty boy?"

Patrick turned pale and held up his hands in mock surrender.

"Sorry, sorry. Just kidding. My hair is off-limits. My stylist would never forgive me."

As everyone was walking out of the class, Adam stepped beside Anger-Management and whispered, "You did that on purpose."

She looked away from him in what—on anyone else—would have been a bashful expression. When she turned back, she'd returned to her usual angry scowl and whispered, "Suck it up, Buttercup. I've had worse in every part of my body."

She pointed to the ear closest to him which must have had nine piercings in it.

"You don't see *me* whining, do you?"

Adam huffed. He didn't like getting schooled in masculinity by a girl. He let it drop.

50
Vandalism

Two periods later, Adam walked in the Shop classroom on the second floor. The Shop giant sat at his desk, looking down at his computer pad. He looked up when Adam entered and beamed his perfect smile in Adam's direction.

"Nice hair."

He gave a thumbs-up.

"Big improvement. I hardly recognize you. Glad you made it. I just got an interesting work request from the football coach. He says the public address system isn't working in the observation tower. Asked us to head down there and take a look at it."

Adam nodded.

"Here," Shop-Boss said, then did something on his computer. "I just sent you a link to all the instruction manuals for everything in the school. Also, I am giving you access to the school PA system in case I need you to do some troubleshooting."

"Thanks," Adam said, as he opened the folder Shop-Boss sent him on his ID card.

It was an enormous file that contained lists upon lists of manuals for everything from hair clippers to industrial air-conditioning systems.

"This is pretty cool."

Mr. Keynes looked at him as if he were suddenly talking gibberish. "Uh... Right," he said without any conviction. "Well, instructions are a tool. And like any tool, you never know when they might come in handy."

Adam looked at Mr. Keynes a little disbelievingly, then shrugged. At least the man was consistent.

Shop-Boss swung two empty toolboxes toward Adam. When Adam took control of the toolboxes, their weight was startling. They weren't empty.

"Take these toolboxes with you when you go down to the field," he was told. "Oh, and pull your sleeves up. Girls like to see a muscular arm at work."

He threw a roguish grin in Adam's direction.

Adam glanced at Mr. Keynes' arms, then his own. He had no idea if what Mr. Keynes said was true, but he put the boxes down and pulled up his sleeves as far as they would go... just in case.

Mr. Keynes slung a large tool belt over one shoulder in the fashion of a professional wrestler showing off his championship belt. Then he grabbed a large tool bucket and they headed down to the field together.

In short order, they arrived at the base of a one-story wooden tower adjacent to the football practice field. Adam climbed up first and Shop-Boss tossed the tool boxes up.

Adam frowned, not liking how the tools clanged and rattled when thrown. He set the boxes down carefully.

While he waited for the Shop giant to climb, Adam looked around and noticed a tarp suspended over the top of the tower— probably to keep the rain and sun off. The sides of the tower were open in all directions, giving a nice view.

The Play Yard seemed smaller from this vantage. At the center of the tower's platform was a cabinet with a gold plate affixed to one side. Shop-Boss waved his ID and the cabinet clicked open, revealing two rows of dials and knobs and buttons at the top and shelves containing microphones near the middle. Shelves with coiled wire were close to the bottom. In the very bottom of the cabinet, fixed to the floor, were rows of plugs.

"Okay," said Mr. Keynes, "first we need to figure out how to turn this on."

Shop-Boss stared in the cabinet a few seconds while rubbing his muscular jaw, then started turning knobs, flipping switches, and pushing buttons.

Seeing his cue to get to work, Adam plopped down where he was and looked for the manual to this thing on his ID. He found it under 'Schoolyard—AV equipment—Public Address System'.

He scanned through the manual frantically, hoping the Shop giant wouldn't break anything before Adam figured out what they were doing. Suddenly a loud screech erupted from speakers all over the schoolyard. Shop-Boss said something unfriendly under his breath, then the squealing stopped.

Adam tried to stay focused and kept searching. The diagrams and labels started to give him an idea of the setup. He got up and moved closer to the machine until he was beside the Shop giant, who was shoving his perfect hair backward in a well-groomed—and probably well-practiced—display of frustration.

Adam leaned forward, pointed to one of the buttons in the top right corner, and said, "Power."

"I figured that much out," Mr. Keynes said dryly.

Adam pointed to several dials near the bottom left.

"Volume controls by region."

Then he pointed to several switches.

"Input selection."

"Nice," Shop-Boss said, holding a thumb up and grinning. "That should be enough to get us started. Let's go through each input and each region and record which ones work and which don't."

For the next ten minutes, they systematically tested and catalogued what worked and what didn't in the system. When they were finished, it appeared that all the input routes worked and all but one region of speakers worked. Next they climbed down from the tower and followed the wires to the affected region. They found that some of the cables were cut along the inside of the west fence.

Adam thought the damage looked haphazard and incomplete—the work of someone with a short attention span and no real objective.

Shop-Boss must have been thinking along the same lines because he said, "This looks like a random work of violence. Probably by someone with too much time on their hands and a sharp knife. It's sad, but that's what juveniles do in their free time—destroy."

He put on a pair of safety glasses.

"Men, on the other hand, build."

Mr. Keynes showed Adam how to use wire strippers to remove a bit of wire insulation on both sides of a cut electric cable then splice the naked ends together. Shop-Boss had Adam repeat the same process on several of the damaged wires. When they'd finished repairing all the damaged wires, Adam ran back to the tower and broadcast a test message to the dead region—except it wasn't dead any more. Adam was filled with a robust sense of accomplishment when he heard the sound of his own voice echo back across the yard.

He ran back to the fence where Shop-Boss had him wrap insulation tape around each of the spliced wire connections. Then they wrapped all the repaired wires in a steel protective cover and fixed it in place with adjustable steel loops.

It was a nice patch job, Mr. Keynes told him. Something to be proud of.

With their work done, Adam looked around and noticed some oddities. For one thing, there was more trash in this one area by the fence than he had seen in all the rest of the Play Yard put together. For another, the fence had scuff marks in short vertical slashes. When Adam followed the scuff marks up the wall, he noticed a tiny piece of cloth attached to an irregular part of the fence near the top.

"See that?" Adam pointed up at the cloth scrap.

The Shop giant looked up.

"Yeah. What do you make of it?"

"The color," Adam said. "It's not our school colors. Whoever climbed over was not a student."

Shop-Boss started looking around too.

"Yeah, this place is kind of a mess. It would be unusual for any of our students to vandalize the school like this, given so many of them are involved in keeping it nice."

Adam put the side of his face up against the fence.

"These scuffs are different colors. I'll bet that means more than one person. And they wore different kinds of shoes."

Adam looked up, then jumped as high as he could. He couldn't make the top of the fence. Shop-Boss offered him a hand up, and Adam scrambled to the top, looked over, and saw a sidewalk on the other side running parallel to the fence line. He hung his head over the edge and noticed holes and cracks along some of the boards that made for natural footholds and handholds. It would be easy to scale. He hopped back down next to Shop-Boss.

"There are some worn out spots outside the fence that would make it easy to climb," he told Shop-Boss. "Also, there is a nearby street lamp but it looks like the glass is broken. So they might have come at night. And unless they had amazing air, it would take two people to climb back out once they dropped down on this side."

Mr. Keynes nodded thoughtfully, then looked at his watch.

"That's enough for today. I'll close up the cabinet and turn the system off. Take those toolboxes back up to the shop. I'll let Officer Ben know about our suspicion of a break-in and I'll add a work request for someone to repair the fence on the other side so it is not easy to climb."

Adam turned toward the tower, following instructions. He had an uneasy feeling in his stomach.

51
Plans

Lunch was next.

Sweet!

Adam ran through the lunch line, piling his plate with every food option. He saw Asuna and asked her to come over to his table when she was free.

With food in hand, Adam went straight for Lee's table. He found the tall boy sitting next to Hal, as before. They both looked up as he set the food tray down.

"Listen to this," Adam said, "I found something strange out on the Play Yard."

He then proceeded to tell Lee and Hal about the evidence of outsiders around the west fence. As soon as he'd released every juicy detail he started inhaling his food.

When he looked up to breathe, he saw Lee and Hal looking at him expectantly.

"What?" Adam asked.

"Who do you think it was?" Lee questioned.

"Gang members would be my guess," Adam replied.

"Gang members?" Lee choked out. "Seriously, what do they want *here*?"

Adam shrugged.

"Who knows? Expand their territory? Put some fear in students who previously felt safe?"

"Maybe they have something to trade?" Hal said.

Both Lee and Adam looked at Hal askance.

"You know. You said there was a bunch of trash on the ground. Maybe they were bringing in something to trade with us."

Lee poked at the food on his plate sourly.

"Food with a little less *healthy* in it might find a favorable audience among the students."

"Possibly," Adam said, still thinking. "Or something with a lot less healthy."

He made an OK sign with his fingers and brought it to his mouth, taking an imaginary puff.

"Let's not get too excited," Lee said. "I'll bet they just want an education and they heard this place offered the best in town."

The smile he used to punctuate the end of the joke looked more pained than happy.

All three stared down at their plates, lost in thought. Adam took the moment to wolf down more food.

A chair scraped and Asuna sat down heavily.

Adam looked up surprised. Lee looked up and paled. Hal looked... the same.

"What's your news?" Asuna whispered across the table toward Adam.

He repeated his story about the apparent break-in and vandalism he'd uncovered in the Play Yard.

Now it was Asuna who looked pale.

"Who could it be?" she asked, nervously.

"I think it might be local gangs," Adam said around a mouthful of food.

Asuna went from looking pale to scared.

"I don't like to think of gangs running around chasing the girls here."

She folded her arms in front of her.

Adam felt an urge to hit something all of a sudden. It was a strange sensation he'd never had before. Kind of like the hot rush before a fight, but different—colder and simmering.

He looked over and thought Lee and Hal must be feeling something similar judging by the looks on their faces.

"We hadn't thought of that," Adam said to the other two boys. "They might be here for the girls."

"I wouldn't let that happen," Hal said as his fist came down like a hammer on the table. The plates and forks rattled from the vibrations and a few people at nearby tables looked over. Hal's expression looked about the same as always, but his eyes looked darker and there was a tension in his jaw.

"Same here," Lee said to Asuna. "I'm a pacifist, but I would place myself in front of any gang if it would buy time for a lady to get to safety."

Adam took a deep breath and sighed.

"Perhaps we should come up with a plan."

"A plan for what?" Lee asked.

"For what we will do if the trespassers come back. A plan for how we will deal with them," Adam said gravely.

"When coyotes invade the farm, you shoot them," Hal said stone-faced.

Lee's jaw dropped open. He sputtered, "Don't you think it might be better to talk to them first? See what they're about before opening fire?"

Adam thought about it a moment.

"Either way, information gathering is necessary. The Shop-Boss—sorry, I mean Mr. Keynes—said he was going to start an investigation. I'll keep you all posted on any information he finds. In the meantime," he turned to Asuna, "could you reach out to the other students and see if anyone else has heard anything about it?"

Asuna pursed her lips and nodded.

Lee spoke up, "I'm in the student council. I'll add it to the next meeting agenda."

Adam spoke next.

"Hal, can you inform some of the hall monitors about our concerns? They might want to watch the Play Yard more closely for any potential trouble."

Hal nodded slowly while chewing his toothpick—also slowly.

Adam continued, "And I think I know someone who could do some information gathering if it turns out gang members are the ones involved. I'll float the concept by her next time I see her."

"A spy..." Lee said conspiratorially. "How very *Art of War* of you, Adam."

"Is that a bad thing?" Adam asked.

"How should I know?" Lee said. "I'm a pacifist. But Sun Tzu—the famous Chinese military tactician—would say, 'What enables the wise sovereign and the good general to strike and conquer and achieve things beyond the reach of ordinary men is knowledge.' And, 'It is only the enlightened ruler and the wise general who will use the highest intelligence for the purpose of spying and thereby achieve great results.'"

Asuna gaped at Lee.

"That was impressive."

Lee smiled shyly.

Hal said, "He has his moments."

Lee's smile faltered a little.

Adam said to Lee, "You're such a paradox."

Lee's smile left altogether. He looked confused and said, "What?"

Adam answered, slightly annoyed.

"What kind of pacifist reads books on military tactics?"

Lee just shrugged.

"And how," Adam continued, "does a panic-stricken introvert get the nerve to run for student council?"

"Ah, well, you see," Lee said nonchalantly while scratching the back of his ear, "no one in my class wanted the job. So we all flipped coins and I lost the most."

52
Honesty First. Always.

Adam went to Statistics and Algebra, then to Work/Study with Boss-Clean.

He found his blanket in the same place he'd left it. It was dry now. He pulled it off the cleaning cart, folded it, and stuffed it in one of the many open shelves on the cart. When he stood up and turned around, though, he locked eyes with Boss-Clean.

She was standing at the other end of the room just inside the doorway, watching him. They looked at each other for a second, then she turned and walked out.

The Boss drove them hard that day. There had been a complaint that there was a moldy smell in the shower rooms. So she had all her student assistants put on lab safety goggles and gloves and scrub the cracks of the shower rooms with toothbrushes and bleach water.

When they were finished and were leaving, Adam stopped at his locker and opened it up. His clothes were drying there, as was their ritual. He pulled them out and inspected the locker for mold. Sure enough, he found green stuff growing around the locker corners. He attacked it with bleach water, a rag, and the tooth brush. It took some effort, but he got it all cleaned and hung his clothes back up, being careful not to let them touch the recently bleached areas.

Mold likes moisture, apparently.

He might have to rethink his laundry solution. Perhaps he'd have to use the lake again.

When the bell rang, Adam pushed his cart back to the great storage room and found Boss-Clean waiting there. She inspected everyone's cart before they left. His was the last. When it was just the two of them in the room, she stopped inspecting his cart and turned to look at him.

"You came out of the boys' locker room long after everyone else. What were you doing?"

Adam looked down and shuffled his feet. "I noticed there was mold on the lockers so I wiped down some of them."

The Boss grunted and looked at the wall in the direction of the locker rooms—as if she could see through them.

"It's a real chore to clean that room correctly. You have to empty out the lockers one at a time and wipe them down. Logistically, it is impossible during the school year. We usually have to do it during the summer when most of them are empty."

Then she shook off her reverie and turned back to Adam.

"Was that your blanket draped over your cart today?"

Crap, Adam thought to himself.

He hadn't gotten away with it.

To Boss-Clean he said, "Yes, it was wet, so I laid it here to dry."

"You know there are dryers you can use, don't you?"

Adam looked at her blankly.

"Come this way," she said, leading him through the back of the closet where his cart was stored. The very next room over was a similarly large space filled with washing machines and dryers and dozens of student workers moving between the machines or folding clothes and placing them in tall, multi-tiered shelves on wheels.

"See?" she said, triumphantly.

"Wow!" Adam said impressed. "Can students use these?"

"They sure can," Boss-Clean said. "There is a nominal fee—like 25¢ or something—to use each machine. Some students have access to special accounts so they don't get charged. Like the Team Manager for the football team can charge the football team's expense account when she has their uniforms cleaned. Personal use gets charged to your personal account though."

"Thanks for showing me this," Adam said, excited by the possibilities.

Ms. Singer changed the subject.

"Are you staying around to work after school today?"

"About that..." Adam said. "I noticed there was some vandalism out on the Play Yard near the west fence. I was wondering if you wouldn't mind if I went there and cleaned it up."

Boss-Clean's eyes went wide.

"Vandalism?"

"Yeah, there was trash all around and marks on the fence and some wires were slashed."

"Grab your cart," she said as she turned and headed back through the door. She made a stern face.

"We're going off-roading."

Adam and Boss-Clean stood outside an area strewn with trash on the west end of the Play Yard. The Boss was uncharacteristically silent as she looked over everything.

Adam pointed out the repaired conduit he and Shop-Boss had fixed earlier that day. Then Boss-Clean had him start picking up trash while she wiped the smudges off the fence.

"These will need re-painted," she said to herself as they worked. "The City is starting to infringe on this safe place."

Then she spoke to Adam.

"I'm the head of the Parent-Teacher Association. I'll need to let them know about this. I'll ask them for some funds to repair this area. I think this might scare them though. This school was built in a rough part of the City. Some parents might want to pull their students out if they thought dangerous people could get in any time they wanted. We might have to consider hiring another security guard."

"Is it wise to tell them about this if it might scare them to do something rash?" Adam asked.

Quick as a striking snake, Ms. Singer reached up and grabbed his left ear and hauled his head down so his eyes were level with hers.

"Honesty first, young man. Always. Understand?"

He tried to nod but it made his ear hurt more and he grimaced instead.

"Repeat after me," she said with religious conviction in her voice.

"Honesty..."

"Honesty..."

"First..."

"First..."

"Always."

"Always."

She released him and started walking back up toward the school muttering about boys needing to go to church.

Adam rubbed his ear, collected his tools, and followed.

When he caught up he asked, "Why did you grab my ear?"

Boss-Clean looked at him sideways, grunted, then said, "Honesty is important. I wanted to help you remember that."

"And pulling on my ear will help me remember?" he asked, skeptical and still rubbing his ear as if to scrub the memory away.

"You'll see," she said sagely. "When you're my age and you think about me, this is what you will remember. You probably won't remember my name or anything else I ever taught you. But *this* you will remember."

"Oh," Adam said. "Thanks."

And he meant it.

53
Mugged

Adam pulled the extra money he'd earned that day from the cash machine in the school's entrance hall and hurried to the bus stop. He got off the bus and walked across three streets until he was back at the thrift store. He went in and found the same pleasant, plump sales clerk working. He waved to her and asked if she had a bag behind the counter for him. She looked blank for a moment, then seemed to remember and reached down. She pulled out the bag with his selections from the day before.

"Great!" Adam said. "I'll be right back."

He went around the store and grabbed a pair of jeans he thought would fit. He picked out a large, sturdy—albeit faded—backpack with lots of zippers and pockets.

Very manly, he thought.

He picked up two more thick blankets that didn't smell overly bad. He also grabbed two plastic water bottles and several more socks. All they had were colored socks.

Whatever, I'll wear dark socks.

Adam flicked through the t-shirt rack until he came across one that said 'Toast' over a picture of buttered bread. That made him laugh. He grabbed it. He also picked up the winter hat and mittens he'd put back the previous evening.

As he was about to head to the register again, something caught his eye. He detoured over to a box full of toys. On top of the pile was a perfect replica of the demon-baby doll from school. Suddenly paranoid, he felt around in his plastic bags to make sure his own baby was still in it. It was, but he had an idea. He picked up the fake demon-baby and added it to his purchases.

Adam got the whole load of stuff for $18 in cash. He'd started with $22, so he had $4 left. He figured he could squeak some sort of dinner out of that.

He went outside the store and started stuffing his purchases in his new, manly backpack. He'd just finished and started walking down the street when he heard a familiar voice come out of the alley just to his left.

"Well, look who showed up on my doorstep again."

Adam spooked and started to run but didn't make it two steps before he was tackled from behind by at least two people. He fell hard to the ground and scraped his cheek and his left knee. He lost all his air for a moment. As he tried to catch his breath, Adam felt the backpack being pulled off and he heard Loud-Talker say, "This is for running."

Then punches started raining down on his back and ribs, and his legs were kicked. Hard. After about thirty seconds, Loud-Talker said, "Enough," and the blows stopped.

Hands searched Adam's pockets. His pants were too small, so whoever was searching could only get two fingers in his pockets, but they managed to fish out his $4.

Maldito, Adam thought. There goes dinner.

Adam felt a hand grab his hair and lift his head up so he was looking in the eyes of Loud-Talker who was crouching in front of him. The older boy looked like he was enjoying himself.

"And so the scholar returns to our turf. Welcome back, Scholar. What did you bring us?"

Loud-Talker released Adam's hair and started pulling items out of the backpack one at a time and tossing them on the ground haphazardly. With each item he pulled out, Loud-Talker looked more and more perplexed. Eventually he shoved one of Adam's new coats in front of Adam's face and said, "Did you actually pay money for this?"

"Beggars can't be choosers," Adam said.

"Beggars?!" Loud-Talker exclaimed. "I wouldn't *give* this stuff away to a beggar. Not even for free. Have you no pride, Scholar? Have you no taste?"

Adam was silent.

Loud-Talker started pulling things out faster and tossed them all on the sidewalk. Then he stopped and looked at Adam with a raised eyebrow as he pulled out the demon-baby doll.

"I can explain that," Adam said.

"How much money did he have on him?" Loud-Talker asked.

"$4" said someone Adam couldn't see.

Loud-Talker tossed the baby doll and the backpack to the ground.

"Look," Loud-Talker said, "I can see that you are poor and that you are stupid and have bad taste. But I already told you we have work you could do. You could earn tons more money than this paltry sum."

He waved the $4 in front of Adam's face.

"Why don't you just join us? Then all this unpleasantness could stop and you could get rich. Think about it. Gold. Cars. Women."

He paused for a moment, looking around at Adam's belongings on the sidewalk.

"Respectable clothing. White socks, even. Come on now, why don't you say yes?"

"Because I think you would ask me to sell drugs or steal," Adam said as defiantly as he could with someone's knee pressing in his back and his arm twisted around behind.

Loud-Talker backhanded him in the face. Not hard enough to injure, just insult. Unfortunately it was on the same side Patrick had punched earlier in the week. Pain from his right jaw blotted out his vision momentarily.

"And what's wrong with that?" Loud-Talker asked.

"Drugs hurt people. Stealing hurts people. Hurting people violates the citizenship agreement."

"What the hell are you talking about?" Loud-Talker asked.

"The citizenship agreement. The agreement not to hurt other people and to help people who are threatened. It is the most effective method for securing and maintaining justice ever devised. Justice is the foundation of prosperity. Prosperity is wealth. Violating the citizenship agreement does not lead to wealth. It leads to poverty."

Adam felt a fist curl tightly in his hair again and his neck was wrenched up painfully. Loud-Talker had his face directly in front of Adam's so that Adam could feel hot breath and spittle in the angry words directed at him.

"I don't know what they are teaching you at that school, Scholar, but it doesn't make any sense out here in the real world. We've got more wealth than you can possibly imagine, which spits in the face of that garbage that just came out of your mouth."

Loud-Talker smacked Adam's face hard against the ground. Adam saw stars in his vision for a moment. Then Loud-Talker released his hair and spit on him.

"Let's go boys. This kid is loco."

Adam walked home that night in the dark. His new walking shoes were a little loose and he felt a blister forming. The bruises on his legs ached with each step. The bruises on his back, not so much. Taking a deep breath hurt though. He hoped he hadn't broken a rib. He had his backpack loaded up. His demon-baby doll was strapped to the side where he could reach it. It was bitter cold again, but the coats he'd just purchased—when layered—were working even better than he'd hoped. As he walked and grew warmer, he'd strip one off, which released more heat. Thus, he kept comfortable and avoided sweating. His belly ached from hunger. His face throbbed.

His newly purchased imposter demon-baby doll was strapped to the back of the pack, facing behind. Adam felt this new mascot reflected his mood nicely. She was cute and small. And innocent and terrible.

His feet hurt, his legs hurt, his back hurt, his pride hurt. But, in spite of everything, he felt optimistic. He'd retained all of his purchases. He would only miss one meal from the money he'd lost. The bruises would heal. He could still walk. He reached behind and rubbed the foot of his new mascot. Perhaps she was lucky.

54
Hope is What's Left

Adam woke the following morning... then wished he hadn't. He hurt everywhere. Trying to move even a few centimeters caused his muscles to seize up and his mind to flood with agony. He considered just lying there in bed all day, then remembered that he was hungry. He groaned in frustration, then rolled back and forth under his blankets trying to get some heat going. It took longer than usual. Eventually he sat up and put on his new clothes. He put on several pairs of socks to fill out his new hiking shoes. The 'Toast' on his new shirt looked good. When his stomach growled, he briefly imagined eating his shirt.

It was still dark outside. The normally effortless task of hauling wood up to the house took ages. His back hated him for even trying. It probably would have unfriended him if it could. He brushed his teeth and filled his new water bottles with water from the sink in the Campground-Lady's mud room. He packed his backpack with school stuff, two of his blankets, the demon-baby, and his mascot. He found a quarter on the floor of his tent.

Bonita!

He walked—slowly—to the local diner in Cow-town. His legs were doing some funny things, so he kept his gait wide. In the diner he ordered water and did his homework. The waitress looked confused and annoyed when he didn't order anything else, but he left her his quarter. As he walked to school he began to warm up, which made the pain everywhere lessen. The real demon-baby doll cried twice on the trip and required feeding and burping. The blister on his foot from yesterday hurt a little but didn't get worse thanks to the extra socks cutting down on the slippage inside his shoe.

Eventually he made it to the edge of the City and took the bus downtown. He walked—hobbled, really—to school and went straight to the locker room. He showered in two minutes. He nearly passed out from the impact of the sprayers on his back. Then he changed to the long-sleeve, long-pants version of the school uniform and took his street clothes and blankets to the laundry room Boss-Clean had showed him yesterday.

Adam looked around the room and found a large bucket full of laundry soap.

Jackpot!

He'd forgotten to buy laundry soap. He threw his laundry in a big washing machine and scanned his ID card. He was happy to see it pulled from his voucher account—which had money left—rather than his private account—which didn't. He hoped he'd have enough to eat and do laundry for the rest of the semester.

Then he remembered something his dad used to say about hoping.

Hope is what's left when you stop working.

His chest ached for a moment and he felt a lump in his throat.

"Don't be lazy," Adam said out loud. "Think."

Some of the students doing laundry nearby looked at him funny.

Adam grabbed his ID and pulled up the calculator.

Semester length was approximately 105 days. He was paying, on average, $12 per day for food. So he needed about $1260 for food over 105 days.

No. Wait. He still had to eat on days when school was out.

So 365/2 = 183 days of eating per semester. 183 days of eating x $12 per day = $2196 for food for half the year. Tuition and fees for all his classes so far totaled $1085.

Laundry averaged 50¢ per day. 50¢ x 105 = $52.50.

School uniforms made his clothing costs negligible.

So his total expenses for his first semester was going to be about $1085 + $2196 + $52.50 = $3333.50.

His voucher was worth $3500. $3500 - $3333.50 = $166.50. That's approximately how much he would have left on his voucher going into the next freshman semester.

Assuming he would need new shoes by then and there might be slightly higher tuition costs, second semester costs would probably cost around $3500. $3500 - $166.50 = $3333.50, which was approximately how much money he needed to earn over the next year to stay fed, clothed, and in school the second semester.

If he worked six days a week, that was… 6 days x 52 weeks = 312 days worked in a year. If he divided the amount he needed to earn—$3333.50—by the number of days he had to work—312—then he needed to earn $3333.50/312 days.

$10.69 per day.

He laid his head on top of the washing machine and sighed.

He was currently earning about $6 per day from his three Work/Study periods. If he worked another 90 minutes after school at the same $4/hour rate, he would earn $12 per day. More than enough to stay fed, clothed, and in school. He'd even have a little left over to save against catastrophe or a growth spurt. Or even a date.

His cheeks flushed at the idea.

He knew he had money stashed behind masonry all over the City but refused to consider touching any of it. If he ever got injured and couldn't work, he'd need that money to eat. It was his hedge against death.

The morning bell rang. Adam—slowly—put on his backpack then headed to first PE class.

55
Dodgeball—Of Course

Naturally, the game that day in first PE was dodgeball. Adam planned to use his hands to defend his battered body and get himself out as soon as possible. The sideline was the only safe place for him today.

Asuna had different ideas. She seemed to catch on to what he was doing and it made her mad. At least, he assumed it did. She put her hair up in a ponytail and put on her game face. Adam hoped he didn't look scared. For the rest of the time, she made it her mission to get past his defenses and whack him on the body. He tried not to pass out or look too terribly wimpy when she got him square on the back. Unfortunately it was hard to look tough on his knees.

When had he fallen to his knees?

Asuna was beside him in a second. She said softly so no one but Adam could hear, "Did I hit you that hard?"

"Not your fault," he gasped out around clenched teeth. "I have some..."

He was about to tell her a lie when Boss-Clean's lesson the previous day echoed through his thoughts and tugged at his ear.

Honesty first. Always.

Not a bad policy with your friends, he admitted to himself.

"I have a bruised back that you managed to hit just right."

"Let me see," she said as she tugged up the back of his shirt.

"NO!" he said louder than he'd intended, grabbing the bottom of his shirt.

Too late.

He heard her gasp behind him.

"Adam," she sounded shaken. "What happened to you?"

He got to his feet clumsily and started walking toward the out-of-play box. He waved the teacher away. Coach-Squarepants had been walking over to investigate why Asuna had stopped playing.

"I'll tell you later," he said to Asuna over his shoulder.

Unless I can figure out a way not to.

56
Words, Actions, Meaning… Poetry

As soon as first PE was over, Asuna attached herself to Adam's side and walked with him to the lockers. He hadn't put up enough effort to sweat, so he skipped the shower and just changed his uniform. The used outfit went in the dirty laundry cart.

He tried to get out of the locker room before Asuna could get ready, but Baby-Demon-Doll decided it needed a diaper change just then.

Asuna was waiting for him when he exited the locker room. She still looked concerned and anxious.

"What happened to you?" she asked as she fell in beside him.

He was walking slowly, but she matched his pace without complaint.

"I got mugged last night," he told her honestly.

"What?!" she said, shocked. She touched his arm out of apparent sympathy. He tried not to flinch but couldn't stop the reflex. She'd found another bruised area.

Asuna pulled away quickly, whispering an apology.

Adam's arm felt tingly and warm where she had touched. It started to cool immediately when she pulled away.

He sighed regretfully.

"I was shopping last night and got ambushed by a bunch of the Street-Angel gang. They took my money and gave me a few… souvenirs."

Asuna made a cute little whimper sound. He tried to look over at her but it hurt, so he just kept walking.

"I'm so sorry," she said. She grabbed his shirt sleeve and pulled him to a stop.

Now he did turn to look at her. She had big fat tears beading up in her eyes.

"Why…?" he asked, confused. He felt his own eyes watering up.

"I nailed you in dodgeball… in the body… more than once."

He laughed—a deep laugh from his belly.

"That's how the game works! And besides, you didn't know."

He started walking again.

She didn't let go of his sleeve and walked beside him.

He was glad for her company.

Adam saw Lee's eyebrows go up as he entered Language class next to Asuna. Apparently they caught Saint-Anne's attention as well. She followed their progress across the room in her peripheral vision as she verified attendance on a computer pad.

Miss Anne was wearing ragged, faded clothes with rips and tears visible in every piece. There was black discoloration under her fingernails. Her hair was a rat's nest of tangles and curls. Her cheeks were smeared with dirt and grime. She had on cloth boots with holes through which yellowed socks were visible. She looked disheveled. She looked pitiful.

Asuna only released Adam's sleeve when he'd gotten to his seat. She reluctantly went to her own seat. Adam shifted in the chair futilely. Comfort was beyond reach.

Miss Anne stood to address the class once Adam and Asuna were situated.

"Poetry," Miss Anne said in a hoarse, breathy voice, "can add power to ideas."

She shuffled a meter across the front of the room toward her desk. Her walk looked uncomfortable, like her joints needed greased. She stumbled a few times before she set down her computer pad and picked up a bottle half full of brown liquid off her desk. She tipped back her head and the bottle and drank deeply. After drinking, she wiped her mouth on her coat sleeve and replaced the bottle on the edge of the desk. She used her right hand to pull back her left sleeve to her elbow. She fished a plastic syringe out of her right pocket and laid it against her exposed forearm.

Adam noted the syringe lacked a needle and was empty besides, but Miss Anne fluttered her eyelids and rolled her eyes back anyway. After a few seconds of standing motionless, she reached in another coat pocket and pulled out a sealed bag of small pills. She emptied half of the bag in her palm and downed all the pills at the same time. She chased the pills with another swallow of the brown liquid. She placed the bottle again on the edge of the desk. Finally, she removed a plastic pipe from a pocket. It looked like a toy. She put it to her lips and brought the flame of a real lighter close to the bowl of the pipe. She puffed her lips and a plume of vapor erupted around her head. The room suddenly smelled of incense.

She wobbled in place while speaking.

"In 1895," Miss Anne slurred, "Mary Lathrap wrote a poem titled 'Judge Softly'. I would like to recite some of it for you now. See if you feel the power in the words and the poem."

She slumped to the side, leaning heavily against her desk. She grabbed the bottle, which unbalanced her further, and she slid down the side of the desk. She ended, a crumpled heap on the floor. She looked like a pile of discarded trash on the ground, barely recognizable as a person. From that position she spoke.

"'Pray, don't find fault with the man that limps
Or stumbles along the road.
Unless you have worn the moccasins he wears,
Or stumbled beneath the same load.'

Saint-Anne lifted herself on one elbow. She placed the brown bottle on the floor in front of her. Her voice became less slurred.

"'There may be tears in his soles that hurt
Though hidden away from view.
The burden he bears placed on your back
May cause you to stumble and fall, too.'

She sat up and placed the plastic bag on the floor in line with the bottle.

"'Don't sneer at the man who is down today
Unless you have felt the same blow
That caused his fall or felt the shame
That only the fallen know.'

She placed the plastic syringe third-in-line with the other contraband on the ground, then rose to her knees. Her words were no longer slurred but her voice remained hoarse and breathy.

"'For you know if the tempter's voice
Should whisper as soft to you
As it did to him when he went astray,
It might cause you to falter, too.'

She stood and dropped the toy pipe on the floor in front of her. Her voice carried, strong and clear.

"'Just walk a mile in his moccasins
Before you abuse, criticize, and accuse.
If just for one hour, you could find a way
To see through his eyes, instead of your own muse.

Brother, there but for the grace of God go you and I.
Just for a moment, slip into his mind and traditions
And see the world through his spirit and eyes
Before you cast a stone or falsely judge his conditions.

Take the time to walk a mile in his moccasins.'"

Miss Anne took another step and, as before, stumbled. Then she regained her balance and bowed slightly to her audience.
The class, almost as one, cheered and clapped boisterously. Even Lee, who was normally so reserved, gave her a standing ovation.
Saint-Anne, grinning through her eyes, thanked the class.

"Just so you know," Miss Anne explained when the clapping ended, "I spoke with my physician while preparing this dramatic presentation. She assures me that, had I actually taken real drugs in the way I modeled for this poem, I would have almost certainly stopped breathing and died right in front of you."

The room was deathly silent as she picked up the drug paraphernalia and dropped it in her desk drawer.

"How could you do that?!" Asuna said, shattering the silence.

Asuna stood up and pressed her hands on her desktop. Her face was red. Her veins stood prominent on her neck.

Miss Anne stiffened before directing her answer cautiously to the entire class.

"Good poetry can affect people strongly."

"How could you model drug use?" Asuna pressed, her voice raised. "Don't you know what that does to people?"

"Each of you," Miss Anne said—again to the class, "will have to make decisions about drug use in your lifetimes. Many of you already have. Drugs are everywhere. And, like all decisions, you will each have to consider the up sides and the down sides of any proposed actions. The benefits of drugs may include euphoria and forgetting. The costs include death and, worse, addiction. Addiction is slavery to craving. This poem was not recommending listeners make the same choices that obviously injure others. Furthermore, it was not recommending or requiring drug use before condemning drugs and drug use in others. Instead, I believe, it recommends humility toward others who have made poor decisions or suffered bad luck."

"Humility?" Asuna repeated, sounding dismayed.

"Humility," Saint-Anne confirmed. "When considering others, keep in mind that, under different circumstances, you could have suffered the same fate or made the same bad choices as the persons you condemn. That is framing a decision through a lens of humility."

Asuna frowned. Emotions warred on her face and across her features for several seconds before her lips calmed to a straight line. She nodded once and sat down again.

Miss Anne returned to the center of the room, clapped her hands together, grinned softly, and started teaching about poetry.

Adam—admittedly more curious about poetry than he'd ever been in his life—could not concentrate on the lesson.

Why, he wondered, does Asuna have such strong feelings about the dangers of drug use? And how would humility influence my own decisions about Loud-Talker and his gang?

By the poet's reasoning, Adam didn't know enough about the Street-Angels to condemn them outright. He'd never lived as they did. He did not live where they lived. He'd never weathered their trials. But he'd been hurt and robbed. Justice had been violated. And justice required remedy.

Can justice be satisfied without my judging?

Could he actively and aggressively—even violently—respond to the Street-Angels' actions without automatically condemning them?

He sighed.

I hurt right now. Of that I'm certain. Isn't that enough? Why would I need to know more?

When he was able to pull his mind back to the classroom, Saint-Anne was teaching about similes and metaphors. She politely overlooked his distraction, if she had even noticed at all.

Something told him she had.

Asuna walked with Adam to his next class, Biology. She stopped at the door as he was walking through. Something about her body language made him look over his shoulder. She was staring at something in the room, chewing on her bottom lip. Then he saw her game face slide over her features, and in two twists of her wrists, her hair was up in a ponytail. He felt the breeze of her passage as she walked past him. He was too uncomfortable to keep up with her, so he made his way to his seat alone, stepping around one of several buckets along the way placed strategically to catch water dripping through discolored ceiling tiles. He plopped his new book bag down next to a desk and sat down gingerly.

He shifted around trying vainly to find a comfortable position. Then the demon-baby started making crying noises from his backpack. He groaned inwardly. It was only an arm's length away, but tending to it was going to hurt a lot—which he supposed was the point of the little thing. He started to shift his weight on to his less-painful butt cheek when he suddenly felt a presence in the space beside him. He smelled spearmint.

Adam stopped shifting and tried to look to his left without actually moving much. Then he heard Ribbon's voice pitched low and close to his left side.

"Don't move," she said quietly. "I'll help."

He heard her messing with the straps that held the demon-doll to the side of his backpack.

After a few seconds, the cries stopped. Then another presence entered his personal space on the right side. He looked up and noticed Asuna. She leaned in close and whispered in his ear. She smelled like frutillas.

"I told Amy what happened to you. I hope you don't mind. I can't stay with you as this isn't my class. So I asked Amy to look after you."

Adam whispered back, "I didn't realize you knew Amy. I should have figured. You're friends with everyone."

"More like long-time rivals," Asuna whispered with a little steel in her voice. "But she's the most capable person I know in this class. I trust her. She'll take good care of you."

With that, she reached forward and squeezed Adam's right arm. He tried not to, but flinched reflexively from the pain. Her squeeze froze and she quickly let up.

"Sorry," she whispered, then turned and fled the classroom.

Adam stared after her momentarily, then turned his attention to his left.

Ribbons was close, holding out a pencil and paper she'd fished from his backpack. He took them gratefully.

"I'll be here if you need anything. Just look me in the eyes and I'll rush up here," Amy said to him quietly.

"I'll be fine," Adam lied. "I don't need any help."

"Is that so?" she asked in a remarkably friendly tone.

Just then he felt her arm across his shoulders. He looked at her a little confused. She was smiling stupidly next to him as if he'd just told a really good joke. Then he felt her pat his right upper back a couple of times—like one football player might do for another who had just scored a field goal. Agony shot through his back. His breath caught. He broke out in a sweat and just barely kept in a moan. To the class it must have looked like she was being chummy.

"Don't do anything manly and stupid," she said to him like a ventriloquist. Then she turned her head so her mouth was close to his ear and whispered, "I've committed to—of all people—Asuna to help you. Don't disrespect me by rejecting my offer."

He stiffened briefly, then sighed and relaxed. He nodded once. Her arm left him and he caught the flash of ribbons as she turned and glided back to her seat. The place where her arm had rested felt hotter than the rest of his body, but it quickly cooled, eventually feeling colder than the rest.

The class went smoothly, all things considered. The teacher, who everyone just called "Coach" was the same Coach-Squarepants as his first-period PE teacher. She had not bothered to change out of her flannel warm-up outfit and matching jacket. She still had her whistle around her neck. Adam wondered if she ever took it off. She looked, for all the world, like a small football linebacker—or perhaps a typical rugby player.

Today he could see grey streaks in her thick, curly black hair as she bent over a microscope, examining a leaf. The view she was seeing in the microscope was projected up on a screen at the front of the room. She pointed out different aspects of the cell structure she had gone over at the beginning of class with a laser pointer on the screen.

Adam thought it was kind of cool to see things moving around— alive—on the screen. It was so much more... dynamic than the still diagrams in the science book he had displayed on his ID card.

Water dripped rhythmically in buckets, making a kind of natural music in the background.

At the end of class, Amy was at his side again, picking up his backpack and helping him climb in to it. She was a little rough with him, probably to gloss over how much she was really doing for him. Hal must not have been fooled by their show. He came over and walked beside Adam as he slowly made his way toward the door. Everyone else had already gone, including the teacher, so that only Hal, Amy, and Adam remained.

"You don't look so good," Hal said to no one in particular while staring fixedly ahead.

Adam grimaced. He shouldn't have come to school today. He should have stayed home and gotten over the worst of it. There was no way he could hide it or cover it up.

"I got beat up a little last night."

Hal nodded easily as if he'd just been told it rained the previous evening. "Anything to do with that little matter by the fence we spoke of yesterday?"

"I don't think so," Adam said. "I was out in the City last night in the evening and wasn't watching my surroundings adequately. It might be the same group of people. I just can't be sure yet."

Without asking where he was going, both Hal and Amy followed him down to his next period in the nurse's office.

Hal's eyebrows rose in a question as he saw where they were heading.

"That bad, huh?"

Adam chuckled dryly, "No... Well, yes... But this is my Work/Study period under Nurse Kacey."

"Ah," Hal said. "Well, let's get you out of this backpack before you go in there. It'll require some explanations if the nurse sees you need two people helping you with something that is normally effortless."

"That's the most words I've ever heard from you at one time," Adam said as he slipped his arms free of the backpack straps.

"Same here," Amy said, off to his other side. "You should do that more often. You're... smart-sounding."

A hint of a smile appeared on Hal's face. Well, more like a turning up of one corner of his mouth, but on Hal it looked like an emotional outburst.

"It's just that words need actions to give them meaning. In this place—school, I mean—actions are prohibited. Which makes words meaningless."

Adam chuckled.

Hal raised an eyebrow.

"'Obras son amores y no buenas razones.'"

Hal raised both eyebrows.

"It translates," Adam explained, "'Works are loves and not good reasons.' But it's used like, 'Actions speak louder than words,' or, 'An action is worth more than a thousand words.' I always thought the translation was funny," Adam said quietly.

He looked to the side, suddenly embarrassed for some reason.

Amy snorted a laugh, then covered her mouth and nose. Her eyes looked merry.

Hal looked amused too as he handed the backpack to Adam.

"I'll be here at the end of the period," Amy said in a brook-no-argument tone. "Wait for me."

She shot him a friend request from her ID card, and both she and Hal headed back down the hall.

57
Healing Patterns

Nurse Bubbly-Boss clapped her hands together when Adam entered her domain.

"Page-Boy, great to see you! How are you?"

Adam put his book bag down.

"Good," he said, "but I'm terribly sore. I added a grueling new exercise to my workout routine and I can barely move today."

"Oh no!" she said. She came over to look him up and down.

"And did your grueling new workout cause this abrasion on your face as well?" she asked innocently.

"Yes," Adam said, turning the injured side of his face away.

She grinned, squinted her eyes, and clapped her hands together.

"Well, I've just the thing for that then."

She padded over to her medicine cabinet and took out some ibuprofen and Tylenol.

"Do you have any allergies to medications?"

"No."

"Have you taken any medications today?"

"No."

"Okay then," Nurse-Bubbly said cheerfully. She handed him two pills and a small glass of water, then said in a loud, theatrical stage voice, "Heal thyself, physician!"

Then she giggled.

Adam couldn't help it—he grinned as he choked down the pills.

"Good boy," she cooed. "Take these..." she handed him a small plastic bag with two pills, "in six hours. The Tylenol and the ibuprofen are both relatively safe, inexpensive, moderately effective pain medicines. But they work in very different ways, so they complement each other nicely when taken together."

Adam might have imagined it, but he was already feeling better.

"Thanks a lot," he told her.

"Now then, let's get to work," Nurse Kacey said as she bustled toward the little waiting room.

That day there were a lot of kids with fevers, body aches, runny noses, coughs, ear discomfort, and sore throats. Nurse-Boss had him give out Tylenol or ibuprofen to each of the kids if they didn't have any allergies to the medicine and hadn't had any of that same kind of medicine within the last four hours. As they worked, she explained viruses to him.

"The common thread between all the symptoms these kids are experiencing is mucus," Nurse-Boss told him.

Adam fought down a chuckle.

"I'm serious," Nurse Bubbly-Boss told him as she slapped him on the shoulder playfully.

Adam's breath caught, then he did some quick breaths through his mouth like women do when pushing out a baby.

"Oh, yeah, sorry," Nurse-Boss said, turtling her head and shoulders while looking at him through one open eye.

She cleared her throat.

"Anyway, your middle ears make mucus, your tonsils and adenoids make mucus, your nose, empty spaces throughout your skull," she giggled, "the insides of your eyelids, the lungs, even the stomach and GI tract all make mucus. There are viruses that LOVE cells that make mucus. They infect them and turn them into tiny virus-making factories, which cause all kinds of damage. That damage triggers an immune response in the body which both fights the viruses and tries to heal the damage at the same time. Additionally, the viruses are really contagious, so if they manage to take up residence in one part of the body, they will quickly spread.

"Quiz time," she told Adam. "If you had some virus on your hand and then rubbed your eye, where is the first place you'd be likely to experience symptoms?"

Adam replied, "That same eye."

"Right," she told him. "And since the eye drains to the nose, where is the second place the symptoms might appear?"

"The nose," Adam said.

"Precisely," Nurse-Boss confirmed. "And it keeps spreading until you have symptoms like a sore throat, runny nose, cough, itchy eyes, ear pain, and sometimes GI symptoms—all places that make mucus."

"I see," Adam said, grimacing as he thought about each symptom in turn.

"Superb," she said, then turned to a sick student lying on a couch nearby.

"Cover your mouth, young lady, when you sneeze. Then wash your hands right away. Each time you sneeze, you send out a shotgun blast of tiny mucus droplets, each of which is swimming with armies of tiny, microscopic viruses. It makes you very contagious. Wash your hands right away and put on this little mask."

The girl looked dubiously at the mask.

"It's not for you, darling," Nurse-Bubbly said in her friendly, disarming way. "It's for everyone else in the room. Now be considerate of others and put it on."

Then she turned back to Adam.

"We discussed the immediate pattern of symptoms and how they are related to the mucus-producing epithelium in the body. Now let's discuss the meta-pattern of the illness."

Adam suppressed a smile. He thought—maybe—he understood what she'd just said from context clues... Maybe.

"The first day symptoms start is designated *day zero*," Nurse-Bubbly said in formal speech. "On day zero, people usually feel their timing is a little off, but not much else. Day number one—the second day of illness—they'll often get a sore throat or runny nose. Each day thereafter, they get symptoms in more parts of their body and they get more severe symptoms in the parts of their body already infected. So the illness spreads. Their complaints peak on the third day of the illness, remain peaked for the fourth day, and begin to slightly improve by day number five. From day six on, they just keep getting better and better every day. Symptoms actually linger for a full three weeks with most respiratory viruses, but by the end of two weeks, the symptoms are usually so mild they don't hinder anyone anymore. So I often tell people they will get better in two weeks."

"Okay," Adam said.

He leaned over a piece of paper and drew out a chart with 'Symptoms' on the Y-axis and 'Time' on the X-axis. He labeled the intersection of the Y- and X-axis '0', then made hash marks at equal intervals along the X-axis and labeled them '1', '2', '3'...

"It sounds like the cold pattern you described to me makes a flat-topped pyramid—the symptoms get worse each day till day three."

He drew an uphill-sloped line between zero and three.

"Then symptoms level off for three days."

The line he was drawing turned at day three then ran horizontally for three more days.

"Then symptoms start improving until they are eventually gone."

The line he was graphing bent down at day six and continued with a downhill slope until it eventually intersected with the X-axis again.

"Well met, Adam. You are quick on your feet. Keep this up and I might have to give you a raise. Who knows? You might even have a career in medicine ahead of you," she said and winked.

"I'm not sure I would like that," Adam confided. "I found it really hard yesterday not being able to talk to anyone about the experience we had with the broken arm."

He'd lowered his voice to protect the privacy of the student they were discussing.

Nurse-Bubbly-Boss sighed.

"I know what you mean. I find a lot of medical people only have friends who are also medical people. Probably so they can talk about their experiences without violating confidentiality. It's a hard thing. Please feel free to talk with me, though. About anything, anytime. We are peers now. We have to lean on each other or... or you won't make it."

He looked out the window. Nurse-Bubbly-Boss was unusually quiet.

Then Adam asked, while still looking out the window, "How long do bruises take to heal?"

Adam felt Nurse Kacey's attention on his face.

"About three weeks," she said. "Same with cuts and abrasions. It's kind of interesting that almost any kind of healing in the body takes about the same time frame and most of the time follows that same viral pattern you drew out earlier."

Adam touched his jaw on the right side.

"So this might hurt more each day for three days, then stay the same for three, then get better over another two weeks?"

"Mmm," she said thoughtfully. "Injuries are a little different. There is no replication or spreading period with injuries like there is in viruses. So the ramp up period only takes one day. The leveling off still lasts three, though. By day four, steady improvement begins and continues for about three weeks."

"Thanks," Adam said. "Just out of curiosity, are there any medical problems that take longer than three weeks?"

Nurse-Boss didn't say anything for a few seconds, then answered, "Bones..." followed shortly after by, "...grief," in an uncharacteristically sober tone.

Adam looked at her in his peripheral vision and found she was looking out the window too. Her hand was resting over the center of her chest.

"Grief takes at least a year."

"Yeah," Adam said, remembering a dark, stormy night in the ocean. "That sounds about right."

58
Acknowledging Friendship

Ribbons and Asuna were both waiting for Adam when he emerged from the nurse's station at the end of the period. There was a palpable tension between the girls.

He smiled at them and said, "Thanks for coming."

Both girls fell in step beside him.

"You're looking better," Asuna commented.

"And moving faster," Amy added.

"Nurse Kacey gave me two over-the-counter pain medicines that are helping a lot. Apparently the trick is to take them together for really bad discomfort. She even gave me a few pills to take later when these wear off. I think I should be able to make it through the day now."

"Good," Asuna said sounding relieved. "Amy and I were discussing forcing you to go home. You were looking really rough."

"I was thinking that too," Adam admitted, "but Nurse Kacey told me it takes several days before I'll begin to feel better. I can't miss that much school."

And he also knew he couldn't afford to miss that much work.

After a few more steps, Adam stopped abruptly. Both girls took another step on each side of him before stopping and turning to look back.

"Listen," he said very seriously, "I don't know what I have done to earn your friendship but I really treasure it. I hope someday I can show you such kindness."

He gave a little bow with his head and shoulders in their direction.

"I told you I'd pay you back some day for your honesty," Asuna said. She smiled warmly. "Maybe this will make us even."

"And *I* am in your debt for my actions that led to your injury at the hands of Patrick in the Play Yard," Amy said. "This is the least I can do."

Adam nearly melted on the inside from happiness. He was connected to these amazing girls through a circle of reciprocal kindness. He felt fortunate, lucky, and extremely grateful. He resumed walking and wondered—for the first time—if this is what love felt like.

59
The Disappearing Crime Illusion.

The girls left him at his next class, Economics, and walked away talking to each other—heads close together. Adam eased himself down in his usual spot and waited for Mr. Geezer to start the class.

The professor began—as now seemed his daily pattern—with review.

Justice was, 'Do no harm, remedy harm done.'

Prosperity was 'the plant that grew from the pot of justice'.

The Big-Problem was 'scarcity'.

The Prosperity-Problem was, 'Wealth attracts woe."

The Big-Idea was 'citizenship'.

Citizenship was 'the agreement between strangers to respect justice and aid each other when threatened'.

After the review, Mr. Geezer rasped out, "Today, my underdeveloped adults, I will solve for you the second great mystery of human civilization."

He paused for dramatic effect.

"What is government?"

Adam thought he could hear crickets chirping outside.

"Can any of you brilliant, healthy, gifted, highly-educated young people tell me what the government is?"

Adam sensed a trap. Apparently everyone else did too because no one was speaking.

Adam huffed air toward the bangs he no longer had, then said, "The police."

"And?" prompted Mr. Geezer while making a 'come-on' motion with both his hands.

"And the army," Adam said.

"And the judiciary," another student added from the back.

"And the legislature," said a girl on Adam's left.

"And?" Mr. Geezer prompted again.

"And health insurance," said a random student off to the right.

"And retirement insurance," said yet another random student.

"And tax collectors," Adam threw in.

"And they issue driver's licenses."

"And they say what drugs are okay to use."

"And they coordinate disaster relief."

"And they maintain bridges."

"And they build roads."

"And they run schools."

"ENOUGH!" Mr. Geezer said loudly and banged his cane on the floor.

He sounded angry and was breathing fast.

After a moment, his breathing slowed and he said in a pleasant voice that sounded forced, "Enough. You are doing a wonderful job, wise children. But if I let you continue, you could keep listing occupations that the government has chosen to meddle in till the end of the period. BUT—and this is important—just because the government does a thing does not mean that thing *is* government."

The class mulled over that one like a moldy dog bone.

"I know that sounds contradictory. How best to explain...?" he asked before answering his own question.

"How about a fable?"

Mr. Geezer cleared his throat, struck a Shakespearean pose, and said:

"Once upon a time, before the citizenship agreement—let's call it the Dark Ages—free men assembled an army to protect themselves from foreign invasion and domestic bandits and the like. The army pushed back invaders and put down bandits. The land was at peace, and prosperity began to sprout. Some soldiers went back to their previous professions, but others chose to remain in the army and prepare for the day when another invasion might come.

"But after many days of preparing for a foe that never came, the army grew restless and bored. It began to look for something else to do. But these soldiers had no skills besides violence. What were they to do without an enemy? The answer—apparently—came down from heaven to the army.

"They were divinely inspired to help everyone else in the nation do their jobs. And who could complain if the army exceeded its initial mandate? The army had swords and clubs and axes and shields and experience in combat. What skills could be better suited for making millions of highly varied and nuanced business decisions on a daily basis? So the army told everyone what to do and no one disagreed. Well, *some* disagreed, but they were thrown in jail, or else tortured, or murdered. Might makes right.

"The army was mighty so, by definition, the army was right. Since it was right, the army was boss. It told people what to do and they did it. But 'telling people what to do' was so different from 'defending against invasion' that a thoughtful person bestowed a new name on this new army—government.

"I'd like to break from the fable for a moment," Mr. Geezer told the class, "to point out that 'telling people what to do' is a description of rationing. If you will recall, rationing is any method that determines who gets what. 'Telling people what to do' is one way to determine who gets what. But I digress. Let us return to our tale:

"Trouble began to brew when the people under the control of the government started to realize that whatever divinity had given the army its mandate to rule had neglected to give it the knowledge and wisdom required to make everyone's decisions *well*. People began to notice that the things they were told to do were often less productive—or even counterproductive—compared to what they were capable of producing when deciding for themselves. The whole nation suffered—relatively speaking—because the people making the decisions were not the people with the best available information for making those decisions.

"Inevitably, the government made the predictable error of punishing people for their lack of productivity, which created a no-win scenario for the populace. They were punished if they did not follow the government's instructions and also punished when they *did* follow its instructions. Whenever a system devolves to 'damned if you do and damned if you don't', then people start looking for change. Enter the citizenship agreement.

"Just one more quick interruption," Mr. Geezer said. "Remember that the citizenship agreement is a combined rationing and security solution. If you have been paying attention, the government-army combination is also a rationing-plus-security solution. They are competitors—so to speak. But anyway, back to the story:

"The people—coordinated through the citizenship agreement—rebelled against all harm, especially the harm inflicted by their government. They defended each other from both well-meaning and ill-meaning people and, at great expense, repealed and replaced the rationing methods of the government.

"Make no mistake," Mr. Geezer said, leaving his Shakespearean pose yet again, "might still made right, but the mightiest force at that time—the unified populace—insisted that justice limit rationing decisions. The government—in general—could not meet such a high hurdle, so it was reduced in size and scope and power to a servant. A servant of the citizens. A servant of the citizenship agreement. A servant of justice."

Adam blurted out, "But, Professor, we already established that our present government is expansive and heavily-involved in nearly every trade and specialization. That doesn't sound like a government restrained and limited by anything. Present reality does not fit your story at all."

"I'm not done!" Mr. Geezer shouted him down, though the twinkle in his eyes and the grin on his face took the sting out of his words.

"You're messing up my story, nitwit."

Adam shrunk back in his seat.

Mr. Geezer resumed his pose and started again.

"The men of the government, like all people, gloried in the prosperity brought about through the citizenship agreement. At the same time, though, they chafed at its restrictions. They just *knew* they could do more good if only they were free from the uncompromising restrictions of citizenship. And then a clever plan emerged: keep the citizenship agreement and—ideally—its prosperity. But change the terms.

"The government's attack was through universal public education. The government persuaded the population to let it run the schools. Shortly after taking over the school system, the citizenship agreement was taught differently. No longer was citizenship a contract voluntarily entered into by consenting adults—it was a right bestowed by the government on any child born within the defendable boundaries of the country. And the obligations of citizenship changed too. Forget protecting each other against violence! Now citizens' only responsibilities were obedience to the law—and the lawmakers—and dutifully paying taxes. Protecting citizens was the sole prerogative of the government. Anyone else was a vigilante, a criminal, or a terrorist. Thus, in a single generation, the virtue of justice was supplanted by the virtue of *obedience*. And, seemingly overnight, the government ascended—once again—from servant to master."

"I don't buy it," said a skeptical boy from the back of the classroom.

"GOOD," Mr. Geezer told him enthusiastically. "Accept nothing without evidence. Economics *is* a science, after all. What will it take to convince you of the truth of this fable?"

"Um," said the boy uncertainly.

"What does it take to prove anything in science?" Mr. G asked the class as a whole.

More crickets.

"An experiment! So let's conduct a little classroom experiment. I need two volunteers. What's-Your-Face, stand up."

Adam, used to his title by now, stood up.

"You also, girly," he said to the girl who sat to Adam's right.

Mr. Geezer gave his cane to Adam and said, "Take her money."

Adam, rather shyly, held the cane like a gun and pointed it at his classmate and said, "Fork over your dough," in his best gangster accent.

She burst out laughing.

"Don't be daft, young lady," Mr. Geezer chided the girl without any heat in his voice. "Science is serious stuff, you know. Here now, take this," and he handed her a dollar bill. Then he turned to Adam.

"Do it again, and do it better this time."

Adam put the cane to the ground and leaned on it leisurely while putting as much menace in his body language as possible. Then he did his best impression of Loud-Talker.

"Money is a burden. It attracts thieves and other... dodgy people. My associates and I want nothing more than to protect you from such vile individuals. If only you would consider handing over your money to us—your *friends*—that we may invest it—for your *protection*—then I feel we could make certain that you would no longer feel threatened... *this* week."

She rolled her eyes at him and said, "Your first one was more believable."

But she handed him the dollar anyway.

"Now, class," Mr. Geezer said, "who here thinks that What's-His-Face harmed this lovely lady—that he stole her money?"

Everyone raised their hands.

Mr. G went on to ask, "And who among you would rush to her aid if you saw this happening to her? Leave your hands up."

Some hands raised, but not all.

"Or take photos for use as evidence against her attackers?"

A few more hands went up.

"Or yell for help?"

Yet more hands.

"Or call the police?"

At this point, every hand in the room was up.

"Good," Mr. Geezer said. "Here is evidence that you are all, at least subconsciously, aware of the citizenship agreement to each other. Stealing is harmful. Harm violates justice. Harm activates the citizenship agreement and you, dear citizens..." he waved his free hand at all the students, "are obligated to intervene. Anyone disagree so far?"

No one did.

"Now watch this," Mr. G said with a twinkle in his eye.

He handed the girl another dollar, then spoke to her.

"Young lady, I am the representative of the government's Internal Revenue Service. My job is to collect taxes. I'm sorry to inform you that we have had to raise your taxes by one dollar more than the previous year. I know you think you need that money and you voted against this tax increase and you even voted for my opponent in the election, but there are other citizens in a much larger voting block who are much worse off than you. They really need that dollar more than you. Now I know you are a prudent, kind person who will pay your taxes like any good, law-abiding citizen, but I just want to remind you that the penalty for *not* paying taxes is a stiff fine—much larger than one dollar—AND a jail sentence, AND a lifetime of yearly IRS audits, AND you will forevermore be labeled a felon.

"Oh, I forgot to mention that the Work Oversight Office cannot issue work permits to felons. So your license to work in your preferred profession will be instantly and forever revoked. And should you try to work without a work permit, we will fine you again and put you in jail again. And, besides, don't you agree that it is selfish to keep that money for yourself? Money is the root of evil, after all. We're doing you a *favor* by taking it from you. And think of your loved ones. If you can't work, then how will you feed your family? And if you're in jail, what kind of role model would you be for your children?"

He held out a hand, palm up.

The girl seemed shaken. She handed over the dollar.

Mr. Geezer pocketed the money, then pulled a fruit basket from behind his desk. He handed the fruit basket to Adam. As an afterthought he said to him, "You might want to vote for my party next election. It would be a shame if the other party took over. They might not continue these policies. Just saying."

He winked.

"Now, once again," Mr. Geezer said to the class, "who here thinks that What's-His-Face harmed this lovely lady? That he stole her money?"

Three people raised their hands.

He went on to ask, "And who among you would rush to her aid if you saw this happening? Leave your hands up."

No one else raised their hand.

"Or take photos for use as evidence against her attackers?"

One hand went up.

"Or yell for help?"

No additional hands.

"Or call the police?"

One more hand went up.

"Good," Mr. Geezer said. "Here is evidence that you are—on average—alarmingly obedient to some authority which you apparently prize greater than justice. Because the same harm occurred in both cases—the same amount of money was taken. She was threatened with violence in both cases. What's-His-Face ended up with the money—or an equivalent—in both cases. The only difference between these two scenarios was that one of them involved the government as middleman. Apparently that tiny change made an enormous difference. So your homework tonight—and probably for the rest of your lives—is to answer this question: 'Where did the crime go?'"

60
No One Ever Told Me

Adam was moving slowly enough that Asuna was able to meet up with him just a few steps out the door of the Economics room. She offered to take his backpack but he shook his head slightly.

"The pain meds are still helping."

They walked together down the hall to Home Economics. Most of the class was already present when they walked in. Little-Fox was beside the door again with her computer pad. Beside her was a large box piled with baby dolls.

Finalmente, Adam thought.

Miss Erica held out her hand.

Asuna handed her baby doll over, then turned and helped unstrap Adam's from the side of his backpack.

Little-Fox had her head turned sideways and her eyebrow raised as she looked over Adam's backpack baby storage solution. Then she closed her eyes and shook her head.

Asuna handed over Adam's baby doll and its bottle.

Little-Fox accepted the problematic teaching tools while glancing curiously back and forth between Adam and Asuna. Eventually her eyes settled on Adam's face. She squinted and leaned closer.

"You're not looking so good," she said.

Adam shrugged. The motion hurt and made him wince. He tried to cover up the reflex with words.

"I'm not feeling well."

Asuna glanced toward Adam and frowned.

Little-Fox frowned also.

"Is it contagious?" Little-Fox asked, looking serious and unhappy and... nervous?

Adam chuckled and managed to mostly suppress another involuntary wince.

"Only if bad luck or bad judgment is catching."

Little-Fox stared up in his eyes for a full second before she flicked her head to continue.

Adam walked toward his seat, pleased he'd gotten past the gate guard. His relief was short-lived, however.

"Wait!" Little-Fox said to Adam's back.

Adam froze.

Crap, he thought miserably. *What gave me away?*

"What's that on your back?"

Adam blinked, momentarily confused, then wrestled down a grin. He reached back and rubbed the foot of the imposter demon-baby doll strapped to his backpack, facing rearwards.

"I found this gem," Adam said over his shoulder, "at the thrift store. It looked exactly like the babies we used in this class. I had to have it."

Little-Fox's mouth formed a sine wave, as if she couldn't decide whether to smile or frown.

"You liked it that much?"

Adam turned halfway back toward Little-Fox.

"'Like' doesn't accurately capture my feelings for these little torture devices. I was actually thinking of having a special ceremony with this one once the class was over."

Her mouth quirked.

"Ceremony, eh? Like what kind?"

"Originally I'd envisioned a very tall bonfire," Adam explained. "But I've decided it's more fitting to, instead, make it my personal mascot."

She stared prettily but her eyes looked kind of vacant.

"How would that work... exactly?"

"I figured I would mount it on the end of a tall pole and parade it ahead of the football team before games to scare our opponents."

A huge grin took up half of Little-Fox's face.

"Scare them... with a baby doll?"

"A *demon* baby doll," Adam corrected. "And yes, anyone who has ever worked with one of these would be scared of it. It can't be helped if the other team pees their pants at the sight of the thing."

She barked out a laugh, then motioned for Asuna and Adam to sit. She walked over to her office door, left the room briefly, and came back, ushering a woman carrying a small bundle of cloth against her chest.

The girls in the class—which was just about everyone in the class—started talking excitedly all at once. Little-Fox showed the other lady to a mat on the floor and helped her sit.

Lee raised his hand.

"Can I get her a chair? It might be more comfortable," he said from his uncomfortable seat.

"Thank you," Little-Fox said. "That was thoughtful, but no. You are all in this class, presumably, to learn. Learning requires making mistakes. If one of those unavoidable errors just happens to be dropping an infant, I'd prefer it enjoy free fall for only a few centimeters, ending on a soft mat."

Lee lowered his hand slowly. His eyes were alarmingly wide.

"Class," Little-Fox said from beside the sitting visitor. "This is my sister, Jayne, and her daughter, Kayla. Kayla is nine months old and you may each hold her for a few seconds. Anyone who wishes to touch the child must first wash their hands for thirty seconds. If you are ill," she looked straight at Adam, "then you may *not* touch the infant. Clear?"

The room buzzed.

"Okay. Get to washing."

Everyone washed their hands and made a circle around Jayne and her child. One at a time, Jayne told each interested student how to hold the baby and carefully transferred the infant. Adam was reminded of the way emperor penguins pass their eggs from one parent to another—carefully. The infant slept for about half the class, then woke up and required feeding, at which point the students took turns feeding the baby pumped breast milk from a bottle. Even Lee took a turn—looking more nervous and excited than many of the girls.

Adam wasn't allowed to get near the infant, so he mostly just watched the reactions of his classmates as they came in contact with the baby. Some seemed to fall into a kind of relaxed trance. Most—like Lee—grew nervous, excited, and agitated. A few—like Asuna—got very businesslike and handled the baby dispassionately.

At the end, Little-Fox asked Jayne if she had any advice for young people who might be considering having children someday.

Jayne patted the infant on her shoulder and said, "Wear condoms."

Adam laughed heartily. No one else did.

Jayne continued, "Get help. Beg for it. Steal it. Hire it. Do whatever it takes, but don't do it alone. Even two people are about half a person short of what it takes to raise a single child. Also," she continued, "be prepared. A child will change you. You'll lose all your friends, too. They won't understand why you can't come out to play until they've had their own kids."

Little-Fox laid a comforting hand on her sister's shoulder.

"Don't get me wrong. Parenting is very rewarding. I wouldn't trade this experience for anything. But it's *so* much work! No one ever told me that." Jayne wiped at her eyes. "I just wanted you to know."

61
Clueless Hand Rest

Asuna walked beside Adam as he headed toward the Play Yard for his second PE period.

"It's not fair," Asuna said out of nowhere.

"What's not?" Adam asked.

"You weren't allowed to hold the baby because Miss Erica thought you were sick. But you're *not* sick. It's not fair."

"Oh, that," Adam chuckled. "I'm good. I got to see you with the baby. That was enough."

Asuna looked at Adam, her emotions unreadable.

Amy strode up and stopped.

Asuna acknowledged her, squeezed Adam's left hand gently, then turned and walked away.

Amy watched her leave, then looked up at Adam, searching.

"The pain meds are still working," he said, trying to guess her question.

The corner of one side of her mouth lifted. She stepped to his right. One of the ribbons in her hair brushed his arm. It felt velvety. She put one hand around the inside of his right forearm.

Adam thought it felt like something between holding hands and escorting someone by the elbow. It was hard to walk that way. He wanted to hold his arm still for her, but his arm wanted to swing with each step. She seemed to notice the problem and slid her hand higher so it rested around his right bicep.

Adam felt as though he were in *The Twilight Zone*. On the one hand, half his body felt brittle and painful—as if it would shatter if someone so much as bumped him. On the other hand, his right arm felt wonderful. It was like, "Oh, right, *that's* what this arm is for—a resting place for Amy's hand."

All those other things he used the arm for seemed trivial at that moment.

They walked that way down to the Play Yard in silence.

62
Surveillance

Adam pleaded ill for his second PE class and walked slowly around the track while everyone else ran. After class, Amy walked him to the Shop room, waved, and disappeared back in the crowd.

Adam entered and found Shop-Boss sitting at a table with electronic equipment spread everywhere. The box Shop-Boss had removed the electronic equipment from was on its side—also on the table.

Before his backpack even settled on the floor, Adam asked, "Did you learn anything about the intruders?"

Shop-Boss looked up. He favored Adam with his shiny smile and said, "I sure did."

Adam sat down, all attention.

Shop-Boss rotated his massive shoulders and stretched his neck in preparation for telling his story, then leaned forward and said conspiratorially, "I spoke with Officer Ben, who is part-time on the police force. The Chief of Police told him the Street-Angel gang has been really active in this area recently. He thinks they are expanding their territory. They have been pushing at their previous boundaries and making headway against some of the other gangs in the City. He figures they must be trying to establish a presence in the school as well—probably in hopes of recruiting new members. Or perhaps selling to students. Something like that."

Adam whistled.

"Yeah," Shop-Boss said. "We might be in the middle of a gang war or something. Could get hairy."

Adam grunted. If the Street-Angels could get a permanent presence on the school grounds, 'hairy' was way too nice a word to describe the fallout.

The Shop giant continued, "So I thought we could set up a surveillance system to watch the walls. That way, at least we can confirm who we are dealing with and formulate a response."

"Good thinking," Adam said as he fished around in the box on the table. He found the instructions looking lonely and undisturbed at the bottom. He started to check off the different parts on the table against the parts list on the first page of the instructions. When he was satisfied Mr. Keynes hadn't lost any parts yet, Adam started to read the manual.

Apparently putting electrical parts in water was bad form. So was touching electrical parts with wet hands or manipulating power circuits with the power still running. He skimmed over the rest of the safety warnings, then jumped forward to Step One.

"It says here," Adam told Shop-Boss, "first we have to identify where we want to mount these. Then we'll mark spots for drilling holes and for running wires. Also, we need a power box to splice these in, or else run them off batteries. Oh, and it says we're supposed to make sure the power is off when we tie these in the electrical circuits. Just thought I'd mention that..."

Shop-Boss sat up and shook a screwdriver at Adam.

"Don't get too uppity just because you read the instructions. Sometimes trial-and-error is the only way to go. And it's *always* the more interesting way to go."

Adam fought down a laugh. It was impossible not to like this man.

They walked to the west end of the building and took the stairs up to the roof. Mr. Keynes's ID opened the roof hatch and they climbed out and walked to the west edge. Adam looked down the three stories and felt vertigo before stepping back.

While sighting over the edge of the roof, Shop-Boss said, "I think we can line up one of those cameras from here to look down on the west fence. I'll bet we can set it to capture most of the length of the Play Yard from here. Then we can do the same on the other two fence lines."

He looked around.

"Powering it is going to be a pain, though. I'll have to ask my buddy, the electrician, to help me with that. Professor Steph, the physics teacher, is good with that sort of thing, too."

Once they'd scouted good viewing angles, Shop-Boss sent Adam down to the front office to request blueprints for the building. Adam did as instructed and Mr. Greene sent a blueprint file to Mr. Keynes' computer. That finished, Adam headed back to the Shop room.

Mr. Keynes made a flicking motion off the edge of his desk computer and a large blueprint file showed up on Adam's ID.

"Listen," Shop-Boss said. "I've got another work request I need to attend to. I've been putting it off."

He shook his head and looked resigned.

"What is it?" Adam asked.

"One of the rooms on the third floor has a leak in the roof. It has for a long time. The leak is getting worse. I should have fixed it ages ago but... the teacher is just so unattractive."

He made a vague gesture around his face, which looked unhappy and disgusted.

"But why would—" Adam began, but was cut off.

"No, no," Shop-Boss said. "I wouldn't think of it. I'll take this one for the team. No sense in both of us having to suffer. Besides, the period will end soon. There's not enough time before the next period bell. You stay here and clean up this mess I've made."

Adam glanced around at the electronics scattered everywhere.

The Shop giant's jaw firmed. He picked up a tool box and a bucket. He took a deep breath, as if for courage.

"Wish me luck," he said, then strode out of the room.

Adam frowned at the door for several seconds, then shook his head as if to clear it. He set about the room, carefully placing all the electronics back in the box along with the instructions. He slid the box under Mr. Keynes desk.

Still unhappy for some reason he couldn't perfectly describe, Adam left for lunch.

63
Forbidden Fruit Conspiracy

The Cafeteria. Heaven on Earth. God so loved man that he created a place with large troughs of never-ending food, offered in great variety, where men could congregate and eat themselves silly without any other concerns. Today, though, Adam sinned by bringing to this shrine an apple off the tree which must not be named.

"I'm puzzled," Adam said to his friends across the table.

Lee raised an eyebrow.

Hal kept eating without looking up.

"Listen to this problem Mr. Geezer gave us," Adam said.

"Mr. who?" Lee asked, snickering.

"Oh, sorry. Mr. G, my Economics teacher," Adam explained.

"Well, I suppose the 'G' could stand for 'Geezer'," Lee muttered.

"Or 'Grouchy'," Hal added.

Adam ignored them both.

"A large group of men walk in a store and hold up the cashier saying, 'Hand over the money!' And the cashier hands over $200 that day. That's a crime, right?"

Both boys nodded, though Hal still hadn't looked up.

"One year later, the same large group of men walk to the voting booth and elect a candidate. That candidate, once elected, raises taxes on that same store by $1000, then redistributes $200 of it to the same gang of men who robbed the store the year before. Now," Adam asked, leaning across the table, "where did the crime go?"

Lee looked indignant, then said, "That is corruption, sir. It is definitely a crime to use the powers of an office for personal gain. That politician should be impeached."

"What?" Adam asked, confused. "Correlation does not imply causation. There is nothing in the story to say the politician raised those taxes or distributed them for personal gain. Only that he raised them and distributed them."

"And those thieves," Lee went on undeterred, "they should have been in prison the first time around, making them felons. They should not have had any right to vote in the election."

Adam waved his hands in a 'stop' gesture.

"No, no. You are missing the point. The crime was theft. The dilemma is, 'Why does the second story not trigger the same alarm as the first?' Why does the gang of robbers deserve to be in prison in the first story, but in the second story, the only punishment that came to your mind was impeachment of the politician?"

Lee rubbed the bridge of his nose as if he had a headache. "Remind me why we are talking about this at lunch?"

"Because it's important to me," Adam said, unable to keep the hurt and anger out of his voice.

Lee sighed, "Very well. As a personal favor to you, I will use my preposterously overpowered intellect to solve your simple riddle."

"Preposterously oversized ego, you mean," Hal said, grinning up at his overly-tall friend.

Lee bared his teeth in Hal's direction and snarled, "Silence, you over-muscled cow herder. I can't think with your endless chattering in my ear."

Then Lee turned back to Adam.

"Now, Adam. Here's the skeleton. Tell me if I get anything wrong. In story number one, a bad group of men takes money from another man, which is theft—a crime. But in story number two, the bad men elect a politician who takes the same money through taxes, then distributes it as government services or whatnot. But there is no crime, even though the same amount of money was taken and ended up with the same people who, in the first story, we all agreed were criminals. Is my summary accurate?"

Adam nodded.

"So we must establish what makes taking the money—in the first story—a crime. Then we figure out why it does not apply in the second story," Lee said while drawing on his napkin. "Why is taking money from a person a crime?"

Adam answered, "It's only a crime if the victim owns the money and doesn't want to trade. Using violence or threats to force him to trade produces a 'Lose-Win' scenario. By definition. My Economics teacher said trades that cause one or both parties to 'lose' is a violation of justice. Justice is the benchmark we use to define crime."

"All right," Lee said, "let's accept the justice argument as true for now. Next question. Is it still a—what did you call it?—'lose-win' trade when the money is removed by the politician through taxes?"

"Yes," Adam reasoned, "the stories are meant to be identical in every way possible. If he does not desire the trade in the first story, he also does not desire the trade in the second."

"Okay," Lee said, still drawing on the napkin. He continued, "Let's assume the victim does not desire the trade in both cases. Is it the fact that *force* was used to make the exchange happen that makes taking the property a violation of justice? Or is it the *particular person* producing the force that makes it a crime?"

"I don't follow," Adam said, bewildered.

"Does it make a difference if the *Pope* tells you that you will go to Hell if you don't give over $200? Versus the President threatening to make your life hell if you don't give up $200? Versus the local drug dealer telling you he will send you to Hell if you don't give him $200? Does justice care who is doing the threatening? Or is justice blind to station and titles and authority?"

Adam rested, chin on hand, and looked at Lee's cute little pictures of the Pope, the President, and a drug dealer all pointing down a long pipe that opened on a fire with horned, pitchforked little goblins dancing around it.

"You're an amazing artist," Adam said.

"Oh, now you've done it," Hal said.

Lee looked at Hal out of the corners of his eyes and bared his canines again, but made no reply before looking back at Adam.

"Stay focused, simpleton. Else I'll never get back to my peaceful, quiet table setting."

Adam suppressed a grin and nodded. "Repeat the question."

Lee repeated himself, stressing each syllable as if dictating something elementary to a particularly slow dog.

"Is justice blind?"

Adam thought for a moment, then said, "Justice is, 'Do no harm, remedy harm done.' No exceptions were made in the definition we were taught. For Popes, or politicians, or anyone."

Lee pursed his lips.

"I see. So the same crime happened in both stories, at least according to your definition of justice. But the second story does not raise the same alarm at the violation in most of the people who hear the stories. What's the difference?"

"A middleman in the second story?" Hal proposed.

"Yes, but no," Lee responded. "The story was specific about the middleman being a government employee. If the middleman had been, say, just another street thug, it would have triggered the same alarm and we wouldn't be having this discussion. There has to be something about the middleman *being* the government that causes us to overlook the crime in the second story. Why would it matter?"

He pulled his lips to one side of his face and tapped his napkin in thought.

Adam spoke up, "Mr. Geezer told us a story where the government took over the school system and taught everyone that obedience—to the government especially—was the cardinal virtue. By 'cardinal', I think he meant that the virtue of obedience overruled all other virtues—including justice. Could it be that we automatically ignore the *in*justice in the second story because doing otherwise would mean we were disobedient to the government?"

"Wolf packs are like that," Hal said while fishing out a new toothpick from a box in his pocket.

Both Lee and Adam looked at Hal.

"What," Lee asked, "could wolf packs have to do with this riddle?"

Hal said, "Lots of mammals—especially carnivores—will form groups with a pyramidal social structure—pups and weaklings are at the bottom. Healthy adults are in the middle. The alpha male is at the top. The alpha male is chosen—in fact, the entire hierarchy is defined—by violent contests. Winning a violent contest elevates your status in the social group to the same level as the defeated opponent. The alpha male, by definition, is the most capable warrior no one else can beat in a fair contest."

"And?" Lee made a 'hurry up' gesture with his hand.

"A really interesting thing about this hierarchical setup," Hal continued at the same pace, "is that everyone else in the group follows the alpha male without question—more or less. So if the alpha male attacks an animal, everyone in the group attacks that same animal. Also interestingly, if the alpha attacks a member of his *own* pack—outside of a formal challenge—then everyone else in the pack either stands back or helps him attack. They just sort of assume that the alpha's actions will benefit *everyone* in the group, even when those actions clearly injure one member of the group."

Lee rubbed his chin.

"That reminds me of an incident I heard in the news once where a pod of whales beached themselves for days. No one could figure out why until the lead whale died. Then the rest, all at once, worked their way back in the ocean. Perhaps the lead whale was the alpha male."

"So you're saying," Adam said, thinking out loud, "that perhaps humans respect the same pyramidal social structure as other mammals? That we overlook the harm to the individual in the second story because we think of the government as the alpha? And we assume the government's actions will benefit everyone, even when they're clearly hurtful to one of the members."

"Yeah," Hal said around his toothpick.

"That kind of fits," Adam admitted. "You said the alpha was the most violent member of the pack?"

"By definition," Hal agreed.

"Well," Adam reasoned, "there is no individual or group more specialized in the art of violent combat than a standing army. And Mr. Geezer keeps telling us the government is the administrative arm of the army."

Lee drummed his fingers.

"If that were the case, your Geezer's conspiracy theory about the government running the schools would be unnecessary. People would react obediently to the alpha *regardless* of what they learned in school. On account of some sort of genetic imperative."

Adam ran both of his hands through his hair.

"A genetic predisposition to value obedience over justice—to treat the most violent among us as God? I don't know. It sounds like a bad design."

"Wouldn't nature select it out if it were bad design?" Hal asked.

"Perhaps it has only just started that process," Lee put in. "Perhaps the climb out of a hierarchical social structure is a recent event. Maybe we are at a decision point in history where natural selection is trying to choose which social design is best. We do seem to be on top of the food chain at the moment."

"Food," Adam said, alarmed. "I forgot to eat."

64
Tag-Team Virtual Giant Porcupine Combat Strike Force

The bell rang and lunch ended. Adam hadn't finished his meal! Desperately he finished the last of his glass of water. Then he dumped what was left of his food in the drinking glass. He drank the meal in enormous gulps, like a lumpy soup.

Forcing down his gag reflex was uncomfortable and his eyes watered.

Perhaps not the best idea I've ever had, Adam thought, wiping his mouth with a napkin.

Asuna walked over as Adam deposited the empty food tray at the kitchen window. Lee and Hal had vanished.

While walking Adam to Statistics class, Asuna grinned and asked, "What were you talking about over lunch? I've never seen you eat so slowly before. You must have been really deep in something."

"It's complicated," he said.

Asuna looked disappointed.

"I asked them if it made sense to elevate obedience above justice," he quickly explained.

"Obedience versus justice," she said, sounding disbelieving but looking amused.

"Yeah," Adam said, "those two—Hal and Lee—don't like to talk much. But they're really smart. I value what they have to say."

"You should ask *me* what I think some time," Asuna said, looking him directly in the eyes.

"Really?" Adam said, getting excited. "Of course I'm interested in your thoughts on justice! I should have asked you before. I didn't realize. I'm so sorry. Do you think justice is different for boys than for girls?"

Her face scrunched up toward the center.

"Well, no... I mean, I don't know. I've never thought about justice before, honestly. I meant about other things."

"Like what?" Adam asked, feeling clueless and off-balance.

Just then they arrived at his Statistics class. She waved goodbye and darted off down the hallway.

He entered class wondering what Asuna liked to talk about and found everyone already in their seats.

He sat through another video of Mr. Hayek giving an amazing lecture, most of which covered in great detail just a few of the myriad ways to screw up simple math.

When the class ended, Adam found Amy waiting at the door.

"How did you know where to find me?" he asked, stepping out in the hall.

She held up her ID.

"We're friends, remember?"

Adam smiled. "That's right."

As they walked toward their next class, Algebra, Adam asked, "Do you think we could be friends in the game world too?"

She was silent.

"I mean, I thought I saw you on the first day. Around the giant wasps. I looked for you everywhere on the second day, but couldn't find you," Adam told her.

"Have you gotten past the porcupines yet?" Ribbons asked.

"No," he said, frustrated. "I can only punch and kick, so far. The porcupines hurt me every time I hit them."

"Yeah," she said, "you need a special tool. Something long and metal—I think—to get past their quills."

"You got past them already?" Adam surmised.

"No. But I've been running around trying to find the right tool for the job," she admitted.

"Mind if I look with you?" he asked.

"I'd rather you didn't," she said.

Adam tried not to look hurt.

"My avatar does not have many clothes. I'd like to avoid other people until I can get a decent wardrobe."

Adam laughed and said through his smile, "That's a good point. I found you rather... distracting on the first day."

Amy lifted her chin and flicked her hand through the hair behind her neck, causing ribbons and braids to flair backward as if blown by a strong gust of air.

"Watch it," she told him, "your endless flattery might get you entangled with me some day."

Adam had the briefest image of himself and Ribbons very close together—arms and legs and ribbons and hair all tangled up. He felt his mouth dry up, his cheeks get hot, and his eyes widen. He must have looked ridiculous. He stopped in his tracks and shook his head trying to get the image out of his mind.

Ribbons stopped and turned back toward him. She looked concerned. Then her face turned red too, and she spun and continued down the hall without him.

Adam tried to catch up but his body wouldn't move quickly no matter how hard he spurred it.

Amy was already hidden behind her desk—wherever it was in that warehouse of a room—when Adam arrived. The teacher—was he really a teacher?—was sitting in his chair, feet up on the desk, reading *Backpacker* magazine.

Adam could see the cover model was a fit, healthy looking man who hadn't shaved in days. In the photo he was sitting in a tent which was hanging off the side of a mountain. That reminded Adam that winter was coming. He sighed.

What is it like sleeping in a tent in the snow? The guy on the magazine looks happy. Maybe there is hope.

The teacher—Adam decided to call him Hippie-Face instead of Hippie-Cheerleader today—wore a different tie-dye shirt, khaki shorts, and beat-up leather sandals. He still wore his shirt open down the front and still had the large medallion in the shape of a gold '$' at its center.

"What?" said Hippie-Face, looking annoyed when he glanced up from the magazine.

"I was just wondering," Adam began, "what kind of tool is required to get past the porcupines?"

Hippie-Face rolled his eyes.

"You don't need tools. This isn't trigonometry. You need health. You just have to have a way to take a beating yet survive the encounter. Try teaming up with a healer, or saving up for some healing potions, or buying more hearts. There are lots of ways to overcome each of the obstacles in this game."

"Oh," Adam said, feeling a little embarrassed that he hadn't thought of that himself. "Thanks."

Adam sat down at his desk and the computer lit up. He entered his password and his avatar dropped to the exact place he'd left off. He jumped right to the shop and looked around for some sort of healing spell. He found one called 'Tiny Heal' for cheap and bought it. Then he went around in the game fighting monsters but intentionally getting the math problems wrong so he would take damage. He activated his 'Tiny Heal' spell by tapping a green icon on the right side of his screen.

To Adam's surprise, a second algebra equation popped on to the screen. Now he had two going simultaneously. He answered the healing question first and was pleased to see his health rise about 10%. Then he answered the other question and dealt the death blow to an angry ostrich. He used another healing spell on himself and was given another problem very different from the first. He solved it too, and his health went up more. Then he went and found a giant wasp. While fighting the wasp, he healed himself several times. He noted that the healing spells seemed to pull problems randomly from any type he had mastered in the past. It was like a math review, but occasionally it would hit him with something that pushed him a little. He noticed the same lectures were available off to the side of the screen if he needed help.

"Okay," he said to himself, "now for plan B."

Next he went to the forest and picked a fight with a porcupine. They were tough and he had to use the instructors at first and also heal himself with review problems. It took about fifteen minutes to overcome the first porcupine, but he was rewarded with $1.

Un dineral! A fortune!

He ran around for a while avoiding fights and looking for Amy. He found her sitting under a tree. She was wearing a sleeveless tank top made out of animal fur that cut off above her abdomen. She'd also found a shredded garment to wear as a skirt. It clashed horribly, he thought, but she still looked attractive.

He entered '/wave' in the command line and his avatar waved at her. After a while she waved back. He targeted her and saw a new button appear along the left upper border of the screen. He hit it and the word 'Invite' flashed across the screen. After a short wait, a small image of her face next to some bars indicating her health popped up in the top left-hand corner of the screen. He motioned for her to come with him and headed to the porcupines. After a pause, she followed.

When they arrived at the forest, his avatar pointed at a porcupine. She stood there. He pointed again. This time she walked forward and engaged the beast. Both of the avatars entered their slow-motion battle stance at the same time. He saw problems come up, as before, and solved the first quickly.

His avatar punched the porcupine—hurting it—but he also took damage. Amy was having the same success and the same difficulties. While she went on to perform her second problem, he did a healing spell on her, completing a review problem for the spell. It raised her health back to full. Then he did the same for himself and went back to work on the porcupine. The porcupine went down faster than when he'd done it alone and they were both awarded 60¢.

"Nice!" Adam said out loud. There was a bonus for grouping.

They fought the porcupines together until the class bell rang.

65
Really... Love... School

Adam and Amy walked side-by-side down to the bottom floor where Adam had his final Work/Study with Boss-Clean.

At the door to the master storage room, Amy turned partway toward him and said, "Thanks."

"What for?" Adam asked. "You walked me here. I should be thanking *you*."

"I told you not to come looking for me, but you did anyway. In the game, I mean. And I had fun. Thanks for taking me to the porcupines."

Adam rubbed the back of his neck with one hand.

"I had fun too. Let's do it again sometime."

She gave a quick, very girly curtsy without making eye contact, then turned and fled down the hall.

Adam watched her pigtails sway until they were gone, out of sight.

He really loved school.

Just then Adam remembered his laundry from earlier that morning. He hadn't moved it over to the dryer. He walked quickly through the large storage room to the back where the washing machines were kept. He found someone had dumped his clothes in a pile on top of one of the washing machines. He sniffed his clothes and thought they smelled pretty good, so he loaded them in a dryer and went back to fetch his supply cart. He sat Demon-Baby-Doll-Mascot on the top and wedged her between a few things to keep her from falling over. He hoped no one would get jealous and steal his new mascota.

Boss-Clean had them washing windows that day on the outside of the school building. It involved a bucket, a squeegee, a water hose, and a really cool platform that raised and lowered the kids up and down the walls. They spent fifteen minutes learning all the different ways to fall off and die, and how to use the safety harness correctly, then Boss-Clean sent several of them up at a time to wash. The rest she deployed inside the building doing windows or along the outside, bottom floor where they could reach the windows with small ladders.

Adam was assigned to the ladder team, which was fine. Given his luck, he'd fall from the top floor and die given even the smallest opportunity. Unacceptable. Dying—right at that moment—would hurt too much.

Washing windows uses a lot of back muscles and climbing ladders uses a lot of leg muscles. Both places he had bruises. So this particular task was not fun at all. Adam popped the extra Tylenol and ibuprofen Nurse-Bubbly had given him and tried to ignore the discomfort. He muddled through.

At the end of the period, Boss-Clean asked if he would stay to continue working, but he had to decline because he had a commitment he had to attend. She nodded and said she'd miss his help, which—oddly—made him feel appreciated and regretful at the same time.

Adam parked his cleaning cart back in the great storage room and checked his laundry. It still needed more drying. He attached the Diablo-Bebé-Mascota to the outside of his backpack—facing behind—and headed to the Play Yard.

66
Life and Death

Adam followed the Friend-Tracker on his ID card to Anger-Management. He found her lying on the bottom of a slide in a section of the Play Yard fenced off for daycare kids.

"Isn't there some rule that says you're not supposed to be in there?" Adam asked through the fence.

Anger-Management rolled her head to look at him, then sat up. She was all tight muscles and swagger. Her brown hair was spiked on the top and short on the sides. Her many piercings glittered in the sun. She walked over to the fence and held a lunch box in front of her. It had a cute kitten on the side.

"This is for you," she said, "if you come through as promised."

"Where?" he asked.

"Right here," she flicked her head at the playground behind her. "School's out for the youngsters and the fence will give us a little privacy. I don't want people to notice while I'm beating the piss out of you."

Adam rolled his eyes, looked around, and prepared to hop the fence. Then he thought better of it as his right leg cramped.

"Is there a door or something?" he asked.

She walked to a different part of the fence. Her ID card opened a gate latch.

Adam lifted an impressed eyebrow in her direction as he walked through the open gate.

"I help babysit the kids in my Work/Study," she said, reading his thoughts.

"Really?" he said.

She pointed an angry finger at his face.

"I will cut you."

Adam laughed and held his hands in front of him in the gesture of surrender.

"I just didn't see that coming," he admitted. "It's a good kind of surprise."

He put on his business face and looked around. He picked a spot near the slide that was free of obstacles and looked pretty soft.

"Okay," Adam said, "you asked me to teach you self-defense."

Adam sat down gingerly on the end of the slide.

"But there are different *kinds* of self-defense. For our purposes, there are two you can choose from today: life-or-death or the other kind. Which are you interested in?"

"Life-or-death," Kat said without hesitation.

Adam leaned forward and looked her directly in the eyes.

"Are you sure? These things I can teach you will cripple, maim, blind, or kill your opponent. This is not the kind of thing you do to someone in a schoolyard brawl or against some prom date rival."

Anger-Management's eyes flashed angrily for a moment, then grew distant—as though she were reliving a memory. Adam thought he saw her eyes change color from a lively brown to lifeless grey in the span of two seconds. Her voice, when she spoke, sounded like dry leaves blowing over a grave.

"Life-or-death."

Adam nodded and asked her, "Which position do you want to defend from?"

She looked confused.

"Like, do you imagine yourself standing? Or are you knocked on your back or on your stomach? Where is your opponent likely to be, do you think?"

"On my back," she said, frowning, edgy, and defensive all at once. Her body language made Adam feel like someone was scratching a blackboard with fingernails.

"All right, lie on your back."

She did as instructed—still looking jumpy.

"Okay," he told her, "I am going to climb *slowly* on top of you. Do *not* hurt me. I'm not going to hurt you. I am simply the fill-in for an attacker, but not a real threat. Got me?"

She nodded.

Adam slowly lowered himself—slowly because it hurt to go any faster and because he didn't want to alarm her—till he was straddling her waist.

"Okay," he told her. "This trick is very effective. It could save your life. It is possible to execute it from this position even if you are dazed or blinded, and even against a much stronger opponent."

Kat nodded.

"First you have to come close together. Either sit up to get closer to me or grab me and pull me closer to you, or both at the same time. You have to get close. It's very important."

She sat up as best she could so her face was close to his chest.

"Now, I'm going to show you what to do. Then you are going to do it to me—everything but the killing blow at the end. Don't do the *actual* strike, or you'll blind me."

Adam reached out with his arms and hugged Anger-Management pulling her in closer. Then he moved his hands up so they were on both sides of her head and he brushed his thumbs over her eyes. Her eyelids closed automatically. He placed a small amount of gentle pressure over her eyes then let up, released her head, and straightened up again.

She looked in his eyes. Her irises were dilated and looked like deep pools.

Then Adam placed his hands in the air as though there was a head between them. He confirmed she was watching, then he thrust his thumbs violently forward through the place where an invisible set of eyes would be.

Katrina let out an involuntary gasp as she realized what he was showing her.

"This will work," Adam explained, "even if their eyes are closed. It only takes fifteen pounds of direct pressure on the eye to fracture the bone behind it—the one in front of the brain. And since there are as many nerves clustered closely together in the eye as there are in your fingertip, it is guaranteed to hurt a whole lot. Ideally enough that your attacker will have bigger things to worry about than attacking you."

Adam looked down at Anger-Management and saw her eyes were still wide and there was extra moisture in them along the bottom.

In a soft voice he asked, "Are you okay to continue?"

She nodded and wiped her eyes with her sleeve.

"Okay then," he told her. "Hug, grasp, position your thumbs over my eyes, and... don't blind me. We're only practicing."

He wagged a finger.

"In a real fight though, don't hesitate. Blind him... or her, I guess. It takes only milliseconds for an attacker to realize you're after his eyes and remove them from your reach. If you are going to do it, you have to do it. No thinking. No threatening. Also, you don't ever want this person coming back after you for revenge or whatnot. So while you're in there, make a good mess of things. Then run. Get away."

She nodded.

"Now you try," Adam told her again, "hug to get close, grasp head, thumb strike."

They practiced several times in slow motion. Then Adam had her speed up. Then he had her practice the same moves with her eyes closed.

"You never know. It might be dark. He might have hit you in the nose or sprayed something in your eyes. Prepare for such a possibility."

They stood up and worked out some ways to use the move in a standing position against a single attacker. Then they practiced some more.

It was all kinds of surreal for Adam. Being so close to Anger-Management felt intimate, yet they were discussing and practicing unmitigated brutality of the worst sort.

After about a half hour, Adam called a halt.

"That's all I can teach you today. Practice with your eyes closed at night to keep what we've rehearsed alive in your muscle memory. Speed is vital for this to work."

She walked over and picked up the lunch box with the little kitty and handed it to him.

"Thanks," she said. "I'll make you one of these every day for the rest of the semester. What you taught me was good."

Adam frowned at the lunch box.

"What?" she asked, annoyed.

"Did it have to be a kitty?"

She grinned evilly.

"Definitely."

67
Viking Invasion

Adam scuffed the ground of the little kids' play area with the toe of his shoe, uncertain how next to broach an awkward subject. When he couldn't come up with anything clever to say, he tried the straight-forward approach.

"Kat," he said, "have you heard of the Street-Angels?"

"Sure, I've heard of them," Katrina said while brushing dirt off her clothes. "They're a local gang. Some of them use the same skin art place I do."

She pointed to a colorful design on her left forearm.

"Do they ever talk about themselves around you?" Adam asked.

"Sure," she answered and shrugged. "It's their favorite subject. They never shut up."

"And what do they talk about?" Adam asked, trying not to look extremely curious.

"They brag about their fights," she answered, sounding bored. "They brag about their girlfriends. They brag about expanding their turf. They brag about their tattoos, and their cars, and their cash, and, well… you get the picture. They like to brag."

"Do they ever talk about this school?" Adam asked, unable to hide his intensity this time.

But she didn't notice. She wasn't listening. Instead, she was squinting at something in the distance. She looked pale.

Adam heard a scream from the direction she was looking and followed her gaze.

At the west end of the Play Yard, distant figures were hopping over the fence two at a time. At least ten had come over already, and more were cresting the top of the fence. Most of the invaders wore black in varying quantities and leather jackets. They were too far away to make out faces.

"It's like the Viking legends," Adam whispered to himself.

The scream, apparently, had come from a group of five girls in school uniforms in the same area. Even at a distance, their body language looked alarmed. Three boys in school uniforms with construction-orange armbands were running toward the disturbance. Adam thought one of them must be Patrick—the hall monitor who'd laid him out earlier in the week.

Adam did some quick math. Even if all three of those boys were world-class fighters, the odds of winning a fair fight with that many opponents—fifteen and still rising—were zero.

"This is not good," Adam said.

"Can you help them?" Anger-Management asked, fear and excitement and tension all mingling in her voice.

Adam felt like cement had been poured around his feet. They didn't want to move. Fear chemicals bathed his blood vessels and brain. Every scenario he imagined all ended horribly for all of them, with or without his help.

"No." Adam said, his voice flat. "I'm no help injured like this. And even if I weren't hurt, I couldn't turn the tide against those numbers."

"What are you, a coward?" Katrina half-yelled.

He held up a hand and said, "Wait. I'm getting an idea."

"What?!" she asked, sounding slightly hysterical.

"Wait," he repeated, letting his mind do its thing.

In his head, chemically enhanced synapses were firing faster than normal. His focus was absolute. He could feel himself breathing deeply and his heart racing, but he couldn't spare any thought to it. He let his body do its work and he waited. Chaotic waves of ideas were exploding all over his thoughtscape—ideas causing ripples that spread out in all directions. Like rain hitting the surface of a pond. Many thoughts were dismissed and disappeared under the surface, but others complemented and connected and grew until...

"I've got it," Adam said and focused his eyes on Katrina beside him. "This is a coordinated attack. It requires a coordinated response. This is exactly the kind of thing the citizenship agreement was designed to handle."

"Say what?"

"Do you have a phone?" Adam asked abruptly.

"Of course," she said, and a phone appeared in her hand so fast it could only be a reflex.

"Good. Call 911. Then run over toward that group, but don't get close. Just start snapping pictures. Some will probably break off and run toward you. If that happens, run away as fast as you can toward the center of the Play Yard."

"You want me to *what*?!" she half-yelled. Fear and disbelief colored her voice.

"You wanted to help," he said, looking toward the center of the Play Yard. "*This* will help."

She was silent. There was a pregnant moment, during which time Adam thought up three alternative plans in the event she refused to follow his advice.

"Okay," she said, managing to sound angry, resigned, and nervous all at once.

Then she ran toward the gate.

Adam followed her but—where she turned and headed toward the trouble—he turned and ran the other direction.

68
Master of Ceremony

Adam's body, which had been nothing but pain and agony all day, now felt perfect. He had no pain. Everything was moving without friction. He sprinted to the watchtower and flew up the ladder—the whole while praying that Shop-Boss hadn't thought to remove his ID privileges after they'd repaired the public address system.

He flashed his card at the cabinet and it unlocked and opened.

"YES!" he said out loud, full of relief.

He crouched in front of the open cabinet, scanned over the controls, then started turning nobs and flicking switches. Once satisfied, he reached down to a shelf and grabbed a microphone and a cable and plugged them into 'Input-1'.

He ran across the top of the tower as far as the cord would allow. He leaned over the railing and scanned the Play Yard. All the different sports teams were practicing on their various fields and something was still going on over by the west fence. He saw some of the invaders running toward a lone female student who was running back toward his position.

Adam flicked on the microphone.

"Citizens of Justice High," Adam's voice rang over every part of the yard except the west region.

"Stop what you are doing immediately. An organized gang has invaded the school property and is threatening your fellow students with violence. The hall monitors are standing against them but are horribly outnumbered. Run, without delay, to the west fence just beyond the preschool playground. Ladies, bring your phones and take pictures of the attackers. Men, grab what weapons you can, but do not delay. I repeat, your peers are outnumbered and in danger and require your assistance. The police have already been called but will take time to get here."

Everything had stopped. No one moved anywhere on the Play Yard. He imagined they were held down by the same fear that had only minutes ago paralyzed him. They needed a push.

"MOVE!" he yelled.

Suddenly everything was in motion—everyone sprinting to the west. From his vantage in the watchtower, Adam could see baseball bats, hockey sticks, tennis rackets, javelins, high jump poles, and shot puts all bouncing up and down in the air as their owners sprinted toward the west wall.

Then the invaders, almost as one, took an involuntary step backward. They must have noticed the horde of students sprinting toward them. Two seconds later, the entire gang turned and ran toward the fence.

Some of the students chased after them, but most stopped at a safe distance, formed a solid wall of people, and yelled, screamed, and roared their defiance at the attackers.

And then it was over. The gang was back over the fence. The yelling died down and silence settled over the Play Yard. Then everyone started talking at once. The excitement in the air was palpable. The solid wall of defiance dissolved to hundreds of clusters of students all talking over each other.

In his side vision, Adam caught movement. He looked over and saw faces in the sparkly clean windows of the school that faced the schoolyard. Adam winced. That was a lot of handprints. Every student still in the school must have been pressed up against them.

Adam was tempted to take advantage of the spectacle. So tempted...

He flicked on the switch for the west region's speakers.

"Well done, citizens," Adam said over the loudspeakers. "The danger has passed. Your defense of the school was triumphant. Be sure to thank Patrick and the other hall monitors for their brave stand against the invaders. Their courage and composure are deserving of our gratitude."

There was a change in the pattern of groups by the west fence, then Adam saw several students with construction-orange armbands lifted up on the shoulders of the crowd before the whole group started parading back toward the tunnel entrance.

Standing outside the main doors was a throng of administrators and teachers, obviously taken aback by the scene. Adam imagined their predicament. There was nothing for them to do. The situation was already resolved. Now it was just a matter of processing the event. Adam saw Principal Greene lay a hand across the shoulder of one of the hall monitors and guide him back in the building. He also saw large gaggles of girls sharing their photos and videos with some of the female teachers. He smiled, glanced at the fence one more time to make sure the gang was not climbing back over, then turned off the loudspeaker system and started putting it back the way he'd found it.

69
This Loudspeaker?

Adam's body was back to feeling like a ninety-year-old cripple. He was a sloth making his way down the ladder, but he couldn't afford to fall—it would break him, he was sure of it. At the bottom of the ladder, Anger-Management stood waiting for him. He also noticed a homeless woman striding toward them from the direction of the main building.

Adam landed on his feet and grunted. He looked up and found Anger-Management staring at him. He wilted under her scrutiny.

"What?" he asked.

She waved her arm in the direction of the west fence. Her mouth worked a couple of times but nothing came out, then she found her words.

"That... that thing you did. That was amazing."

Now he really felt uncomfortable.

"And it was no accident. I saw you PLAN it! How on earth did you know that would happen?"

"Ah, well, hmm," Adam dissembled, uncertain how to deal with anything other than scorn and anger from Katrina.

"It's just... there is a model in economics that predicts this is what happens. I just recognized the pattern and applied the model."

Anger-Management made a disbelieving face followed quickly by an angry face.

"You had me run directly at a small army because of a *theory*?"

Her volume rose with each word.

"Do you know what they would have done to me if your plan *hadn't* worked?!"

She yelled the last few words—her face scarlet.

"They would have broken your phone," Adam guessed, grinning sheepishly. "Did you get any good pictures?"

She looked down at the phone, then back at Adam. The tide of her anger seemed to recede. She tossed the phone dismissively at his chest and said, "I'm still mad at you," as he clumsily tried to catch it.

He righted the phone and scrolled through the pictures. Adam stopped on a photo of Loud-Talker in the front line, flanked by Ogre. In the picture it looked like Loud-Talker was shouting at a set of hall monitors only partly captured in the frame.

"Darn," Adam said, letting out a long, slow breath. "I was right. It was the Street-Angels. That's going to make getting home tonight a problem."

"What do you mean?" Kat asked him.

"See this guy in your picture at the center of everything?" he handed the phone back to her. "I think that is the leader, or one of the leaders, of the Street-Angels gang. They know me. I've run into them a couple of times outside of school and it gets uglier each time. There's a chance he might have recognized my voice over the loudspeaker even though I cut the feeds to that part of the Play Yard. I think if they catch me tonight I might not survive to tomorrow."

"Adam," a second voice intruded on their conversation, "was that you on the loudspeaker?"

Adam looked to Kat's left and saw the VW-Saint approaching. She was still dressed in her homeless person costume, though she now sported stylish black boots in place of the air-conditioned, holey cloth boots. Her hair was now combed. Her face was washed. He could not tell from her voice or the look on her face if she was angry.

"*This* loudspeaker?" Adam said in his most innocent voice while pointing a finger up at the tower.

"Don't play games with me," Saint-Anne told him as she planted herself directly in front of him. "This is serious. Was. It. You?" she repeated, poking him in the chest once for each syllable.

Adam looked off to the side, then over her head, then back down to her eyes—huge, pretty eyes.

"Yes. It was me."

Saint-Anne looked down at the ground and said, "I thought so," almost to herself.

She looked back up at him and said, "You've got to come with me. The teachers and staff are having an emergency meeting. We're even calling the teachers who have gone home to come back in. We need you to tell us what happened."

Adam nodded. "I'll come."

"I've got other places to be," Anger-Management said stiffly and started to walk away.

"Oh no, Katrina. You come too," Saint-Anne said in a commanding voice.

Anger-Management grimaced and stared longingly off in the distance before she turned reluctantly and followed Saint-Anne and Adam back to the building.

70
Running with the Torch

The school's combined faculty and staff were gathered in the library. A large space in front of the front desk had been cleared of the normal study tables, and now there were rows of chairs facing the elevated front desk. Every seat was filled and there were people standing all around the sides of the room. Saint-Anne had Adam stand against the wall as she went forward through the crowd. He saw Principal Greene standing behind the front desk. A microphone stand was on top of the desk. Next to Mr. Greene were three boys. One of them, Patrick, was giving a description of what happened on the Play Yard.

Patrick explained that someone had informed the hall monitors that there were suspicious findings on the west fence which suggested a group from outside the school had broken in and vandalized the area. The hall monitors had been watching the area closely for the last several days for any signs of intrusion. That afternoon, one of them noticed a group of girls on that end of the field looking scared. Then a large group of people in black clothing and leather jackets started jumping over the fence. He'd called the other hall monitors still on campus after school to come and help him investigate. By the time they'd gotten there, though, there were way too many outsiders for them to handle.

"Why didn't you call for more help?" asked Coach-Squarepants from the audience on the floor.

"We felt pinned in place," Patrick said in the microphone, his amplified voice emitting from speakers hidden in the overly-tall library counter. "We felt we needed as many people together as possible to slow the advance, and that any of our number leaving the area would put the girls there at increased risk. We needed the invaders to stay focused on us."

"Why didn't the girls run for help?" Coach-Squarepants asked again.

A tall, mousy brunette student was ushered up to the microphone by Mr. Greene.

"At first I was too scared to move," the girl sniffled, "and by the time I thought to run, some of the people coming over the wall had cut off our escape—penned us in. They were coming closer—kind of driving us up against the fence line—when one of them shouted an alarm. Then they were all running after a girl who started taking pictures from a distance."

"Did they catch her? Is she okay," Coach-Slaven asked. His military bravado made him easy to hear over the noise in the room.

Adam saw Saint-Anne wave to Anger-Management to come forward.

Katrina stood frozen in place.

Adam grabbed Katrina's wrist and pulled her along to the front of the room. He handed her off to Saint-Anne who guided her to the microphone.

Anger-Management looked terrified at being the center of all the attention.

"Are you all right?" Coach-Slaven repeated.

"I'm…" Kat croaked, then faltered, then collected herself again. "I'm fine."

"That was quick thinking, young lady," Mr. Greene said beside her. "Who would have thought a camera could strike such fear in the hearts of a mob?"

"It wasn't my idea," Kat said in a voice Adam had never heard from her before. It was like a little kid—a terrified little kid. Words just spilled out of her.

"It was Adam's idea. He told me to get close enough to take pictures, then run away if they came toward me."

"Why didn't the boy stay to protect you?" Coach-Slaven asked.

"He had a plan."

Her answers were automatic. Adam wondered if she was able to think or just recite facts.

"I ran one way, he ran the other. I didn't see him for a while. I took pictures. When they noticed me, a large number of the people coming over the fence started running after me. I ran toward the center of the Play Yard. I thought they would catch me. Then I heard Adam's voice over the loudspeakers. It was distant, but I could make it out. He had a plan. At first nothing happened, but then there was noise coming everywhere from the Play Yard all at once. Then students were all running toward me. It looked like all the sports teams. They were still in their gear. They ran past me. When I turned, the invaders were running back toward the fence. Some were already climbing back over. The noise was terrible. My heart swelled with it. I wasn't afraid. It felt like I was being washed down a river with a really strong current. I wanted to run with them. I wanted to add my voice to theirs."

Kat's eyes glistened.

"Thank you, young lady," Mr. Greene told her. "You were really outstanding today."

The principal put a hand on her tattooed shoulder, then ushered her back away from the microphone.

The assembled teachers started clapping. The clapping lasted for several minutes before Mr. Greene tapped on the microphone and it stopped.

"Is the boy here? The one who spoke on the loudspeakers?" Mr. Greene asked.

Saint-Anne grabbed Adam's wrist and tugged him toward the stairs to stand behind the elevated front desk. The microphone was intimidating. He broke the ice on something simple.

"My name is Adam Smith. I'm a new freshman transfer student."

"How did you get access to the public address system?" Jello-Lady asked from the audience.

"Shop-Boss and I did some repairs this week on the PA system. That's when we found evidence that someone had come over the fence. I still had access through my ID," Adam explained.

"Shop-Boss?" Mr. Greene asked curiously.

"Ah, that would probably be me," Mr. Keynes said, standing up from the crowd. He ran his hand through his hair as if embarrassed by the attention.

"We found some knife cuts to wires and also some damage to the west fence suggesting more than one person had scaled it."

"Why weren't we told about this?" said another frustrated teacher in the room.

Boss-Clean stood now and said, "Adam brought it to my attention yesterday and I added it to the next Parent-Teacher Organization agenda, but that's two weeks off."

"How did you know," Mr. Geezer's dry, crackly tinder voice came from the crowd, "that the other students would recklessly throw themselves at a highly questionable and probably dangerous situation when you decided to take over the public address system?"

Adam smiled down at Mr. Geezer. The old man had pitched a soft, slow ball right down the center.

"There was no question they would come," Adam explained. "This is the Tower of Justice. Its citizens would be aware of their obligation to the citizenship agreement thanks to the excellent education you provide for them. The only question was how to make them aware of the threat to their friends. Also, I was not sure how many would be close by, given this attack took place after school."

"The 'citizenship agreement'?" Mr. Geezer asked, apparently playing dumb for the moment. "What is *that* and what does it have to do with you getting on the PA system?"

Adam recited confidently from memory.

"It is the two-part agreement to uphold justice and aid other citizens whenever they are threatened. I simply informed the students practicing out on the Play Yard that some of their peers were being threatened. They did the rest on their own."

"Clever," Mr. Geezer said, sitting down.

"What's to keep this from happening again?" Hippie-Face from Algebra asked.

Shop-Boss spoke up again.

"Adam and I have already started the process of installing cameras on the top of the building. They will record any activity along the fences. That should help."

Patrick stepped up to the front row of chairs and said loudly enough to be heard, "The hall monitors have put in a grant request so each of us can carry a walkie-talkie. That should improve our coordination and response time. In addition, we have hired the karate club to teach the hall monitors defense techniques once a week, starting next week."

Officer-Red spoke up. "It would be expensive, but we should at least consider hiring a second school guard to walk the boundaries of the Play Yard, especially after hours."

Ideas were thrown around for another half hour till there were no more suggestions.

"We'll all need to consider what we've heard today," Mr. Greene said, taking the microphone back from Adam. I will have my secretary distribute a summary of the minutes of this meeting to every teacher tomorrow and my office will prepare a press release tonight. Also, my office will prepare an official email for parents by end of school tomorrow. I'll run the rough draft by each department head by noon for review and suggestions."

Adam felt the meeting coming to a close and grew nervous. His palms were sweating and his heart raced. They hadn't thought ahead far enough. He needed to do something. He raised his hand. No one noticed. He took the initiative and stepped up beside Mr. Greene, speaking in the microphone from the side.

"You haven't considered something very important."

The room fell silent. Mr. Greene stared at him a moment, then said, "What do you mean?" before sliding back a bit, giving Adam more room by the microphone.

"Everything we talked about this afternoon is excellent. But making this Tower and its grounds an impenetrable fortress won't end the problem. It just displaces the problem outward. As soon as the students and teachers step out the doors and on the streets, we are vulnerable to that same danger. I saw the pictures Katrina took," he nodded at Anger-Management who still stood on the stage by him. "I recognize some of the players. They call themselves the Street-Angels. They are one of the gangs in this city and they're currently involved in a successful turf war. Their territory has been expanding. What we saw today is probably just a small-scale example of what is going on all over the City."

The room was chilly and quiet, then someone spoke up and said, "We aren't politicians or policemen—with the possible exception of Officer Ben. We have no power to influence what happens outside the confines of the school proper."

"I'm sorry, but you're wrong," Adam said, finding it hard to keep some anger out of his voice. "The people outside this school are just like us. They have jobs and kids and homes and hopes and fears. In fact, as soon as school lets out, we ARE those people."

Silence again. Then Boss-Clean spoke up.

"What do you propose we do, young man?"

Adam thought for a moment, then said, "The difference between the people out there and those in here is that *we* know the secret. We know about the citizenship agreement and have even seen it in action today. We know the results are spectacular. I propose we do what we are best at. Education. Let us, as a student body and leaders in the community, go out and—in an organized fashion—teach the people of this community about the citizenship agreement. I used a public address system to coordinate a unified response to the threat we faced today. Perhaps we can help the greater community set up some systems for coordinating *their* responses—like call chains or text hubs or local TV emergency broadcasts or radio alerts. We can get out and show them how to establish justice around their homes and shops. If we don't, I fear we will become a safe island surrounded by waters infested with hungry sharks."

Little-Fox climbed up and stood on the seat of her chair.

"What you say sounds great. But isn't this exactly the kind of problem we pay the police to handle?"

"The police are overwhelmed," Adam answered forcefully. Then he shrugged. "Otherwise we wouldn't be having this discussion."

The only sound in the room was Adam's rapid breathing over the microphone. He hadn't realized how worked up he'd gotten. This was really important to him. He cared about the people in this room, but also feared for the people outside its walls. He wanted to help them all, and he thought he knew a way to do just that.

Little-Fox sat back down, looking pensive.

Nurse Kacey spoke up for the first time that evening.

"Adam's plan sounds a lot like a modified neighborhood watch system. I saw that program established in the city where I lived before moving here. The results were excellent. Perhaps we could research how it went in other cities and modify it to fit our particular brand of... what did you call it? Citizenship."

A few more people threw in supplemental ideas for Adam's plan. There were no detractors.

"All right then," Mr. Greene took the podium back again. "I am ever impressed by the quality of students we have in this school."

"Big thinkers!" someone in the audience said in agreement.

"Let's go home and consider what we've talked about today. We all have a lot to think about in the coming days, and it looks like a lot to do over the next several years. Thank you all for coming on such short notice. Be careful going home tonight."

Then Mr. Greene turned off the microphone and the meeting adjourned.

71
Confidant

Adam had a hard time getting out of the library on account of everyone in the room wanting to shake his hand, starting with Mr. Greene. His current teachers seemed to shake his hand more vigorously than strangers and seemed more inclined to clap him on the back. He tried really hard not to flinch but wasn't above dodging a little to the right or left—room permitting—when he saw someone reaching for his shoulder.

At the same time, he tried to listen to all the other conversations going on around him. After a few minutes, his brain started to weave bits and pieces of the things he heard as a story. His mind interpreted the seeming chaos as a festival, one where everyone around him was trying to sell him something—something about themselves, or about him, or about some idea, or about the school or the community. None of the selling was evil—at least, it didn't feel evil. And, after a few short conversations with adults around him, Adam started to think he had something to sell too.

"Well done, Adam," Shop-Boss was saying. "I had no idea I had such a brilliant student working under me. I hope I have a modest, but positive, impact on you. You certainly did shine today."

Shop-Boss was favoring Adam with his best smile and trying to convey his sincerity and excitement at their shared experience through his over-muscled hand. Adam felt the fingers in his hand move in directions God never intended them to travel.

"We're only just getting started," Adam said, as pain in his hand caused his eyes to tear up. "You are an amazing communicator. Sharing and spreading the citizenship agreement—its obligations and practical applications—will take a great deal of work. Your skills at winning people over will make that effort a lot more fun and a lot more successful. I hope I can count on you in the days to come to help expand the justice enjoyed by this great institution to the people outside its walls."

Shop-Boss blinked as if in surprise, then smiled even broader—though Adam would have thought such a thing impossible had he not seen it for himself.

"Well said, Adam," Mr. Keynes chuckled. "You're not just brilliant, you're dangerous. I'm still not giving you enough credit."

He went to clap Adam on the back.

Adam was saved by Mr. Geezer shouldering his bony way between them and yelling in Adam's ear.

"Great work, What's-Your-Face! But don't get too full of yourself. I've a lot more to teach you. Keep coming to class."

"Thanks for your help," Adam yelled back. "Your leading questions were home runs for me every time."

Mr. Geezer nodded. "I like hot dog buns too! I'll see you tomorrow."

One after another, teachers and administrators shook hands with Adam. He gave each of them a pitch for spreading the citizenship agreement to the community.

At last, there was no one left in the room who wanted to shake Adam's hand, which was fine with him. He felt exhausted. Greeting people—particularly that many people—was such an intense experience. Add to that the rollercoaster of excitement that led up to this meeting, the lingering injuries on his back and legs, and the pain meds wearing off. Suddenly he wasn't sure he would make it to the door, much less all the way home.

Adam heard a soft voice say his name as he entered the hall outside the library. He turned and found a wide-eyed Saint-Anne looking at him.

"Katrina told me you might need a ride tonight. I know I head home the same direction you walk, so I told her I would take you home if you still needed a ride. Katrina said she had to get going and left right after the meeting."

He found it a little hard to take her seriously, dressed down as she was, but he was so tired that he didn't have the energy to laugh or make a joke.

"Miss Anne. I would be eternally grateful to you if I could ride even partway home in your lovely car. I'm quite sure I wouldn't make it home tonight otherwise."

"No problem," she told him. "Can you meet me at the front door of the school in five minutes?"

"Can we make it ten minutes?" he asked, rubbing his sore legs.

"See you in ten," she said and disappeared up the nearby stairs.

Adam went down to the laundry room and found his laundry in a pile on the floor under the dryer where he'd left it so much earlier in the day. He quickly folded the two blankets and walked to the locker room. He threw his school uniform in the laundry hamper and dressed in his own clothes. He pulled on his backpack, Diablo-Bebé-Mascota still hanging off the back, and walked to the front doors of the building.

Saint-Anne was waiting. She wore tight jeans and the stylish black boots he'd noticed earlier. She wore a soft flannel, short-sleeve, baby blue t-shirt with a deep V neckline that looked really great on her. Her hair was tied back in a ponytail, but her hair was so curly the tail looked like a hair bun. Most of the dirt and grease from her earlier costume was washed off, but he could still see traces of the paint on her lower left eyelid and a spot below her bottom lip.

"You got some new clothes," she said as they walked out of the building.

"Finally," he said. "I was about to split the seams on my old ones. Those clothes look nice on you," he said sleepily as they got into the car.

"Watch it, youngster," she responded, sounding amused. Then she drove her VW beetle out of the City.

In mere minutes, Adam found he was struggling to keep his eyes open. His head kept falling forward and he had to jerk it back upright.

"I don't really know where you live," Saint-Anne said.

"Oh," Adam replied, thickly. "I just needed out of the City. You can let me out anywhere. I can make it home the rest of the way."

"Nonsense," the Saint said. "You can't keep your eyes open two minutes. You'll get run over by the first car that comes along. Tell me where you live so I can get you there alive."

Adam looked across the Yellow-Beetlebug cabin at its driver. Saint-Anne's eyes were on the road. She had large eyes, which looked even larger driving at night.

Can I trust her?

He didn't know. She could seriously be his undoing, tearing down in a moment everything he'd built over the last several months.

Do I even have a choice?

If he got caught by the Street-Angels again he might not survive. He needed a ride. He needed help—help she was offering. She just didn't realize how badly he needed her help, or how much.

"Miss Anne," he said softly, "You're right. I won't make it home tonight without your help, but…"

She looked at him out of the corner of her eye, still keeping some attention on the road.

"But you can't tell anyone else where I live. I know it's unfair to ask for a favor and then attach strings to it…"

He looked out the window. "No, that's terrible," he berated himself. "I should offer you a trade—something to compensate you for your time and …for keeping my secret."

Adam felt her hand on the back of his.

"You don't have to offer me anything. I'll keep your secret. Let me help you."

She squeezed his hand gently, then removed hers.

He looked down at the back of his hand where hers had rested just a moment before. Her touch didn't burn hot like Asuna's or Amy's. It felt warm in the center and cool around the edges. He wondered if she felt different because she was communicating something different. Or perhaps because she was a different person. Or maybe it was because she was older.

Adam gave Saint-Anne directions to Cow-town—which she told him was actually called Liberty when she figured out where he was describing. He took her past the motel to the gravel road that led back to the campground. He was fighting sleep the entire time. He hugged the two blankets that were folded on his lap but resisted the urge to lay his head on them.

Eventually they arrived at the campground.

"Okay, where now?" Saint-Anne asked.

"This is it," Adam said yawning. Then he climbed out of the car and pulled his backpack from the rear seat.

"What?" Saint-Anne said and got out of the car. "There's nothing here."

"It's dark," Adam said gently. "You just can't see it."

He walked over to his tent and unzipped the front and tossed his blankets in first, followed by his backpack. Then he turned to thank her and his shoulder ran into hers. Pain lanced through his shoulder and he gasped and fell backward in the tent. He landed on blankets—which was good—but also on his back—which was not good. New pain from his back overwhelmed his other senses. He gasped and couldn't breathe momentarily. The pain quickly receded to a nice, tolerable level and he took a deep breath again.

"Oww..." he groaned.

"I'm so sorry," Saint-Anne said, crouching in the mouth of his tent looking down at him.

"Are you hurt? I was just trying to look past you and you turned and bumped me. Come to think of it, we didn't bump hard. Why are you acting like I just punched you in the gut?"

Adam grimaced. This really wasn't going how he'd hoped.

"I've had a really rough week. That's all. I've got some bruises that need healing."

He hoped she'd be satisfied with that. He hadn't lied.

"How did you get bruises?"

He could only make out the vaguest outline of her face and hair in the little bit of glow her car's headlights gave off—pointed, as they were, into the woods.

"Anne," he said pleading, "I don't want to..."

"No," she insisted, "you have to tell me. Why do you have bruises? Why are you living in a tent when it's freezing out here? Is someone abusing you? Have you run away from home? What's going on?"

"No one's abusing me."

Adam tried to reassure her as he started to cover himself up with blankets.

"I didn't run away from home."

He curled the covers up around him and pulled the demon-doll off his backpack to use as a pillow.

"This is my home," he said weakly. "I just need some sleep. Everything will be better in the morning. You'll see. Just... need... sleep..."

72
Fireside Revelations

Adam woke. He was freezing. He needed to pee. Muscles in his back and legs were screaming agony. He rolled around under his blankets for several minutes trying to warm his battered body. While he worked, he tried to remember the dream. It was a doozy. Then he froze.

That was no dream. Anne had been here. She'd brought him home. She'd been grilling him on all his secrets and she'd sounded angry.

He groaned, despair over losing his secrets mingling with the discomfort in his body. He was going to lose it all. He couldn't see a way out.

Sighing, he got back to work warming up. He slipped all three of his coats on and his shoes. Odd though, he didn't remember getting out of his shoes... But they were sitting together, arranged neatly by the door. He usually left them outside the tent.

Whatever.

He put them on and grabbed his toothbrush, heading outside.

He picked up the wood at the end of the property and piled some of it by the back door of the mud room. Next, he peed like a racehorse. After washing his hands, he styled his hair and brushed his teeth. Then he walked out of the mud room and almost ran into Saint-Anne again.

She was bundled in a huge, puffy, purple winter coat. She wore a knitted cap. Mittens covered both of her hands and she was nursing a steaming cup of something that smelled like coffee with milk.

"Saint-Anne!" Adam said, surprised.

"Is this where your parents live?" Saint-Anne asked, getting straight to the point.

"This? No," Adam said, laughing slightly. "This belongs to the campground's owner," he explained, indicating the cabin behind him. "Campground-Lady lets me sleep on her property and use that tent someone left here. In return, I carry wood to her house each morning. She also lets me use the bathroom in the mud room here. She's very nice, though I never see her."

Saint-Anne looked around at the firewood stacked by the door and inside the mud room. Then she followed Adam back toward his tent.

"She's not the one hitting you?" the Saint asked gravely.

"Good grief, no," Adam chuckled. "She can barely walk. It was the Street-Angles who hit me, right before they stole my money. That's why I needed a ride out of the City so badly last night. I'm in no condition to face them again. Not yet, anyway."

They walked in silence for a few steps until Saint-Anne said, "I thought about it all night. I was certain you were lying to me."

"About what?" Adam croaked.

"About everything," she told him. "Every. Single. Thing. You *had* to be lying, because this kind of thing," she waved her hand vaguely at the forest around them, "doesn't happen in America."

"It's not bad, Miss Anne," Adam explained, voice recovering. "I really like it. I'm just a little poor right now. It's not a permanent thing."

"This isn't 'poor'," she told him, sounding a bit unstable. "Poor is living in a mobile home instead of a brick house. Poor is eating subsidized, store-brand sugar bombs instead of proper Raisin Bran. I don't have the slightest idea what this is, but it's not like any 'poor' I've ever seen."

Unable to think of a reply, Adam went about packing his school bag. As he did, he came across Anger-Management's picnic box. He'd been too busy and then too tired to eat it last night. His hands shook as he opened the lid. Inside was a peanut butter and jelly sandwich, apple slices, and cut carrots. He was so happy tears formed in his eyes.

"What's wrong?" she asked.

"Here," he said, wiping the tears from his eyes. "Sit down and have breakfast with me."

He sat down on a stump beside an old fire pit near his campsite and motioned for her to take up a spot on one next to him. She came over and sat on the stump he indicated.

Quizzically she asked, "Is that a kitten on your lunch box?"

Adam blushed. "I can explain."

She laughed, "Don't bother. It's what's on the inside that matters."

He handed her half of the peanut butter and jelly sandwich, then devoured his half in two bites. It was dry in his mouth, making it hard to swallow, so he ran over to the tent and pulled his water bottle off the backpack, then ran back to the fire ring. Anne hadn't eaten hers yet.

"You don't like peanut butter?" Adam asked, then sprayed water down his open mouth.

She peered at him over the sandwich in her hand. She looked puzzled and somewhat angry.

"What did you eat for dinner last night?" she asked.

He thought about her question while he fished some of the carrots out of the lunch box. He stopped the motion halfway to his mouth, grimaced, then offered them to her.

"Do you like carrots?"

She ignored the offer.

"What did you eat for dinner last night?" she repeated.

"This was supposed to be my dinner," he said, "but I got too busy with the whole saving-the-school thing, then the meeting that followed, and by the time I got home, I was too tired. So nothing, I guess."

He grinned suddenly. "Now it's my turn. Do you like carrots?"

"Yes," she said. Then, "No. I mean, I like carrots, but not for breakfast."

He frowned at the carrot in his hand, then looked at her.

"Mind if I eat yours then?" he asked.

"No, of course not. Eat all of it. In fact, eat this too," and she handed him back her half of the peanut butter and jelly sandwich. "It's no wonder you're so thin."

Miss Anne moved over and sat next to him on his stump. He tried to make room for her. He was confused why she would come so close. He figured it out quickly as she grabbed the apple slices in the lunch box and tried to force the food in his mouth.

"Eat," she said, making threatening gestures with the apple slices.

He pulled away laughing. "I can eat on my own."

She seemed to realize what she was doing and gave him some space. He polished off the rest of the sandwich, the remaining carrots, and all the apple slices in thirty seconds.

"Adam?" she asked, not mincing words. "Where are your parents?"

He frowned while still chewing, uncertain how to answer.

Anne waited in silence.

"They didn't make it," he said finally.

Something other than food formed a lump in his throat.

She flinched, grew sad, and finally looked away toward the woods. Without turning back, she asked, "What happened?"

"I can't remember," he started to say, but his voice cracked and he was unable to say more.

They sat like that, quietly, for a while.

Eventually Adam said, "I have to start walking to school now. Thanks for coming by and keeping me company. I hadn't realized how dull this place can be without company."

"What are you talking about?" Miss Anne scolded him. "I didn't come here to keep you company. I came here to prove you were pulling my leg last night. But now I can see you weren't. You really live here—in a tent. You really walk over sixteen kilometers to school every day. You really didn't eat dinner last night. You really are living by yourself. And I feel like I've only scratched the surface of your secrets. Adam, I've got to get you out of here."

"Why?" Adam asked, confused.

"Because no one can live like this!" Anne yelled the words of frustration in his direction. "Because it's inhuman. It's *barbaric*. Even prisoners in this country live better than you."

Now there were tears spilling down her cheeks. "Your life is crueler than I would wish on even my worst enemy."

"Anne," Adam said gently, rubbing the tears off her cheeks with the cuff of his coat. "I like it. I'm free here. I can make my own way. Expand or shrink. Succeed or fail. And it's just temporary. I'm going to a great school. I'm learning how to be productive and earn enough money to live in a trailer, and then maybe a house someday. I'm going places. This is just a..." his hand moved in the air as though trying to catch a hummingbird, "...a temporary thing."

She sniffed.

Adam broke eye contact and looked at the empty fire pit.

"I'll grant you there have been times I was worried I wouldn't make it home, but my friends have always come through when things got bad. You, Miss Anne, and your wonderful Yellow-Beetlebug, have saved me on more than one occasion. Last night was one of them. In fact, that's why I started calling you the Saint—the VW-Saint."

"Saint," she said, balancing equally between laughing and crying.

"Hmm," Adam muttered, "maybe I shouldn't have told you that."

She laughed several times from her belly, then grinned.

"I thought you were making fun of me when you called me 'Saint-Anne'. No one has ever called me a saint before. It's probably a sin, but my ego really likes it."

"You are 'Saint-Anne' to me," Adam told her, grinning like a fool. Then he said seriously, "I really do have to get going to school now. It takes a while to get there. Do you think you could give me a ride home tonight again? The streets aren't really safe for me in the evenings."

Anne looked at him sideways with one eyebrow raised. "And they're safe in the mornings?"

"I think so," he said. "The gangs seem to stay up late and sleep till the afternoon. At least, that's the impression I got watching them before I started school."

"So you don't want a ride to school?" she asked, serious once more.

"I don't want to be a burden…" Adam started to say.

"Get in the car," Anne ordered. "You're not a burden."

"But…" Adam tried to get a word in.

Anne cut him off.

"If you really feel like a burden, then we can work out some sort of trade later."

"I'd like it," Adam told her, "if we could work out some kind of trade."

"I'll think on it," she said.

They shuffled through dead leaves to her car. Close enough to bump each other. The creak of the handle of Adam's empty lunch box and the swish of their winter clothes provided musical accompaniment to the silent colliding of worlds.

73
Heaven is Coming. Prepare for the Worst.

Saint-Anne parked in the teachers' lot. She and Adam agreed on a time to meet after school. She had a frown on her face as she turned and walked away with a purposeful stride.

Adam chewed his lower lip as he watched her disappear in the building. So much was riding on her. He hoped she was up to it.

That day was Adam's sixth day of school—Saturday. Why had he chosen a school with a six-day work week? Oh yeah, because he got paid to go to school. He really loved this life.

He showered, changed into uniform, and threw his laundry in the wash along with two more of his blankets. Then he went to the library. He found it eerily deserted and dark, but the room seemed to sense his presence and the lights warmed up dimly as he entered. That felt good—like he was a king entering a room that lit up just for him.

He picked an empty desk, sat, and pulled his homework out of the backpack. He went through, subject by subject, completing each task until they were all finished. Then he turned his attention to the ID card.

Adam pulled up the blueprints Shop-Boss had asked him to look over. What he saw looked like a ghost of a school rather than the school as he saw it. All the edges were visible, but everything in between was transparent. Inside those huge, transparent spaces were lines and colors and symbols of all types. He could sense a pattern to the jumble—it looked as though it all followed some very strict discipline—but right now it only looked like spaghetti to him.

He flashed his ID card at a nearby computer and it lit up. He researched 'making blueprints' in the library web portal and reserved two books. They thumped, one at a time, in the front desk about five meters away. He walked over and flashed his card. The panels in the front desk opened. He grabbed the books and went back to his seat where he skimmed the table of contents, then the chapters he thought might help in each book.

Adam found tables with symbols in one of the books and he propped it up so the lists were visible for reference. In the other book, he found a chapter titled 'Common Conventions of Drafting Blueprints'. He read that chapter completely while constantly referring to his ID to see if the conventions talked about in the book were used in the school blueprints. It was a close fit. But looking at a huge blueprint on his tiny ID card was annoying.

He remembered the motion Shop-Boss had used to toss the blueprints to Adam's ID card. He repeated the same motion—swiping two fingers across the surface of his ID card toward the desktop computer next to him. The motion was like—he imagined—sliding a piece of paper off the top of a stack of papers and trying to get it to land on the nearby desktop. When his fingers left the edge of his ID card, the blueprints shrank on his ID to a small postage stamp icon. Then the blueprint reappeared and expanded on the desktop computer monitor next to him.

"Mágico," Adam purred.

He bent to deciphering the blueprints in earnest. What started as a bowl of spaghetti and symbols began to look more like roads and rivers on a map. Then, as he continued to decipher, it started to look like a circuit board.

"These are doors," Adam said to himself, "and these are wall outlets. This must be a circuit breaker box. That's a conduit passage through a wall. These are floor level designations," and on and on.

He started to feel like the blueprint was three-dimensional—like he could walk around inside it. It wasn't spaghetti anymore. It was a living, breathing building. He 'walked' through the building to where he and Shop-Boss had discussed putting up video cameras, then highlighted the closest power junctions and network access points. Whatever blueprint software the school was using let him make notes and draw pictures and highlight areas of the blueprint in different colors with his mouse cursor—like attaching Post-it notes, only inside the computer screen rather than on top of the screen.

It just floored Adam that people could design programs so intuitive and responsive, even for someone using it the first time. Humanity was capable of some really neat stuff.

A feminine sounding, "Oh," broke Adam from his reverie. He turned his head and found Amy standing in the door to the library. She was not yet in her school uniform. She was wearing black leggings that fit so well he could make out the lines between her muscles. She wore a short black skirt over the leggings. She wore black boots that only went above the ankles, then turned out in a flare like something Robin Hood might have worn in a 1940s movie. She wore a black leather jacket rolled at the sleeves, leaving her forearms bare. He could see thin black ribbons around both her wrists, the same color and style as the one around her neck and the two flowing down her hair. The bottom of the black leather jacket was short, only reaching her mid-abdomen and the center looked like it was designed to remain open. It was probably too small to button down the center. It had tiny pieces of metal artfully placed. The jacket, Adam decided, had zero utility aside from drawing the eye and funneling it to the center of her t-shirt and the buttered piece of bread displayed proudly over the simple slogan—'Toast'.

"I have that shirt," Adam breathed out in astonishment.

"What?" Ribbons said, clearly taken aback.

"Toast!" Adam said in amazement. "That's my shirt. You're wearing my shirt. I wore it to school this morning and just now put it in the wash. How did you find it? How did you get it to dry so quickly? And how did you get it to look so good? Why can't it look that good when I wear it?"

She cocked her head sideways like a bird looking at a worm.

"What *are* you babbling about? This is *my* shirt. No one has this shirt. I only have it because I was willing to date a very nerdy guy to get it. I convinced him to give it to me as a gift. And now no one is ever allowed to ever have this shirt but me. It's special, not only because it's one of a kind, but because it's awesome!"

Adam suddenly feared for his own Toast shirt.

"Um," he said, "I must have been mistaken. That's not my Toast shirt. In fact, I've never seen a Toast shirt that awesome before. Forget I said anything."

He turned back to his project table.

He felt Amy come beside him.

"What are you doing?" she asked, glancing at the books propped open all over the table.

"These are blueprints of the school," Adam gestured toward the computer screen. "Shop-Boss… er, Mr. Keynes asked me to look them over so we could jury-rig some cameras to look at the fence lines of the Play Yard."

"But why?" she asked, sitting down in a chair next to him. "I heard you already took care of the problem. The whole town is lit up over it. Everyone is talking about it."

"That's just the opening salvo of a greater war," Adam told her as he squinted over the school blueprints without really seeing them.

"This idea of justice represents a marked departure from the present reality of this city. To adopt justice, the people of the City will have to embrace something different—which means they will have to change. And if there is one thing I know for certain about people, it's that they hate change. They fear it. They *fight* it. If I'm right," Adam said, frowning, "you are going to see a lot of intense action in the next few months—some of it ugly. I've never done this sort of thing before, but I have a sneaky suspicion we're going to find out who our true friends are very soon. And I've got a feeling it will be a frighteningly small number. We need to be prepared for a whole lot of the worst humanity can offer. Ultimately though, I think this war is winnable. More importantly, though, I think this is a war worth fighting.

"I think," he continued with barely a pause, "it is possible to make Justice the Alpha. Not a king, or an elected official, or a scholar, or a philosopher, or a committee, or a government. Not a person of any kind, but a principle. I think we can create a world where justice and security exist for everyone equally. And I think, under those conditions, prosperity will blossom everywhere. That's what I'm hoping for anyway and—God help us all—that's the direction I'm taking us."

Adam emerged from his speech and looked over at Amy—confused that she hadn't said anything. He found her staring back. She looked... odd. Her lips were parted. She was breathing quickly. Her pupils were dilated. Her lips were swollen and her cheeks were flushed. She looked... hungry, almost.

"Are you okay?" Adam asked, a little concerned. "Did I say something wrong?"

"No," she said as she suddenly stood up and hugged her shoulders so that her arms crossed in front of her chest. Then she spun around, sending her hair and ribbons in a brief spiral.

"I just remembered somewhere I need to be. I'll... I'll talk with you later."

And with that, Amy was gone.

Adam stared at the empty doorway in disbelief, then flopped back in his chair and clapped both hands against his forehead.

What did I do this time?

Why did God surround him with amazing girls but fail to give even the slightest clue how to talk with them or even vaguely understand them.

"It makes no sense!" he shouted at the ceiling. He banged his feet repeatedly on the ground in a miniature tantrum before taking a deep breath and letting it out slowly. He opened his senses and listened intensely, hoping perhaps God would send down an answer to his shouted complaint. Instead, his stomach growled and he was filled with a really strong craving for toast.

74
Freedom from Fear

From the first moment he entered his first class, Adam discovered he wasn't going to get any learning done that day. Not even the teachers wanted to talk about their lessons. All anyone wanted to talk about was what happened on the Play Yard the previous evening. Adam found himself singled out in every class to retell the story of the conflict and how he handled it.

Each time he told it, he tried to give his audience some background on the citizenship agreement that had shaped his plan and how it had worked out in practical terms. At the conclusion of each story, he tried to muscle in a blurb about the potential expansion of that citizenship agreement and its benefits to the people in the community—security from violence and theft.

In his own mind, Adam saw no boundaries to the possibilities. Ultimately, he thought the citizenship agreement could expand out of the City to the state, then to the country, then to the continent, and then to the world.

But he kept that to himself.

He also didn't mention the prosperity that would likely flourish following the expansion of justice.

Too many steps.

Too far off.

La esperanza espera.

So Adam shared the simplified message—freedom from fear; justice and security for everyone through a simple, contractual commitment.

He told it to anyone who would listen.

75
New Beginnings

Several minutes after the start of his last period, Work/Study, the border around the back of Adam's ID card started flashing red.

That's new, Adam thought.

Adam walked over to Boss-Clean. She was giving directions to a student on proper mopping technique. He caught the name on her uniform out of the corner of his eye.

"Ms. Singer?" Adam said as he approached.

Adam was holding the ID card in his palm, with the screen on the back facing up so she was able to see the flashing red border. Her lips pursed thoughtfully.

"My ID has never done this before," he told her. "Is it broken?"

"It could mean a lot of things," Boss-Clean told him. "Touch the screen and see what it tells you."

Adam touched the screen and a message came up that read, 'Please report to the principal's office immediately.'

He felt his stomach drop to the floor. He showed the message to Boss-Clean. Her eyebrows rose.

"You'd better go and see what that's about," she told him. "I'll clean and stow your cleaning cart for you. Go there straight away."

Adam walked slowly down the hall, trying to work out in his mind what the principal might want with him. His mind started to weave different world-ending scenarios. Perhaps Miss-Anne had turned him in—given over his secrets—and the police had come to pull him out of school. Perhaps someone had seen him working illegally and the police were there to take him to jail or an orphanage. And what would happen to the people and businesses who were caught paying him for work? Or perhaps the government had changed its mind about his voucher. Adam would have to leave school for certain in that case. He'd have to save up a long time before he could afford to return.

With each new horrible thought, he felt more and more ill. His hands began to sweat. He felt nausea and his mouth grew dry. His gait slowed even more.

Maybe if I don't go, it will just blow over.

He ducked in a bathroom—feeling like he might throw up. He splashed some water on his face and looked in the mirror. The face looking back at him was somewhat alien. He looked older, healthier. His neck was wider—his cheeks less gaunt. The new haircut helped. It was rough in some spots, but better than he could have done on his own. His eyes, though, looked nervous. Scared.

Adam backed to a corner in the room and squatted down. He rested elbows on knees and his mouth against clasped hands held in front of his body. He racked his brain for some way out. The worst part was he didn't know what was coming. He couldn't prepare for it. He closed his eyes and took several deep breaths. He said a quick prayer.

God, protect the people who took me in and gave me work.

Mid-prayer, a memory sprang to life unbidden: his father looking down on him—hands on his shoulders. The young Adam was scared and crying. He couldn't remember why.

Adam's father had a mellow voice. Caring, but also firm.

"There was a man once named Winston Churchill. He was a famous historian and war hero, but spent most of his life as a politician. He was the Prime Minister of England during World War II—a long, terrible conflict that killed at least 50 million people. It was during the early years of World War II that Churchill gave a speech to the students of his former grade school—a school where he had done poorly academically. He told the young people there, 'Never give in. Never give in. Never, never, never, never—in nothing, great or small, large or petty—never give in except to convictions of honor and good sense.'"

Adam's father had continued, "I heard that story when I was a young man and it helped me, so now I pass it on to you. Never give up, son. Never give up. Never, never, never, never give up."

Adam took one final deep breath, then wrapped resolve around like a cloak. Fear still swam all through his body and mind, but now it was peripheral. His center was something stern and hard and resilient. Trials in life were not unique to him. Everyone faced hardship sometimes. He was not ever alone in that regard. He would face whatever life threw at him. He would survive this.

Adam resumed his walk to the principal's office. As soon as he came through the door, Jell-O-Lady popped out of her seat. He'd never seen her move so fast. Her eyes glittered. She was wrestling with a smug smile.

I know that look, Adam thought.

Ms. Gladys knew a secret.

She escorted him behind her counter to the hallway in the back of the room. It led past several open doors. Adam peeked in each and saw small offices with desks and computers. Men and women in business suits and ties sat at those desks. They looked busy.

The door at the end of the short hall was closed. Jello-Lady knocked, then pushed it open and announced him.

"Adam Smith here to see you, Mr. Greene."

Adam's hands clenched involuntarily. He glanced quickly around the room. No police. That was good at least.

Mr. Greene's office was larger than the other offices he'd seen along the hall outside. The walls were covered with awards and plaques of achievement—some were scholastic, some were athletic, some were career milestones. The majority of the collection, however, didn't have anything to do with Mr. Greene. They were pictures of students. Many were wearing graduation gowns. Some were holding up awards or projects. Nearly all the students in the pictures looked proud and happy.

Adam experienced a brief, but strong desire to have his picture on that wall.

Mr. Greene allowed him time to peruse the walls, then said gently, "Please have a seat, Adam. We have much to talk about."

Dread—briefly forgotten—flared again. Adam sat down in a large, soft leather chair in front of Mr. Greene's desk and tried to remember to keep breathing.

"Thank you for coming on such short notice," Mr. Greene told him. "I know it can sometimes be frightening to get a summons to the principal's office. But I felt this was important."

Adam nodded. He couldn't bring himself to look Mr. Greene in the eyes.

"As you might imagine, there has been a great deal of discussion regarding the trespassing incident in the Play Yard yesterday. You were at that incident and played an important role. You were also at the meeting afterward and demonstrated impressive foresight and maturity in front of so many of your peers and teachers. Over the course of today, I have had many conversations with department heads and instructors. One thing we all agree on is to move forward with your proposal to expand our efforts to improve security beyond the boundaries of this school."

Adam rocked back in his chair. They had taken his proposal seriously! He felt off balance. He had been prepared for his world to end. He wasn't ready for... this.

Mr. Greene continued, "We have chosen, as a school, to assemble a team dedicated to interfacing with the City and its people."

Adam's eyes glittered—partly from relief and partly from excitement. He smiled despite himself.

"Adam, I know you have a lot on your plate already. You are only a freshman and have only been at this school for one week. That has got to feel overwhelming. But several of your current teachers have spoken up on your behalf. They suspect you will do great things—are already doing great things—and they think you can manage even more."

Adam cocked his head to the side. He was curious now, having no idea what to expect.

"So in recognition of your demonstrated leadership and also in recognition of the fact that this was your idea to begin with, Charter 7 would like to make you an offer."

The room grew silent. Adam was dumbstruck. Mr. Greene sat back in his chair and looked at some of the pictures on the wall before speaking again.

"Several people even suggested you lead the effort but, as remarkable as you have proven yourself, I feel it is important that you remain focused on your studies, your classes, and just being a kid. So I've vetoed the idea of you being the project team leader."

Adam blinked.

"Still, I would like you on board with this project in an important capacity."

Mr. Greene pulled up something on his computer.

"I took the liberty of looking at your schedule. I don't think you have joined any after-school activities outside of Work/Study. Is that correct?"

Adam nodded.

"Here is my thought," Mr. Greene said. "We could have the outreach team meet every day after school for an hour and a half or more as conditions dictate. We will assign a teacher to be the project leader and have student representatives from every part of the school. We might even ask the entire student council to participate. The team will have access to all teachers and staff in the building. We are giving it high priority. Your job, if you choose to accept it, would be as a consultant."

"Consultant?" Adam whispered, mystified.

Mr. Greene nodded.

"That way," he explained, "you can come and go as you please. Help or not as you please. Get involved or not. It is entirely up to you. I think that role will leave you the freedom to take on only as much responsibility as your time allows. You can focus on your studies as you need. You can focus on being a kid, if that's what you want. The downside of being a consultant, though, is you are confined to a role that is advisory only. You will not have a vote."

Adam's eyes grew large as he pondered the possibilities.

"Oh, and," Mr. Greene said, as if in afterthought, "in exchange for your time and effort as a consultant to the task force, Charter 7 will pay you $15 per hour worked."

Adam choked.

Mr. Greene handed him a tissue.

Adam, once recovered, steepled his fingers in front of his face and looked at Mr. Greene over them.

"If you need time to think..." the principal offered.

"Yes," Adam interrupted him. "Sí. Pefecto. Absolutamente. I accept!"

76
Postlude

Adam emerged from a flower shop with four roses—one red, one pink, one yellow, and one dark violet. He'd had to pay for them with a withdrawal from one of the hiding holes behind a dumpster, since he hadn't yet earned anything as a hired consultant for the Charter 7 Special Committee on City Security.

The flowers were expensive, he admitted, but pretty and smelled nice—like the girls for whom they were intended.

The red was for Anger-Management, pink for Saint-Anne, violet for Ribbons, and yellow for Asuna. His chest swelled at the thought of giving the flowers away. The colorful, fragrant plants were meant as a gesture of appreciation for some of the wonderful people in his life, but they were small and their existence fleeting.

Which is fine, Adam told himself, given the circumstances.

They were the best he could do. In the long run, though, he hoped to shower his friends in treasure, so they would know how precious they were. But even that wouldn't be enough. He hoped to someday give them a gift on par with what he'd received—something grand and epic.

Something valuable beyond measure. He wanted to give them security. He wanted to protect them. He wanted to give them justice.

He was lucky to be alive, he knew. And even luckier to attend school. To have a job and money. To have a healthy body. And, especially, to have friends. His eyes grew blurry as he walked along the sidewalk contemplating the small bouquet and the amazing people in his life. It felt almost as if he were part of a family again.

A deep ache settled in his chest. He missed his old family, but wiped his eyes deliberately. The past was gone. He couldn't touch it now. His friends, this City, this life were all he had. He needed to take care of them. He brushed his fingers gently over the fragile flower petals, then glanced around, conscious of how he must look. He needed to stay alert. He'd learned this lesson many times: The City was exciting, but also dangerous.

Aware of his surroundings now, Adam heard police sirens far off to the north. In another direction, but still far away, he heard small popping sounds in rhythmic succession that might have been firecrackers, or even gunfire. At the same time, he passed under a window and heard angry, raised voices in heated argument. Up ahead, coming from a small gathering of young men in leather jackets congregating on the street corner, he heard voices full of bravado, pitched loud so that everyone nearby would hear and, perhaps, fear. He frowned at the cacophony—unsettled, yet unsurprised. The contrast between the soft petals against his fingers and the abrasive sounds against his ears could not have been more severe.

The City needed saving, he told himself. Moreover, the City was *worth* saving.

He was just one man, but he had an advantage. He saw the problem from two distinct vantages—on the ground at street level and looking down from the lofty heights of the Tower. It was like seeing a battle from the front lines as a soldier, but also from a command tent positioned above the fray. He observed both simultaneously. He felt the City's dilemma both intimately and abstractly. Equally important, Adam Smith had a workable solution and a plan to make that solution happen.

It was time to get to work.

Appendix A
Creative References

Warner, Gertrude Chandler. *The Boxcar Children.* Rand McNally. 1924.

Paulsen, Gary. *Hatchet.* 1987.

Smith, Adam. An Inquiry into the Nature and Causes of the Wealth of Nations. 1776.

Smith, Adam. The Theory of Moral Sentiments. 1759.

Friedman, Milton and Rose. Free to Choose: A Personal Statement. 1979.

Roberts, Russ. "Econtalk". 2006 – Present.

Munger, Michael; Munger, Kevin. *Choosing in Groups: Analytical Politics Revisited.* Cambridge University Press. 2015.

Rand, Ayn. *Atlas Shrugged.* Random House. 1957.

Skousen, Mark. The Making of Modern Economics: The Lives and Ideas of the Great Thinkers. Taylor and Francis Group. 2016.

Kahneman, Daniel. Thinking Fast and Slow. 2011.

Hayek, F.A. The Fatal Conceit: The Errors of Socialism. 1988.

Hayek, F.A. The Road to Serfdom. 1944.

Gladwell, Malcolm. Outliers: The Story of Success. 2008.

Millay, Katja. *The Sea of Tranquility.* Simon & Schuster. 2012.

Silver, Nate. The Signal and the Noise. 1994.

Ratey, John. Spark: The Revolutionary New Science of Exercise and the Brain. 2008.

Sowell, Thomas. Basic Economics: A Common Sense Guide to the Economy. 2007.

Cooper, Heron, Heward. Applied Behavior Analysis (2nd Edition). 2007.

Rothfuss, Patrick. *The Name of the Wind.* 2009.

Herbert, Frank. *Dune.* 1965.

Tolkien, J.R.R. *The Hobbit.* 1937.

McCullough, David. *John Adams.* 2001.

Waal, Frans De. *Our Inner Ape.* 2005.

Jordan, Robert. *The Wheel of Time.* 1990.

Doidge, Norman. The Brain that Changes Itself: Personal Triumphs from the Frontiers of Brain Science. 2008.

Moon, Elizabeth. *The Speed of Dark.* 2002.

Steakley, John. *Armor.* 1984.

Card, Orsen Scott. *Ender's Game.* Tor Books. 1985.

Watari, Wataru. "My Teen Romantic Comedy is Wrong: As I Expected" (Television). 2011-2013.

Shirane, Hideki. "Is it Wrong to Pick Up Girls in a Dungeon?" (Television). 2015.

Sanbe, Kei. "Erased" (Television). 2016.

Sato, Dai. "Eureka Seven" (Television). 2005.

Takayama, Kattsuhiko. "Aldnoah.Zero" (Television). 2014

Anthony, Piers. *Bio of an Ogre*. 1982.

King, Stephen. *On Writing*. 1999.

Verant Interactive. *Everquest*. 1999.

The Bible.

Appendix B
Adam's Spanish to English Dictionary

Absolutamente – Absolutely.

Aspirante – Candidate.

Ay, Dios mío – Oh my God.

Bandito – Bandit.

Bonita – Beautiful.

Con buena hambre, no hay mal pan – 'with good hunger, there is no bad bread' or 'Beggars can't be choosers'.

Delicioso – Delicious.

Diablo-Bebé-Mascota – Devil-baby-mascot.

Estúpido – Stupid.

Finalmente – Finally.

Frutillas – Strawberries.

Increíble – Incredible.

La esperanza espera – Hope waits.

Maldito – Damn or wretched

Mágico – magic.

Mascota – pet or mascot.

Muy estúpido – very stupid.

Negativo – Negative.

Número Tres – Number three.

No manches – No way.

Obras son amores y no buenas razones – 'Works are loves and not good reasons' or 'Actions speak louder than words,' or 'An action is worth more than a thousand words.'

Pefecto – Perfect.

Qué chévere – Cool.

Que chido – How cool.

Salud – Cheers. (Used when toasting).

Señoras – Ladies.

Serio – Serious.

Sí – Yes.

Un dineral – A pretty penny.

Made in the USA
Lexington, KY
27 February 2018